DETONATE

A TYRONE KING NOVEL

DAVID GREENE

"Always forgive your enemies; nothing annoys them so much."

OSCAR WILDE

ONE

At 10:30 AM Amtrak train number 64, the Maple Leaf, traveling from Toronto to New York, pulled into the last station on the Canadian side at Niagara Falls, Ontario. The train was eight minutes late.

King sat in a regular coach class seat. A couple sitting across the aisle from him gave him the once-over. He was used to that. Some people thought his dreadlocks meant he was a drug dealer. Other people wondered if he sang reggae. But the couple sitting across from him wasn't an ordinary couple.

Two hours earlier, King had watched them when they boarded the train. The young man had pulled a black roller bag, the young woman a pastel pink one. *Cute,* King had thought. *Gender-coordinated luggage colors.*

They'd climbed aboard the train and made their way down the aisle to the seats across from him. While the man heaved the pink and black bags up to the overhead bin, the woman took off her shawl. After the man sat in the window seat, the woman placed her purse beneath the aisle seat, then sat down beside him.

The woman wore a lime green hijab that covered her head in a crinkly, crepe-like fabric. The man wore jeans and an olive green t-shirt. His hair was curly jet-black. His beard, also black, was on the verge of being scruffy. But his clothes were wrinkle free, as if he'd just ironed them. His posture was formal. He held his head steady and erect. He stared forward. He appeared to be deep in thought.

Since boarding, the couple hadn't spoken. But now, as the train came to a stop at the Niagara Falls station, the young man turned to the woman and said, "The time has come."

The man spoke in Arabic, but King understood what he said. Five years earlier, he'd been a U. S. Army interpreter/translator. He spoke Arabic. But the man across the aisle had no way of knowing that.

"Jasmeen," the young man said gently. "You must get off now." He put his arm around her shoulder. "Before the child is born."

Jasmeen frowned. A curl of raven hair peeked from beneath her scarf. Her eyelashes and brows were thick and dark. Her eyes, like her scarf, were emerald green. She did not look pregnant.

"If the child is not born, they will take you off the train," she replied, also in Arabic. "You'll have trouble on the American side." She pulled his arm off her shoulder. "Kareem..." She fixed her eyes upon him. "The child must come before that."

King tried to place where they were from. The dialect sounded like Iraq, he thought. Or possibly Syria.

Kareem nodded. "Do not worry," he said. "The child will be born on time. I will call you from the caves at one o'clock."

Jasmeen stood and bowed. "Allāhu Akbar," she said. Then she picked up her shawl, which hung on the back of the seat, and wrapped it over her shoulders. She reached beneath the seat in front of her and pulled out her handbag. Without another word, she turned and made her way to the back of the car.

A moment later, King saw her step onto the train platform and walk toward the station. Then she stopped. She looked back at the train. She opened her handbag and dug around. She pulled out something that looked like a phone. But then she put it back, turned, and walked into the station.

To King, it looked like she was leaving and not coming back. He looked up at the overhead shelf across from him. The pastel pink roller bag was still there. *Something is wrong*, he thought.

King stood and stepped into the aisle. He leaned over to speak to Kareem. "Excuse me," he said. "I wonder if your companion has forgotten her suitcase." He pointed up to the overhead shelf.

Kareem was startled by the interruption. His face was expressionless, but he blinked several times. He glanced up at the pink bag on the overhead shelf. He shrugged. He closed his eyes for a moment, then opened them, and said. "Thank you, but she did not forget the bag. I am taking the luggage to New York for her. She will join me there in two days."

King nodded, and then sat back down in his seat. *OK, fine.* He looked out the window at the station. The woman, Jasmeen, was gone. The station platform was quickly emptying out. King looked at his watch. The train was due to leave in less than a minute.

King was puzzled. He mentally replayed the couple's conversation. She'd spoken of a child coming soon—but she didn't appear pregnant. She'd warned Kareem that he'd have 'trouble' on the American side and that the child must be born before that. King thought he heard Kareem say he'd call her from the caves at one o'clock. Maybe his Arabic was getting rusty. But he doubted it.

The train began to move. Soon the Maple Leaf would cross the bridge over the Niagara River and enter the United States. King looked across the aisle at Kareem. He had something in his hand. It looked like a mobile phone, but it had a thick short antenna and bore the word Cobra on it. King had seen a device like that before. It was a GMRS radio, a two-way radio, like a walkie-talkie, but higher quality. In the U.S., a person who wanted to use a two-way radio had to get a license. But in Canada, anyone could use a short-range device.

The last time King had seen one of those radios was in Afghanistan. A Taliban insurgent had used a GMRS to detonate an improvised explosive device that blew up the Humvee traveling in front of him. Why would a man on a train need a walkie-talkie instead of a cell phone? King thought about the security admonition he'd heard hundreds of times. *If you see something, say something.* Perhaps he ought to say something to the conductor. But what would he say? There was nothing incriminating to report. But King couldn't just disregard his suspicions. *If you see something, say something.*

On impulse, King stood again, put one foot into the aisle and faced Kareem. With a pleasant smile, he said in Arabic, "I hope you aren't planning to blow up something with that."

Kareem's face went ashen. He stood and said, "Excuse me." He set the two-way radio on the window seat and stepped into the aisle. King stepped back out of the aisle. He relaxed a bit when he saw the device was out of Kareem's hands.

Kareem pivoted toward the overhead shelf that held his luggage. He pulled the black roller bag down, and set it on the aisle seat. He turned his back to King, unzipped the outer pouch of the bag, and pulled something out of it. He picked up the two-way radio from the window seat. Then he turned around to face King. He held a handgun. He pointed it at King's chest.

King raised his eyebrows. Before he'd joined the army, he'd trained in Aikido, the Japanese martial art also called 'the Art of Peace.' It emphasized the ability to relax the mind and body, even in the stress of dangerous circumstances.

King stood six feet tall—which was four inches taller than Kareem. He kept the smile on his face, even when Kareem said, in English, "Don't move."

King assessed the situation. The two-way radio was in Kareem's left hand. The gun was in his right. King had studied Aikido, but this called for improvisation. He glanced around the car at the other passengers. There were only a few. Most had already left the train on the Canadian side of the falls. A woman with a boy sat three seats away. She stared at the gun with a look of incomprehension. King spoke in her direction, "Don't worry, ma'am," he said. "He won't use it."

Kareem turned his head for a split second toward the woman and the boy. In that moment, King executed an Aikido technique called nikyō, a pronating wristlock that torques the arm and applies painful nerve pressure. He silently counted his breaths.

One. He dropped down and to the left. With his right hand he knocked the barrel of the gun down and to the right. Instantly Kareem fired the gun. With a loud report, the bullet ripped into the velvet blue fabric that covered the padding on the seat cushion. The woman nearby screamed.

Two. Coming back up, King gripped Kareem's right wrist with his left hand. Using nikyō torque, he applied nerve pressure until Kareem could no longer hold onto the gun, which fell to the floor.

Three. Extending leverage to Kareem's wrist and arm, King bent him down and to the side. Kareem swung out his right arm to try to keep his balance.

Four. King spun and gripped Kareem's right wrist, which held the detonator. King applied pronating torque to the wrist until the detonator clattered to the floor.

Five. King pushed him all the way down to the right and pinned him on the floor.

Once on the floor, Kareem grunted. King could tell his wrists and arms were hurt. He waited until Kareem lay completely still. Then he focused on the roller bag on the aisle seat. He considered the various ways a bomb inside it could be detonated. Kareem's two-way radio was on the floor nearby. But King had also seen Jasmeen remove something that looked just like it from her purse. Maybe she was the backup plan. She could use her detonator if she was anywhere within a two-mile range. They might also have rigged the bomb with a timer. King decided he'd better get the luggage off the train and away from people as soon as possible. But he couldn't think of a way to do that and subdue Kareem at the same time.

He made a snap decision. He released Kareem from the pin. He picked up the pistol from the floor with his right hand. At the same time, he used his left leg like a shuffleboard stick to push the detonator and shoot it down the aisle.

He cradled the gun in the palm of his hand. It was a Sig Sauer P220. He hefted it, gauging its weight. He had to decide what to do with it. He had only an instant to decide. It would be easy to point it at Kareem, but it was a matter of principle with him. He'd renounced the use of weapons. Although he wasn't willing to use the gun on Kareem, he had to be sure no one else could use it either.

He stood and removed the magazine from the gun. Then he ejected the round from the chamber and stuffed the magazine in his pocket. He put the empty gun back into the open compartment on the bag and re-zipped it. He grabbed the handle on the roller bag and pulled it off the seat. He stepped over Kareem and put the bag on the floor.

Kareem had flopped onto his stomach. He held his sorest arm, his right arm, out in front of him. King stood between him and the roller bag. Kareem rolled onto his back, holding his right arm, and grimaced. He said in English, "What are you going to do?"

King said in Arabic, "I'm going to look inside your bag and see what's in it."

Kareem blinked. He rolled onto his stomach to look for the radio. King had kicked it a good distance down the aisle. It had come to rest near a young woman. The woman stood at her seat, frozen in place, with one foot in the aisle. She stared at King. She had headphone earbuds in each ear. She pulled one of the wires until the earbud popped out of her left ear.

King pointed to the radio on the floor. "Pick that device up right now," he said to her. "But don't push any buttons on it. Keep it away from this man, and bring it to a conductor."

The young woman popped the earbud from her right ear, but didn't move. She looked at the radio. "What is it?" she asked.

King sized her up. Her clothes looked expensive. She wore a

blue satin blouse with black silk crepe pants. A gold ankle bracelet glistened above the sandal on her foot. Her toenails were painted with pale lavender polish. He focused on her eyes. He tried to gauge her ki. In Aikido, ki was synonymous with life energy. He had a sense of strong ki from her. Would she have the courage to do what he needed her to do? He hoped she would. But she'd have to trust him. He knew it was a good idea to address a stranger by name if you wanted his or her trust.

"What's your name?" King asked her.

She looked at him, then at the man on the floor, and then back at him. She waited a moment before answering. She was obviously sizing him up. Then she said, "Sarah."

"Sarah, that device is a two-way radio," he said. "It might be a detonator. There might be a bomb in this suitcase." He held the suitcase up. "I'm going to get rid of the suitcase. While I do, you need to keep that thing away from him. If he gets to it, he'll explode the bomb."

Sarah looked back down at Kareem, who was crawling along the aisle, inching toward the detonator.

"Sarah, do it now," King yelled. "Do you understand?"

She nodded. She looked at the object at her feet, and then around the train car. There was no one else. The woman with the boy had already scuttled away. Sarah bent and picked up the Cobra radio. She held it out at arm's length in front of her. Her arm trembled.

Kareem had crawled close enough to her to reach out and grab at her leg. He closed his hand around her ankle bracelet, but his damaged wrist was in pain. He flinched.

Sarah felt him pull at her ankle. She let out a short, startled cry. She pulled back hard, and yanked her leg out of his grasp.

"Sarah, run," King shouted. "Run now."

King, Kareem and Sarah were in the second from the last car of a seven-car train. Sarah ran toward the front of the train. She ran without looking back. Within a moment, Kareem was on his feet, running after her.

TWO

King was not sure if the bomb might be in the black or the pink bag—or maybe there were bombs in both bags. He changed his mind about opening the bags to look inside. There might not be time. He pulled the pink bag down from the rack, then looked out the window. The train was moving faster, but they were still in Canada.

He was strong enough to hold both bags up at once—one in each hand. He held the pink one in front of him, the black one behind him. He marched them carefully toward the rear of his car. He stepped into the passage that joined his car with the café car, the last car on the train. He saw a yellow stool, used to bridge the gap between the bottom train step and the platform.

He studied the doors on both sides of the train. He looked at the door mechanism to see how it worked. The design of the door allowed the top half to open separately from the bottom half. He put down the bags, the pink one on the stool, the black one on the floor. He grabbed the lever on the top half of the door, and pulled it up until the lock disengaged. Then he swung the door's top half open. Air rushed in from the opening. The train was rapidly gaining speed.

The train was traveling too fast for him to jump off. He wanted to get rid of the bags, but he had to be careful about when to eject them. At any moment, Kareem might catch Sarah and grab the detonator. He had to be sure the bags went out at a safe spot. He lifted the pink bag off the stool, and put his foot in its place to steady himself.

Sarah had cleared the fifth car, but still hadn't seen a conductor. Now she ran into the fourth car. She was heading toward the front of the train. In the fourth car, three people stood in the aisle, blocking her way. She shouted at them. "Watch out. Let me through." Then she turned and pointed behind her. "Stop that guy!"

The people in the aisle, two men and one woman, turned to look at her. Without speaking, they ducked out of her way. But as she passed by, she could tell none of them was going to step in the aisle to block Kareem. He was going to get past them.

She continued to run. As she ran, the long thin wires from her earbuds dangled from her right pocket. The wires flailed and slapped against her pant leg. As she passed the restroom at the end of the fourth car, one of the wires lassoed out. It hooked on the lever of the handle to the restroom door. Her iPhone was upside down in her pocket with the wire wrapped around it. When it caught, the phone pulled up and snagged in her pocket, which jerked her to a stop.

She pulled hard against the cord, but couldn't move. It took her a moment to realize she had to stop pressing forward. She had to back up enough to put slack in the cord so she could get the phone out of her pocket. She fumbled the phone out of her pocket, and yanked it toward her. But the earbud cord, still snagged on the handle, popped out of the phone jack. Now she had the two-way radio in her left hand and the phone in her right. She heard Kareem coming up behind her. He was very close.

She decided to drop the phone to divert him. But she panicked. She looked at her hands. She couldn't remember which device was which. She stared at each hand—first one, then the other. The object in each hand was about the same size. Her heart was racing.

She looked around and saw the headphone buds dangling from the doorway to her right. Just as Kareem lunged to grab her, she dropped the device in her right hand onto the floor. When he saw the device fall from her hand, he knelt down and snatched it up.

King felt an abrupt change in the roadbed as the train rolled onto the bridge over the Niagara River. He looked at his watch. It was 10:38 AM. The Maple Leaf crossed the Niagara River at the point where the rapids began. The deep gorge that held the river as it streamed away from the falls narrowed at this point. The narrowing canyon forced millions of gallons of water in the river into an accelerating trough that formed dangerous white water rapids.

King held the pink bag against his knee. It was a Samsonite hardside spinner. He made an instinctive assessment. He concluded that Jasmeen wouldn't have left the pink bag behind had it not been meant for a purpose. He got up on the stool and brought the bag up to waist height. He propped his right foot on the ledge of the unopened bottom half of the door. He saw the trestles holding the bridge sliding sideways before him. He calculated he'd have to aim carefully to hit the open space between the girders, or else go high and throw the bag above the upper beam of the structure. He went high. He steadied his leg on its perch on the door. He swung his arms back and lobbed the Samsonite—up and over the top of the beam. Then, without waiting to see what happened to the first bag, he jumped down, grabbed the black bag, and did the same thing with it.

This time he watched. The black bag fell 300 feet from the top of the bridge down into the gorge and splashed into the rapids behind the pink bag, which was already rushing downriver like a raft.

Along the boardwalk at the White Water Walk tourist attraction on the Canadian side, a little girl tugged her mother's arm. She pointed at the pink bag. Her mother smiled when she saw the pink and black Samsonites racing down the rapids. A group of tourists on the boardwalk moved toward the railing and leaned over the railing to watch the roller bags cascading down the rapids.

Kareem punched at the surface of the phone until he realized it was the wrong device. He threw it on the floor. He screamed at Sarah, "Stop, I have a gun. I will shoot you if you do not stop."

She stopped. She was too frightened to turn around. Kareem came up behind her. He didn't have a gun, but he snatched the two-way radio from her left hand. Then he fell to his knees and concentrated on punching buttons on the device. Breathing hard, he stopped and stared at the key pad. He slapped his hand on the floor and swore. He hit the cancel button.

The bags weaved and bobbed. The raging cascades hurled them forward until giant boulders in the river knocked them like pinballs. They ricocheted from rock to spray and back to rock, all the while zigzagging downstream. Some of the tourists raced along the boardwalk to keep in line with the floating luggage as it coursed alongside them twenty feet away. The bags were rushing toward the massive whirlpool that was half a mile beyond the boardwalk at a hairpin bend in the Niagara River.

Kareem pushed the buttons again. This time he pressed them slowly and deliberately. He entered the detonation code numbers on the Cobra keypad. When he was done, he opened his eyes wide. He punched on the "Call" button. The device emitted a chatter of fast high-pitched beeps.

More than a mile from the bridge, an enormous explosion erupted in the gorge. The roller bags had traveled at thirty miles per hour past the end of the white water boardwalk. But they hadn't yet reached the whirlpool rapids. The bombs exploded from deep in the gorge somewhere between Ferguson Street on the Canadian side and Findlay Drive on the American side in a gigantic blast of water and rock, which flew up hundreds of feet into the air above the river, and then clattered back down to the rocks with a torrent of water. The shrapnel fell entirely within the chasm, causing a monstrous noise. A piece of it fell on a teenage boy who had run to the end of the boardwalk to watch the luggage. The projectile sliced open a gash in his right arm above the elbow. It took him a moment to process what happened. Then he cried out. All around him, the other tourists had ducked beneath an overhang on the canyon side of the walk just as the debris rained down. No one but the boy was hurt.

Kareem looked up when he heard the explosion. He shouted, "Muhammad," and clasped his hands together as if in prayer. He whispered, "Peace be upon Him." But then he lowered his gaze. He wasn't sure how to interpret the magnitude of the explosion. Something was off. The sound was too far away. He rushed to look out the small window in the exit door of his car. He pressed his face to the glass. Within a moment, he saw what had happened. His mission had failed. He dropped back down to his knees and bowed his head into his hands.

King stared out through the open space of his exit door. He saw that the bombs had gone off past the end of the boardwalk. He heard footsteps and turned to see the uniformed Amtrak café attendant standing across from him at the doorway of the café car.

"What the hell are you doing?" the man yelled.

"Had to get some fresh air," King said. Then he turned from the attendant, and began to run back toward the front of the train. It was obvious Kareem had wrested the two-way radio from Sarah. But he wasn't sure what Kareem would do next.

THREE

When the Maple Leaf finished crossing the bridge over the river, it arrived in the United States. The train approached the depot in Niagara Falls, New York. The Amtrak conductor had heard the explosive sound that echoed like booming thunderclaps, but that didn't stop him from making his standard announcement.

"Ladies and gentlemen, our next stop will be Niagara Falls, New York. Before we arrive at the station, U. S. Customs agents will board the train to conduct a border inspection. You must remain in your seats at this time. Have your passports ready and available for inspection. Please remain in your seats until the Customs agents have completed their inspection and cleared the train."

King did not sit down in a seat. He made his way to the third car, where he saw Sarah, sitting near the back of the car, her body rigid. King asked her, "Are you all right?"

She nodded. "Was anyone hurt?"

"I don't know," he said. "The bags landed in the rapids. They blew up down river in the gorge. They were past the boardwalk when they exploded. I think they were far enough away so that no one was hurt. But I'm not sure. It could have been much worse."

She stared at him. "Who are you?" she asked.

"I'm Tyrone King."

"What are you? A cop?"

"No."

"Who's that guy?"

"His name's Kareem."

"Is he a terrorist?"

"No doubt," King said. "But thanks to you, I think he's only a would-be terrorist."

She had retrieved her phone. She held it up now in her left hand, then grabbed her left wrist with her right hand to steady it. "He got the detonator away from me. He set off the bomb. He told me he had a gun. But he didn't."

"It doesn't matter," King said. "You kept him away from the detonator long enough to keep him from blowing up the train. You were brave."

She grimaced. "Then how come my hand is still shaking?"

King shrugged. "That's how bravery works. Feel the fear and do it anyway."

"Now what happens?"

"Difficult to say," King said. "It depends on him."

"Won't they catch him? The border agents?"

"If he stays on the train. But I have a feeling he won't."

King looked out the window. The Maple Leaf was slowing as it entered the railyard. Multiple sets of tracks fanned out into the yard. A quarter-mile away, at the far end of the yard, a line of seven tanker cars sat on a track. An engine began to push the tankers. It pushed them 200 feet, and then stopped abruptly. All the cars stopped except the seventh car, the one farthest from the engine. The seventh car uncoupled from the train, then kept going. The decoupled tanker rolled down the track until it shunted off onto a sidetrack and kept rolling.

A minute later, the engine began to move again. It pushed the remaining tanker cars another 200 feet, then stopped. Once again, the last tanker detached and kept going. King realized the freight crew was using this technique to sort the tanker cars onto different sidetracks.

Meanwhile, the Maple Leaf had come to a complete stop. King turned from Sarah and made his way cautiously toward the front of the train. As he crept down the aisle, he glimpsed something moving outside the window to his right. Kareem was running across the railyard, headed toward the tanker cars. King looked out the window on the left side of the train. There he saw a group of U. S. border agents preparing to board.

King spoke to the passengers sitting near the end of the second car.

"How'd that man get out?"

A boy in a Yankee's baseball cap pointed to an emergency exit window on the right side of the train. The window dangled outward, unanchored from its frame. Kareem must have jumped off the right side of the train while the customs agents were boarding from the left. King hesitated as he considered what to do. He could go right now to the border agents and tell them what had happened, tell them about the man who was getting away on the other side of the train. He knew they'd detain him and question him. At best, it might take them twenty or thirty minutes to realize that they should pursue Kareem.

He looked out the window. Kareem was headed across the railyard toward the tanker cars. If he got on the other side of those cars, he'd be out of sight. In twenty or thirty minutes he'd have disappeared completely. And once he escaped, he'd be free, free to try to blow up something else.

King decided he couldn't let Kareem get away, no matter the consequences. He went to the emergency exit window and pushed it out. He folded his body and perched himself on the window frame. He looked down. He gauged it to be a seven-foot drop onto a paved surface. Should be easy.

He jumped out the window, but he landed wrong. His feet hit the ground first, out ahead of him, then his knees snapped back. He flung his arms backwards to break the fall. He came down hard on his hands, which took the brunt of the impact. Small bits of gravel in the pavement gashed his palms and ripped the skin of his fingers. He eased himself forward and sat on the ground, staring at his bloodied palms. His hands stung. Blood rushed from his head as he tilted his head back. He looked up at the open window.

Sarah stuck her head out the window above him. "Are you OK?" she yelled.

"I think so."

"That jump was not too graceful."

"Thanks."

"Now he's getting away," she said.

"I know."

King looked out toward the tanker cars. Then he looked back toward Sarah. "Tell the agents what happened," he shouted. "I don't want to get shot out here."

He tried to stand up. But when he did, his legs wobbled and gave way beneath him. He fell back down to the ground. His right knee hurt. The blood rushed from his head again, making him dizzy. He leaned forward, hung his head below his knees, and closed his eyes.

Then King heard the sound of metal clanking. He turned to look over his shoulder at the door on the end of the second car. The door swung open. An arm dropped the yellow stool out. Then he saw Sarah. She carried a lavender Prada handbag. She stepped down onto the stool, paused, then gently hopped from the stool onto the pavement. She ran over to him.

"What are you doing?" King asked. "The border agents don't like it when a passenger jumps off."

"I'm not the one who jumped off," she said. "I think I detrained quite gracefully."

"Why? Why'd you get off the train?"

"Because you're obviously hurt," she said. "And meanwhile the guy is getting away."

"I'll be all right."

"Can you stand?"

"I think so." He started to stand up again. She grabbed him by the arm to help lift him up. She steadied him on his feet.

They both looked across the railyard. There were four cars left on the tanker train. Kareem had climbed onto the side of the fourth tanker car. He was climbing up the rungs leading to the top of the tanker. They watched as he went up over the top and onto the other side. He was no longer visible from the Maple Leaf.

"Uh oh," Sarah said. "I think he got away."

King started to move toward the tankers. But his knees still felt weak. He had to hobble. Sarah moved with him, half-holding him up.

"He can't have gone too far. You should go back," King said.

She shook her head. "You can't walk on your own."

"I'll be all right in a minute."

"He'll be long gone by then."

They kept moving toward the tankers, King hobbling and Sarah propping him up by his left arm. After a few minutes, when his knees had stretched out some, he felt better. He pulled away from Sarah. He tried to walk on his own. He tottered forward.

The engine maneuvering the tankers began to move. It pushed the tanker cars forward. As before, after two hundred feet, the engine stopped abruptly. The fourth tanker, with Kareem hanging on its far side, detached from the train and kept rolling down the track. It shot off to the right side of the main track.

King and Sarah shuffled quickly toward the third tanker car. When they got there, King reached up, grabbed the lowest rung, and climbed onto the side. Then he twisted around and called to Sarah. "Go back to the train."

But she stood still and watched him. The tanker engine started up again. It pushed the last three cars 200 feet forward, then stopped. The third car shot loose, with King hanging onto its side. It shunted off toward the left sidetrack and rolled slowly forward. King leaned out as far as he could from his car to see what had happened to Kareem. But he couldn't see him or his tanker.

Meanwhile three border agents and two other men in dark blue jackets imprinted with "Homeland Security" in bright yellow scrambled off the train at the exit door that Sarah had opened. All the men hit the ground running. The two men from homeland security had their guns drawn.

FOUR

When his tanker car began to slow, King jumped off it. He gauged he had traveled at least a quarter mile. As the car rolled past him, he looped around the back of it. Then he saw Kareem running toward a gap in the fence at the far side of the railyard. King looked back toward the Maple Leaf. The border agents and security men had stopped for a huddle near the tanker engine. One of the men was talking into his phone.

Then King saw the second tanker car—the one that had been next in line after his—coast to a stop along the same track onto which Kareem's car had gone. Coming round the side, he saw a flash of gold near the ground, then above it the black crepe, and then the blue satin. Sarah was running toward him, waving her purse.

He stood and waited for her to catch up with him.

"What the hell are you doing?" he yelled. "You should go back to the train." King waved his arms toward the train like a traffic cop. "Go back right now. Put your hands in the air. Walk slowly toward the agents with your hands raised. Then tell them what's going on here."

"I can't," she said. "It isn't safe."

"No, listen. It'll be safer for you if you go back. They won't shoot you."

"Oh really? They just did shoot at me," she said. "Several times." Her voice mixed anger and fear.

King looked back toward the agents. The two from Homeland Security were running again, with guns out. "Damn," he said. "They must've already had a report about the bombs exploding."

"Seeing as how they're shooting at us," Sarah said. "I think we better run. When we're in the clear, we can call somebody and explain what happened."

King turned toward the gap in the fence. It opened onto a city street. Kareem was at the end of the street, moving out of sight.

"There he goes again," Sarah said. "He keeps disappearing."

King and Sarah ran after him. They ran through the gap in the fence and onto the street. They ran along the sidewalk, then turned right where they had seem Kareem turn. But when they got around the corner, he was nowhere to be seen.

"He must've gone between the houses," King said.

They hurried a few hundred feet, then dashed across the street toward a parking lot that sat between a house and a one-story industrial building. At the back was an alley. The far side of the alley opened onto the backyard of another house. There was no fence, so they ran through the lot, across the alley, into the yard, past the house, and out onto another street.

Then they repeated the same pattern. They continued moving between houses as they made their way in a straight line away from the railyard. They crossed two more streets. When they got to the third, King waved his hand to signal Sarah to turn right.

They turned onto the sidewalk and stopped running. Kareem was nowhere in sight. A middle-aged woman sat on her front porch across the street. She had a book in her hand, but she looked up when she saw King and Sarah.

King reached out and took Sarah's hand.

"We should act like a couple," he said.

She looked at him doubtfully. "Yeah. OK. I guess."

They walked hand in hand down the street. A busy intersection was just ahead of them. "We ought to catch a cab or get a bus," King said. "Do you have any American money?"

She nodded, and lifted her purse. "I'm rolling in it."

When they got to the intersection, the signs told them they were at the corner of Ontario and Hyde Park Boulevard. On the other side of Ontario was a Sunoco gas station. There was also a bus stop. The sign said the Route 52A Hyde Park bus went to the Niagara Transit Center. A paper schedule was taped to the sign pole.

King studied the schedule. "What time is it?" he asked.

Sarah had a watch that looked like a bracelet. The watch face was so small she had to bring her wrist close to her eyes to read it. "It's 11:15," she said.

"A bus stops here in five minutes." He looked down Hyde Park Boulevard for signs of the homeland security agents. They weren't in sight.

A helicopter buzzed up in the sky. They both looked up. A large blue helicopter was circling above the railyard. Without speaking, King yanked on Sarah's hand and pulled her toward the Sunoco.

"Would you stop pulling me along like some luggage?"

"There's a chopper up there. Don't you understand? They're looking for us."

"Yeah, I understand. I get it. But let's walk normally—no one dragging anyone else. It reads better from the air."

"OK. Fine."

Inside the gas station, King asked the man at the cash register, "How much is the bus?"

"Where you headed?"

"All over. We're sightseeing," King said.

The man nodded. "You want an all-day pass. They cost four bucks. You can buy one on the bus."

"Do we need exact change?" Sarah asked.

The man smiled at her. "The drivers don't make change," he

said. "But I do. You need some singles?"

Sarah had already taken a ten-dollar bill from her handbag. "How about a five and five ones?" she said. To King she said, "I'll pay for us both."

The man took the ten, pushed a button on his cash register and counted out the bills. He looked up. "You better hurry," he said, and pointed out the window. "The bus is coming now."

King and Sarah ran back to the bus stop. The blue helicopter circled low in the sky half a mile away, then turned in their direction. The bus belched a sound from its brakes when it stopped in front of them. They climbed in. The helicopter passed overhead as the bus doors closed. Sarah stuffed eight dollars in the cash box, and the driver gave her two passes. They made their way down the aisle and sat near the exit door.

They sat in silence looking out the window as the bus traveled down Hyde Park Boulevard. Then King said to her, "I was just thinking, I told you my full name, but I don't know yours."

"I'm Sarah Gaber," she said. She extended her hand toward him. "You said your name is Tyrone King, right?"

"Yeah, but hey..." He shook her hand. "Fellow runaways generally call me Ty."

"Do they?" She smiled, but then she withdrew her hand, and tilted her head. "OK, Ty. Do you have any kind of a plan?"

"I think we should go where there is a crowd—somewhere with plenty of witnesses." King lowered his voice. "They won't shoot at us in that case. At least I don't think so. And then we ought to call the FBI to explain."

"What about Kareem? You think he got on a bus too?" As she spoke, she looked around to assure herself that he wasn't on their bus.

"Kareem had a plan," King said. "I overheard him tell the woman with him called Jasmeen that he would call her from the caves at 1:00 PM. What time is it now?"

Sarah held the tiny watch up to her face again. "It's 11:29," she said. "Is that like a joke? Terrorists don't actually live in caves, right?"

"That device Kareem had is a two-way radio. It's a walkie-talkie. It has a range of only a mile or two. That means he has to be close enough to Jasmeen to be within range when he contacts her. But she got off the train before we crossed the border. So he's going to have to get himself somewhere near Canada, while staying on this side of the river. My guess is he's going to the Cave of the Winds."

"Cave of the what?"

King leaned forward in his seat and faced her. "It's a tourist attraction on the American side called Cave of the Winds. I went there when I was a kid. You go down an elevator. They've built wooden walkways so you can walk out from the base of the cliff close to the falls. From anywhere out on those walkways he'd have a clear range to Jasmeen on the Canadian side of the river."

Sarah stared at a poster above the window touting a business school degree. "OK, but wouldn't people see him?"

"They'd see a guy talking on his phone. Everyone on the cave tour is given a raincoat to wear because of all the mist and splashing from the falls. The raincoat would help him blend in with the crowd. It would help us blend in too."

"Us?" She looked at him in disbelief. "You want us to chase after him?"

"It would be easier to prove what happened, if we nabbed him."

"If *we* nabbed him?" She made a face.

"Well OK, if I nabbed him."

"But you said you're not a cop, right?"

"No, I'm not a cop. I was in the army. In an earlier life I worked in counter-intelligence in Afghanistan."

She leaned her head back and studied the ceiling of the bus. "I don't know," she said. "It seems too dangerous."

"He doesn't have a weapon. I can take care of him."

The bus stopped at a red light. Sarah looked at the woman

across the aisle who was staring ahead blankly. She wondered if the woman could hear any of their conversation. "You'd take care of him how?"

"The same way I took away his gun. Using Aikido. It's a martial art."

"You mean like Kung Fu?"

"Kung Fu is Chinese. Aikido is Japanese. You learn how to defend yourself while protecting your attacker from injury."

Sarah thought about that. Protecting the attacker seemed counterproductive. "You protect the attacker?"

"Absolutely."

This made no sense to her. "Why?" she asked. "Why would you want to protect your attacker?"

"Aikido is non-violent—even in the face of violence. The point is, if you believe in non-violence, you don't change your belief just because someone else is violent."

"That reminds me," said Sarah. "Why the hell didn't you use that gun to keep Kareem in line instead of letting him chase me and the detonator all over the train?"

"I don't believe in using guns."

"That's it? You don't believe in using guns? What if someone was hurt in that explosion? A lot of people could have been hurt or killed. You risked all that just because you don't believe in guns?"

"It wasn't an easy decision." King lowered his head. "I didn't have much time to think about it. I had a picture of myself being able to get rid of the suitcases before he got to the detonator. And I had faith that you'd keep the detonator away from him."

"Oh, that's reassuring. You had a picture."

"If I'd had more time to think about it, I might not have handled it that way. I don't know."

"Don't you think you have to use force against violent people like Kareem? You have to threaten people like that with violence. Otherwise they don't get the message."

"I think they do," King said. "It's just not the message they expect."

Sarah thought about that for a moment. Then she said, "I think the message they get is that you're weak."

King remembered when he first saw her. *Strong ki.* He wasn't going to argue with her about guns. He let it drop. "Maybe," he said.

Neither of them spoke. Then Sarah asked, "So are you good at this Aikido thing?"

"I'm just a beginner. I have a lot to learn."

Sarah looked at him and nodded. "I guess in Aikido they don't teach you how to jump from a six-foot high train window."

"That jump was at least seven feet," King protested. "I lost my balance on the ledge. The window was small; I had to fold myself in two like a clamshell cell phone. But you're right. I screwed it up."

Sarah said nothing. She sat in silence staring out the window as the bus pulled into the transit center. She thought about what King had said. His 'protect the attacker' thing was idealistic and impractical. And the gun thing was foolish. He'd put people's lives in jeopardy. His idealism might be noble, but it was going to get him in trouble. He needed someone to look out for him.

"OK," she said. "Let's go nab him. But I can't believe I'm doing this. And if you get hold of a gun again, give it to me. I won't have a problem using it."

FIVE

King and Sarah got off the bus at the transit center and boarded a trolley, which the driver said would take them close to Goat Island for the Cave of the Winds tour.

It was 12:11 PM by Sarah's watch when they got off the trolley at Rainbow Boulevard and First Street. They walked across the bridge on First Street to Goat Island, where signs directed them to the Cave of the Winds.

They bought tickets in a small stone building, which housed a gift shop and an elevator that brought tourists down to the base of the American falls. A handful of tourists browsed the gift shop. None of them was Kareem. They walked to the rear of the building and waited for the elevator.

When it came, they rode it 175 feet down into the gorge. The base opened onto a staging area, where an attendant handed them yellow-hooded raincoats, beach sandals, and a bag to check their shoes. They donned their gear, checked their shoes, and then advanced to a wooden walkway that went out to the base. The walkway led visitors up a series of staircases to the "Hurricane Deck," which sat twenty feet from the billowing torrents of Bridal

Veil Falls. They huddled in a corner near the bottom walkway, staying close to the elevator.

They felt safely anonymous in their raincoats. Inside the hoods, their hair and the sides of their faces were hidden. They gazed at the water crashing into the Niagara River. Every few minutes the elevator disgorged another group of tourists. Each time it did, King and Sarah turned to glance at the faces of the people coming onto the walkway. It was fifteen minutes before they saw him. Even with his face obscured by raingear, his dark beard made him obvious.

He walked straight toward them. King leaned down, put his arms around Sarah, drew her close, and pretended to kiss her. As he did so, he used his fingers to close the gap between their hoods so their faces were hidden completely. He knew this kissing ruse was a cliché. But he thought it was the safest thing to do. He put his mouth against her cheek, and whispered, "Sorry. It's only until he gets past us."

"You're kidding, right? This is a cheap move."

"What else am I supposed to do?" King whispered back. "Should I stop him and ask to take his picture?"

Sarah squirmed around, but she didn't break away. She whispered more loudly, "As a matter of fact, my iPhone is also a camera. I could take it out, turn you around and take your picture against the falls." Then she lowered her voice. "It seems to me that would hoodwink him as much as this move."

"I'm just being careful. With these rain hats smooshed together like this, he can't see our faces, and I figured that was the safest bet."

"Yeah, but can you see him?" Sarah darted her eyes. She could see nothing but the inside of their hoods. "The way you're holding me, I can't see anything except your ear lobe. What is that in your ear, by the way?"

"In my ear?"

"Yeah. It sparkles."

"Oh it's a stud." King moved his eyes sideways as if looking at his ear. "You know—an earring, a diamond stud."

"Diamond?"

"Well, rhinestone."

"Cute."

"Thanks."

"Here's the problem," she said. "We can't see him. How do we know he hasn't recognized us, turned around, and run out of here?"

King lifted his head slightly and opened a view along the edge of his hood. "It's OK. He's still here. He's about fifteen feet away. He's leaning over the railing. He's got his radio out. He's punching codes in the radio."

"Jesus. I hope something else isn't going to blow up."

King thought back to Kareem's conversation on the train. "I don't think so. He must be calling Jasmeen on it."

"So are you going to nab him or what?"

"I want to get closer. If he's calling Jasmeen, I want to hear what he says to her before I grab him."

"You must be crazy, Ty. He's gonna recognize you if we crowd him so close."

"Not if we stay in this kissing position. Besides, I don't think he has the faintest idea that we're here. When he mentioned the cave thing to Jasmeen, he didn't know I was eavesdropping. Anyway, he's looking out across the gorge. He must be hoping to see her on the other side."

"Can he see us?"

"I suppose so. But as far as he's concerned, we're just a couple of lovebirds."

"Yeah, right. In your dreams."

"Hey, give me a break. I'm not doing anything out of line here except talking with my mouth very close to your cheek."

"Yeah, well feeling your breath go up my nose makes me nervous."

"I brushed my teeth this morning."

"It's not that. I don't like confined spaces. This hood makes me claustrophobic. It's like being trapped in a burqa with a horn dog."

"A horn dog? Really? You know what? If I was making a move on you, you'd know it."

"Where is your hand?"

"It's on your shoulder. Is that OK?"

"Not that hand, the other one."

"It's on your waist—like we're waltzing. It's pretty tame."

"I thought I felt something goose me a bit lower down."

"That was some people walking by us on the walkway. Would you please relax? A group just came out of the elevator. Let's move with them as they go by."

With his arms around her, King pulled Sarah along the wooden railing, sidling with her until they were five feet from Kareem. Holding the walkie-talkie to his ear, Kareem glanced in their direction and pursed his lips, but then he looked back toward the Canadian side of the gorge and said "Hello" as his call was answered.

The roar of the falls made it difficult to hear. But King picked up the gist of what Kareem said. He told Jasmeen he was safe. He told her some guy had attacked him, and that guy had thrown the bags down into the river. But, he had escaped. He told her not to worry, that he would redeem himself. But he'd have to wait for Abdul to make a new plan in New York. He said he would meet her at the hotel, as agreed. Then he shoved the radio in his pocket and walked up toward the Hurricane Deck.

"OK. He's gone up the stairs. We can relax for a minute," King said. He backed away from the feigned kiss. They turned to look out at the river again.

"So what now?" she asked.

"I changed my mind," King said. "I don't think this is a good place to grab him. There are too many people around. I'd have to subdue him, then get him into the elevator. Besides, I just heard him say that he and Jasmeen are planning to hook up with some guy named Abdul so they can try some new stunt in New York."

"Shit!"

"Yeah." King let it sink in. Kareem was going to try again. There was no way he could stand by and let that happen. "I think I should follow him," he said. "I have to find out who he's meeting in New York, and stop whatever they have in mind."

"Wouldn't this be a good time to call the FBI?"

"Maybe. But they'll haul me in for interrogation. Then I won't be able to follow him."

"But if you told them where Kareem and Jasmeen are right now, on the phone? Couldn't they get someone in the government to follow them?"

"It would depend on how fast they could decide, and who they had nearby to work undercover. Logistically, it's a problem. I think it would be better if I do it. In fact, it's the kind of thing I trained for."

"You trained undercover?"

"Yes. I speak Arabic. I can make myself look Middle Eastern." He put his hand up to his chin and stroked it as if he was stroking facial hair. "It helps if I wear a beard." He looked around as if to check if anyone else was listening. "I spent three weeks under-cover in Kabul."

Sarah raised an eyebrow. "At the moment you look more Rasta than Al Qaida. It's your hair. Your hair looks wrong with those dreadlocks." She squinted, to picture him without his locks. "I guess your skin is about the right color to look Middle Eastern."

A parade of yellow rain-coated children filed past them. King turned to look up at the falls. The sheer volume of water endlessly pouring over the precipice was mindboggling. He'd always thought of Niagara Falls as a romantic spot—a place for honeymooners. By rights, he should be here with his arm around his sweetheart. But it was clear that Sarah had no interest in flirting with him. It was a pity. He liked her. She was beautiful and brave. He wished they had time to get to know each other better.

He explained about his coloring. "My mother was white," he said. "My father was black."

"So you got his hair and her skin?"

"Mostly," he said. "But my skin is darker than hers. She was Irish, very pale, but with black curly hair." He waggled his fingers above his head to simulate playing with curly hair.

Sarah smiled.

King smiled back. He sized her up once again. There was something unique about her appearance. "What about you?" he asked. "You don't look exactly Anglo Saxon."

Sarah shrugged. "Like you, I'm a combo platter. But not in the same way. My combo is more heavy duty than yours."

"Combo of what? Your skin is olive. Your hair is black. Nice eyes by the way."

"It's not a racial kind of combo; it's a religious and ethnic kind of combo."

"Interdenominational?"

"You could say that. My mother is Jewish. My father is Muslim. Since being Jewish is based on maternal lineage, I'm officially a Jew. My parents split up a long time ago. When they met, it was an 'opposites attract' thing. But then it stopped working." Sarah had been watching the Maid of the Mist, filled with tourists in blue raincoats, maneuver its way around the river. Now she looked back toward the elevator. "I'm not sure what to do. Do you want me to stay with you? I'm not much good at nabbing guys with beards."

"No. You should turn yourself in. Tell them everything. I'll stay on him."

"Where is he now?"

"He's up on the Hurricane Deck. I guess he's taking in the view of the falls."

"Listen, Bruce Lee. Are you sure you'll be all right?"

"I'm sure. He doesn't have a weapon. I can handle him."

At Niagara, it was always possible for the spray from the rushing water to create tropical storm-like conditions. Now the breeze was picking up. Sarah pulled her raincoat tighter around her body. "OK," she said. "It's getting windy. I think I should leave now. I'm going to go back up top. I want to call my father. I have to let him know what's going on. He's expecting to meet me at Penn Station on the Maple Leaf."

"Do you live in New York?"

"No. I live in Toronto with my mother." Sarah glanced at the elevator, which was loading for a trip up, but she didn't move toward it. "My father lives in New York. But I keep things at his place for when I visit. What about you?"

King said, "I live in Chicago."

Sarah didn't catch what he said because the wind and spray muffled it. "Where? Did you say Chicago?"

"Yes, Chicago." King shouted now to make himself heard above the wind. "I'm on vacation. Or I was. I went first to Toronto, then I planned to go to to New York."

Sarah nodded. "Do you have money?"

"I have some cash. I can get more. I have my phone and my wallet and credit card in my pocket."

"Should I give you some time before I call the FBI?"

"Give me an hour. Otherwise, they might jump on me before I get out of here."

"What should I tell them about you?" A big gust of wind doused the deck with spray just as Sarah spoke.

King shouted, "I can't hear you."

Sarah moved next to King and signaled him to come closer. She pulled the sides of her hood out toward him, and he did the same. She eyed him warily. "I said, what do you want me to tell the FBI about you?"

"Tell them to look up my military record. That should clarify which side I'm on. Tell them not to shoot me. Be sure you tell a journalist about me too."

"A journalist?"

"Yeah."

"Don't you trust the government?"

"Yes...well...mostly. I like insurance."

"OK." Sarah stepped back and looked up toward the Hurricane Deck. She saw several figures in yellow raincoats playing in the mist. Behind them, the cascade from the Bridal Veil crashed on the rocks. Vapor sprayed everyone on the deck. "Well," she said, "I guess this is good-bye." She looked at the elevator, then back at King. "You can't jump for shit. But you're pretty good with bomb disposal."

"Thanks," King said. "Don't let those federal men push you around."

"OK."

King stepped backward a foot to gaze at her. The mist from the falls had soaked her raincoat and her face. "How old are you anyway?" he asked.

"28," she said. "Why? How old are you?"

"I'm 31. It's just that you look much younger."

"Oil of Olay."

"When this is over, we should hook up again," he shouted over the spray.

"We should what?"

"We should hook up again," he shouted again.

"Hook up?" Her otherwise smooth brow suddenly wrinkled.

The wind died down and suddenly it was quieter. "You know what I mean," King said. "You make me feel tongue-tied. I only mean we have a lot to talk about, after what's happened here to us."

"Yeah, I suppose we do. It's been unreal—but also kind of a blast."

"Ha. Ha," King said, and smiled broadly.

She opened her handbag and pulled out her phone. "We'd better trade phone numbers. You should call me if you get in a jam—or if you catch him—or whatever. In fact, why don't you call me about 3 o'clock and let me know what's going on? Otherwise I'm gonna worry."

King pulled out his own phone from his pocket. They exchanged phones and keyed in each other's numbers. Then, after trading them back, they shook hands, and Sarah walked to the elevator. Just before she reached the elevator, she turned and called back, "Don't lose your phone!"

King nodded and began to make his way up the stairs toward the Hurricane Deck.

SIX

When King reached the Hurricane Deck, he counted fourteen yellow raincoats. To his surprise, Kareem was not standing by himself. He stood at the far corner, where he was speaking like a tour guide to a family of four. The husband and wife listened to him attentively as he pointed up toward the falls, then back down toward the river.

The teenage son wasn't paying attention. He shuffled around, slowly tracing a circle around the perimeter of the group formed by Kareem and his parents. All of the son's attention was on the portable game device in his hand.

The younger daughter had her hand stuck through the railing and was attempting to reach the water cascade. Her maneuvers grew more contorted as she shoved her arms and shoulders through the opening.

King had put his phone back in his pocket, but now he took it out again. Sarah's parting admonition, 'Don't lose your phone,' had launched a series of thoughts. At first he thought that he needn't worry if he lost his phone, because when he bought it, he'd installed an app on the phone called SignalSecure that was designed to help recover lost or stolen phones.

He could activate the software remotely. He could use it to turn the phone off or on, wipe its memory, or track its location on a map via GPS. If a thief stole the phone and inserted a new SIM card to change the phone number, the software would lock the phone automatically.

King quickly navigated through the file menu of his phone. First, he verified that SignalSecure was installed and operational. He opened the entry he'd made for Sarah's phone number and memorized it. Then he deleted all the names in his contact list except one. He left the entry for his business partner back in Chicago, which was listed simply as "Melanie." He made Melanie the first listing in his contact list. Then he entered some invented contact names and gave them phony addresses in New York, but no phone numbers. He erased all his text messages and emails. He changed the name of the phone account owner to Judith Goldman. Finally, he set the phone's ringer to "off." Then he looked up and continued to survey the movements of people around him.

As he did so, he called Melanie. He left her a voice mail. He told her that if she were to receive another call from this same phone number, she should answer the phone by saying, "Hi, Judith; how's Niagara Falls?" He explained that the call would be from a man named Kareem—if he spoke, she should insist on asking where Judith was.

After leaving the message, King watched as the son circled further from his parents—absorbed by the video game in his hand. King pulled the plastic strap that tightened his hood until his hair was covered. He walked toward the boy, stood next to him, bent down, and pretended to pick up something near the boy's feet. He did it in such a way that the boy couldn't help but notice him. When he stood up, he tried to hand the phone to the boy. But he didn't take it.

King said, "That guy with the beard back there dropped this." King pointed at Kareem. "It fell out of his raincoat. Can you give it back to him?"

The boy looked back at Kareem, then at King, and said, "I don't know him. You give it back."

King said, "No time. My girlfriend's waiting for me up top. If I don't get up there right away, she's gonna throw a fit." King set the phone down on the deck at the boy's feet. He said. "But if you don't want to deal with it—just leave it here, OK? Maybe the guy will find it later—whatever. I gotta go." Then King turned and walked a few steps toward the top of the stairs.

"Oh…all right," the boy said. He reached down and picked up the phone.

King dashed down the stairs. From the bottom platform, he paused long enough to watch the boy interrupt Kareem, speak to him and hand him the phone. But before Kareem could react— and look around—King ducked his head. He went immediately to the elevator, got in, and rode back to the top.

He was gambling that the boy would say simply that "some guy" had seen it fall from Kareem's pocket. He was sure the kid couldn't have noticed the dreads under his hood—or much else in the way of description. And he was counting on the sparse speaking habits of American teenagers around adults.

The real gamble was, would Kareem fall for the bait? Would he find a reason to keep the phone for some purpose of his own— or just throw it away?

It was a big gamble. King sacrificed his only convenient form of communication for this scheme. Now he had to find a way to get online to activate the phone's security program, and set it to track the GPS coordinates. He also had to find a way to call Sarah as soon as possible and tell her the plan; otherwise, she might call his number and start talking to Kareem instead.

When he got to the top, he went to the cashier in the gift shop and said to her, "Excuse me. I gave my cell phone to my son half an hour ago. Now I can't find him and I'm getting worried. Will you loan me your phone so I can call him and find out where he is?"

The woman hesitated, then nodded. "OK, but I'm not supposed to do this—so make it quick." She handed King a cordless phone from somewhere behind her counter.

"Do you happen to have a paper and pencil?" King asked.

The woman made a face. But she reached down below the counter and came back with both.

King had memorized Sarah's number. But to be safe, he wrote it down, handed the pencil back to the cashier, then stepped out of the cashier's earshot. He dialed Sarah's number. After three rings, she answered.

"Hello."

"Sarah, it's Tyrone."

"The caller ID says 'Niagara Park District.' I almost didn't answer. What's going on?"

"That's why I'm calling. I ditched my phone with Kareem. I am using it to track where he's going. But that means you shouldn't call me on that number."

"What do you mean you ditched it with Kareem? How did you do that?"

"I'll explain in a minute. I borrowed a phone from the gift shop and I don't have much time. Where are you anyway?"

"I'm walking on a street headed toward a hotel. Where are you?"

"I'm still at the Cave of the Winds. Did you talk to your father?"

"Yes." Long pause. "Ty, there are some new twists in the situation. I'm not going to be able to call the FBI after all."

"Why not?"

"It's a long story."

"What hotel are you going to?"

"The Crowne Plaza"

"OK, I'll meet you there. Where is it?"

"It's at 300 Third Street. Easy to remember. How did you pass the phone to Kareem?"

"I had a kid walk it up to him and tell him someone saw it fall out of his pocket."

"Why?"

"Because if he holds onto it, I can track his position through GPS. It's tailor-made for tailing him."

"Why would he keep it?"

"Why wouldn't he? If he thinks a woman named Judith lost it, then it's just a free phone for him to use. No one can connect it to him. He's operating in the shadows, right? Just like we are"

"Yeah, just like we are. But what if he doesn't fall for it?"

"Then I'll have to trail him the old-fashioned way. In which case, I won't be able to meet you at the hotel."

"How am I supposed to reach you?"

"You can't. If I don't show up at the hotel, I'll find a way to call you back in about an hour."

"OK."

"OK. Good-bye again. And thanks, Sarah."

They hung up. King returned the phone to the cashier. Then he looked around the shop, while he waited for Kareem to come back up. He busied himself browsing souvenirs. He found a nondescript hat that was big enough to fit over his hair. He took it to the cashier and bought it. He put on the hat, and stuffed his dreds under the brim until they were completely hidden.

He settled on a strategic spot to wait. He stood by a postcard kiosk and surveyed the people who came off the elevator. He waited forty minutes before Kareem finally came back up.

King circled the display until he was behind it. He took a postcard in his hand to inspect it. As he did so, he peered through the wire structure of the kiosk.

He watched as Kareem walked out the front door of the gift shop. Through the window he saw Kareem stand outside the building and hold the phone—King's phone—in his hand. Kareem pushed buttons on the phone. He studied its content. Then he held it up to his ear, as if making a call. He listened for a moment. Then he abruptly pulled it from his ear and pushed a button. He smiled and put it in his pocket.

King smiled too. He watched as Kareem walked onto the First Street Bridge and crossed back to the mainland. After a moment, King followed him on the bridge, crossed the river, and left Goat Island. He headed toward the Crowne Plaza.

SEVEN

Sarah sat on the bed in her hotel room, thinking about her conversation with her father. Her parents had separated when she was five. She grew up living with her mother, and she had mostly adopted her mother's view of her father. Her mother thought he was a domineering schmuck. 'The man lacks any insight into what is humanly appropriate and what is not,' was how her mother put it. Sarah had vague memories of them arguing with each other. But she did not know what they had argued about or why her mother had become so disillusioned.

It wasn't until Sarah became an adult that she began to form her own opinions about her father. She felt awkward around him, in part because his manner was always formal and solemn. It took her some time to understand that this wasn't from a lack of affection, but from his sense of propriety. The formality was his way of modeling decency and virtue. Her mother was emotional, expressive, and funny, while her father, the opposite in every way, was reserved, quiet, and serious.

Whenever they saw each other, her father pampered her with gifts and money. Intellectually, she knew this was his way of showing affection. She supposed he felt guilty about being absent from her life. But she had told him more than once that she didn't want his money or gifts. It didn't matter. He didn't understand. He reacted as if she was rejecting him. He couldn't grasp that she wanted intimacy—real intimacy—more than money.

This trip to New York was to be her opportunity to spend time with him and get to know him better. But then this chance episode with Kareem and King and the bomb had thrown her plans up in the air. Her father reacted with uncharacteristic emotion when she told him what was going on. There was no worse fate in his mind than finding himself associated in some way with terrorists. She had never heard his voice so animated. He told her he hated the way the terrorists had twisted everything good about Islam. "Peace and mercy," he said, "are the foundation of the prophet's teaching. Do we not say 'peace be upon him?' Do we not say 'In the name of Allah, the merciful, the compassionate?' What does Islam have to do with exploding bombs and killing innocent people? Where are the mercy, compassion, and peace in that? We are patient, faithful, praying, fasting, charitable servants of Allah, not terrorists! Shame on those people! Shame on them!"

Sarah was flabbergasted at how much her father had sounded like her mother. It would have been just what her mother would have said, "Shame on you!" when someone did something wrong.

Sarah had asked her father, "So are you a pacifist then?" He'd said, "No. I wouldn't transgress against anyone, but with Allah's help I would kick butt in self defense." Despite herself, she'd laughed when he said 'kick butt.' It was the most uncharacteristic phrase she'd ever heard him say. But when she told him she had to call the FBI, he'd grown quiet. He'd been silent for a long time and then it seemed almost as if he might cry. That was too much. Anger and then tears all in the same conversation.

Her heart went out to him when she saw his struggle. He didn't care about the trouble it would bring him. But he worried about her. He also worried about his friends and about his charities. So many good people would find themselves made guilty by association if it got out that his daughter had a connection to the Niagara bombing. There were too many Americans who believed that all Muslims were terrorists, he said.

He didn't doubt that the man she was helping was innocent. But he also was certain that the Americans would mix all of them up in an indiscriminate blend of guilt. It was bigotry, pure and simple. She could come to him, he said. She could bring the African-American man to him to hide out, if that was what they wanted to do. But if she went to the FBI, there was no telling where they would all end up.

She told her father that it had just been a fluke that she'd become mixed up in the situation. She'd been in the wrong place at the wrong time. She told him she did what she had to do when King asked her to take away the detonator. It had to be done. There was no one else around to do it. So why not her? Then later, when she saw that King had hurt himself jumping out the window, she only thought it right to go out and help him. It was what her mother had taught her. If people needed help, you helped them.

All she was doing was helping the guy walk, because he couldn't walk on his own. The bad guy was getting away and someone had to stop him. But then at some moment in that sequence, she'd walked too far. She'd known it was risky. She'd understood the stakes of the situation. But she couldn't just let go of King and run back to the safety of the train. She thought he might fall down at any moment, the way he was limping. He was an odd mix of courage and impracticality. He needed her help—and at some level that made her come alive. Her father said that was all good. He was proud of her. But he also said he didn't think that the FBI would believe her. 'Look at what has happened already,' he said. 'They already shot at you, didn't they? And based on what? Guilt by association, Sarah. This whole thing will get out of hand. Mark my words.'

She'd soon discovered that her father might be right. She went online after talking to her father and found King's picture was all over the media. They said he was a 'person of interest,' and she knew that meant he was, in fact, a suspect. The media didn't have any information about her.

She realized then that if she wanted to, she could just bow out. No one knew she was connected to King. She could just walk away. It would be as if she was never involved. But she knew she wouldn't. She figured it was in her DNA. From an early age her mother had taught her to be a mensch—a person of integrity and honor. Her mother said 'You might get the idea that you have to be a man to be a mensch. That's crazy. The word mensch doesn't mean man, it means human being. You've got to be a human being of noble character, Sarah.'

So just like there was no way she was going to leave King stranded out in the railyard on his own, there was no way she was going to abandon him now. But what a mess it had become. In the midst of her thoughts, the phone in her room rang so loudly that it made her jump.

She picked up the phone. "Hello."

"I'm in the lobby," King said.

There was a pause while Sarah digested this. "So he took the bait?"

"Yes. I saw him make a call, which was probably to my friend Melanie."

"So what now?"

"Now I have to get online. I have to make sure that the Signal-Secure GPS feature is working."

"What's SignalSecure?"

"That's the GPS program on the phone that will show me where the phone is."

"You can use my phone to go online. You want to come up?"

King looked around the lobby. No one was paying any attention to him. "I would," he said. "What room are you in?"

"They didn't tell you?"

"No. They just patched me through to your phone. I guess

that's their standard security precaution when a horn dog asks for a woman's room number."

"Funny. I'm in room 708."

"I'll be right up."

King arrived at the room a few minutes later. But before he could knock, he heard the sound of Sarah undoing the chain inside. Sarah opened the door. She said, "We've got trouble."

"We do?"

"I'm afraid so. Come in and sit down, and I'll tell you about it."

The room was a typical modern hotel room. On the wall opposite the door was a wide window hung with sheer drapery. In the middle of the room, a king-size bed held a flock of decorator pillows. The bed faced a dresser, on which sat a widescreen TV. Near the window was a desk and chair. King came in and settled into the desk chair. "What's wrong?" he asked.

Sarah sat on the bed. "I went online after you called. The media has a story about the bomb posted. They have a picture of you to go with it."

"A picture of me?"

"Did you leave something behind on the train?"

"My luggage."

"Well, they found it."

"Damn it, my passport was in there. What about you? Do they mention you?"

"They don't know about me."

"That's good." King looked out the window at the lighted sign on the casino across the street. The sign entreated tourists to come and play. He wished he and Sarah could go join the fun. "It's probably a matter of time," he said to her, "before they connect you to me."

Sarah shook her head. "One witness said a young woman *may* have left the train. But he wasn't sure. The homeland security agents who fired at me saw me from behind. But they must be keeping mum. They don't have any way of knowing that the woman is me." She laid her head back on the headboard of the bed. "Ty, I don't think anyone knows I was on that train. I got on in Niagara Falls, Canada. The conductor never took my ticket. He must collect the tickets after the customs inspection. But I didn't get that far."

"You got on the train in Niagara Falls, Canada?" This surprised King. He thought that Sarah had boarded in Toronto, as he had.

"Yes, I had just boarded the train and was sitting there minding my own business when you and Kareem started shooting off that gun. Five minutes later I was off the train, in the U.S., and running around like a fugitive with you."

"I thought you said you're from Toronto."

"I am. I was visiting Niagara Falls. With my mother. We spent a couple of days sightseeing. This morning she got on the train going back to Toronto, and I got on the train going to New York."

"What happened to your luggage?"

"I didn't bring luggage. Like I told you, I keep a set of things at my father's place in New York. I don't like schlepping bags around. My mother took most of what I brought with me to the falls back to Toronto. Everything else I brought on the trip is in my bag." She pointed at the handbag on the bed. "I wasn't plan-ning on an overnight detour here."

King looked at the Prada purse sitting on the bed. That Sarah would travel with nothing else was telling. She was a rich woman with plenty of self-confidence. He said, "We need to find out when the next train to New York leaves."

"I already checked. From here in Niagara Falls, the next train is tomorrow. We could still catch a train to New York today from Buffalo, which isn't far from here. But my father thinks I should stay in Niagara Falls tonight."

"Oh right. Your father. You said you talked to him. And then you changed your mind about calling the FBI."

Sarah blinked. "I did change my mind." She looked at him with a solemn expression. "I changed my mind because of my father. It would complicate things for him. He's Muslim. He's involved with charities. The FBI would be all over him and most of his friends the minute they connected his name to this bombing thing." She shook her head. "I can't do that to him."

King nodded. He wanted to ask her more about her father, but he decided to wait.

"Besides, the fact that I'm not connected to this thing and the fact that nobody knows about me makes it easier for me to help you." She got off the bed and began to pace the room. "You're gonna need help. You are a seriously wanted man. You probably can't even use your credit card now without some alert going off at Homeland Security. By tomorrow, your picture is going to be all over the newspapers. Deranged ex-soldier bombs Niagara River. Lucky for you, nobody was seriously hurt. A teenage boy got a cut on his arm from some debris when the bomb went off, but that's it."

"Thank God." King was relieved. He'd been agonizing about his decision not to use the gun on Kareem. "Wait a minute," he said. "What about Kareem? Don't those news stories say something about him?"

"Not by name. They just mention a guy with a beard who jumped off the train."

King scowled. "Damn. That's it? A guy with a beard? That means they don't know who he is. He must not have left anything on the train either." King thought about it for a moment. "I guess that must have been his plan all along."

"That's the way I see it, too," Sarah said. "I think he and his girlfriend bought tickets only as far as Niagara Falls, Canada—so the authorities would have no way of knowing he was still on the train when it crossed the border. He must have planned to jump off the train before he set off the bomb. He seems to have known about the tanker cars, and about how they shunt them around the railyard. He probably researched the whole thing in advance. All in all, it leaves you holding the bag...so to speak."

"That's great. The café car attendant saw me throw the bags

off the train. But some people must have seen Kareem too. There was a kid in a Yankee's cap. He pointed me to the emergency window that Kareem used. That kid must have told the police about him."

"The way the news story has it, several witnesses saw people get off the train. Two people saw a man with a beard—that would be Kareem; three people saw the bomber, described as a man with dreadlocks—that would be you—and one guy said he thought he spotted, quote, 'an attractive young woman,' end quote, getting off—that would be yours truly."

"They said that? They called me the bomber and called you an attractive young woman?"

"Hah, you're the bomber and I'm the bombshell."

King put on an affected smile. "I guess you think it's funny."

"Yeah, well, not really. You want to see the article?" Sarah picked up her phone and navigated onto a news site. She handed the phone to King. "See for yourself."

King read the article. It read just as she said. The picture of him was from his passport. He'd had the picture taken at a post office. He'd widened his eyes just as the camera flashed. As a result, he had a 'deer in the headlights' expression on his face. He hated that photo. But he'd been in a hurry and didn't want to take the time to take another one. He hadn't expected anyone other than bored customs agents to see it. Now he was looking at it on CNN.

"That's nice. Very nice. They don't mention anything about my service in Afghanistan. All they care about is that I threw out a bomb that exploded on the border between two countries. Doesn't it register with them that the bomb blew up far away from anyone? Do they think that was an accident?"

"Don't worry. They'll figure it out eventually."

"In the meantime, Kareem is on the loose." He handed the phone back to Sarah. "Can you go to the SignalSecure site? I want to see where he's at."

Sarah sat back down on the bed. "You want me to go to SignalSecure.com?"

"Yes. SignalSecure.com." King waited for her to navigate. "When you get there, I'll give you my sign in."

"OK. I'm there. I'm signing in. It says, 'What's your username or email?'"

"My username is 'cappuccino.'"

"Cappuccino?"

"Yeah. It's a nickname I had when I was a kid. All lower case letters."

"Cute. OK, now it wants your PIN or password."

"atqs8hz9"

"You remember that?"

King smiled and blinked his eyes. "I have a good memory."

"OK, it says, 'Do you want to restore data, lock and secure your phone, wipe your data, or track and locate your phone?' I guess you want to track and locate, right?"

"Right."

Sarah pushed buttons until she got to a map page. "Bingo. He's still in town. It looks like he's a few blocks away. It's pointing near the intersection of First and Buffalo Avenue. There is a Holiday Inn there."

"That fits. Holiday Inn was the first hotel I saw after crossing the bridge. Maybe he's going to stay in town overnight too."

"What about you?" Sarah asked. "Are you planning to stay in town tonight?"

"I'm doing whatever he's doing."

"OK, but how are you going to get a room? Right now, it's not safe for you to show your face. If anyone recognized you and called the cops, Homeland Security would grab you in a heartbeat." She shook her head. "For all I know they'd shoot you on sight."

"I guess I'll have to disguise myself."

"Yeah. I think you'd better do that." Sarah got off the bed. She went to the desk where King sat, turned on the desk lamp, and appraised him. "First of all, the dreadlocks have got to go. They're the most telltale thing about you."

"So, I'll go to a barbershop."

"Right … and if the barber has been sitting there watching CNN, he'll know just what kind of haircut you want."

"So what are you saying? I should cut my hair off with some office scissors?"

"I'll take care of it."

"You?"

"Yes me. I can do it. It just so happens that I was a theater major in college. I have first-hand experience with costume and makeup. First, I'm going to have to pick up some supplies. Then I'm going to give you a makeover."

"A makeover?"

"Under the circumstances, you seriously need a makeover. I'll get some decent scissors so I can cut off those dreadlocks." She appraised his face. "I want to give you some facial hair too— maybe a goatee. You might look halfway decent if you had one."

"Thanks." King scowled. "Maybe you can throw in some Oil of Olay to make me look younger."

"Oil of Olay doesn't work that fast. Besides, it's too subtle."

"I was joking."

"Actually, I could get some makeup to change your skin tone. I don't know if it's better to go lighter or darker."

King was skeptical of the whole project. "It's all the same to me. You choose."

"I guess it would be better to make you look more whitish. That would be the conventional wisdom. Black guys are suspicious."

"Yeah, but what if I went super black?" King stood and walked around the bed, with a bouncing, rhythmic stride. "I could be a drug dealer and, you know, get down with some street lingo."

"Street lingo?"

King stuck out his hand with his fist closed and said, "Hey

now, look here, I got something you might can use. I got some real wicked dank."

Sarah rolled her eyes. "Are you kidding?"

"Yeah baby, don't pay me no mind."

"You sound ridiculous."

"Or, how about this? How about if I put on dark sunglasses? Like a movie star." King ran his hand over his head and struck a pose.

"Possibly," she said. "Your eyes are distinctive." She stared at him. "Or maybe it's your eyebrows."

"Please don't get any ideas about doing something to my eyebrows. I don't want to end up looking like a drag queen."

"Why not? That would throw people off—especially Kareem. He's the most likely one to recognize you."

"Yeah, well what about you? Kareem might recognize you too."

"I don't think so."

"He saw you, didn't he?"

Sarah shook her head. "He saw my feet and my back. He saw my feet when he was crawling on the floor toward me to get the walkie-talkie. Then he saw me from behind when I was running away from him. When he caught up with me, I didn't turn around. I thought he had a gun. He grabbed the walkie-talkie from behind me. I'm sure he never saw my face. I never looked at him. In fact, I didn't know what he looked like until he was off the train." She smiled. "So the way I see it, all I have to do is change my outfit and ditch the ankle bracelets. He saw my feet for sure."

"You better get rid of the lavender toe-nail polish too."

She nodded. "I guess he saw you when you were Aikido-ing him and all that."

"I talked to him about Jasmeen's luggage in Arabic. He saw me plain as day—but he was distracted and nervous."

Sarah began navigating on her phone. "All right. You stay here and don't answer the door," she said. She studied the screen on her phone. "I'm going on a shopping expedition. I'm going to a theatrical supply house. According to Google, there's a place here in town called Production Supply Company on Niagara Falls Boulevard." She navigated to the Google Maps site. "Whoa, it's like eight miles away. I'll have to take a cab."

EIGHT

When Sarah returned from her expedition, she had two shopping bags full of stuff. She dumped both onto the bed in the hotel
room. King looked over the contents. There were scissors, an electric razor, and a plastic bag with a 'false beard kit.' The kit was
labeled '3 point Goatee.' It included a bottle of Spirit Gum and a
bottle of remover. There was also a makeup kit. It included an
assortment of foundations, some rouge, an eyebrow pencil, a lip
pencil, a cake of translucent face powder, a bottle of hydra
cleanse, a rouge brush, a velour powder puff, a latex sponge, a
stipple sponge and swab applicators.

"My God," King said, "how many people are you planning to
make up?"

"This kit was the easiest and cheapest thing to buy. Relax. I
don't have to use everything in it."

"That's good. And remember, no eyebrow pencil, OK? I told
you I don't want you to mess with my eyebrows."

"You seem insecure about your masculinity."

"I'm not insecure. I just don't like to have my eyebrows
changed around. It has nothing to do with masculinity."

"OK, fine. No eyebrows."

Sarah dumped out the second bag of stuff. In this bag were sunglasses, a gray hooded sweatshirt, a blue t-shirt, a pair of black pants, socks and several pairs of underwear, both men's and women's.

King smiled. "You bought me socks and underwear?"

"Yes. I bought some for me and I bought some for you. I assume you're not planning to wear the same socks and underwear for the next few days."

King inspected the clothes. "How did you know my size?"

"I didn't know. I guessed."

He went through the clothes, checking the sizes. "You got large pants and underwear. That's right. But you got an extralarge t-shirt and sweatshirt. I usually don't wear extra large."

"Yeah, well, the shirt you have on is too tight in the arms. This way you won't look so muscular. You're supposed to be in disguise here, not dancing with the Chippendales."

"OK. I can pay you for these clothes," King said. "But I don't have the cash for it right now."

"It doesn't matter."

"So what's the plan? Do you want to do this right now?"

"No time like the present," she said. "We better do it in the bathroom. It's going to make a mess."

In the bathroom, Sarah handed King a towel. "Put this over your shoulders while I cut."

She proceeded meticulously, gradually cutting each of King's dreadlocks off. When she was done, she used the electric razor and the scissors, alternating between them, to trim his hair to a 3/8 inch length all around. Then she used an applicator to apply foundation to his face, followed by powder—both in lighter tones than King's natural color, which left an obvious line on his neck.

"Time to take off your shirt," she said. "I'm going to have to put the makeup on until it is down below your neck line. Then I have to put it on your arms and hands. Your skin color has to match everywhere, or it won't look right."

King took off his shirt.

She stared unabashedly at his chest. "Wow," she said. "I guess you are kind of a Chippendale dancer."

"I work out," he said.

"Turn around. I have to get this stuff on the back of your neck."

She continued applying the makeup. When she was finished, she inspected him in the mirror. "It looks good," she said. "But it's too even. I should dab on some blush to vary the tones. Or is that too girlish for you?"

King cringed. "Put on the blush."

She dabbed blush on his cheeks, then worked it in with the brush. She painted spirit gum above his upper lip. She took the two mustache pieces from the goatee and pressed them in place. Then she gummed his chin and applied the beard. When she was done, she turned him around to see the effects of her work.

He looked odd because the makeup only went to the bottom of his neck and up to the top of his arms. His chest, back and belly were his natural color, which was darker.

"You better put on your shirt," she said. "I can't get the full effect of the makeup until you do."

"Do you want me to wear the new t-shirt?"

"Yes. And you should change into the new pants too. You stay here. I'll hand you the clothes so you can close the door and change."

After a few minutes, King emerged from the bathroom. "What do you think?" he asked.

She looked him up and down, inspecting him with a professional eye. He looked surprisingly different, and not just because of the haircut, the beard, and the lighter skin. The baggy clothes made a difference too. "Not bad," she said.

"I never had a goatee before. I think I like it."

"You should grow your own. It will look more natural than the fake one."

"Can I do that? I mean if I let my beard grow won't the fake beard look lumpy?"

"Not right away. Your beard will provide texture that will help anchor the glue so the fake one will stay put. By the time you have enough real beard that it's starting to get in the way, you won't need the fake one anymore."

"But in bright light, it must be obvious that I have makeup on."

"It is. For now, you're gonna have to be a vampire: only come out at night. Stay out of the bright lights."

He studied himself in the mirror near the window. It was sunset. The light outside had diminished considerably. In the light of dusk, he looked plausibly white. "It's weird," King said. He pinched his nose. "If only my nose was different, I'd look Middle Eastern in this skin color."

"Well, that's perfect, since you're a known bomb thrower."

"No, seriously. It could help me go undercover. Maybe I can infiltrate Kareem's group."

Sarah threw up her hands. "Oh, for God's sake. That's crazy and dangerous. Don't you think Kareem would recognize you?"

King put on the sunglasses. "What about now?" He looked in the mirror again. "I hardly recognize me."

"I admit you look different. But it's too risky. If Kareem saw you up close for any length of time, how could he not recognize you? You can't take that chance."

"It's the best way for me to find out what they're planning. I have to get into their circle somehow."

"Ty, it's too dangerous."

"So you're concerned about me?"

"Of course I am. Why wouldn't I be?"

"I feel like you have a mixed opinion of me."

Sarah shrugged. "I don't have a mixed opinion. Earlier I was irritated because you were trying to drag me around like a roller bag. And then there was that fake kissing scene. But actually, I have a pretty decent opinion of you. I think you're brave, even if you are nuts with the non-violence bullshit."

"Really?"

"Yeah. What you're doing is heroic."

"Really?"

"Yeah, but don't get all mushy on me. I'm not looking to go to bed with you."

"Who said anything about that?"

"Well it's just that you're going to have to stay in my room tonight to be safe." Sarah pointed at the bed. "I'll sleep there. And I want it clear from the get go that you will sleep on the floor."

"Yeah. Yeah. Fine. I will sleep on the floor. You know it's a bit irritating to me that you're so certain that I'm all hot for you."

"So you're not?"

"I didn't say that. I just don't like you being so sure of it."

"So what are you saying?"

"I don't know what I'm saying. I just wish you'd relax a bit. Why don't we go and have dinner somewhere nearby? Let's see if this disguise can pass a field test."

"OK. I'm starving."

NINE

Sarah proposed that they eat in the casino. "My mother says casino food is usually a good value. We ate in casinos on the Canadian side. They like to lure you into the restaurant with cheap food, knowing you'll probably drop a few bucks in the slot machines before you leave."

Inside the casino, they found a sign that advertised several dining choices: Java Café, Morrie's Express, Thunder Falls Buffet, Koi, la Cascata, and the Blues Burger Bar.

"What about Koi?" King said. "The ad says 'the best of Pan-Asian innovation meets timeless traditions. Where high energy meets high style, from the shimmering décor to the central view of the display cooking line.'"

"Fine."

"Would you rather have a burger?" King asked.

"No. No. I think high energy meets high style sounds like our kind of place."

"OK, then Koi."

Inside the restaurant, the host seated them at a table with a white tablecloth. He handed them a menu of cocktails and wine.

"I could use a drink," Sarah said. She read from the menu.

"They have a 'Green Tea Martini' made from Zen Green Tea Liqueur and Absolut Mandarin Vodka."

"What is green tea liqueur?"

Sarah shrugged. "I have no idea. I wonder if it has health benefits. How about an 'Acai Blueberry Burst?' It's made with Vincent Van Gogh Acai Blueberry Vodka and a splash of Sierra Mist."

King grimaced. "They lost me with the splash of soda pop."

"Do you think there really is vodka called 'Vincent Van Gogh Vodka?'"

"Of course," said King. "Manufacturers have mastered the art of naming products so they sound sexy."

"What's sexy about Van Gogh?" Sarah was genuinely puzzled by this.

"I don't know."

"So what are you having?"

"I'll try the 'Green Tea Martini.'"

Sarah made a face. "Not for me. The mandarin Vodka part sounds good. But green tea? I want a drink, not a Zen experience." She looked again at the menu. "I think I'll go with Van Gogh. I like carbonation. And I like blueberries."

"Très bien."

"What? You're speaking French?"

"Mais bien sûr," King said. "That means 'but, of course."

"I know what it means. But why are you speaking French?"

"Because of Van Gogh."

"I thought he was Dutch."

"Och, dat het recht van! … that means 'Oh, that's right.'"

Sarah tapped her finger on the table. "In what language?"

"In Dutch, of course."

"So what are you, like a United Nations translator or what?"

"I like languages."

"How many do you speak?"

"Eight, more or less."

Sarah's eyes went wide. "You're kidding me."

"No, I'm serious. It's my hobby. And I have, you know, a good memory. Are you surprised?"

Sarah was indeed surprised by this. No one looking at King would take him to be a simple man; but she had not figured him to be quite so complex as to speak eight languages. Sarah said, "That's amazing. I'm impressed. The best I can do in a foreign language is say a bunch of French-Canadian words, and I only know those because of Canadian TV. I can also order 'pollo' on my tacos."

"I started young with the language thing," King said. "My father worked as a trade negotiator for a coffee company. Every few years we moved to another country. By the time I was eighteen, I'd lived in six foreign countries."

"Like where?"

"We lived in Berlin, in Geneva, in Panama during the canal transfer, in Taipei, in Rome, and then in Dubai."

"I guess everybody likes coffee."

"I prefer tea."

Sarah had mixed feelings about her own international family life. She took pride in the breadth of the worldview that her background had given her. She was a citizen of two countries that were close allies. But she was also the child of two parents and two religions that often clashed. She did not fully belong to either country or either religion or either parent. She was an outsider constantly forced to mediate her allegiances. At times, she envied people whose cultural identity was simple. She knew that hers could never be. But this was a point of commonality with King. He too must know the feeling of being both a person of the world and a perpetual outsider.

"The waiter is coming to get our drink order," Sarah said. "Have you decided what you want to eat?"

King looked again at the menu. "I want that hot and sour soup, and maybe some red curry shrimp. You want to order for us?"

"OK. Do you want to share some dishes?"

"Let's share, why not?"

"How about this Indonesian thing, 'nasi goreng'?"

"What's in it?"

"Spiced fried rice with chicken satay."

"Sounds good."

"And maybe an order of spring rolls?"

"I can only eat one spring roll," King said. "I'll have the soup too."

"OK."

"Is anyone staring at me?" King asked.

"At you?"

"Yeah, I mean because of my disguise. I don't think this skin tone you came up with looks natural. I feel like Michael Jackson."

"Relax. No one's looking at you. In this light, the makeup doesn't stand out. It's only in bright light that it looks strange."

"If I go undercover, I can't use this makeup. It's too risky. There won't be any way to control the lighting conditions I might find myself in."

Sarah knew she did a good job of blending King's makeup. She applied it conscientiously to all the parts of him that might have betrayed the disguise. But still she could not regard his lighter skin color as natural. She said, "Yeah. OK. I have to admit it. You're right. But you should keep the beard. The beard looks convincing."

"Does that mean you've come around to the idea of my going undercover?"

"No. I think it's a lousy idea. But I've already figured out that you're stubborn as hell. So why would it matter what I think?"

"It does matter. I care what you think. I won't do it, if you think I shouldn't."

"Don't do it."

King frowned. "I knew you'd say that. You're exasperating. You're not even giving it a chance. You're more stubborn than I am."

"Possibly."

"Can we at least talk about it?"

"I don't see how it can work. Kareem is going to make you. If not at first, he will with time. These are dangerous people. Why would you take that kind of chance?"

"If I don't do something, they will. I don't want to take *that* chance."

Sarah didn't have a snappy rejoinder to that. She understood the stakes of the threat. She said, "Tell me again why we can't just contact the authorities."

"We could. But if we did, then they'd take both of us into custody for a while…maybe even a long while. We might convince them to track Kareem and we might not. They might get onto him before he's slipped away or they might not. They might get someone with as much experience as I have on the case, or they might not. It might work…."

"OK, I get it. And it might not."

The waiter came. Sarah ordered the drinks and the food. King said nothing. He was thinking about Sarah's advice. He knew she was right. Going undercover was dangerous. He couldn't argue with that. A disguise would only go so far. Even if Kareem had never seen him before, King could easily make a mistake and blow his cover. The encounter on the train with Kareem only made it trickier. But when he thought of the alternative, when he thought of going to the authorities and having to rehash everything, starting with his discharge from the Army, it made him shudder. He knew that he'd have to talk to the authorities eventually. But if he had to do it, he'd feel a hell of a lot better about it if he had stopped Kareem and company first. He trusted his instincts. He thought about the bomb blast going off in the Niagara River. He thought about what might have happened if he hadn't followed his instincts on the train. How was this any different?

After the waiter left, King said to her, "Why are you here?"

"What do you mean?"

"I'm just wondering why you're here. Most people would have stayed on the train. But you didn't."

"I got off the train because you looked like you needed help. You were lying on the ground and it looked like you hurt yourself. That's all."

"Yeah, but you kept going. You walked with me. I mean if you had wanted to stop me from chasing Kareem you wouldn't have kept saying things like 'he's getting away.'"

"What's your point?"

"My point is that the same thing that made you get off the train and put yourself into this risky situation is the same thing that makes me want to see this all the way through. I can't leave the job half-done. If a bomb were to go off somewhere in the next few days while I was sitting in a government office defending my innocence, how could I live with that?"

Sarah understood that. She felt the same way. But King's plan was not rational. "How are you going to stop them?" she asked. "You can't just walk up to Kareem and Jasmeen and say 'Hey dudes, I speak Arabic, see, so how about if I hook up with you and see what's going on?' How would you even begin to gain their confidence?"

"I could make a pass at Jasmeen."

"You've got to be kidding." Sarah rolled her eyes. "She's about as likely to go for that as I am. I hate to tell you this, but your technique is lame."

"You could help me work on it."

"Right. I'm going to help you figure out how to put the make on a nice Muslim girl."

"You must know something about it. You're part Muslim, aren't you?"

"Not really." She thought about it for a moment. Then she said, "Well technically I am, but not like that. You're talking about a woman who observes proper Islamic dress and who apparently believes in jihad. I don't know anything about any part of what goes on in her mind. Besides, she's married to Kareem, isn't she—

or she's his girlfriend or something. Even if you were the Sheik of Araby I don't see how you'd expect her to flirt with you for God's sake. She's spoken for."

"I'm not so sure. I mean, you're right...at first glance they seemed like a couple. But what if they're not? What if their relationship is strictly...professional? Maybe she was just his contact—or a way to give him cover, make him seem less threatening, someone to help him blend in better. You can't take these things at face value. Almost nobody is who he or she seems to be at first glance. She could be his cousin for all we know."

"Yeah, and maybe she's a lesbian." Sarah laughed. "Maybe I should put the make on her."

King cocked his head, and said, "Are you gay?"

"Oh come on. Just because I didn't jump at the chance to suck face with you under the raincoat, you think..."

"No, I don't think anything," King cut her off. "Take it easy. It's a simple question. I don't make assumptions about anyone."

At this point, the waiter returned with their drinks. For a moment, they sipped them without speaking.

Then Sarah said, "It's too far-fetched. Even if you were right, even if it was true that she isn't already attached to Kareem, and even if it was plausible that she might be inclined to find you mildly attractive—how would this work, Mata Hari? Are you going to get her in the sack and then trick her into mentioning their next bomb plot?"

"As it happens, I had a mission in Afghanistan that was similar."

Sarah looked at him with disbelief. "Are you saying your job in the Army was to seduce some woman and get her to tell you something?"

"More or less. Of course, I had more intelligence to work with in that case. They knew that she was a valuable asset and that she was...well...lonely and unhappy. So it made it easier for me."

"This is what our tax dollars are spent on?"

"I thought you were Canadian. I'm sure no Canadian taxes were spent in support of my mission."

"That's not the point. I'm a U.S. citizen too. And I was speaking on behalf of my fellow U.S. citizens."

"Well, OK. What do you think counter-intelligence is about… taking photos on microfilm of secret documents? It's about relationships. That's what I was trained to do…make nice with the enemy."

"The enemy?"

"Sorry, that's the wrong word. It isn't the word I would use… but that was the Army culture. I should have said make nice with the locals. I never thought of her as an enemy. She was just lonely. I had mixed feelings. I felt bad about the whole thing."

"So you went through with it? I can't believe you seduced some woman as part of your job." Sarah sipped her drink. "This is good," she said. "How is yours?"

King drank from his glass. "It's OK." Then he shrugged. "I don't know, I guess I don't like it."

Sarah gave him a triumphant look. "My rule is no green tea for liquor or ice cream."

King said, "Anyway, I didn't seduce my source. I wasn't able to finish the mission. Something else came up." King played with his cocktail glass, but he didn't drink it. "That's why, in a way, I feel like this might be a chance to finish the job."

"Finish what job?"

"The job I was trained for."

"They trained you? You're an Army-trained gigolo?"

"Damn, you make it sound so crass. It wasn't like that. I was trained in a general way to live undercover and blend in culturally. They didn't give me actual tips on how to make a pass. They took for granted that the seduction part of it was a default skill… a universal skill. But it isn't. That's one reason I thought you might help me."

"Help you with your default skill?"

"Yes. I'm serious. I was too embarrassed to talk about this

sort of thing with the other guys in the Army. Anyway…those lady-killers wouldn't have had the kinds of insights you might have."

"Insights?"

"Right. You know. I thought you would be able to help me think of ways to approach her."

"Wow." Sarah shook her head. "I just don't know what to say."

"You understand why, right? It's not because I'm hot for her."

"No?"

"Well, not like that. I mean sure, Jasmeen is beautiful. But I have no personal interest in her."

"No personal interest."

"Well, no. I mean she's a fucking terrorist. What do you think I am?"

"Beats the hell out of me. I don't see how anyone could think the way you do. It's like some macho James Bond fantasy."

"You're wrong. I'm not like that at all. There isn't a sexual kick in this for me. It's about me trying to use my skills with language to do good in the world."

"So you don't have any ethical difficulty with this concept?"

"Not if it means stopping a bomb that might kill innocent people. Sex is just sex. It's not evil. I did have a problem with the thing in Afghanistan because that woman wasn't a bad person. She was caught in the middle of complex circumstances. After I met her, I found that I liked her—and that was the only reason I thought I'd go through with the mission."

"So let me get this straight. If the woman is good you have to like her personally to trick her into bed, but if the woman is bad, then you don't have to like her personally to trick her into bed— and either way it's OK because it's all in the cause of saving lives."

"OK, forget it. Forget I mentioned it. I'll see if I can make friends with some of the men in their group and find out what I can. You make me feel like a jerk. Why do you see everything I do as some kind of sex-crazed thing? That isn't it at all. You don't know anything about me."

The waiter was back now with the spring rolls and soup. They sat in silence while he served the dishes. Even after he left, they did not speak for several minutes.

At last, King said, "Maybe we shouldn't talk about Jasmeen or Kareem tonight. Maybe we should take some time to get to know each other."

"OK. What do you want to know?"

"You said you were a theater major in college. Do you work in theater?"

Sarah shrugged. "No. I tried it for a few years. But eventually I figured out that I had to make a living."

"So you were an actress?"

"I was a director. I did some acting. But I was much more interested in directing."

"That fits."

"What's that supposed to mean?"

"I just mean you don't seem like the actress type; you seem too catholic."

"I told you I'm officially Jewish. But what does religion have to do with directing?"

"I don't mean Catholic religion. I mean catholic as in a universalist, a generalist—someone who would rather be involved in the whole play than in acting just one part in the play."

"You mean I'm a control freak."

"That's not what I meant. Why are you so defensive?"

"I don't know." Sarah scowled and took a bite of her spring roll. Then she looked around the room. She knew that it was true, of course. All her life she'd been accused of being controlling. But was that so bad? Was it wrong to want to control your life, to be the master of your own story? She said, "I suppose it's because I am pretty much a control freak." She looked back at him. "Someone like you brings it out in me."

"I do."

"Yeah. You're a weird mix of bravery and vulnerability. It makes me want to discourage your bluster and protect the parts of you that seem vulnerable."

King was silent while he thought about this. He supposed that he was no more or less vulnerable than anyone else. It wasn't something he had analyzed about himself. "You think I'm vulnerable? How do I seem vulnerable?"

"It's difficult to put my finger on it. I just remember how you hurt yourself when you jumped off the train."

"I was going too fast. I didn't take enough time to gauge the jump."

"And then this thing with the woman in Afghanistan—and how you now want to 'finish the mission' as you put it with Jasmeen. It's like you have to prove something about yourself."

King nodded. She was right to recognize that the incomplete mission was a sensitive matter for him. "Yeah. OK. Fair enough. So maybe I do want to prove something about myself. The army didn't give me the chance to do what I was trained to do and it pissed me off. So, yeah, on some level I want to show them that they made a mistake."

"What happened?"

"I don't want to go into it right now. Could we talk about something else?"

Now the waiter arrived with the Indonesian fried rice and chicken satay. He placed the dishes on the table and said, "Enjoy."

King took a few bites from his food, then said. "Look. Many times when two people meet, they start out getting to know each other with simple conventional questions, like 'what do you do?' Somehow we missed that step between us."

"You're right."

"So what do you do?"

"I work in a hospice. I take care of people who are dying."

"That's intense. Are you a nurse?"

"More of a social worker." Sarah ate some rice. She was not

fond of talking about her work. She knew that death was a taboo topic. Most people reacted to her profession with a mixture of morbid curiosity and discomfort. "What about you? What do you do?"

"I'm a private investigator."

"You're kidding!"

"No, I am. I have an Illinois licensed private detective identification card and everything. I have an office in Chicago. I have an assistant named Melanie. What I don't have are many clients."

"So what do you investigate?"

"Domestic problems, like infidelities, or missing persons, or insurance fraud. I don't get to use my language skills very often. I wish I could figure out how I could. That's one of the reasons I'm so interested in … well … I said we weren't going to talk about them, but you know who I mean."

"Isn't it kind of icky to get involved in people's personal lives like that?"

"Icky?"

"I mean it's such an invasion of privacy. I think people have a right to privacy."

"A guy doesn't have a right to privacy if he's missing and everyone is worried about him, or if there's reason to believe he's seriously doing something wrong."

"OK, but infidelity?"

"Yeah, well…I've only taken two of those cases—and I took them when I was just starting out—and you're right, I didn't like doing that. It would have been better if the couples involved had just patched it up or broken up and moved on with their lives. The wives who hired me were more or less throwing gasoline on the fire." King hadn't finished his soup, and now he spooned up the last of it. Then he said, "Doesn't it depress you to be around people who are dying?"

"I wouldn't do the job if it did. Death doesn't depress me. Most people are more afraid of death than I am. That's why it's a good job for me. My patients can see that I accept it as a natural thing."

"I'd think it was natural if the dying person was old. But are all your patients old?"

"No. But their age doesn't matter. At least, it doesn't change how I feel about death. Many of the patients who are dying are so sick that death will release them from suffering.

"It sounds like you believe in euthanasia."

"No. No. I don't do that. At least not in any legal sense."

"Then you do do something?"

"When it feels to me like they can handle it, I encourage people to let go. Most people don't realize how much of a role that plays—whether someone is hanging on or not. It's intangible. You can't explain it scientifically. But I can see that indirect forces play a role in the timing of death—like when someone important shows up for a last visit—or if someone feels like the medical costs are getting too high—or the pain is getting too much. Different people have different guiding forces about why they stay or leave."

"So aren't you getting into people's private space too?"

"Yes, but not uninvited. I'm not spying on them."

King was done eating and he saw that Sarah was too. He said, "Do you want dessert?"

"No. I'm exhausted. It's been a long day."

"Yes," King agreed. "It has."

"Since you don't have any money," Sarah said, "I'll pay the bill. And then let's go back to the room."

"OK." King nodded. "I'll fix up bedding on the floor."

TEN

Kareem and Jasmeen sat down to eat in the dining room of the Red Coach Inn. They sat in soft, oversized floral-print chairs at a white-clothed candlelit table beside a picture window hung with heavy drapes. It was a romantic setting in a room embellished with dark woodwork, subdued tapestries, and a view toward the Niagara River rapids.

Kareem supposed that many of the couples who sat at similar tables around the room were honeymooning or indulging in a romantic night out. The food was expensive, but this was of no concern to him or Jasmeen.

After the bombs exploded, the authorities closed the Rainbow Bridge for four hours. At 5 PM, the bridge was reopened. In advance of the mission, Abdul had obtained a U.S. passport for Jasmeen, which she used to walk across the bridge from Canada to join Kareem at his hotel on the American side. There they discussed once again what happened on the train. Kareem could not explain how the dreadlocked man had known about the bombs. Nor could he explain how the man had managed to throw the luggage into the river in a way that the bombs didn't explode with destructive results.

The Maple Leaf bombs were the consummation of months of planning by Abdul and the mujahedeen who had helped him organize the mission. They'd planned an event that would affect both Canada and the United States. They'd wanted to let the world know that the Great Satan's allies would not be spared the mujahedeen's revenge. But it was not to be.

Abdul was angry. He was certain the dreadlocked Negro on the train was an American. So he channeled his anger into a new plan to attack an American target. Abdul already had the technology he needed to strike a tremendous blow—a blow that would send a message to the entire world. He would take down the Statue of Liberty. He'd acquired an invincible new weapon, one the security systems wouldn't be able to stop. But now that he had the means, he also needed the opportunity. Jasmeen and Kareem would meet him in New York to plan how to create the right opportunity.

Jasmeen had argued against an attack in New York. She still wanted to find a way to send a message to the Canadians. Her visit to Toronto had convinced her that the Canadians were as bad as the Americans were—maybe worse.

When Abdul ignored her arguments, she accepted the idea of an attack in New York. But then she tried to persuade him that Wall Street was a better target than the Statue. A chance to argue her position was the most Jasmeen could hope to obtain. She'd never be allowed to make a final decision. She'd never be a primary actor in their plans. But all her arguments were dismissed.

In Kareem's hotel room, they'd watched the reports on television. CNN showed a picture of the man with dreadlocks. His name was Tyrone King. The authorities were seeking him in connection with the bombing. Witnesses also described seeing a bearded man and a woman running through the train. But there was no name and no picture of the man with the beard. The authorities did not know—could not know—that the bearded man was Kareem. Both Kareem and Jasmeen had bought tickets only as far as Niagara Falls, Ontario. No one but Tyrone King knew that Jasmeen had left the train by herself at the last Canadian station.

It had been difficult for them to separate. Jasmeen was unmarried. It was improper for her to travel alone. But they had planned to separate only for a short time. The plan had been for Kareem to leave the bombs in the car where they'd sat, which had been the second from the last car of the train. They knew from their practice runs that the train always crossed the bridge over the Niagara River slowly.

After Jasmeen left the train in Canada, Kareem was to have waited a few minutes and then walked to the first passenger car of the train. Then as soon as the front of the train had crossed the bridge, he would have opened a window and jumped out. In their trial run, they had calculated that he would have had enough time to get a safe distance from the train before the car with the bomb got onto the bridge. Kareem would then have detonated the bomb just as it came onto the bridge. He would have destroyed both the bridge and the back half of the train. It would have been easy for him to get away in the confusion. He would have met Jasmeen just as they did—when the Rainbow Bridge was opened so that she could walk across it.

For Kareem it was a matter of faith that the failed mission had been the will of Allah. He told Jasmeen it must have been an audition, a trial through which Allah had tested him. If so, he'd proven his courage. He'd shown his willingness to do the deadly thing. Everything would have gone according to plan if the man with the dreadlocks had not intervened.

There was nothing for them to do but to carry on with the remaining parts of their getaway plan. At 7:30 PM, after watching the news, they prepared disguises. Kareem shaved off his beard and mustache. He changed into the new set of clothes Jasmeen had brought for him. Jasmeen removed her hijab. It was immodest for her to be uncovered in public. But to continue on to a new mission they must pass among the general population without suspicion.

Now they sat in the restaurant and looked at each other without talking. Each was unused to seeing the other looking as they did in their disguises. Kareem's face, now clean-shaven, was unhidden. His beard had been full. It had overpowered his face. Without the beard, his youthful and refined features were more apparent.

Jasmeen was undoubtedly beautiful, even within the frame of her hijab. But without the hijab, with all her raven curls revealed, she was still more striking.

Kareem did not tell her this. It would embarrass her to be reminded of her immodest appearance. Were she not his sister, it would be improper to sit and look at her. Kareem was, above all, a faithful adherent of Islam.

As a child, he had been a quiet boy. He had been studious in nature. But his father, Omar, and his older brother, Abdul, wanted more from him. They wished him to act with boldness and manliness.

Kareem took it for granted that his father's will was an expression of the will of Allah. In his daily prayers, Kareem sought guidance to help him live up to his father's expectations. He became more and more pious in his devotions. Kareem hoped his piety would please his father—but it did not.

Jasmeen and Abdul imagined a way for Kareem to prove himself to their father. At Abdul's urging, Jasmeen steered Kareem toward the redeeming virtues of jihad. She was confident in the sincerity of her brother's spiritual faith. When called to the struggle against evil, he would find the boldness he lacked. By encouraging her brother, Jasmeen could also fulfill her own ambition. Had she been a man, she would certainly have been a jihadi.

When she came of age, she felt the eyes of men upon her. She did not wish to corrupt any man, but she observed the lewd force her body aroused. She understood the power of that lewdness.

Unchecked, she believed, it could only lead to the downfall of morality. It would foment degeneracy. Because of this, she believed in the wisdom of the veil. She wore it gladly. She vowed to repudiate the lewdness of infidels who treated women with disrespect by leaving them uncovered and vulnerable.

Throughout history infidels had, without provocation, invaded and sought to conquer and subdue Muslims. Jasmeen was certain this was the result of coarseness and disrespect for women.

Kareem was her surrogate and willing disciple. Together they were on a holy crusade. She provided the background accompaniment that made his actions possible. The irony was that now, in order to disguise herself, she must participate in the infidel's lewdness. And here in the dining room of the Red Coach Inn, the devils were all around her.

Jasmeen was not vain. She'd done nothing to sully her body, which was pure and untouched. She wore an emerald ring because it was a gift from her father. The gift may have come from a certain pride in Omar, but she did not wear it from immodesty. She wore it as a dutiful daughter.

She wore no makeup. Her body was unembellished. It was just as Allah had created it. And Allah had created great beauty in her. She knew that without the veil, she embodied temptation. Even in the romantic setting of the restaurant at the Red Coach Inn, she felt the men's eyes. It was disconcerting. An indecent curiosity made her want to glance back at them. Instead, she looked at Kareem. She regarded how handsome he was. He was her mirror. She saw that he too looked openly at her.

Kareem said, "The absence of the beard makes me feel lighter. It is as if I have one less possession. Since I am seeking detachment and tranquility, this is good, is it not?"

"It is not lack of possessions that leads to detachment," said Jasmeen. "It is a lack of self-absorption."

"Then I am not detached," said Kareem. "I want to purify

myself of all earthly things. I want to lose myself in the love of Allah."

"Brother, you are pure. What earthly thing do you possess? You possess nothing that matters to you, I think."

"But I am not detached from myself. I cannot stop the chatter in my mind of thoughts about myself and my desires."

"Are there things you desire?"

Kareem lowered his eyes. "Of course. That is the test given us by Allah."

"If you need to concentrate your mind, Kareem, you should focus on our mission, on the jihad. That will take you outside yourself."

"I feel badly about what happened today."

"You must think about the days to come in New York. Despite what happened today, the event in New York will go ahead. And it will succeed."

"You are so confident."

"Abdul has planned everything."

"There are always risks," said Kareem.

Jasmeen rapped her fist on the table. "The Statue will fall," she said.

She said the Arabic word for 'fall' so loudly that Kareem put his finger up to his lips. "We don't know who might be listening," he said.

Jasmeen looked around the room. "There is no one who can understand us," she said impatiently. "But I'll speak more softly."

Kareem was surprised by Jasmeen's sudden enthusiasm. He knew that she and Abdul had disagreed about blowing up the Statue. He'd heard her argue that the Stock Exchange should be their target. "I know the Statue was not the choice you wanted," he said.

Jasmeen shrugged. "No, but it is not my decision," she said. "Abdul has made that clear."

"The destruction of the Statue will be a great wound," said Kareem. "He is right about that, isn't he?"

"The destruction of the Stock Exchange would be an even deeper wound."

"Perhaps." Kareem nodded to acknowledge her point. "But Abdul wants all of them to care. Too many Americans would not care if we blew up the Stock Exchange. Look at these Wall Street protests. The destruction of the Statue will hurt them all. And not just the Americans. The French too. It was their gift."

"Yes. Yes. I understand his reasons. He wants to send an international message without actually being on the border."

"So why do you still object?"

"The Statue is chastely dressed, Kareem. Her robes are modestly draped. They hide the shape of her body. They touch her feet. In fact, they cover her feet entirely." Jasmeen folded her hands onto her head. "Even her head is covered."

"Yes," Kareem nodded. "These are things you and I can see. But Abdul is thinking of the Americans and the French. The Americans, especially, don't even notice such things. They don't see things literally. They only see the allegory, the symbolism, the lamp lighting the way to the open door." Kareem lifted the candle that sat in the middle of their table several inches by way of illustration.

"But the open door is halaal," said Jasmeen, "to welcome strangers, to honor visitors, to embrace travelers. This is the courtesy that Islam encourages."

"You and I can see that. But none of the Americans will think of that, Jasmeen. The Americans do not think. They will only cry out from the wound to their pride. For them it is all pride."

"Yes. They will cry out. And the sound of their cry will bring justice. But to destroy the Exchange would bring more than crying. It would wound their power, not just their pride."

"You have to picture it," said Kareem. "The Statue will be decapitated." He picked up his butter knife and sliced it against his palm. "The head will fall. The torch will fall. It will be a great humiliation."

"I do not like us to use a woman this way," said Jasmeen. "However, I have learned to set aside my opinion. I defer to Abdul's judgment, and to yours."

"I would have supported your plan too, sister. You are wise. You see very deeply into things. But this is Abdul's decision. And we must carry it out."

"Yes. We will carry it out. And it will be a great victory," said Jasmeen.

A waiter approached them and announced, "Hello, my name is Dylan. I'll be your server."

Kareem nodded. He tried to fix Dylan's gaze to stop him from looking directly at Jasmeen. But Dylan turned to Jasmeen and said in a cheerful voice, "How are you this evening?"

Kareem answered. "We're fine," making his English as curt as possible.

Dylan looked back at Kareem. "Are you visiting the Falls?"

"Yes," said Kareem. He put a sour expression on his face with the hope that it would discourage the waiter from further banter.

But Dylan continued with a meaningless patter as he filled their water glasses. "I'm working here this summer while I'm at school. I'm studying to be an architect. It's great. I love the Falls. They're so awesome. You guys have the best table. It's a great view from here."

Kareem nodded without looking out the window to confirm Dylan's assessment.

"Would you like something to drink to start this evening?"

"No thank you," said Kareem. "The water is fine."

"Have you had a chance to look at the menu? Are you ready to order—or would you like me to give you some more time?"

"Perhaps you'd better come back."

Dylan smiled. "Of course. I'll check back in a few minutes."

Jasmeen looked up at Kareem and fluttered her eyes. She raised her arm from the table and let her hand dangle next to the candle. Her emerald ring glinted in the candle light, flashing a green sparkle onto the white tablecloth. She swished her hand back and forth and let her wrist go limp. "I'm studying to be an architect," she said in Arabic in an affected tone.

"The falls are awesome," Kareem said in English.

"We better choose something to eat," said Jasmeen.

ELEVEN

The next morning, King awoke on the floor of Sarah's room. He looked at the bed and saw that she was still asleep. It annoyed him that she was so certain that he found her attractive. But he couldn't deny it. Even with her eyes closed, and her hair a mess, she was beautiful. A shaft of morning light fell softly on her face.

Sleeping on the floor was a pain. His back was sore from the hard surface. He studied the shape of her body beneath the covers. He wondered what her reaction might be if he slipped into the bed next to her. He could whisper, "My back hurts," then slide in the bed and see what happened.

But he knew the odds that something pleasant might happen weren't very good. She'd made it clear she had no interest in sleeping with him. He knew they'd had little time to get to know each other. Yet the fate they'd shared made him think they'd become more intimate with each other than they would have in less remarkable circumstances.

He thought about getting up. He had to pee, but he was still waiting for his morning erection to ease up. Looking at Sarah hadn't helped that problem. He was wearing the boxer shorts she'd bought for him. If he were to stand up now, it would look like he was pitching a tent. It'd be just his luck, he thought, for her to open her eyes when he stood up, and then she'd see that view at eye level.

So he lay back on the floor. He summoned into his imagination a certain image that was for him reliably un-erotic. His friend Walter, a gay music professor back in Chicago, referred to such imagery as the "detumescence stockpile." Walter claimed that many men had formed a collection of dependable imagery to use for this purpose.

King thought of an unfortunate visual memory from a visit to a nude beach, but despite his best effort, the images weren't enough to tame the beast. And so he was in a quandary. Not only did he have to pee, he was also eager to check up on Kareem. He didn't want to use Sarah's phone without her permission, so the only thing he could do was to wake her up.

While lying on the floor, he gently called her name.

She opened her eyes and, after a moment, looked down at him. She yawned, then asked, "What time is it?"

"I don't have my watch on. But judging from the light coming through the drapes, I'd say it's about 6:00."

She looked at the window. "We should get up," she said. "Are you getting up now?"

"In a moment."

She looked down at King and focused on his figure lying on the floor. "What happened to your beard?"

"I took it off. I couldn't sleep with it on. I tried, but it was itchy. It felt weird. And anyway, I didn't want to get it all creased up. You can put it back on with some more glue, can't you? "

"Yeah. Yeah. I'll glue it back on." She leaned over the bed and cocked her eyebrow. "Aren't you going to get up?"

"I'm having a morning problem."

"A morning problem?"

"Yes." King nodded. "You know, some guys call it 'morning wood.'" He saw that she still looked confused. "You know, it's like what happens when a guy takes Viagra."

That made it clear to Sarah what he was talking about. "Oh," she said.

"So if you wouldn't mind, I'd appreciate it if you'd turn the other way while I get up to go use the bathroom."

"OK." She turned back toward the drapes. "Go ahead. But don't come out 'till I tell you. I'm going to get dressed while you're in there."

"Fine. Could you also check the tracking program on your phone to see if Kareem is still here? He might be an early riser. I don't want to lose him."

"Yeah. OK. I'll check it in a minute."

King scooped up his clothes and headed into the bathroom. He did some yoga stretches until his back felt less creaky.

After a few minutes, Sarah called, "OK. You can come out now."

He came out fully dressed. She, too, was dressed and sitting in the chair by the window studying her phone.

"He's still here," she said. "But he must be on the move. The little dot shifts slightly every time I refresh the page."

"Which way is he headed?" King asked.

Sarah slid her finger across the phone screen to zoom out the image. "I'm not sure." She turned the phone to the horizontal position. "It looks like he's headed back to the train station."

"That fits." King nodded. "He's gonna get back on the train to New York."

"Why would he do that?" Sarah thought that was the last place he'd go. "It seems risky."

"Not at all," King said. "Not for him anyway. Nobody has identified him. And now that he's in the U.S., he can buy a new ticket. No one will ask to see his passport at the train station. Check the train schedule. We better find out when the next train leaves."

She tapped and swiped through screens on her phone until she found the Amtrak schedule. "There's an Empire Service train that leaves at 7:05 AM," she said. "After that, the Maple Leaf comes through here at 12:25 PM. That's the one we were on yesterday."

"What time is it now?"

"It's 6:40."

"He has to be trying for the 7:05. How close is he to the station?"

"About half a mile away. He must be on a bus or in a cab. The dot is moving faster."

"Could he be going somewhere else?"

"Like where?" Sarah swiped the phone surface to zoom out. She studied the wider map.

"Is there anything else nearby? A restaurant or something?"

"You think he's just going to eat."

"Probably not. In my experience, terrorists are gung ho types. He probably ate already. No point sitting around the hotel when there's a bombing to do."

"Jesus, Ty. I wish you wouldn't say that."

"Well, it's true. That's what this is about."

"What should we do?"

"We better check out of here and head to the station."

"We can't make the next train." Sarah shrugged. "It leaves in less than 25 minutes. We don't even have tickets."

"Maybe you could rent a car," King suggested.

"And then what? Drive alongside the train like a couple of bank robbers?"

"Yeah, actually. Then if we catch up with the train, or get ahead of it, we could board it at Buffalo or Rochester."

"That's just what I need, a car chase," Sarah said. "I wish you woke me up sooner. I don't like driving, especially not fast."

"Hey, don't blame me. I only woke up a few minutes before I woke you. With the drapes shut, I couldn't tell how late it was." King came up behind her to see what was on the screen of her phone. She was on the Hertz rental site. "Anyway," he said. "I can drive if you want."

"You're going to have to stay out of sight. That means I won't be able to put you down as an additional driver on the rental form. They have to see your driver's license for that."

King swiveled around and rolled his eyes. "You know what? The police are already chasing me on account of I like, you know, threw a bomb off the Maple Leaf. I truly don't suppose that driving a rental car without being listed as an additional driver is gonna add much to my rap sheet. You feel me?"

"OK. Save the sarcasm. You might be used to being a fugitive from justice. But I'm not."

King was busy packing up his old clothes and the makeup kit. "How about this? How about if you go down to the front desk and check out of the room? While you're there, you can ask about car rentals. I'll pack up everything and meet you down in the lobby in about ten minutes."

"You can't go yet. You don't have your beard on."

"There's no time for that now. You can glue it on me in the car. I'll be OK. I'm only going to be in public a little while. Before I leave the room I'll put on that hoodie and those sunglasses you bought, and my Cave of the Winds hat."

"You shouldn't wear a hat with a hoodie. It's too unnatural. You have to try not to look like you're in hiding."

"Fine. I'll leave the hood down and put the hat on."

"And don't make eye contact with anyone."

"How is that natural?"

"I don't know. Act like you're shy. Lots of people are shy."

"All right. All right. You'd better check Kareem's position before you make car arrangements. We won't need a car if he doesn't get on the 7:05 train."

Sarah looked back at her phone to check the car rental site. "This Hertz place is the closest car rental, but it's at the airport four miles from here. We'll have to take a cab to get there. I'm going to make a reservation right now just in case. I can cancel it if we don't need it."

"Good idea. I'll call the concierge on the room phone and ask him to get us a cab. Then I'll bring down our stuff and wait shyly in the shadows by the front door."

"OK. That's a plan." Sarah did some more searching. "The Empire Service train arrives in downtown Buffalo at 7:43. That doesn't give us much time to catch up with it. After that the next stop is Rochester, NY at 9:00."

"I'd think it will be less chancy if we shoot for Rochester. But we have to get there by 8:30 to have enough time to buy tickets."

"What are we going to do with the car? We can't just abandon it."

"We can park it somewhere—anywhere. It doesn't matter. I'll come back for it later and return it. Don't worry about the cost. I can pay you for it."

"I'm not worried about cost. I just don't think you can leave a rental car sitting around for weeks unattended. It would be better if it were in a garage or in someone's driveway."

"We can't put it in a public garage because then it will be noticed for sure. I think we should look for a residential street near the train station and park it there."

"And what if the city puts up signs for street cleaning? Then the car will get ticketed."

King had picked up the phone to call the concierge. But now he put it down. He said, "Sarah, I understand you are worried about these things. But don't you think those are minor problems compared to letting a bomb go off in New York City? The worst-case scenario is that the car may be ticketed or towed. All it would do is add something to the cost. I will pay for it."

"Out of what? Your private detective salary?"

"Yes, as a matter of fact."

"You don't have to pay for it. My dad has plenty of money. If I know him, he'll want to give us money for these expenses when he understands the circumstances. That's what he always does." She said this with disapproval. "He proffers money."

"You say that like it's a bad thing."

"Yeah, well I have issues with him. Money is his answer to

everything. Cash is cold. I'd like it better if he had even a little interest in me. I'd like it if he wanted to know something about my life. But, all he ever wants to do is give me money. He never asks me anything about myself. It drives me crazy."

King picked up the phone again. "Look, we can talk about this in the car. We have to hurry."

"OK. I'll see you in the lobby."

Sarah left the room, while King made the call to the concierge. Then he began methodically to inspect the room for anything left that might be evidence of their identity.

TWELVE

Cathy Chin of the Buffalo field office was the FBI Special Agent in charge of the Niagara River bombing case. She was short and thin with smooth bisque-colored skin. In spite of her short stature, Special Agent Chin exerted authority with ease. Her straight black hair was impeccably cut. Her clothes were classic and well-fitted. Her habits were formal. Her posture was confident. When she moved, her bearing was graceful, but with a deliberateness that conveyed self-assurance.

By 7 PM on the night of the bombing, she had studied the written testimony gathered from eyewitnesses. She had personally interviewed the border inspectors, the homeland security agents, and the train crew.

Chin's investigative team had already created a file on Tyrone King. From the documents in the file, she learned that King had been an Arabic interpreter/translator for the U.S. Army. He had been first an intelligence analyst in Iraq, and then a counter-intelligence agent in Afghanistan. In his last tour of duty, he'd participated in a covert counter-intelligence mission in Kabul, where he'd established a relationship with an Afghani intelligence asset with the code-name Reema.

None of these credentials matched the media's portrayal of him as a suspected domestic terrorist. Most of what the media reported came from interviews with the Amtrak café car attendant, Mr. Bowens, who testified that King threw the bombs from the train.

Then Chin came to the matter of Tyrone King's discharge from the Army. The file indicated that he had been discharged under the Army's "Don't Ask, Don't Tell" policy. During his hearing, King had condemned the circumstances of his discharge.

He swore that his accuser had framed him and falsified the evidence. He claimed that a man he was investigating was behind it. But the hearing panel concluded that the evidence presented by the accuser was substantial. The panel also was unable to establish a credible link between the accuser and the man who had been the subject of King's investigation.

On the hearing panel's recommendation, the Army discharged King, despite the fact that he hadn't yet completed his intelligence operation. The record indicated that no other Army agent was subsequently able to take up contact with Reema. As a result, the Army abandoned the covert operation and was unable to gather any intelligence from King's Afghani contacts.

Subsequent reports showed that Tyrone King's frustration with the way his case had been handled continued after his discharge. He joined a political organization dedicated to the repeal of the "Don't Ask, Don't Tell" policy.

There was nothing specific in the file about any homosexual relationship King may have had. The file did indicate that King had married a woman named Sandra Watson in Chicago when he was 24. They were divorced two years later through mutual consent. Another record in the file showed that Sandra Watson had married a woman named Susan Chapman in Iowa City, Iowa four months after her divorce from Tyrone King.

Chin was not able to conclude from these facts whether or not King's frustrations about his discharge might have led him to undertake a violent act of terrorism against the United States. It seemed unlikely. The reports of his military service from his commanding officers before his discharge were complimentary.

But since King was identified by Mr. Bowens as the person who last had possession of the bombs before they exploded, she had no choice but to classify him as a person of interest. His disappearance after the explosion did not support a presumption of innocence.

There were reports in the file of two other people seen leaving the train in the Niagara Falls train yard. A boy on the train told investigators that he'd witnessed a bearded man jump off the train through an emergency exit window—and that Mr. King had used the same window to leave the train moments later.

Other witnesses testified that a bearded man and a young woman had run down the aisle of the train just before the explosion. Three of these witnesses described the man as chasing the woman.

All the tickets collected from passengers, except for Mr. King's, belonged to passengers who remained on the train. Investigators had interrogated all of these passengers, and cleared them of any involvement with the incident.

By 10 PM, Special Agent Marsh, Chin's digital forensics investigator, had determined from the historical record that Mr. King had used his cell phone from a location near the Cave of the Winds to make two phone calls; both were to the cell phone of a woman named Melanie Kahn in Chicago. This first call, at 1:50 PM, lasted 38 seconds. The second call, forty-five minutes later, only lasted 14 seconds.

Marsh compiled records about Melanie Kahn, and provided Chin with a photograph of her from her Facebook page. The news media didn't know about Melanie Kahn, and Chin wanted to keep it that way. It was better that Ms. Kahn remained unaware that she was being monitored.

Mr. King, on the other hand, was clearly on his guard. He could not have missed the fact that his photograph was all over the media. He had not used his phone since the call to Melanie

Kahn at the Cave of the Winds. But the computer forensic team was still able to trace the phone's whereabouts through GPS.

Marsh explained to Chin that in order to be tracked, a mobile phone has to be turned on, has to be within range of a cell tower, and has to be able to receive signals from the GPS satellites. He'd found that King's phone was pinging the cell towers at regular intervals all night long. That meant that either King was keeping his phone turned on all night, or that he'd installed and was running security software that was performing the pings in the background. Using signal triangulation from the cell towers, Marsh could track the location of the phone within 328 feet.

According to the historical tracking information from these pings, King appeared to have spent several hours in the Holiday Inn hotel in Niagara Falls after leaving the Cave of the Winds. Then he'd gone out to the Red Coach Inn restaurant. After that, he'd returned to the Holiday Inn where the phone remained.

Chin had assigned two field agents, Cassidy and Walters, to perform reconnaissance at those locations. But they were unable to identify King visually at either location. Chin acknowledged that King may have taken steps to disguise himself.

She'd thought about closing the hotel and having agents perform a room-to-room search. But it would be difficult to do that without alerting the media. There'd be many questions, many disgruntled guests, and much media commotion. The hubbub would get in the way of her main goal, which was to gather intelligence quietly about all aspects of the bombing incident.

Chin took for granted that King was only one actor in the story. She did not want the other actors to know anything about the investigation. So she asked Marsh to set up a team to monitor King's phone overnight and alert her to any movements.

Their first alert came just as she arrived at her office the next day. According to the monitoring team, King's phone—and presumably King—left the hotel at 6:00 AM. Chin immediately sent Cassidy and Walters to follow the phone, which led them to the Amtrak station.

At 7:00, the phone appeared to move onboard the Amtrak Empire Service train. Chin told Cassidy and Walters to board the train and look for King.

Melanie Kahn's phone, in the meantime, had pinged from a residence in the Andersonville neighborhood of Chicago. Marsh had set up an on screen map that would track the movement of both Mr. King's and Ms. Kahn's phones in real time.

Chin watched the movement of King's phone along the Amtrak route headed toward Buffalo. When Cassidy called in to report, he said he'd been unable to locate King anywhere on the train. He'd borrowed an Amtrak conductor's cap. He'd followed the real conductor. He'd inspected every passenger on the train. No one fit King's description. No one even came close. While the conductor audited the tickets, Cassidy's partner, Walters, watched to make sure no one was hiding in a restroom or between the cars.

Chin speculated that Tyrone King could have boarded the train, left his phone, and then exited before it left the Niagara Falls station. That would be one explanation for why his phone was on board, but he wasn't. He'd been trained in counter-intelligence. It may well have occurred to him that the FBI would trace his phone. He might have put it on the train as a red herring, and then escaped through a different route.

With that in mind, Chin had enlisted the assistance of the local Niagara Falls police to continue surveillance for King in the area of the Amtrak station and the Holiday Inn hotel where he'd spent the night.

It was also possible that King could have boarded the train and disguised himself so effectively that Cassidy and Walters couldn't recognize him.

At this point Chin called Marsh. "Cassidy and Walters haven't located anyone who looks like King. Can you be more precise about where the phone is located? Can you pinpoint its exact location on the train?"

"Right now," said Marsh, "the train is moving. That means I can see the phone moving—but I can't see where it is on the train without another reference coordinate. Give me the mobile phone number for one of your field agents, then find out which car he's in. Then I can calculate the distance between his phone and the suspect's phone. If they both stay put, I'll have a better idea where the suspect is."

Chin called Walters and asked him which car he was in. Then she relayed his number and location to Marsh.

"Here's what it looks like," said Marsh. "Since Walters is in the first car, the suspect's phone is probably in the third car."

Chin called Walters and told him to stay put. She called Cassidy and asked him to re-inspect the third car. She told him to make it a covert inspection. If he tried to interrogate passengers individually, it would alert King and might prompt him to take evasive maneuvers.

After fifteen minutes, Cassidy called back. He'd worked his way down the aisle of the third car of the train. He'd seen no one who matched King's description.

Chin rapped her fingers on her desk. She was beginning to think King must have put the phone on the train as a red herring. She could have the third car evacuated. Cassidy and Walters could look for the damn phone. But then if King were actually on the train in disguise, an evacuation would tip him off. The less there was to warn him, the easier it would be to apprehend and subdue him before he could do anything dangerous. If he was carrying another bomb, he might detonate it the moment he saw trouble.

Chin looked at the little dot on her screen. It showed the phone moving toward New York City. If King wasn't on the train, what did it matter? She could just as well wait until the train got to Penn Station. Then, after all the passengers got off, she could have it searched for an abandoned phone without tipping anyone off. That was the safest course.

In the meantime, she instructed her team to arrange for field agents to meet the Amtrak train at each stop along its route. An agent at each stop would don a red cap and pretend to be a baggage handler. That way her agents could size up the passengers as they exited the train. The surveillance had to be discreet. She didn't want the media or anyone on board to notice it. If her computer monitor showed the phone being taken off the train at any of these stops, she'd have the Red Cap agent follow the signal and identify who was carrying it. Once the agent was at a safe distance from anyone who might be hurt, he could subdue the suspect before any violent action occurred.

After this plan was in place, Chin could only wait. There was nothing else to do. The Niagara Falls police were conducting a local dragnet in case King had ditched the phone on the train without boarding. But if he had boarded the train, her agents would be in position all along the route ready to seize him.

THIRTEEN

KAREEM AND JASMEEN sat in the third car of the Empire Service train. The phone Kareem picked up at the Cave of the Winds was in his pocket. He figured that if he had to, he could use it to call his brother in New York City. But Jasmeen convinced him they should avoid mobile calls except in an emergency. She'd studied the surveillance policy of the U.S. National Security Administration. If national security was at stake, the agency could monitor phone calls without warrants if it involved any party outside the U.S., even if the other end of the communication was within the U.S. But Jasmeen didn't trust the Americans to be bound by this policy. She believed the agency would monitor any calls they wished to monitor.

She felt it would be safest to use her two-way radio for communication. But it would only work when they were within a two-mile range. Their brother Abdul had a similar device tuned to the same frequency. Her instructions were to call him on the two-way radio as soon as they got within two miles of his apartment.

Kareem had tossed his walkie-talkie into the torrent of the Bridal Veil Falls after he'd spoken with Abdul the day before.

Kareem and Abdul had made a covenant. Abdul had come up with a plan that would require Kareem to become a martyr. He believed they couldn't be certain of success at the Statue unless Kareem was inside it when the deadly moment came.

Kareem had taken this news calmly. His courage impressed Jasmeen. She couldn't bear to lose him. But she knew she couldn't react any less bravely than he had. She tried to hide her feelings. But once she knew what they'd decided, she found herself watching Kareem closely. She was looking for signs of doubt. If he needed her to be strong, she would be.

Out of habit, Kareem studied the passengers seated nearby. A mother and her teenage son sat in the seats across the aisle. The son had a tablet on his lap and earphones in his ears. He was watching a movie, while his mother was reading an eBook.

"These Americans are obsessed with their electronic gadgets," Kareem said in Arabic.

"Of course," said Jasmeen. "They are materialistic. They believe only in this world. Even those who claim to be religious, from what I can observe, have little thought for what is to come."

"Do you ever doubt what is to come?" Kareem asked.

"Ordinary doubts cannot be avoided," said Jasmeen. "But true faith allows these doubts to be set aside. Everyone would have faith if doubts did not exist. The cultivation of purity and the daily practice of prayer keep away the devils of doubt."

"Yes, it is prayer that I find most helpful."

"But why do you ask? Are you having second thoughts?"

Kareem didn't want to hide anything from her. "It is not a matter of courage. I have the courage to do what I have to do. Because it is necessary, I will die. I am not afraid to die. But I sometimes have doubts about how I will feel in Paradise. I know it is said to be a place of all that is good. But I have so little practice with the kinds of contentment that are promised, that I sometimes wonder how I will experience those joys."

Jasmeen smiled. "You mean, because you are a virgin?"

Kareem blushed. "I have never been with a woman," he admitted.

"Kareem, your purity is such that you will be rewarded for it. If Allah the most beneficent, the most merciful, can open Paradise to men less pure than you, do you not see how your rank in Paradise will be that much greater?"

"Yes, but it is said that Paradise will have gardens and grape yards, and …." Kareem paused, "….young women."

"Yes, of course," said Jasmeen. "The Prophet has said that you will find beautiful young women in Paradise. Such pleasures will surely be yours, Kareem."

"But I have never known pleasure with women," said Kareem. "When I die, Inshallah, I will go to Paradise—but I will go there with no experience. It is my inexperience that gives me doubt."

"Are you afraid that you won't know what to do when the lovely-eyed women of Paradise come to you? I cannot imagine that the pleasures of Paradise will be kept from you on that account."

"Yes. That is it. I won't know what to do."

"Perhaps you wonder if it might be better, in preparation for what is to come, that you should have an experience with a woman here on Earth before your martyrdom."

"I have considered it," Kareem said. "I do not wish to diminish my purity. I would like to be martyred with no earthly blemish upon me. But I would feel more prepared for what is to come if I had some practice with it."

"You must pray about it, Kareem. Allah, the beneficent, will guide you."

Jasmeen and Kareem looked up. A man carrying a tray with drinks stopped in the aisle next to them. He grabbed the back of the seat in front of them to steady himself. Kareem looked up at him and said in English, "The train is so unsteady."

The man nodded, but he continued working his way down

the aisle—stopping at every seat to grab the seatback to keep his balance.

"Maybe I should offer to help him," Kareem said in Arabic when the man had passed. "I could carry his drinks. It would be much easier for him."

"You must not call attention to yourself," Jasmeen said. "Besides, such men do not like to be helped." She frowned. "I do not know why this man is so unsteady. He is not an old man, yet he acts like one."

"Maybe he has a handicap," said Kareem. "I should help him." He stood up. He stepped out into the aisle.

Instantly Jasmeen called to him in English, "Jack, wait, don't go. I changed my mind. I don't want to eat now."

Kareem came back to his seat and sat down.

In Buffalo, Special Agent Marsh called Special Agent Chin.

"Did you see that?"

"See what?" Chin looked at her screen, but everything looked the same to her. The dots were moving steadily along Amtrak's Empire route.

"I think the suspect's phone just moved a few feet forward. Then it went back to where it was," said Marsh. "Either the phone moved relative to your agent's phone, or your agent moved. Or it might be noise in the signal strength from one of the phones."

Chin called Walters in the first car. "Tom, did you just move your position?"

"Negative," he said.

"Not even a few feet?"

"Cassidy's walking around, but I haven't moved an inch. I'm sitting in my seat. I haven't budged."

Chin returned to the conversation with Marsh. "Walters didn't move. It must've been the other phone. Maybe it's on the floor and slid along on its own," she said. "Did the train just change elevation?"

Marsh overlaid an elevation map over the section through which the train had just passed. "No," he said. "There's nothing in the elevation that would have caused the phone to slide."

"Maybe the train slowed, and then sped back up. That could make it slide."

Marsh rewound his tracking program. He turned on a function that displayed the train's speed. Then he replayed the previous five minutes of the train's travel. "Negative," he said. "No change in speed."

"Well," said Chin, "If something caused the phone to change position, someone must have it on them."

"That seems likely," Marsh agreed.

Chin called Cassidy, but he didn't answer. Four minutes later, he called her back. He was with Walters in the first car. He told her he'd been carrying a tray of sodas down the aisle and couldn't answer the phone when she'd called.

"Did you see anyone get up or move in that car?"

"No," he said. "But if someone moved after I passed by them, I wouldn't know it. I wasn't checking behind me."

"Go back to the third car. Find a seat in the back row. Sit where you can see everyone. And keep your phone ready. If we see the suspect's phone move again, we'll call you to make visual verification of who has it."

"Roger that," said Cassidy. He made his way to a seat in the back row. From there he could see everyone in the car.

FOURTEEN

King drove a white Nissan Sentra on Interstate 90. Sarah sat beside him with her phone tuned to Google Maps for navigation. They had just passed Buffalo.

"How's our time?" King asked.

Sarah pinched and tapped through forms on her phone. "Google says the trip from Niagara Falls to Rochester should take 90 minutes," she said. "But if we're going to ditch the car and buy tickets, we've got to make it in 60 minutes. Even then, it's gonna be close. How fast are you going?"

"I'm going 80," King said. "The speed limit is 70. I don't want to be stopped by the cops. Help me keep an eye out."

"God, this is nerve-wracking," she said. "What about your disguise?"

"What about it?"

"Don't you think I should put your beard on now? There's not going to be time to do it after we get to Rochester."

"You can't do it while I'm driving. You'll block my view."

"No I won't. Don't worry."

Sarah rummaged through the paper bag of theatrical supplies, which King had hastily packed. She emptied the contents of the bag onto the floor of the passenger seat. She dug through the pile until she found the glue. "In order for me to do this," she said, "You'd better slow down and turn your head slightly toward me, but keep your eyes on the road."

"Slow down? Really?"

"We've got to do this now, and I don't want you to crash. If we don't get to Rochester in time, we can keep going to Syracuse. The train doesn't arrive in Syracuse until 10:30. In fact, I think we should change our plan and bypass Rochester. Waiting until Syracuse gives us more time to get ahead of the train."

"OK. Fine. But then you'll have to double-check on Kareem to make sure he doesn't get off the train before that."

"Sure. Sure. I'll keep an eye on Kareem. Let's see what's happening with your skin," Sarah said. "The fake beard won't stick to greasy skin." She ran her fingers along his cheek to test the oiliness of it.

King could smell a faint smell of honeysuckle on her fingers as they came close to his nose. She only brushed his skin briefly, but it felt like a caress. He wished he could close his eyes, but he kept his head fixed in a forward position and his eyes open. "What's the verdict?"

"Not bad. But I'd better swab you with some alcohol first. It'll dry your skin completely."

"Swab me."

She put a cotton ball like a cork on a bottle of rubbing alcohol and inverted it. Then she dabbed the chilling liquid all around King's chin and cheeks. When she ran it over his upper lip, his nose twitched. She said, "I see you can wiggle your nose."

"It's a family talent."

"Nice."

"So?" King asked. "Is my face de-grease-ified enough for you now?"

Sarah felt his cheek again. "It's drier. But rough. The stubble from your real beard is like sandpaper."

"I haven't shaved for two days."

"OK, now turn your head toward me."

King turned his head.

"But keep watching the road."

King turned his eyes back toward the road without moving his head. "I'll try. This is an awkward position."

"You'd better slow down more. We'll make up the time later." Sarah applied the glue to the right side of King's chin, which was turned toward her. Then she positioned a ribbon of hair on it. When the right side of his face was done, she assessed the left side. "Turn more toward me."

"You sound like a dentist. You'd better work fast. I can only turn my eyes so far in their sockets. I can't see the left side of the road with my head twisted like this."

Sarah reached across King's chin from below to avoid blocking his view. She dabbed the glue, then placed another ribbon of hair on his left chin. King glanced at her face. Her lips were pursed in concentration, which made them look especially full. She was focused on her task and didn't seem to notice his glance. He felt wafts of her breath on his neck. She fussed with another small piece of beard below his lips. Then she repeated the process with the left and right sides of his upper lip.

"I'm almost done," she said. "And quit looking at me. You're supposed to watch the road."

"I'm not looking at you. I just peeked for a second to see what you're doing."

"You know what I'm doing."

"We're coming up to road construction," King said. "I'm gonna have to turn my head back in about fifteen seconds to navigate a lane change."

"OK. OK. One more dab. There. Now you can turn back."

King glanced at himself in the rear view mirror. "I look better than last night."

"Yes," Sarah agreed. "Without the skin lightener, you look more natural."

Orange cones appeared on the road to force the lanes to merge for the construction work. King slowed to allow a tanker truck on his right to pull in front of him. When the merge was completed, King drove at a steady pace behind the truck. Three miles later, the orange cones gave way and the lanes opened up again. King accelerated back into the left lane. "So, what's happening with Kareem?"

Sarah checked her phone. "He's either still on the train or he's running alongside it at a fast clip."

"Just like us."

"Actually, we're slightly ahead of the train. But I don't think we're enough ahead of it to buy tickets at Rochester." Then she said, "Amtrak isn't very fast. I don't know why anyone rides it."

"I like trains," King said.

"So do I." Sarah put her phone back into her purse. "I just wish the trains were halfway decent in the U.S. The trains in Europe are much better."

"What about Canada?"

"Better than Amtrak," said Sarah. "But not as good as Europe or Japan or China or…" She closed her eyes, trying to think of another example. Then she finished with, "… or Scandinavia."

"*Vous avez fait le tour du monde?*" King asked.

"I've been around some of the world. Not everywhere."

"*Où avez-vous visité?*"

"I've visited England, France, Germany, the Netherlands, Switzerland, Denmark, and parts of Asia. And please don't speak French. It's annoying."

"Sorry. I just like to practice when I can."

"Say something in Arabic, then."

"Like what?"

"Say, 'Jasmeen, you're so beautiful.'"

"'*al-Yāsmyn 'Nt Jmylh Jdā,*'" King said. "How does that sound?"

"It's worse than French."

"I have no interest in Jasmeen," King said. "Except as a source of information."

"I know. You're as honorable as a Canadian Mountie."

"Whereas I am interested in you, and it has nothing to do with terrorism."

"What do you mean … interested how?"

"I've been looking for a makeup assistant."

"Right."

"It would make a nice addition to my private-eye service. I could disguise myself and spy on my clients."

"Why would you do that?"

"Sometimes the people who hire me have hidden agendas. I have to check them out. Right now I have an associate who does that for me."

"You have a partner?"

"Yes. She's a friend, who helps out occasionally."

"A friend? You mean like a girlfriend?"

"No. We're just friends. She's Jewish."

"What does that mean, 'we're just friends; she's Jewish?' Are you saying there's a connection?"

"No, there's no connection." King tapped his fingers on the steering wheel. "But I get tongue-tied whenever I mention a woman, because you assume there's a sexual angle."

"I just asked if she was your girlfriend. Why are you so defensive about it?"

"I already told you I don't have a girlfriend."

"No. You didn't say one way or another."

"Well I don't," King said matter-of-factly. "I'm single. And I'm not seeing anyone."

Sarah nodded. "So I guess we're both single."

King turned to face her. "You're single too?" He cocked his head. "I'm surprised."

"Maybe I should hire you as an investigator," she said with a shrug. "To investigate why Sarah Gaber is still single."

"Must be a hidden defect," King observed.

"No," Sarah shook her head. "You're supposed to say 'it must be a terrible mistake.' Or 'how could this be?' Or 'the right guy hasn't come along.'"

"OK. The right guy hasn't come along. Or he has but you haven't picked up on it."

"What? You think I don't know the right man when I see him?"

"It's very common. People are often drawn to the wrong types and overlook the right ones."

"I see."

"Hey," King said suddenly. "What about Kareem?"

"He's not my type."

"Ha. Ha. You'd better check the GPS to make sure he didn't get off the train. The train should be at Rochester by now."

Sarah pulled her phone from her Prada bag, switched it on, and opened the SignalSecure page. "The train must've stopped," she said. "Kareem's dot isn't moving."

"Is the dot at the Rochester train station?"

"It's on the map next to a little train symbol labeled Rochester Amtrak. When I switch to satellite view and zoom in, I can see the tracks, the station house, and a little u-shaped parking lot behind the station. There's a train on the tracks at the station, but it looks like a freight train."

"The Google satellite picture isn't real time. That's just the image of a train that was sitting there when Google took their picture. But the dot is real time. So watch if it moves toward the station house. That might mean he's getting off the train."

"I'm watching," Sarah said. "It's not moving at all."

"Good."

"Do you think he's sitting there with another bomb?" Sarah asked.

"I don't see how he could have another bomb already. I think he's going to New York to hook up with some people to set up the next … event."

"I hope you're right," Sarah said. "I'd hate to be sitting here looking at my screen and see that little red dot blow up."

"The dot would probably just disappear."

"Yeah, along with the people on the train. Let's hope the dot stays lit."

FIFTEEN

When Kareem was back in his seat, Jasmeen leaned over and, even though she spoke in Arabic, she whispered in his ear, "You mustn't do anything to call attention to yourself."

"Do you think someone is watching?" Kareem asked.

"Maybe. Maybe not," Jasmeen said. "But it is possible. They may have decided to watch all the trains in this area now."

The teenage boy across the aisle had finished the movie on his iPad. Now he sat with his head laid back on his seat and tilted to the side. He looked at Kareem with a bored expression. His mother still held the eBook reader in her hand, but she too had her head back on her seat. She was falling asleep.

Kareem turned to Jasmeen. "The boy across the aisle is staring at me," he said.

Jasmeen glanced at the boy. "He is just bored," she said. "He hears us speaking, but he doesn't understand our language."

"I suppose if the FBI was watching for us, it wouldn't be a boy staring, but a man who tried not to look at us."

"Yes," said Jasmeen. "It would be a man or woman who is alert and feigning indifference. But you must not look around the train. I think we should just sit here quietly." She glanced at the boy across the aisle, who still wore his headphones. He appeared to be listening to something. "It would be better if we had music players like everyone else."

"Maybe the phone I found has music on it," Kareem said. He fished the phone out of his pocket, turned it on, and scrolled through the apps.

"Tell me again," said Jasmeen. "How did you get this phone?"

"I was at the Cave of the Winds. A boy found it and thought it was mine. He gave it to me."

Jasmeen nodded, but said nothing for a while. Then she asked, "Was it a boy like that?"

Kareem looked at the boy across the aisle, then back at Jasmeen. "Yes."

"But not the same boy, surely?"

Kareem looked across the aisle again. "No," he said. "The boy at the falls was similar. But I'm sure it's not him. How could it be? That would be too much coincidence."

Jasmeen looked at the phone in Kareem's hands. "Did you find music on the phone?"

"I'm still looking?"

"You said that you called someone with the phone."

"Yes, I called someone in the contact list named 'Melanie.' A woman answered and said 'Hello Judith,' but I hung up without speaking to her."

"Judith?"

"Yes. And the phone shows 'Judith Goldman' as the owner in the account settings."

"She sounds like a Jew."

"There are some photos here in the 'My Pictures' folder." Kareem paged through the photos. "Here is a picture of the CN Tower in Toronto."

"Is this Judith Goldman a Canadian?"

Kareem looked back through the contact list. "The addresses she has are all in New York."

"So the woman from New York was in Niagara Falls, but she

must have also been in Toronto to photograph the CN tower. Perhaps she was on the train," said Jasmeen. "Are there other pictures?"

Kareem paged through the photographs on the phone. "Yes, most of the photos are pictures of people, some men, some women."

"Are they American?"

"I don't know. They look American."

"How old?"

"Most of them look like they are in their twenties or thirties. Here is a picture of a Negro soldier."

"A soldier?"

"Yes."

"In what uniform?"

Kareem spread his fingers on the phone screen to zoom in the image. "The uniform is U.S. Army." Kareem tapped the screen to go to the next image. "After that there is another picture of several more soldiers. They are in a military camp somewhere." Kareem tapped the phone again. "Next is a photo of a woman in a hijab. I don't know where it was taken, but it doesn't look like the U.S."

"Kareem, this is very strange. Why would a Jewish woman in New York have these pictures?"

"Perhaps her husband is in the Army and emailed her these photos."

The train had pulled into the station at Rochester. Jasmeen looked out the window and saw passengers getting off. She saw nothing out of the ordinary.

"Yes, but wouldn't he have emailed photos of himself?"

"Maybe the Negro soldier is her husband."

"I suppose that is possible," said Jasmeen. "But why would he email her a photo of a Muslim woman?"

"Perhaps the woman is a friend of his."

"I don't think soldiers send their wives photos of their female friends from overseas—even in America. And if an American soldier knows a Muslim woman, I do not think it is very likely that it is a matter of friendship."

"Yes, but maybe the husband sent her this photo as a souvenir. He may have wanted to show his wife how women dress differently in the country he is visiting."

"You can invent a story to explain anything, Kareem. But that does not make it believable. Something about this story does not seem right to me. It may be true that there is a Jewish New York woman named Judith with a Negro husband who is fighting in the Middle East and who has sent her a photo of a Muslim woman. But why would she keep this photo on her phone? The CN tower, a Negro soldier, and a Muslim woman—it does not fit."

"What does it matter? Do you think I should get rid of the phone because it has these pictures?"

"Yes, I do," said Jasmeen. "I don't like taking any chances."

"I can take the phone right now to the restroom at the end of the car," Kareem said. "I'll leave it there." He began to get up.

"No, wait," said Jasmeen. "I don't think you should do anything right now. Just sit here. Wait until we get off the train. Then you can leave the phone behind in the seat."

"Very well." Kareem had only risen a few inches from his seat. Now he sat back down. "But you are making me anxious. You make it seem like someone is watching our every move."

"Yes, I know. I cannot explain it," said Jasmeen. "It is just a feeling I have. Perhaps I am being too cautious. But do not forget, there is a reason I have two sugar packets in my purse."

Kareem spoke slowly in Arabic. "Abdul gave you those packets filled with poison," he said, and then he frowned. "Abdul was not right to do that. Suicide is forbidden."

"Abdul says if you are caught and tortured, you will have to use one of those sugar packets if you think they might break you."

"I would never take poison," said Kareem. "Do you not know what the Prophet said? He said, 'whoever drinks poison and kills himself with it, he will be carrying his poison in his hand and drinking it in the fire wherein he will abide eternally forever.'" Kareem shrugged. "I think that is very clear."

"But that is about suicide," said Jasmeen. "Abdul says it is not really suicide if you are fighting in a war."

"I do not believe Abdul." Kareem shook his head. "If you are a prisoner, you are no longer fighting in the war. Why did he give you two of them?" Kareem asked. "Is one of them meant for you?"

"Yes, of course." Jasmeen shrugged. "The Americans might capture me just as easily as you. I could not withstand the torture. I know this."

"Please, sister," said Kareem. "You must promise me you won't use it. Abdul has not studied the Prophet's teaching on this matter. You will end up drinking the poison forever in Hell."

Jasmeen was silent for a moment. "All right, Kareem. I promise not to take the poison."

"I think you should get rid of those packets."

"Yes. All right. I'll throw them in the river when we reach New York."

"Do not worry," said Kareem. "You will not be tortured. They will not catch us."

"Only if we remain vigilant," said Jasmeen. "That is why you must not leave anything to chance. And you must pray, brother."

"OK." Kareem looked around the train. "I don't see anything unusual," he said. "But I will sit here and think about what is to come. And I will pray for guidance about my preparations for Paradise."

"You mean you will think about the lovely-eyed women of Paradise?" Jasmeen smiled.

"Yes. Perhaps." He smiled back. "I will think of those things that give me courage."

Kareem lay back in his seat. He closed his eyes. He thought of Paradise. And he hoped that when he got there all his doubts would be erased.

SIXTEEN

Special Agent Marsh told Special Agent Chin, "The phone may have moved again. It was just a small movement."

Chin, in turn, said to Cassidy in the back row of the third car, "We saw a small movement of the phone just now. Did you see anyone move?"

"Two people moved in the last minute," he said. "A woman got up to get a book from her bag on the luggage rack. Also, a teenage boy left his seat. I think he went to the restroom."

Chin asked Marsh, "Could the movement you saw have been made by a woman getting up to take something off the luggage rack?"

"Perhaps," he said. "But it was only a movement of a couple feet at most."

"Understood," said Chin to Marsh. She switched back to the line with Cassidy. "Keep watching, Jay," she told him. "We don't think it was the boy. It might have been the woman."

King and Sarah drove past the exit for Seneca Falls. According to Google maps, they were halfway between Rochester and Syracuse on the New York State Thruway, in the middle of the Finger Lakes region. Sarah watched the red dot of King's phone, as it moved along the Amtrak route. The dot had just left Rochester a few moments earlier. She estimated they were now forty or fifty minutes ahead of the train.

"What else does the SignalSecure program do?" she asked. "Besides show you where the phone is."

"You can use it to turn the phone off, so whoever has it can't make any calls."

"OK. But that doesn't help us. What else does it do?"

King shrugged. "I don't remember what else. Look on the help system. What are you trying to do?"

"I was hoping I could tell if Kareem has made any phone calls with your phone. Maybe it would lead us to his contacts."

Sarah opened the help system and began to read about the functions and features of SignalSecure. "Oh, this is cool," she said. "According to this, we can turn the remote phone's microphone on and use it to eavesdrop on whoever has it."

"Do it," said King. "Let's see if Kareem has anything to say."

Sarah followed the instructions in the help system to turn on the remote phone's microphone. Then she held her phone up to her ear. "I hear the sound of the train," she said. "At least that's what I think it is. It's like a background noise. It's mostly static, but I can hear a faint clickety-clack underneath it."

"Clickety-clack? That's it?" asked King. "He's not talking."

"Not at the moment."

"Keep listening."

"Wait a minute," said Sarah. "Someone is talking now. It's a woman's voice. But I can't make out what she's saying."

"Do you mean you can't understand it because she's not audible, or because she's not speaking English?"

"Wait." Sarah pressed her ear to the phone and cupped her hand around her other ear. "Yes. I can hear her talking. But you're right. She's not speaking English."

"Let me listen," said King.

Sarah held the phone up to King's ear. "Do you hear her?"

"Push it close," he said. "It's difficult to hear." He cupped his hand over his left ear while Sarah pressed the phone tight against his right ear. "OK," he said. "I hear the woman talking. She's speaking Arabic. She's saying something about women in Paradise." King blinked his eyes. "Wait. Now Kareem's talking. He's says he's thinking of things that will give him courage." King looked at Sarah. "You're sure they can't hear us, right?"

Sarah pulled the phone back from King's ear. She navigated back to the help system and read the description of the eavesdrop feature. "No. That wouldn't make sense," she said. "The whole idea is to eavesdrop. It's like a one-way mirror. We can hear them but they can't hear us."

"OK." said King. "Let me listen again. I'll tell you what they're saying."

Sarah put the phone back up to King's ear. "If that's Kareem talking," she asked, "Who's he talking to?

King listened intently. "It must be Jasmeen. It has to be. She's the only one who could have boarded the train with him in Niagara Falls. She's saying that Allah will give him courage. She is saying Abdul can arrange for Kareem to … to spend time with a woman who will help him prepare for Paradise."

"By doing what?" asked Sarah. "By making him some bombs to use?"

"No. Apparently she's talking about a woman that Abdul knows who will have sex with Kareem."

"Sex? You've got to be kidding."

"No, seriously. I think she's telling Kareem how he can get laid before he blows himself up."

"You mean she wants him to have sex with another woman? I guess she's not his wife or girlfriend after all."

"Apparently not." King held up his hand to indicate that he was listening again. Then he said, "She's telling Kareem that since he has been so pure all of his life, this one experience will not sully him."

"Pure, huh." Sarah grimaced. "The guy's a murdering terrorist for God's sake."

"I don't think they count that as a negative," said King.

"But why is she pimping for him? Who is she?"

"Maybe she's an Al Qaeda operative—someone who arranges things for up and coming terrorists."

"Do they allow women to do that?" Sarah asked. "Do they let women play an active role in planning attacks?"

"Definitely," said King. "They're fine with women being suicide bombers. They crossed that line some time ago—once they saw it added an element of surprise."

"Now what's he saying?"

"Nada. Neither of them is speaking. But I can hear the conductor. He's announcing that the snack car is open."

"My arm is getting tired holding this phone to your ear. How about if I turn it on speakerphone?"

"Fine."

She switched on the speakerphone, and resumed her navigation on Google maps."

"What are you doing?"

"Trying to figure out where we can ditch the car and be close to the train station."

"We should leave the car right in front of the station."

"But the rental is in my name," said Sarah. "If the car's abandoned, it'll call attention to me. So far, I've been under the radar."

"OK. Fine."

"According to this, we can get off at Hiawatha Boulevard and park near Hiawatha and 1st Street. That's less than half a mile from the station. It would be a ten-minute walk at most."

"Ten minutes is a long time. Do we have that much time?"

"We can make it," Sarah said. "But you'll have to drive faster."

SEVENTEEN

Amtrak Empire Service train 284 was running nine minutes late for its 10:30 AM arrival in Syracuse. King and Sarah wouldn't have missed the train even if it had been on schedule. They arrived at the Syracuse station at 10:20. No one was in line at the ticket counter. They bought two tickets with cash, and were ready to board the train by 10:25. Now they sat on a wooden bench in the waiting room.

"You see," said King. "All that rushing, and now the train isn't here."

Sarah took out her phone and visited the screen that showed the location of King's phone. "The train is getting close," she said. "It can't be more than fifteen minutes away."

"Maybe we should get something to eat," King ventured.

Sarah looked around the room. "From where?"

He pointed at the vending machines along the wall.

Sarah lifted her finger to her mouth and made a mock gagging gesture. "I'd rather starve."

"OK," he said. "Suit yourself. What time do we arrive in New York?"

"If it isn't late, we arrive at Penn station at 4:35 PM."

"Long time with no food."

"So fine," said Sarah. "If you're hungry, get something from the vending machine."

"Do they have a snack car on the train?" King asked.

Sarah looked at the schedule again. "There's a picture of a little coffee cup next to the train number."

"The coffee cup symbol means there's a café car. We can get something to eat there. I don't like vending machine food, you know."

"Uh huh." She looked back at her phone. "The train is arriving. We better go out to the platform."

They both stood up. Sarah picked up her shopping bag. King had nothing to stand in for luggage.

"Let's try for the rear car," he said. "We should stay back of Kareem so he won't see us."

"What if he's in the last car?"

"Then we'll sit in the car in front of that."

They went to a spot on the platform that would place them near the back of the train. But when the train arrived, the conductor only opened one car door for boarding new passengers —and that car was in the middle of the train.

King got on first. After they'd boarded, he said to Sarah, "So we're going to walk to the last car, right?"

"Right. But let me go first. If we see him, he's less likely to recognize me."

"What am I supposed to do? Hide behind you?"

"Just lower your head if he's there. Don't make eye contact."

Sarah went first. They walked slowly toward the rear of the car. She saw Kareem in an aisle seat in the middle of the car on the left side. She barely recognized him. He was clean-shaven. His face appeared softer without the distracting beard. He was dressed in dark cotton slacks and a crisp light grey shirt open at the collar. He looked down at something he held in his hand.

Next to Kareem was a beautiful woman. Sarah assumed it must be Jasmeen. She wore a green silk blouse with a string of opaline pearls. She looked wealthy, like a woman of the world. No headscarf covered her curly black hair.

Jasmeen watched the arriving passengers as they came down the aisle. It was clear she was scrutinizing everyone.

Sarah didn't hesitate. She walked at a steady pace. She held her shopping bag out in front of her.

King had no luggage. When he saw Kareem and Jasmeen, he turned his head away, as if he was looking for a seat on the other side of the train.

When they got close to Kareem, Sarah turned to King. She said cheerily, "Let's sit back there, honey." She gestured toward a spot at the back of the car. Kareem looked up at the sound of Sarah's voice. Sarah looked right at him and smiled. She smelled a spicy-sweet fragrance, which could have been his cologne or Jasmeen's perfume.

Kareem smiled back in a friendly way. But then he cocked his head, suddenly perplexed. A beautiful woman was smiling at him. His smile faltered. Color rose in his face, and he blinked. But he didn't look down at Sarah's legs to check for an ankle-bracelet. Her distracting smile kept him from noticing King.

After they passed Kareem, Sarah pointed at an open pair of seats near the rear of the car. She looked at King with a questioning look, but he frowned and shook his head. So she continued, left the third car and went to the fourth car. There she saw a pair of open seats near the front. She took the seat by the window.

As soon as they'd sat down, Sarah said, "You saw him, right?"

"Of course I saw him. And he saw you. He got a good look at you. Were you looking at him?"

"I looked right at him. I made eye contact. I smiled at him. I wanted a diversion. I didn't want him to look at you."

"OK, but now he's probably sitting there thinking about you. He's probably trying to remember where he saw you before."

She shook her head. "I don't think so. Back on the Maple Leaf, he never saw my face. He only saw me from behind. Mostly he saw my feet.."

"I hope you're right."

"So the woman next to him, that was Jasmeen?"

"Yes."

Sarah hadn't watched her closely, since she'd been so focused on Kareem. "Did she see you?"

King nodded. "She looked at me. She looked at you. She was looking at everyone. But if she recognized me, she didn't show it."

"I only got a glimpse of her. She's beautiful."

"I suppose," King said. "In an exotic way."

"You know what's funny?"

"What?"

"Kareem shaved his beard to disguise himself. Did you notice? It's the opposite of you. He took his off. You put one on. Too bad he couldn't loan you his beard."

King smirked. "Yeah, funny."

"He's actually quite good-looking."

"So?"

"So, nothing."

It annoyed King that Sarah, who had said little that was flattering to King, was now pointedly complimenting Kareem's looks. But he let it pass.

"You wouldn't know from looking at either one of them that they're terrorists," said Sarah. "How do people like that get like that?"

King didn't answer. Instead, he lowered his tray table and propped his head in his hands on it. He closed his eyes. After a moment, he turned and said, "I don't know."

"It's crazy."

"It's crazy to us," King said. "But not to them. To them it has to do with religion and jihad. These people have a grandiose sense of destiny. They think Allah has whispered in their ears and told them to 'Go destroy the infidels.' They think they're doing something altruistic. They think they're heroes. It's not easy for us to comprehend. But it's exactly the same motive that drew Christian crusaders to kill Muslims."

"I don't understand it." Sarah shook her head. "Why would a religion want you to kill innocent people? My father is a devout Muslim, and he would never dream of hurting anyone."

"Religion is their excuse. Our excuse was supposed to be weapons of mass destruction." King's expression and his voice changed. "Do you know how many innocent Iraqis died because of that excuse? I saw things I wish I'd never seen."

Sarah saw the pain in King's face. "I'm sorry," she said.

King had his head propped in his hand on the tray table. He was looking out the window of the train. "What the hell was I doing over there?" he asked loudly. Then he lowered his voice. "One day in Afghanistan I was talking to my intelligence source about a friend of hers. She told me her friend was killed by an American bomb. His only crime was that he was in the wrong place at the wrong time. It dawned on me that her friend was as innocent as the people who went to work on September 11th at the World Trade Center."

"I broke down that day. I realized I couldn't go on pretending the collateral damage was justifiable. I mean, there I was trying to get information out of my source, which might well lead to a tactical attack on the enemy. But I couldn't tell who was the enemy and who was innocent. From my source's perspective, her friends were just ordinary people fighting an invader. And now, here, we're the ordinary people fighting Kareem and Jasmeen. Now they're the invaders. Now they've come to our country to fight us."

King was whispering. They were on a train in public space. But the quiet volume of his voice didn't hide the emotion behind his words. Sarah had been watching him with her eyes darting back and forth, as if she could keep him within some emotional boundary through the movement of her eyes. When he stopped speaking, they both sat in silence, listening to the murmur of conversations taking place elsewhere in their car.

After a while, Sarah said, "But we have to fight them. We have to stop them."

King nodded. "Yes, of course. But I don't want to see any more collateral damage—ever." He lifted his elbows off the tray table and put it back up in its cradle in the seatback. "Don't worry," he said. "I'll snap out of it."

"What should we do now?" she asked. "Maybe we should try to listen in on their conversation."

"Yes. If Kareem has any suspicions about us, they'd probably be talking about it."

Sarah called up the SignalSecure program on her phone and set it to eavesdrop. She handed the phone to King. "You'd better listen. If they're talking about us, I guess it won't be in English."

King held the phone to his ear. After a minute he said, "Nothing. They aren't talking."

"So that's good, right?"

"That's good."

The train had been stopped for what seemed like a long time at the Syracuse station. But now it began to move. Sarah looked out the window. She saw a Red Cap standing on the platform talking into a phone. "It's weird that they still have Red Caps," she said. "Just about everyone uses roller bags now."

King looked out the window too. The platform was mostly empty. A matronly black woman stood in the center of a group of assorted suitcases. Her luggage, which had no wheels, looked like it came from another era. She turned her head from side to side, peering in all directions. She looked like she could use some help. But the lone Red Cap, talking on his mobile phone, didn't notice her.

"Red Caps are the last vestige of the glory days of train travel," King said. He imagined the train platform as if in a scene from an old movie: filled with travelers wearing coats and hats, holding luggage with handles that still had to be lugged, surrounded by a swarm of uniformed Red Caps. "It almost makes me want to travel with a big steamer trunk."

Sarah smiled. "How gay!" she said brightly. "But shouldn't I be the one with the big trunk? And a big fur coat to go with it. Men are just supposed to carry a valise."

"A valise?"

"Yeah. Men aren't supposed to cart around a lot of junk. Not if you're going by the way things were in the old days."

"I see. So if I had a big trunk, that would be gay?"

"Well, yeah."

"It seems to me you've got a pretty stereotyped view of what's gay."

"Come on. You don't think Elton John has a big trunk to carry around his outfits?"

"That's just one person." King said. "But now that you mention it, I guess I can picture him with a trunk and a fur coat."

"And a couple of small dogs. And he'd have three or four Red Caps trailing behind him with all the baggage."

King looked back out the window. "There aren't enough Elton John's in the world to keep Red Caps in business. That Red Cap looks pitiful. And he doesn't seem to be too interested in carrying any luggage."

At that moment, the Red Cap at Syracuse was speaking on his cell phone to Special Agent Chin. He told her that no one getting off the train resembled the suspect Tyrone King.

EIGHTEEN

As Empire Service train 284 made its way east, it stopped at stations along the Interstate 90 corridor: Rome, Utica, Schenectady, and Albany. The train followed a well-traveled path along the Erie Canal and the Mohawk River between the Adirondacks and Berkshires to the north and east, and the Catskills to the south. From Albany, the train turned south to run along the east bank of the Hudson River. Passengers on the right side saw spectacular views of the river, as it passed between the eastern slopes of the Catskills and the western slopes of the Berkshires.

At 2:30, the train arrived at Hudson, a small city on the east side of the river. Jasmeen surveyed the station platform. She was watching for unusual activity. When the train arrived, she saw a Red Cap waiting beneath the red-roofed platform. He held a phone to his ear. He wasn't the first porter she'd noticed talking on a phone instead of helping passengers. At earlier stations, she'd thought it might be a coincidence. "These station porters must not have enough to do," she'd thought. "Maybe they are in a union. Maybe they are so certain of their jobs it does not bother them to talk on the phone instead of working."

But now she watched the Red Cap who was on the phone

more closely. He could see the passengers as they got off the train. A woman with two roller bags was right in front of him. She was looking at him. She must need help. But the Red Cap just stood there, holding his phone to his ear. He didn't move. He didn't speak. Why didn't he offer to help her? Jasmeen turned to Kareem and said in Arabic, "Something is not right with that porter."

Kareem leaned over and looked out the window.

"You see?" Jasmeen pointed at the man. "That man holds a phone, but he doesn't talk to anyone. He wears a red cap, but he does nothing to help that woman with her bags. Why would he choose such a busy moment to make a phone call?"

Kareem yawned and lay back in his seat. "Someone must have called him. He's listening to someone talk. He's distracted."

"No, Kareem." She took his arm. "Look. Something is not right. This is the fifth station where I've seen this—a Red Cap who talks on his phone just when the train arrives."

"Maybe that's how they coordinate with their dispatcher."

"Coordinate? What is there to coordinate? The only thing these porters have to do is come out to meet the train, watch for people who need help with bags, then help them. There is nothing to coordinate!"

Kareem had been napping. Now he felt groggy. He rolled his head sideways on the headrest. "You worry too much," he said in English.

"And you who are napping have become too complacent," Jasmeen replied in Arabic. "The American news media will not tell us what is happening in the hunt for the bomber. But I can promise you, brother, that there are men looking for you. The fact that no one has stopped us does not mean we are not under observation. We have to be careful, Kareem. We will lead them right to Abdul."

"You think they are following us?"

"I think those Red Caps are watching for someone. They might not know it is you they are looking for. But maybe they do.

It is too much of a risk. I think we should split up. If they follow you, I can go to Abdul while you stay away."

Kareem frowned. "Split up? Oh no, Jasmeen. That is not a good idea. You cannot continue to travel alone, an unmarried woman. It was bad enough you were alone for several hours yesterday. That was the extent of what we agreed to—and that was because we knew it would only be for a short time."

"I am serious, brother. I know it is improper. I would not even consider separating from you, except that so much is at stake. We cannot take any chance of leading the Americans to Abdul. It does not have to be for a long time—just until we get to New York—perhaps less than a day."

"But how would we communicate? I no longer have my two-way radio. I threw it into the falls. We have no way to talk to each other if we split up."

"What does it matter? We can still rendezvous in New York—but it just must be somewhere away from Abdul."

"What about this?" Kareem held up King's phone. "You could call me on this phone."

"The phone of Judith Goldman?" Jasmeen snickered. "No Kareem, I do not like that phone. I already told you. We must get rid of that phone. It may have come to you by accident as you say. But what if it did not? It is too risky. There is something wrong about the photos on that phone—they are not right."

Kareem shrugged. "How will we split up?"

"You should get off the train. Then we can see if someone follows you."

"You want me to get off the train before you?"

"Yes—but not at a station. These Red Caps are watching every station. I am sure of it. It will be better if you get off when no one is looking. You can get off the next time the train stops between stations."

"What if it does not stop between stations?"

"The train has already stopped several times to wait for freight trains. Do you not remember? The conductor announced what was happening each time. We only have to wait for another announcement. Then you can go between the cars. When the train stops, you can open the door and get off where no one will see you."

"But that could be anywhere? It might be in a remote location. How would I travel from there?"

"Have you no faith, brother? Do you doubt that Allah is watching over us? You will find a way to travel. You found your way in Niagara Falls, did you not?"

"Yes, but that was in a city with paved streets and buses and hotels and places where there were crowds of people. If I am in a remote area, I will stand out. There are many uncertainties."

"Yes. There are uncertainties. Jihad is not an exercise in certainty, Kareem. You must improvise."

"I will need money to travel."

"I will give you money. I have more than enough American money for both of us." Jasmeen retrieved her purse from the floor beneath the seat in front of her. "Here." She counted out ten fifty dollar bills and handed them to Kareem. "That is five hundred dollars." She fished around in the seatback pocket in front of her. She pulled out the timetable and studied it. "See here? We are only two hours from New York City. It is only 120 miles from here. Perhaps you can find a map on the Judith Goldman phone that will show you how to get to a nearby town."

"But you want to get rid of the phone."

"Yes, yes. But if you can find a map on the phone now, we can draw the map on paper before you get rid it. After you get off the train, you can walk to the nearest town and take a bus into the city. At this distance from New York, there must be many such towns."

Kareem still held King's phone in his lap. He turned it on and studied the icons until he found the one for browsing the Internet. He went to Google maps and pulled up a map of the area from Hudson to New York City. "There are many towns on this side of the river," he said. "Rhinebeck ... Poughkeepsie."

Jasmeen looked again at the timetable. "The train stops in Rhinebeck and Poughkeepsie. If you go to one of these towns, you must stay away from the train station."

The moment Kareem turned on King's phone in the third car, Sarah's phone in the fourth car beeped.

"Did you hear that?" Sarah asked. "It beeped." She picked up her phone and opened the SignalSecure program. "He just turned on your phone." She showed the message on the screen to King. "You see? Before we got on the train I configured it to beep whenever someone turned it on, and it just beeped."

King had been watching the passengers get off at the Hudson station. "Can you set it to eavesdrop? I want to hear what he's saying."

Sarah set the mode to eavesdrop and handed him the phone.

As King listened, he relayed what he heard. "Jasmeen just said something about the train stopping at Rhinebeck and Poughkeepsie. She said 'if you go to one of these towns you should stay away from the train station."

"Who's she talking to?"

"She must be talking to Kareem."

"What does she mean, 'If you go to one of these towns'?" Sarah pulled out the schedule from her seat back pocket. "The train stops in both those towns. How can Kareem stay away from the stations if the train stops at them? It doesn't make sense."

King held up his hand. "Shhh."

Jasmeen took a pen and a sheet of paper from her purse. "Look up the addresses for the bus stations in Rhinebeck and Poughkeepsie," she said to Kareem. "I will write them down." He found the addresses and she wrote them down. "Now show me the maps," she said. "I will draw maps on this paper to show you how to get there."

Kareem did as she requested. Jasmeen sketched a rough map for each bus station and handed the paper to Kareem. "Here," she said. "If anyone follows you, or if you see any of the men in red caps, be careful. Try to shake them off your trail. Even if it looks like no one is following you, you must be careful."

Kareem nodded. "But where will you be?" he asked.

"I will go to meet Abdul in New York. But Kareem, when you get to New York, you must stay away from Abdul's apartment. You can change one of these bills and get coins. Find a public phone, call this number and ask for me." She handed him another small piece of paper on which she'd written a number. "Now I think it is time to turn off the Judith Goldman phone and leave it in the seatback pocket."

King handed Sarah's phone back to her. "He just turned off my phone," he said. "Jasmeen told him to put it in the seat pocket." He pondered what he'd just heard. "I think they're planning to split up. I may be wrong, but it sounded to me like he's planning to get off the train, but not at a station. She talked about meeting up with him later in New York."

"Why would they split up?" Sarah asked.

"Jasmeen thinks someone is following him."

"She must have recognized you."

"I don't think so," he said. "She said something about men in red caps." He looked out the window. "I've been wondering about it myself."

"About what?"

"At every station I've seen Red Caps. But I didn't think these smaller Amtrak stations had any Red Caps. I don't remember seeing any Red Caps at the smaller stops when I took the train to Toronto. There were a lot of them in Chicago, but that was it. Now, all of a sudden, here along this New York route, I've seen a Red Cap at every one of these little stations. It isn't normal. I think they're looking for us."

"The Red Caps?" Sarah peered out the window.

King rose slightly from his seat and pointed down on the platform. "See that one there? The guy is talking on his phone." King sat back down, then looked around. None of the nearby passengers was paying any attention to him. Even so, he suddenly felt paranoid. He lowered his voice. "He's probably an agent dressed as a Red Cap. FBI, or Homeland Security, or something like that."

"Jesus." Sarah matched King's hushed tone. "You think the FBI is looking for you on the train?"

"What else could it be? I'm the one whose picture is all over the news."

Sarah pondered this. It seemed implausible to her. "That's pretty far-fetched," she said. "Why Red Caps?"

"Why not?"

"How would they know you're on the train?"

King shrugged. It was a good question. He thought about how the FBI would proceed. Probably, they'd put together a dossier about him. They'd analyze his life story for clues to his whereabouts. They might interview his friends. They'd talk to his assistant Melanie. Then it dawned on him. "I bet they traced my phone," he said. "It would be easy for them to get my phone number. Then all they'd have to do is track the location of my phone, same as we are. But since Kareem has the phone instead of me—they're confused."

Sarah considered this. It made sense that the FBI could do the same thing they were doing. "OK. Maybe. But maybe they're looking for Kareem too."

"They don't have his picture."

"What if they have a picture of him but they're keeping it under wraps? Maybe they're using the hunt for you to give him a false sense of security."

"If that's their plan, it isn't working," King said. "Jasmeen definitely doesn't have a sense of security. She's suspicious of the Red Caps. She wants Kareem to take a bus to the city. She's drawn a map of the bus stations in each of the towns coming up.

She's instructed him to call her from a pay phone when he gets to New York. She's warned him against going directly to their meeting. She doesn't want him to lead the authorities to them."

"If they split up, what should we do?" Sarah asked.

King thought about it for a minute. "Here's what I think—when Kareem gets off the train, I should get off too. I'll follow him." King looked across the car. Through the window on the other side of the aisle, he saw that another train was moving along side them. It was passing slowly in the opposite direction. He wasn't happy about the idea of getting off the train. He looked at Sarah. "And I think you should stay on the train with Jasmeen. She's suspicious of everyone. But she never saw you. You got on the Maple Leaf yesterday after she got off. There's no way she could recognize you."

"She saw me with you just now when we walked down the aisle."

"But she didn't recognize me, so she won't connect you to me. I'm sure she'd have said something to Kareem if she'd recognized me. She's suspicious of the phone I planted. But she obviously doesn't know we can eavesdrop through it, since she's been discussing their rendezvous plans."

The train lurched. It began to move away from the Hudson station. Sarah looked down again at the Red Cap on the platform. He continued talking on his phone. She glanced around the train car. Everyone around them sat quietly, except for a couple that was talking about something she couldn't make out. She tried to picture how this plan of King's would work. "If I stay on the train with Jasmeen," she said, "what exactly am I supposed to do?"

"All you have to do is follow her. If we're lucky, she'll lead you to the others. But you need to keep your distance. Just stay back and watch. Find out where the others are. Don't get close enough to get involved."

"And you're going to follow Kareem? How will you do that? He's bound to recognize you."

"He hasn't recognized me so far. Maybe he won't."

"But if you and I split up, I won't be able to communicate with you. You don't have a phone."

"Kareem is supposed to call Jasmeen from a pay phone when he gets to New York. I can do the same with you."

"That's fine for you, but what if I need to talk to you? I won't have any way to reach you. I'll be out there on my own."

"If you run into problems, you can call the authorities," King said. "Dial 911. Ask for the FBI."

"The picture I end up with when I play that out in my mind is a picture of me in an orange jump suit at Guantanamo Bay?"

"You're a U.S. citizen, aren't you?"

"Yes, but my father is a Muslim."

"Do you really think it's that bad?"

"I don't know. Maybe."

"Well hell, if that's how you feel about it, why don't we just split up? You can forget all of this. No one will ever know you were involved."

"That's not what I mean."

"If I thought it was that bad, I'd move to Canada."

"Come on, Ty. There's a lot of paranoia out there. In a situation like this, they're bound to be suspicious of everyone, and doubly suspicious of anyone with a connection to Islam."

"OK. But if you don't believe it matters that you're innocent—you shouldn't get involved. You should just walk away."

Sarah stared at him. "And then what?" Her voice raised a notch and began to bristle. "You're going to go on alone? You're going to keep track of them both?"

"I can't track them both. But I can track him." King's voice was bristling too. "He's the one who punched the detonator codes. He's the one who's ready to blow himself up and everyone else along with him. She's like the brass in the military. She keeps her hands clean, and gets someone else to do the dirty work."

"Why are you so hostile all of a sudden?"

"American justice is a touchy subject with me. It's a long story. I had a negative experience in the military." He softened his tone.

"Look, I'm sorry. The truth is I have no right to ask you to follow her. It is too much to ask. It could be dangerous."

"Here's what I don't understand," Sarah said. "I don't understand why you think this is your personal mission any more than it's mine. Why do you feel like you have to save the day? I think we should talk to the FBI now—both of us. We should let them handle this."

It was true. Turning things over to the FBI now might be a good idea. He knew he should consider it. "Maybe," he said. He gazed out the window. They were traveling along the Hudson River. Across the river, spectacular cliffs rose in a line along the riverbank. Several mansions dotted the crests of the cliffs. He imagined what it would be like to live in a mansion on a cliff over the river. He envisioned himself sitting in a wing back chair reading a book, glancing out a picture window at the long silver Amtrak train rolling down the rails on the other side of the river.

"I understand that you're qualified to do this job," Sarah said. "But you have to decide if this is a way of proving something about yourself—or if this really is the best way to proceed."

King raised an eyebrow. "What do you think, Dr. Freud?"

"I think I should get off the train at the next stop, tell one of those red cap FBI agents to follow me back onto the train, tell him what's been going on, and point out to him where Kareem and Jasmeen are sitting."

"And what about me?"

"It's up to you. You could join me, or you could sneak off at another door when I bring the agent on. Then you could just go away and stay out of sight for a while."

"So, that way, maybe later I can work on trying to spring you out of Guantanamo. Is that it?" He smiled so she'd know he was teasing her.

"OK. OK." Sarah shrugged. "I guess I was being paranoid about that. Once they have the real terrorists, it would be crazy for them to think I had anything to do with it—especially if I help them catch the bad guys."

King closed his eyes. He knew she was right. At this point, everything was in place to hand this off to the agents. The FBI would have the resources to follow Kareem and Jasmeen better than he could. The Bureau wouldn't miss a beat—even if someone did take him in and detain him for a while. "All right," he said. "Let's go to the FBI. But I'm not going to run away. There's no point. How could I justify that? I'll turn myself in."

A look of alarm crossed Sarah's face. "You'd better wait until I've had a chance to explain everything before you do that. If they really are gunning for you, I don't want them to shoot first and ask questions later."

"OK, fine."

Sarah fiddled with her phone. She called up the Amtrak route guide. "The next stop is Rhinebeck—in about twenty minutes. After that, it's Poughkeepsie."

"We might as well do this at the next stop," King said. "Why wait?"

"Right."

"I'll watch you from the window," King said. "You'd better start by finding whatever Red Cap is on a phone and tell him the short version of what happened. Then get the agent on the train and show him where Kareem and Jasmeen are sitting; but don't let them see the agent—or at least make sure he takes off his cap before they see him. Then you can bring him to me."

Sarah looked at him. "If I think there's going to be any trouble," she said. "I won't tell the agent about you. If I don't bring him to you, you can assume there is a good reason."

"Roger that." King nodded.

The train was chugging along. The twenty minutes would go by quickly.

"They'll probably separate us," King said. "In order to compare our stories."

"Shouldn't be a problem. We both have the same story, right?"

"Right." He looked her in the eyes. "I'm not sure when I'll see you again. It could be a while."

Sarah returned his gaze. The adventure was about to end. And King was right; they could be kept apart for some time. She reached out to put her hand around his neck. She leaned in close to his face. "It's been an amazing experience," she said.

To King's surprise, when he felt her hand on his neck, he blushed. She looked at him with such emotional intensity that he was startled. Her touch felt momentous. He blinked, unable to act on the moment. Sarah squeezed his neck. He let out an audible sigh. He closed his eyes.

Then suddenly he felt their lips pressing together. Both his arms went around her. She put her other arm around him too—and, in that instant, a cascade of feelings yanked them out of time and space. He felt like they were orbiting—their arms around each other—like a satellite in outer space. They had turned, side to side, in their seats—and they began to sway forward—until King realized they were being pulled forward by inertia. King swung his hand out. He grabbed the seat in front of them to keep them from falling into it. The train was stopping. A low-pitched squeal sounded as the braking train wheels bore down on the metal tracks.

NINETEEN

"We're stopping," King said.

Sarah had her eyes closed. But now she opened them and looked out the window. The train shuddered to a stop. They had come to a stop in the middle of nowhere. The train was a few feet from the Hudson River on the right and ten yards from a wooded embankment on the left.

The loudspeaker sputtered with static. Then the conductor said, "Ladies and gentlemen, we're stopped here waiting for signal clearance. We'll only be here for a few minutes. We should be moving again shortly."

King suddenly stood up. "Damn. This is it," he said.

"This is what?"

"This is where he's planning to get off. They must have been waiting for one of these delays. He's going to get off the train here, in between stations."

"Are you sure?"

"That has to be their plan. Why else would she have told him to stay away from the train station and find a bus station? If he gets off here, no one will see him."

"Should we alert the FBI?"

"We can't do that now," King said. "There's no time. I have to follow him." King stepped into the aisle.

"Wait." Sarah grabbed King's arm. "What if he doesn't get off?"

"If he doesn't get off, I'll come back and we can go back to the original plan."

"And if he does?"

"I'll call you from a pay phone in New York," he said. "Stay with Jasmeen, but keep your distance. If it looks like anything bad is about to happen, get away and call the authorities."

"You have my number?"

"I memorized it."

"Ty, be careful. That guy is dangerous."

"You be careful too."

"OK. Good bye," she said. Then she said, "Wait!" She scooped up her purse from the floor and dug around in it. She took out a roll of money and handed it to him. "You'll need this," she said. "For the bus and pay phone."

King nodded. "Thank you," he said. He looked at the roll of money. "How much is this?"

"About three hundred," she said.

King leaned down and kissed her again. Then he turned and walked toward the car where Kareem and Jasmeen had been sitting. He saw Jasmine was now sitting alone. He walked up behind her slowly, and then walked quickly past her. He kept going until he got to the connecting vestibule. There he saw that the door was open on the left side of the train.

This train car was a different model than the car he'd been in yesterday in Canada. In this car, instead of a manual lever there were buttons that controlled the door. Kareem must have pressed the button to open the door, and then jumped off. King leaned out and looked at the embankment. There was no sign of him.

King was just about to pull his head in, when he saw him. Kareem was moving on the ground alongside the train—crouched down low and close in to the cars, below the sightline of the passenger windows. King peered along the edge of the open door and watched as Kareem sidled all the way to the back of the train. When he cleared the last car and was out of sight of the windows, he turned and made his way up the steep embankment, which was lined by a row of trees and shrubs. Kareem climbed up into the woods and out of sight.

King looked down through the open door. This time the jump was only about three feet. He had a momentary vision of himself landing badly again—and Sarah once again having to make her way down to help him. He erased that vision and replaced it with a picture of a cat landing gracefully on the ground. He didn't want to leave the door open. It would only alert the train crew that someone had made an unauthorized exit. He pressed the "close door" button, then quickly crouched, doing his best imitation of a cat, and jumped just before the door rolled close.

His left foot slipped on the gravel when he landed, but he quickly regained his balance. He glanced up and down the length of the train. He saw no one. He imitated Kareem's strategy, creeping toward the back of the train, keeping low near the wheels. When he got past the end of the train, he too headed straight up the embankment and into the cover of shrubs and trees beyond. He had to climb about twenty feet up a hill before the land leveled out.

Once behind the wall of trees and shrubs, King paused to look back at the train. He waited two full minutes to be sure no one else left the train. But the two minutes came at a cost. He only had a short time to find Kareem. He assumed Kareem would travel toward the nearest town. But without a map, he had no way of knowing if the nearest town with a bus station was north or south of his present position. He decided to look for the closest north/south road. If necessary, he'd try to hitch a ride.

King checked his watch. It was 2:40. Since it was early September, he would have four or five hours of daylight left. He tried to get his bearings. He turned around, peering as far as he could in every direction. When he turned north, he saw that the train, before it stopped, had passed under a bridge that crossed the Hudson River. The bridge was a quarter mile north. He reasoned it was likely that a bridge traveling east to west would also intersect with a north/south thoroughfare. But he had to consider Kareem. Would Kareem have turned around and spotted the bridge? Would he too have made the calculation that it was a logical way to find a route through the woods?

While he thought about this, King kept walking east. He hoped the woods would open onto a field or some clearing where it would be easier to spot Kareem. But the woods stretched out indefinitely to the east. There was nothing resembling a path—which made it difficult to move quickly. He had to step around fallen trunks and through tangles of bushes just to move thirty feet.

Once he got deeper into the woods, he realized there were no other reference points besides the bridge. He could no longer see the train through the trees. The bridge, because it rose up to an elevation needed to cross the river, was the only thing he could see.

He stopped and listened. If Kareem was anywhere nearby, either he was moving very quietly, or he had stopped too. With the maze of brush and the crunchy leaves on the ground, moving quietly was impossible. It didn't seem likely that Kareem would remain stopped for very long. King kept still for a full minute and listened.

He heard a slight rustling sound. But the disturbance only lasted a few seconds. Kareem couldn't be that stealthy. The noise had to be from a squirrel or a bird. He turned until he was facing the bridge. He began to make his way toward it through the woods.

Special Agent Cassidy looked at his watch. The train had been stopped for nine minutes waiting for signal clearance. Now it was moving again. He watched the people who came and went from the third car. For the most part, people got up, went to the café car, and eventually returned with cups of soda, bags of chips, etc. Others went to and from the restrooms at the end of the car. Some coming from other cars were just walking through. Cassidy kept track of each of them.

At the moment, he was keeping an eye out for two passengers from his car who'd left their seats while the train was stopped, but hadn't returned. One was a well-dressed man with dark hair, who'd been sitting with a pretty woman. He'd gone toward the café car. The other was a teen-age girl who'd been sitting with an older woman that he assumed was her mother. She'd gone to the restroom. Now she was coming back to her seat.

If the man didn't come back soon, Cassidy would go look for him. He'd noticed that most of the trips to the café car lasted anywhere from eight to twenty minutes. The dark-haired man had only been gone ten minutes, which was well within normal range. Now he watched as someone else got up. This time it was an older man, who made his way to the restroom.

Sarah put her hand on the empty seat beside her. She'd seen King get off the train—but only because she'd been watching for him. The moment he'd hit the ground, he'd moved close to the train and disappeared. He'd only been visible for about fifteen seconds. She doubted anyone had noticed. Since then she'd been watching the embankment for signs of movement. She hadn't seen any. Now the train was moving again. She relaxed enough to begin to feel the significance of what had happened. She and King had kissed. And now he was gone.

Kareem went straight up to the top of the embankment. He looked back over his shoulder only for a few seconds, until he was sure no one was coming after him. Then he walked east into the woods for twenty feet, just far enough that he could still make out the train through the trees. Then he turned south. He intended to follow the train line south. His plan was to keep out of sight by staying in the woods while walking parallel to the track.

After he'd walked for ten minutes, he noticed through the trees that the train was moving again. He stopped at that point and waited for the train to pass. When it had passed completely, he kept still—listening to the silence around him. Then he knelt down between two trees and said a prayer. *O Allah, lighten this journey and make its distance easy. O Allah, You are my Companion on the road and the One in Whose care I leave my sister.*

When the train began to move, Jasmeen looked at her hands. She realized she'd been sitting with her fists clenched, one hand grasping the other, for the entire time that the train had stood still. Now she separated her hands and relaxed them. She picked up her purse from the floor and took out her wallet. She counted how much money she had left. She had just over five hundred Canadian dollars and about a thousand U.S. dollars. She put the wallet back in her purse and the purse back on the floor. She leaned back in her seat and closed her eyes. She wanted to sleep. She let her thoughts drift. She tilted her head to the side until it rested on the window. She summoned up a memory of a day when she and Kareem had been children playing. They'd made believe they were riding on a train even though they were actually sitting in adjacent cardboard boxes. Kareem was in the front box. He was the engineer. She was the passenger. "Where are you taking me?" she had asked. "Jannah," he'd said. "It is a garden." It was the Arabic word for Paradise.

Jasmeen was awakened by the sound of a phone ringing. She blinked open her eyes and looked instantly at the Judith Goldman phone in the seat pocket in front of her. She dared not answer it. She contemplated picking it up and taking it to the restroom at the end of the car. She could leave it there. She reached into the seat pocket and put her hand on it. Suddenly, she had a sinking feeling. There was someone standing behind her.

She could tell without turning her head that someone behind her was watching her. She let go of the phone. She sat back in the seat and waited. The phone stopped ringing.

After a moment, the man who'd been standing behind her stepped close beside her. She could tell he was looking at the space along the overhead bin above her seat where the conductor had placed the tabs of paper that showed the destination stops for her and Kareem. She knew exactly what he saw. He saw two tabs marked PENN STATION hanging above their seats. But of course, he only saw one person sitting in the seats below, not two. Jasmeen turned toward the window so the man couldn't see her face.

Special Agent Chin saw the incoming call on her monitor. She instantly contacted Cassidy in the third car. "Melanie Kahn is calling Tyrone King," she told him. "Find out where the ringing phone is located."

A few minutes later Cassidy called back with his report. "The phone is in a seat pocket near the middle of the car at a seat occupied by a woman. When I got there, she had her hand on the phone, but she didn't answer it. Earlier I saw a man sitting next to her, but the man left his seat about twenty minutes ago. He hasn't come back. He must have gone to the café car. The ticket stubs above those seats show two passengers for Penn Station," Cassidy said.

"Do you remember what the man looked like?"

"He had dark hair—nicely dressed. I'd say both he and the woman were Middle Eastern."

"Really?"

"Really."

"But did the man look like Tyrone King?"

"Negative. I didn't see him close up. But he didn't look

anything like the picture you gave us of King. Different guy. I'm sure of it."

"OK," said Chin. "Can you describe the woman?"

"She's nicely dressed—green silk blouse, pearls. She has dark curly hair. But I couldn't see her face—she was looking out the window."

"Watch the woman, and get a picture of her."

Now Chin contacted Special Agent Marsh. "Robert? Did Ms. Kahn leave a voice message?"

Marsh waited a few beats in case the voice mail system was still recording. But it was obvious from his monitoring equipment that it wasn't. "No," he said. "She hung up without leaving a message."

"Where was she when she called?"

"She made the call from her apartment in Chicago."

"Did she make or receive any other calls?"

"No. There haven't been any calls to or from Melanie Kahn's phone since she received the second call from King yesterday."

Chin considered this. Then she said, "Robert, Cassidy just reported that a man and woman in the third car appear to have King's phone. Cassidy says the man left his seat after the Hudson stop—but he hasn't returned."

"So the phone rang, but she didn't answer it?"

"Cassidy says the woman had her hand around the phone when he saw her—but she didn't answer it."

"Well, it's King's phone—not hers."

"But Cassidy insists the man he saw is not King."

Marsh was skeptical. "It has to be King," he said. "He must be in disguise. You better have Cassidy double-check that."

"Until the man returns to his seat, that's going to be impossible," said Chin. She thought about how to proceed. She dialed Cassidy. When he answered, she said, "Jay, go to the café car and find the man you saw sitting next to the woman. Check carefully to be sure he's not Tyrone King. If he's not, we need to find out who he is. Get a picture of him. While you're at it, also get a photo of the woman he was sitting next to." She looked at the train schedule. "You won't have much time. The train is scheduled to arrive at Rhinebeck in less than ten minutes. If either the man or the woman gets off I need to know about it so we can hand off surveillance to the agent in Rhinebeck."

Chin looked at her roster of station agents. She called the field agent assigned to meet the train at Rhinebeck. She told him they were now monitoring both a man and a woman. She wanted to be ready in case either the man or the woman or both got off at Rhinebeck.

TWENTY

It took King twenty minutes to get to the bridge. The woods had narrowed so that by the time he reached the bridge, he was in a strip of woods about fifty feet wide. To his left, the bridge rose up over the train tracks on its way out over the Hudson River. To his right, the bridge ramped down to a road, which crossed a field that held regular rows of plants arranged like tufted dots of fabric on a bedspread. He saw cars on the road, but he couldn't see anyone on foot anywhere near the field.

When he looked back toward the bridge, he saw a sign identifying it as the Rip Van Winkle Bridge, Route 23, which connected to the New York State Thruway on the other side of the river. He made his way through the field, walking in a direction parallel to Route 23. At the end of the field was a paved side road that dead-ended at a cluster of houses. He crossed the road and a second field, until he came to another thicket of woods. He kept going. When he came out of the woods he found himself at a two-lane highway identified as Route 9G.

King stood on a wide space on the shoulder of Route 9G. A sign said Rhinebeck was 25 miles away. Rhinebeck was one of the towns Jasmeen had mentioned when she gave Kareem directions to the local bus stations. He figured it would take six or seven hours to walk 25 miles. He knew Kareem couldn't make the walk any faster than he could. They wouldn't get to Rhinebeck until after 10 PM. It seemed unlikely they'd find a bus to New York at that hour.

But what was the alternative? Hitchhiking didn't seem like a good idea for a wanted man. Of course, Kareem wasn't wanted. Only King's picture was in the news. But anyone who saw his picture saw a clean-shaven man with dreadlocks. After Sarah's makeover, his hair was short and he wore a beard. It seemed plausible that with these changes he might go unrecognized.

King had hitchhiked twice when he was in college. On one occasion, the driver was going somewhere else and had to let him off ten miles short of where he wanted to go. He'd had to walk the rest of the way. On the other occasion, the men in the car he got into were so obviously drunk that he chose to get out when they stopped at a rest stop.

He considered the alternatives. If Kareem hitchhiked to Rhinebeck but King didn't, he would lose the trail completely. He decided he'd better hitchhike.

He stood in the shoulder and stuck out his thumb. For the first ten minutes, he analyzed the cars as they came by. When he saw a car in the distance, he'd speculate if it might stop, based on the kind of car it was. Then, once the car got close enough so he could see who was in it, he'd refine his assessment. It didn't matter. All the speculations got him nowhere. No one stopped.

Women with children didn't stop. Men driving alone didn't stop. Old men, young men, taxi drivers, truck drivers—some of them slowed to gape, but none of them stopped. He concluded that the demographics didn't make any difference. Hitchhiking had become nearly impossible. Everyone had seen too many horror movies.

After twenty minutes, King saw a car coming that was going slower than most of the others. It was an older model. From what he could tell, the driver was steering down the middle of the road. But eventually the car drifted completely into the right lane and slowed even more as it came nearer to him.

When it came close enough, he saw the driver was a gray-haired older woman. She was alone in the car. When King realized she was slowing so she could inspect him, he straightened his shoulders. He made his body language as unthreatening as he could. He moved his hand—the one with the thumb extended—in a tentative arc. At the same time, he tilted his head to the side and smiled as sweetly as he could.

The car stopped twenty feet in front of him. He ran up to the side of the car. It was old and shabby, but it had electric windows. The woman pressed a button and the passenger side window rolled down.

"Thank you for stopping," King said. "I'm looking for a ride to Rhinebeck."

"I'm going past Rhinebeck on my way to Poughkeepsie," the woman said.

He saw her more clearly now. He guessed her to be in her late fifties. Her un-dyed hair was mostly gray, but still showed some darker streaks. Her hair was loose, but neat. Her skin was unwrinkled, except at the edges of her eyes and on her neck. Her eyes were bright and intelligent. But her expression was scolding.

"Why are you out here hitchhiking?" she asked. Her tone was that of a mother reproaching a teenage son.

The question surprised him. "It's a long story," he began.

"Tell me," she said.

King considered telling her the truth or at least part of it. Something told him the truth was key to gaining her trust.

"I'm a private investigator," he began. "I've been following a man. We were on an Amtrak train to New York an hour ago when the train stopped near here to wait for another train." King gestured vaguely in the direction of the train tracks behind him. "While the train was stopped, the man got off the train unexpectedly. I think he was suspicious of being followed. I had to get off at the same time in order to try to continue to follow him. I think he's going to Rhinebeck to get a bus to New York City. So, I'm aiming to do the same thing."

The woman looked at him quizzically. She said, "You say you're a private investigator?"

"Yes," he said. "My license is from Illinois. I live and work in Chicago." He fished his wallet out of his pocket and showed her his Illinois private detective ID.

She pushed a button on her console and unlocked the door. "Well, get in then," she said.

King got in the car. "Thank you. I really appreciate this."

She drove off the shoulder and back onto the highway. Soon she was driving at a normal speed. The car bounced and swayed, as if the tires were worn or underinflated. She drove with two hands on the wheel to try to keep it straight and steady.

"Who is this man you're following?" she asked.

King wasn't sure how to answer that. If she'd seen the news at all, she'd know about the bombing at Niagara Falls. If he mentioned that, she might connect his face to the photograph of the wanted man. "His name is Gaber," he said, and left it at that.

"Mr. Gaber?" she repeated the name in a tone that sounded as if she knew him. "What's he done?" she asked.

"That's what I'm hoping to find out," King said. He turned his head so he wasn't looking at her. "His wife hired me to follow him. She suspects him of cheating on her."

"Oh, I see," said the woman. She shook her head. "What kind of a marriage is that when a woman has to hire a detective to check up on her husband?" She looked at King. "Whether the man has done anything or not, I don't see how that can be a good marriage."

King nodded, but said nothing.

The woman drove for a while in silence, pondering what King had told her. Then she said, "Seems like a rather extreme thing to do." She looked at King. "Don't you think? Jumping off a train just to avoid being followed. I mean if he's cheating on his wife and he thinks his wife is having him followed, why not just have out with it? What good does it do him to hide from you? He must know the cat is out of the bag."

This was the trouble with lying. Now King was going to have to improvise based on his made up story. At least he'd used a situation that he knew something about. "In my experience," King said, "people in relationships sometimes go to extremes. When jealousy is involved, rational behavior is generally in short supply."

They'd driven about two miles when King saw a figure walking on the side of the road ahead. King was sure it had to be Kareem. Who else would be out walking down this road? The man was walking at a steady pace a few feet off the shoulder. Though he wasn't facing the oncoming traffic, he had his thumb stuck out in a half-hearted attempt at hitchhiking. He continued walking when they approached.

The woman slowed the car. "Oh," she said. "There's another one walking out here!"

Although the woman slowed, she didn't stop. They drove past him. The man never looked at them and never stopped walking. When they'd passed, King turned so he could see the man's face. "That's him," he said.

"That's the man you're following?"

"Yes."

"Well he's never going to get a ride hitchhiking like that."

"The odds aren't good."

"What do you want to do? Do you want to get out?" She slowed the car again.

King had to decide what to do. He could get out up ahead and hide in the woods until Kareem caught up. Then he could continue to follow him from a safe distance on foot. But they'd still have to walk for six or seven hours to reach Rhinebeck.

King turned to the woman. "Would you be willing to give him a ride?"

She tilted her head. "What do you mean? Are you saying you

want me to let you out, then turn around and go back and offer him a ride?"

"No, I was thinking I would stay in the car and we'd both go back to offer him a ride."

"I don't understand," the woman said. "If he got off the train to avoid you, why would he get in a car with you?"

"He doesn't know it's me who's following him," King said. "He has a reason to think he's being followed, but he doesn't know who's doing it."

The woman hesitated. "I don't know," she said. "This is really more than I bargained for." She looked at her watch. "I have to get to Poughkeepsie by four."

King considered offering her money. It was a risk. For some people, money was an appropriate incentive. But King worried that this woman would take offense. She'd been a Good Samaritan. Offering her money might be seen as questioning her generosity. He decided, instead, to appeal to her generosity. "It would mean a lot to me," he said. "I have to get this case wrapped up quickly and get back to Chicago. I doubt either Mr. Gaber or I will find anyone else willing to give strangers a ride."

"Won't he find it suspicious, to be picked up with another hitchhiker?"

"He wouldn't have to know I'm a hitchhiker," King said. "I was hoping you might be willing to pretend to be my mother."

The woman looked at King. "Your mother?"

He guessed she was looking at his skin color. "Actually, you do look like my mother. My father was black. My mother was white like you."

The woman frowned. "I'm not very good at playacting. It makes me uncomfortable."

"You wouldn't have to say anything," King said. "I can do all the talking." He appealed once more to her generosity. "It would save us both hours of walking."

She waggled her head in a way that seemed halfway between yes and no. "I really don't like to drive fast if I can help it." She looked at her watch again. "I guess there's enough time." She looked at King. "You know, I had a son who would have been about your age now, but he died two years ago."

King wasn't sure what to say. "I'm sorry," he said meekly.

"I was thinking about John when I stopped for you," she continued. "I don't know if he ever hitchhiked—but he might have. It's just the kind of thing he would have done." She sighed, and took her right hand off the wheel. She pointed toward a sign further down the road. "There's a road sign coming up," she said. "If it's a sign for an exit, I'll get off. I don't believe in turning around in the median."

King assumed this meant she was willing to go back and get Kareem. "Thank you for doing this," he said. Then he squinted so he could read the sign. "The sign is for Oak Hill and Fox Creek Road," he said. "Do you know where we are?"

"Yes," she said. "I know these roads quite well. I can get off on Oak Hill. That road just goes back north. I can take it back north to Greendale—then get back on 9G at Greendale and come back south again. I drive this road to Poughkeepsie every week, and I can tell you, I've never seen anyone hitchhiking on this road. And now two in one day!"

They got off at the exit for Oak Hill Road. In a short time, they arrived at Greendale Road and made a sharp turn back onto 9G.

"One more thing before we pick him up," King said. "Do you know how to get to the bus station in Rhinebeck?"

"I do," the woman said. "I used to take John in to catch that bus sometimes. The bus to New York leaves at five every day." She looked at her watch. "You should have plenty of time to catch it."

TWENTY-ONE

Kareem had walked in the woods parallel to the train tracks for a quarter mile when he came to the road. Walking in the woods had been difficult. He was glad to be able to walk on pavement instead. The road ran along the tracks for another quarter mile, then turned east. He followed it a short way until it crossed Highway 9G. A road sign told him Rhinebeck was 23 miles away.

He walked along highway 9G, with his thumb held out. He didn't think it was likely anyone would stop to offer him a ride. But he thought it was far more likely to happen if he prayed. And so, as he walked, he prayed. *O Allah, lighten this journey and make its distance easy.*

After half an hour, he saw a boxy green car pull onto the shoulder a hundred feet in front of him. Allah had answered his prayer. He approached the car. He saw an older woman and a young man inside it. The woman was driving. When he got to the car, the passenger window was down. He looked at the man and blinked, as if he was surprised.

"Where are you headed?" the man asked.

"I am going to Rhinebeck," Kareem said.

The man smiled. "That's where we're headed," he said. "My

mom is dropping me off there." The man pointed to the woman who was driving.

Kareem looked at the man who spoke. His skin was darker than the skin of the woman he called mother. Kareem's father did not approve of the mixing of the races. But Kareem was more open-minded than his father was. There was no prohibition against interracial marriage in the Qur'an. "Can you give me a ride?" Kareem asked.

"Of course," the man said. He turned to the woman. "Is the back door unlocked?"

The woman glanced at him and then at Kareem. She pushed a button on the console. Everyone heard the click as the doors unlocked. "Please get in. I have to be in Poughkeepsie by four." She looked at her watch.

Kareem got into the back seat. The woman drove the car back onto the road. For the first few minutes, no one spoke. The man finally broke the silence. "So where are you going in Rhinebeck?" he asked.

Kareem hesitated. He couldn't think of any reason he shouldn't be honest about where he was going. "I'm going to the bus station," he said.

"That's a stroke of luck," the man said. "We're going to the bus station too. I've gotta catch the bus to New York. I'm going to visit my sister."

Kareem nodded. He said, "I am also going to New York." He considered asking the man what time the bus to New York departed. But he decided it would be better not to reveal that he didn't know the bus schedule.

After waiting a few beats, the man said, "You must be taking the 5 o'clock bus."

"Yes," Kareem said, and his eyes widened. It was as if the man could read his mind. But then as he thought about it, he realized it was only natural that the man should wonder if they were going to be taking the same bus.

"I guess we'll be riding the bus together," the man said.

· · ·

They drove on in silence for several minutes. King turned sideways in the front seat, and put the back of his head against the passenger window. It allowed him to face the woman, but it also let him see the backseat well enough to give Kareem the once-over.

Kareem looked younger than he had on the train. He'd shaved his beard. Yesterday he'd looked like he might be about thirty. But clean-shaven he looked more like twenty-five. His eyes, with long lashes, were light brown. His skin was smooth, his hair black and curly.

King studied the woman too. She had a nice smile, but she kept blinking. Hoping to relax her, King spoke to her in an upbeat tone. "I was thinking of getting Sarah an iPad." He turned to Kareem. "Sarah's my sister. She's starting school at Columbia in the fall." Then he turned to the woman. "You think she'd like it?"

The woman was annoyed. Her forced smile became a genuine frown. She'd told him she didn't like play-acting. "I don't know," she said hesitantly. She looked in the rear-view mirror to glance at her backseat passenger, and saw that his eyes were lowered. She looked at King with a "what gives?" expression. Then she said, "Doesn't Sarah already have a computer?"

"Yes, but an iPad is so much easier to carry around," King replied. "She could bring it to class to take notes. It's much lighter than her laptop."

The woman simply nodded. "Whatever you think," she said. "I don't know about computers."

After that, everyone was silent again. King decided to leave it there. He didn't want to push his luck. He'd said enough to set up his back-story. If he and Kareem were going to be on a long bus ride together, he wanted them to have something to talk about. It would be nice to be able to talk about Sarah. But it was obvious to King that talking with Kareem was going to be difficult.

Ever since Kareem had stepped up to the car window, King had watched him for a sign of recognition. He hadn't noticed any. In fact, Kareem barely appeared to regard him. He glanced at King only briefly. He seemed shy, anxious about talking. When he spoke, his tone was meek. He kept his eyes lowered, his head slightly bowed. He seemed distracted, caught up in some private thoughts. He might have been preoccupied with how he was going to make his way to the city—or with what would happen after he got there. Regardless, it was difficult for King to reconcile this timidity with the violent behavior he had seen the day before.

In order to infiltrate whatever operation Kareem and his friends were planning, King would need to find a way to break through Kareem's shyness. He had to find a way into his confidence. He had trained for this. Both his counter-intelligence training and his Aikido training had taught him to look for a way to empathize with and identify with his opponents.

But when he tried to project himself into Kareem's point of view, he couldn't get a feel for it. Something blocked his understanding. He didn't think Islam or Middle Eastern culture were the obstacles. King had studied both Islam and the culture of the Middle East extensively. It had been a standard part of his training in the Army. He had been curious enough about the culture that he'd gone beyond the standard training. He'd spent much of his own time reading the Qur'an and the teachings of Islamic scholars.

Although he was fascinated by them, he was also dismayed by the behaviors they inspired. He was appalled by the stark moral judgments, the strict gender codes of behavior, the subjugation of women, the puritanical restrictions against pleasures of all kinds, and the harsh punishments for homosexuality or sexual infidelity.

At the same time, he was fascinated by the aesthetics of Islamic art, with its immaculate patterns and geometry. He loved the meditative rituals of morning and evening prayers. He respected the personal humility expressed through daily prostration. He was moved by the eerie soulfulness of the Adhan, the call to prayer. He was inspired by the writings of the Sufi mystic Rumi, whose spiritual teachings of tolerance and charity were expressed in poetry.

That he was appalled and enthralled by the various parts of Islam didn't surprise him. He'd studied other religions and found a similar paradox in most of them—doctrinaire support for those who were self-righteousness and judgmental on the one hand, and for those who were kind and humble on the other. While in the short run the impact of the self-righteous and judgmental often seemed more far-reaching than the impact of the humble and kind, he was idealistic enough to hope that in the long view the kind and humble would prevail.

Kindness was the cornerstone of King's own moral code. But its practice was a constant challenge for him. Sitting in the car with a jihadi terrorist in the back seat challenged his idealism. He knew about, and thought he understood, the principles of jihad, which simply meant 'the struggle.' But that meant one thing for its most visible practitioners, those for whom it was an aggressive, militant, and violent endeavor. It meant something else for the more inconspicuous believers. For them it was a personal, peaceful, and spiritual struggle. King couldn't understand how Kareem had ended up on the violent side of the paradox.

If Kareem was truly shy, it gave him hope. King thought he might be able to connect with Kareem through the humble side of Islam. He might be able to pretend to a degree of ambivalence about jihad, but he knew himself well enough to realize that he couldn't fake being a violent jihadist. He might be able to plant seeds of doubt in Kareem about violence, seeds that fell from the same tree that Kareem worshipped. But before he could do that, he had to discover more about the man who sat so quietly in the back seat.

The woman, now, was equally quiet. She continued to drive with both hands on the wheel. She kept firmly to the speed limit.

King could only imagine how she would feel if she knew who she was transporting! He was grateful for her generosity. He wished he could convey his gratitude without blowing his cover. Even though King had been disillusioned and disappointed by people on many occasions, he did from time to time witness kindnesses that reminded him that selfishness was not universal.

The drive to Rhinebeck took only half an hour. True to her word, the woman knew exactly where the bus station was—and she drove them straight to it. When they arrived, King and Kareem got out of the car. Then Kareem leaned back in and said to the woman, formally and politely, "Thank you, Mrs., for giving me a ride." Then he turned and headed for the door of the station.

King walked around to the driver side window and leaned down to thank her. "Thanks for everything." He smiled at her.

The woman looked at Kareem, who was just walking into the bus station and out of earshot. "I noticed he isn't wearing a wedding ring," she said. "He doesn't seem very happy."

King shook his head. "He's not happy. I think he's out on a limb."

"Too bad," the woman said. "Maybe he'll make amends and go back to her."

"It's hard to make amends when you've gone as far out on the limb as he has."

"Is it that bad?"

King nodded. "I'm afraid so."

"Well, it's a pity," she said. "He has nice eyes. It just goes to show you; I'm a terrible judge of character."

"Some people are hard to judge," King said. "People are complicated. Even the worst have endearing qualities."

"Ah," she said, "I guess you're an idealist—like me."

"I am," King said, and he tapped the side of the car. "Take care, mom." King winked at her, then walked into the bus station.

TWENTY-TWO

Jasmeen glared at the Judith Goldman phone. Ever since it had rung, she'd been fretting about what to do. She was sure the man who'd been standing by her when the phone rang was a government agent. She'd recognized him. He was the same man she saw carrying the drinks an hour earlier. Kareem had wanted to help him because he wobbled like an old man. But he wasn't an old man. And now that he'd seen her holding the phone, he would certainly try to follow her. She couldn't allow that. She couldn't risk leading a government agent to Abdul in New York.

She still had two advantages. First, the government agent couldn't know who she was. When she'd bought her train ticket, she hadn't had to show her passport. She'd shown the ticket agent the false ID Abdul had given her, and paid with cash. Second, no one in the government knew what she looked like. Just now, when the phone rang, she'd kept her head averted and listened carefully while the man came to study the tickets above her seat. She was certain he hadn't taken her picture. There'd been no telltale click. She'd felt his hands resting on her seat back. She'd remained turned away from him so he couldn't see her face, and he hadn't walked in front of her. She sensed that he'd gone back to the back of the car to wait.

If she could get away before anyone got a picture of her, then all the government would have would be the agent's description of her clothes. Her odds of disappearing were much better if she could keep it that way: no name, no face, no picture.

But to get away meant she'd have to do what Kareem had done. She'd have to jump off the train between stops. And then she too would have to find another way to get to New York. She had to get away soon. At any moment, the man who'd seen her could walk by. If he had a camera phone, he might try to snap her picture.

Now that the agent knew her location, she wondered how she could get off the train without him following her. He was sitting back there watching her. She was sure of it. She had to find a way to shake him. She thought about getting up and going to the café car. If she did, he'd probably follow her. If he didn't, well fine, she'd jump off the train the next time it stopped.

But if he followed her, she'd get in line to buy food at the café car. Then he'd have to stand in line behind her as if he was buying a snack too. He had to keep up a pretense. He had no way of knowing she was on to him. He couldn't just stand and watch her brazenly.

She could take advantage of this. If she could stay in the café car after buying her tea and slowly and deliberately add cream and sugar to it, he'd have to remain standing in line to watch her. If she waited just until the moment when he got to the head of the line, once he ordered his food, he'd have to follow through with it.

Then, she might have enough time—while he was interacting with the cashier—to get away. She would walk slowly out of the café car, then, once she was out of sight, she could run quickly back through the cars. She'd hide in a restroom. Then she could stay there until the train stopped again. Once the train stopped, she'd have to leave the restroom and quickly get off the train—and hope he wasn't nearby.

It was a risky proposition. Once he saw she was gone, he might become suspicious of the restrooms. And there was no telling when the train would make an unscheduled stop again. But she couldn't think of anywhere else to hide from him—and he couldn't watch all the restrooms at the same time. She'd have to risk it.

Jasmeen rose from her seat and walked toward the front of the train. At the front of the car, she paused and turned around for just a moment. She saw the agent had risen from his seat. Just as she thought, he was following her. She turned and walked straight through two cars until she came to the café car. She got in line behind three people who waited to buy food. After a moment, she sensed someone fall into line behind her. She thought about retrieving the mirror she had in her purse. She didn't normally wear makeup. She'd bought a pocket mirror so she could use it to check her look, if the need arose. Now she realized she could hold the mirror up to see behind her while she pretended to fuss with her hair. But with the agent standing right there, the ploy might be too obvious.

She resisted the temptation to turn around. She waited until she got to the front of the line and bought some tea. After she paid, she stepped over to a side counter that had cream, sugar, and stirrers. She busied herself there. She put sugar in her tea. She stirred it and put the lid on it. Then she heard the man order. Quickly she turned to face him. But when she did so, she saw her mistake. The man who had been directly behind her was not the agent. The agent had come in just after the man behind her. The agent had been two behind her in line.

As soon as she turned, the agent held up his phone. She heard a click—and she knew he'd taken her picture.

Jasmeen quickly turned back to the condiments counter. She had to think what to do. She took the lid off her tea and added more sugar to it. She had to wait until the agent ordered something before she could get away. She was furious with herself. Now the man had her picture. She took a new stirrer and stirred her tea rapidly.

The agent was next in line. He spoke to the attendant. "I'd like coffee with cream and sugar."

The attendant pointed, "The cream and sugar are on the table behind you."

Jasmeen was about to walk away. But then she had an idea. She opened her purse. She took out the two packets of poison. Abdul had disguised the poison in packets of sugar. She looked at the row of sugar packets neatly arranged in a box on the condiments counter. They were packets of Domino sugar, but her poison was in C&H packets. She turned her body so it obscured anyone from seeing the table. She took the two C&H packets out of her purse and set them at the front of the row of sugar packets. If the agent used two sugars in his coffee, he'd uncover the Domino packets, and he might notice the difference in brands. If he only used one, the one behind it would match the one he took.

Now she stepped back from the table, still stirring her tea. She dawdled as the agent brought his coffee over to the table. She watched over his shoulder. He picked up a single serve cup of half-and-half and poured it into his coffee. Then he picked up the first C&H sugar packet. He opened it and poured it into his coffee. She waited to see if he would take the second packet of poison. He didn't. He took a stirrer and began to stir the coffee.

Now was the time for her to move. She looked at the second C&H packet. If she picked it up, the agent might notice that the remaining packets were Domino brand, not C&H. If he were well-trained, that difference might make him suspicious. But if she left the second packet in place, another passenger would get the poison. She wavered for a moment. *Infidels. I should leave it.* Then she shrugged. She turned and picked it up, as she smiled at the agent to distract him.

She returned to her seat to wait. She no longer had to run and hide in a restroom. All she had to do now was to wait for the agent to drink his coffee. One packet was enough to do the job. Abdul had assured her of that. The moment the man died, she could quietly take away his phone before anyone noticed. Then she would destroy the phone and eliminate the photo.

Jasmeen went back to her seat. She watched as the agent walked back down the aisle with his coffee. Once again she looked at him openly. What did it matter? He had already taken her picture. But the agent pretended not to see her. He stared at the coffee in his hand as he passed by her seat. He did not look at her, except to steal a glance at her breasts. Like most men, she realized—his eyes were upon her.

The conductor announced the train's arrival in Rhinebeck.

TWENTY-THREE

At the Rhinebeck bus terminal, Kareem boarded the Coach USA bus to New York. It was a big, boxy, modern air-conditioned bus with tinted windows. He sat in a window seat near the back of the bus. When King boarded a few minutes later, he only had a moment to decide whether or not to sit next to Kareem. If he sat somewhere else—he'd be able to keep an eye on him during the bus trip. But after that, he'd have to follow Kareem surreptitiously. It would be nearly impossible to do that now that Kareem had seen him with a beard and no dreadlocks. He couldn't change his disguise again.

On the other hand, if he sat next to Kareem, he could talk to him. It meant furthering the chance that Kareem might remember him from the Maple Leaf. But it was also the only way he could think of to find out what Kareem and the others were planning for New York. In order to get Kareem to confide in him, King would have to show that he was trustworthy. In order to do that, he planned to play the role of a devout Muslim.

He sat in the seat next to Kareem, and said, "Salaam," in a sociable tone.

Kareem nodded and replied, "Salaam." But his tone was matter-of-fact.

King launched immediately into friendly banter. "I guess I'm just like you," he said. "I prefer to sit in the back."

The expression on Kareem's face was stiff and aloof. King supposed that Kareem would prefer to be left alone. But he was counting on the politeness he'd previously observed. Kareem looked out the window, then turned back to King and said indifferently, "I like the window."

"These windows are huge," King said. He pressed a button on the side of his seat to try out the recliner. "Nice comfortable seats." He wiggled around in his seat by way of demonstration, then put his seat back in the upright position. "By the way…," He leaned toward Kareem. "We didn't get introduced in the car. My name is Omar."

Kareem raised an eyebrow, then nodded. He said, "Omar is my father's name."

"Really?" King said. "I was named after Omar Khayyám."

Kareem blinked. If he recognized the name, he didn't show it.

"Khayyám was a mathematician and poet," King continued. "He wrote a line you might have heard of: 'The Moving Finger writes; and, having writ, Moves on…' My mother says my name reminds her not to take things for granted."

Kareem nodded, but said nothing.

King persevered in a chipper tone. "A lot of people look at my mother, then they look at me, and they wonder how we're related. My parents met in Marrakesh. Back then, my mother owned a shop selling antiques and rugs. She went to Morocco on a buying expedition. That's where she met my father. He was a carpet dealer."

Kareem continued to wear a blank look.

"He was North African," King said.

Kareem pursed his lips in what seemed like a disapproving expression.

King continued, "When my parents got married, they made a

bargain. He agreed to come to live in America and she agreed to convert to Islam."

Now Kareem gave him a quizzical look. "Your mother did not seem religious," he said.

King shook his head. "My parents are divorced. The bargain she made with my father didn't last. She's an apostate. She doesn't cover her head. She drives a car." King winked. "Now she picks up hitchhikers too. Perhaps that's for the good. She's kind to travelers. That is halaal, isn't it?"

Kareem nodded. "Yes. It was kind of her to offer me a ride."

King paused. "I suppose we must judge people for their kindnesses as well as their faults."

"It is for Allah to judge," said Kareem.

"Yes, brother." King smiled. "According to our intentions."

He let that sink in. He knew Muslims believed that Allah judged people as much by their intentions as by their deeds. He hoped to show Kareem that he was familiar with Islamic maxims.

"I live with my mother in Hudson," King continued. "It's a very nice place. God willing, I will stay here and raise a family. How about you? Where are you from?"

"I am from Canada."

"Oh you're Canadian? It's a good country. I guess it's somewhat cold. But maybe not much colder than here in New York."

"It is often cold," Kareem said. His tone had grown cool again, as well.

King looked at Kareem's hand. There was no ring. "You're not married?"

Kareem squirmed. The question seemed to make him uncomfortable. "No."

"Neither am I," King said. "I suppose I'm choosy. I have prayed to find the right woman. She must be someone who is pure and who has submitted to Allah." King paused. Then he shrugged. "In other words, she cannot be like my mother."

Now they sat in silence for a while. King had pressed hard and fast to this point. He wanted to pull back, to slacken the line.

His experience with Reema in Afghanistan had taught him to be cautious. It had taken time for her to trust him. Kareem wasn't as approachable as she had been. He was so quiet it was hard to read him. He seemed as preoccupied as he had been on the Maple Leaf. He stared forward.

Then at last, he turned to King and said, "I too have prayed to be with someone pure. I have tried to be worthy of someone like that."

King said, "Has your family never proposed such a worthy woman for you?"

Kareem shrugged. "I have not had the opportunity to consider marriage," he said.

"I don't really know any women, except for my sister," King said. "I talk with her all the time."

Kareem nodded. "It is the same for me. I am close to my sister."

King smiled. "Maybe, you could mention me to your sister, and I can mention you to mine. Perhaps it's something for our parents to consider?"

"Perhaps."

King asked, "Where are you staying in New York?"

Kareem hesitated. He had no idea where he was going to stay. But he had to say something. "I am meeting my sister in New York. She is coming from another location. I must make arrangements with her. We will choose a hotel. But we have not yet done so."

King smiled. "Since you don't have a hotel yet, perhaps you and your sister would consider staying with us." He was taking a big risk. He had a vague notion of how he could bring Sarah and her father into the situation. "My sister doesn't have the same father as I do," he began, then paused and shrugged. "My mother remarried after she and my father divorced. My sister lives with her father in New York. Perhaps her father will have room for two more. I can ask him about it."

"It is kind of you to offer," Kareem said. "But I doubt that my sister would want to stay with strangers. She is very modest."

"Yes." King nodded. "I understand." He was silent for a moment. Then he said, "Modesty is becoming to a woman. My sister isn't quite as modest as that."

"She is like your mother?"

"No." King shook his head. "Sarah submits to Allah. She's not like my mother."

King wondered if there was any chance of arranging a meeting between Kareem and Sarah. It would be a risk. He'd have to warn her in advance. The meeting would have to be chaperoned. Sarah would have to cover her head. Kareem may not have seen her face on the Maple Leaf, but he'd seen her on the Empire Service train when she'd smiled at him. Whether or not that one glance would be enough for him to remember her, King couldn't tell.

King continued, "I just mean that when she's chaperoned, she's comfortable being around men who are respectful. But if she feels disrespected, she'll show it."

"Jasmeen also does not tolerate disrespect," said Kareem.

He said Jasmeen's name so casually he seemed unaware it was a revelation. King was pleased that he'd finally been given a name. Kareem had not said what his own name was. King had to remind himself not to use it by accident. But now he could refer to Jasmeen without checking himself.

"Is your sister older than you, or younger?" He hoped this show of interest was not too forward.

"We are close in age. She is one year older."

"Sarah's three years younger than me," King said. "She's old enough for marriage. But we haven't found prospects for her. I assume Jasmeen isn't married."

"No. She is not."

King smiled. He paused again. It was too soon to suggest anything further about the possibility of his meeting Jasmeen—or about the possibility of Kareem meeting Sarah. But this was how

Muslim men and women were supposed to meet—through the intercession of siblings and parents.

Of course, King didn't know if marriage was even a real possibility for Kareem. If his upcoming mission in New York was a suicide mission, any effort to fix him up with Sarah would be a waste of time. Likewise, if Jasmeen were planning to participate, she'd never agree to a meeting with King, even a chaperoned one.

But regardless of whether he might meet Jasmeen, or Kareem might meet Sarah, chatting about it was a good way for King to deepen his connection with Kareem, who could only regard it as a sign of good will.

"Jasmeen is a very pretty name. It's the name of a flower, isn't it?"

"Yes," said Kareem. "A sweet Persian flower."

"Ah? Does your family come from Iran?" King realized that the reference to Persia might have been a slip.

Kareem tilted his head from side to side. "Yes," he said. "Originally."

King knew that Kareem and Jasmeen spoke Arabic, not Persian. He guessed they were Iraqi, but that their parents or grandparents came from Iran. "Well, that explains it," said King. "Persians are the most beautiful people."

Now Kareem looked at King directly. For a moment, it seemed as if his shyness had lifted and Kareem had shaken himself out of his daydream. He seemed to examine King carefully for the first time, like an appraiser who has suddenly noticed an attribute that is crucial to his evaluation. "My name is Kareem," he said, "which means 'generous,' but I do not know if my parents chose the best name for me." He paused, then asked, "Do you like flowers?"

"I think flowers give us a glimpse of Paradise," said King. "Spring flowers are my favorite. They come up after everything has died, they're vigorous." King wasn't sure what he meant to imply by that, except that he was trying to take a serious tone. He saw that Kareem was fully engaged in the conversation for the first time, and he didn't want to lose it.

Kareem looked at him directly. "Tulips come from Turkey, you know. The Dutch would like people to think tulips are from Holland, but they are not."

King nodded. "My mother has lots of tulips. She likes the big red ones. But I like the white ones. They look untainted—like the virgins of Jannah." King remembered the conversation he overheard in which it sounded like Jasmeen wanted to fix Kareem up with a woman so he'd have some experience before he got to Paradise. Kareem seemed so buttoned-up and repressed, it was difficult to imagine him relaxed enough to seduce a woman. King wondered what would happen if he tried to help him get laid. He might be appreciative, or he might be shocked and offended. Still, it seemed worth throwing out a feeler. He said, "Do you like white tulips?"

Kareem nodded.

"There are places in New York where you can see tulips in the spring. But the city isn't the best place to enjoy flowers. There's so much corruption." King laughed nervously, then said, "In the city, Kareem, men can enjoy the services of women, but they aren't virgins."

"Yes," said Kareem. "I have heard about the prostitutes."

"The city has many temptations. I sometimes have to pray to avoid temptation," King said. He wanted to find a way in the conversation to throw out the possibility of getting laid. He thought for a moment about how to put this in Kareem's terms. He said, "I always wonder why we face so many temptations. Is it because we're tested, or are we meant to take a bite from the apple in order to know its taste?"

Kareem frowned. "No, Omar. You must not bite any bad apples. I think we are tested. I have had my own troubles biting a bad apple. But I have found that prayer strengthens me."

King nodded. It was obvious he wasn't going to take Kareem

bar hopping. "Yes," he said. "Prayer and a cold shower, perhaps?"

"I prefer a sweet treat to a cold shower," said Kareem. "I think it is best to eat a piece of baklava."

"A piece of baklava?"

"Yes. If you want to distract yourself from lustful thoughts, it is much better to eat baklava than to take a cold shower. There is no pleasure in a cold shower. At least with the baklava, you can feel some pleasure."

"I see," said King. "Well, when we get to New York we'll find a place that sells baklava with whipped cream and pistachios. How's that?"

Kareem smiled. "Yes, all right. As long as it's Turkish baklava. Not Greek."

TWENTY-FOUR

Jasmeen lowered the tray table in the seat next to her and set her tea on it. Then she took the pocket mirror out of her purse. She held it up so she could see what was going on behind her. She was in the middle of the car. She moved the mirror until she saw the agent. He was in the aisle seat on the opposite side at the end of the car. She saw him take the lid off his coffee. Then he looked up and looked directly at her. He saw her looking at him in the mirror. He got up and moved to the window seat.

When he moved, she couldn't see him as clearly. She could only see the right half of his head. But she could still see enough of his face to see him take a sip from the coffee. She held her breath. She didn't know how quickly the poison worked. She waited. She saw him take another sip. He looked at her again, with a sly smile on his face. He took another sip.

Then she watched as his smile twisted. He opened his mouth, as if he was about to speak. She saw a look of distress appear on his face. She hoped the poison would work fast. She didn't want him to stand up and scream. But he did stand up. He stood about halfway up in his seat. Jasmeen's hand began to tremble. She had to grab the pocket mirror with her other hand to steady it.

She turned the mirror wildly trying to find him. Then she saw him. His face had gone red. He was choking. She saw his mouth move as if he was trying to say something—but he couldn't speak. His eyes rolled in his head. His forehead creased. Jasmeen sucked in her breath so intensely that it came out like a yelp. She saw his left arm go up helplessly in the air. With his right arm, he grabbed onto the seat in front of him. Then he gagged violently and collapsed back in his seat. He fell sideways against the window, motionless.

Instantly Jasmeen stood up and turned. She looked back at the rear of the car and saw that no one was sitting in the last row across from him. The passengers in the seats in front of him were either asleep or wearing headphones. She studied their faces. It appeared that no one had registered what had happened. The man had been unable to cry out.

Jasmeen walked back to the last row. She sat down in the seat next to the dead agent. His body leaned against the window, moving only with the jiggling of the train. His mouth and his eyes were both open. He didn't look natural. She reached up and pushed his eyelids closed. Then she looked around. No one was watching. She put her fingers on his face to close his mouth, but she couldn't get his lips to close. She gave up and searched for his phone. She found it in his right pocket. She fished it out, stood up, picked up his cup of coffee, and went back to her seat. She turned one more time to survey the other passengers. No one had paid her any attention.

She set the poisoned coffee next to her tea on the tray table. Then she inspected the agent's phone. She wasn't sure how to work it. She knew it had her picture on it. She hoped he had not transmitted it or emailed it. She didn't see how he could've had time to do anything with it. She'd watched him come down the aisle just seconds after she came back from the café car. Then she'd watched him through her pocket mirror after he sat down. He'd sipped the coffee. He hadn't done anything with his phone.

So now she had to destroy the phone. She couldn't just carry it with her. She assumed they would be able to track her with it just as they had done with the other phone. They'd follow her. But unlike the Judith Goldman phone, she couldn't just abandon it and walk away. It had her picture on it. She had to destroy it.

Maybe when she jumped off the train she could place it on the track and let the train wheels crush it. Then she realized that she no longer had to jump off the train. All she really had to do was move to another seat—away from the Judith Goldman phone. No one but the agent had seen her. No one else would know who she was.

She took a Kleenex out of her purse and picked up the Judith Goldman phone with it. She carefully wiped it. She didn't think her fingerprints were on file anywhere. But why would she give them her prints now? She dropped the phone back in the seat pocket.

Then she stood and put the agent's phone in her purse. She grabbed the two tabs of paper that designated her and Kareem's stop from their perch above her seat and put those in her purse as well. Then she walked to the restroom, carrying her purse, her cup of tea, and the remains of the agent's coffee.

Inside the restroom, she dumped the coffee and tea into the toilet and flushed it. She thought about dumping the phone in the toilet and flushing it down as well. But then she realized it would just get flushed into some cistern beneath the train where they might be able to get to it eventually. She didn't know whether the liquids would ruin it or not. They might still be able to find her picture.

Still, she thought, *liquid might be enough to ruin it.* She fished the phone out of her purse with her handkerchief and dropped it into the basin of the restroom sink. She put the stopper on the drain, and filled the basin with water. Using a rolled-up paper towel as a stirring rod, she swished the phone around in the water. That might short the thing out and stop it from sending off signals. But she didn't know if wetting it was really enough. She wished she knew more about these things. Her brother

Abdul would know what to do, but she had no way to contact him.

She picked up the wet phone with the paper towel and looked at it closely. She looked for any latches or screws or any other way that she might disassemble it so she could scatter its parts. But there was no latch, no screw. There was nothing but a smooth metal case.

She thought about stomping on the phone. But the flat rectangular device looked like it could withstand her flat shoe with no problem. Maybe if she had a high-heeled shoe, something with a spike. Then she could drive the point of the heel into the shoe with enough force to shatter the glass. But how could she get such a shoe? She couldn't just steal a high-heel shoe. But maybe she could. She thought about how many people were napping. Perhaps she could find a woman somewhere on the train who was napping, a woman who had taken off her shoes. It wasn't impossible.

She'd go look for such a woman. But she didn't want to take the phone with her. She opened the latch on the paper towel dispenser and dropped the phone on top of the stack of towels. Then she left the restroom and began to walk down the aisle, looking for a woman asleep.

Sarah leaned her head against the train window and closed her eyes, but she couldn't sleep. All she could do was think about the kiss. She hadn't expected it. Yet the moment it happened, she'd felt certain it was what she wanted. Up until now, she hadn't had much luck with men. Her relationships with men always seemed to end badly. She thought about the men she'd been with. In some ways, they were all like her father—cool and detached. *Jesus*, she thought. It was all so predictable—her seeking love from her father in whatever form she could find it. But Tyrone was different. He was playful and funny like her mother. She hadn't given him much opportunity to be affectionate, but she was sure that he would be. Based on what she knew of him, she guessed he was a romantic fool. All that idealism—that dedication to non-violence—what was it but a romantic view of the world? His pacifism was another way he was unlike her father. He certainly had a different idea of how to kick butt.

There was that phrase again—and it made her think about Tyrone's body. There was no doubt the man was well-built. She'd had her hands on his butt for a few seconds when they were pretending to kiss at the Bridal Veil Falls. He'd put his hands around her waist and she'd had to grab him to steady herself.

She smiled as she recalled the moment. She opened her eyes and looked out the window. The Hudson River was rolling by—a big, wide channel of blue gray water. She sensed someone coming down the aisle. She glanced to the side and saw it was Jasmeen. She quickly half-closed her eyes. She kept her head still, leaning against the window, as if she were asleep. She watched through her barely open eyes as Jasmeen walked right up to her seat, put her hand on the seat back, and stopped, as if she was resting. Jasmeen studied her for a moment. Sarah had the impression that Jasmeen was looking at her feet. Had Kareem told her about the gold ankle bracelets? Thank God, she didn't have them on. But why would Jasmeen look at her at all? She couldn't possibly know who Sarah was.

Then, Jasmeen went on down the aisle. Sarah saw her stop again at another seat. Again, she grabbed the seat back and paused as if she was resting and she examined the woman sitting there. *What is she doing?* Sarah sat up now and opened her eyes wide. She saw Jasmeen walk still further down the aisle and stop again. Once again, she looked carefully at the woman, examining her. The woman was asleep. So, in fact, had been the previous woman. Then Sarah wondered, "Why is she looking at sleeping women?"

Jasmeen had to walk through three cars before she found the right woman. In the third car, a woman sat in a row by herself, sound asleep. The woman was leaning partly against the seat rest and partly against the window. Her eyes were closed. Her mouth was open. She was snoring softly but steadily. The woman's feet were bare. On the floor in front of the aisle seat was a pair of scarlet red high heels.

Even better, the seats across the aisle from the sleeping woman were empty. Jasmeen opened her purse and took out one of the tabs of paper that indicated her stop. She stuck it in the band at the base of the luggage rack above the empty seats. Then she sat her purse on the aisle seat.

While still standing in the aisle, she leaned down and took off her shoes. Then she bent over in the direction of the sleeping woman's seat in such a way that she blocked the aisle, and, she hoped, the view of what she was doing.

She picked up the red high heels and put her own shoes in their place. Then she lifted her purse from the empty aisle seat and sat down across from the woman. She looked at the woman sleeping. The woman was still snoring softly. Jasmeen watched her steadily while she tried the high heels on for size. The shoes were a size too big, but there was nothing to do about that. She pushed her feet as firmly as she could into the shoes, picked up her purse, stood and tried walking down the aisle. She could manage it, she felt, if she walked slowly. Carrying her purse, she walked slowly and carefully back toward the front of the train, back toward the restroom where she'd left the agent's phone.

Sarah saw Jasmeen coming back down the aisle, returning from wherever she'd gone. She was walking slowly down the aisle, staring straight ahead. She was no longer stopping and looking at sleeping women. She was acting somewhat oddly, like there was something wrong with her legs. Sarah shrugged. She was beginning to suspect that Jasmeen was up to something. She couldn't imagine what it was, but she decided to follow her. She waited until Jasmeen had passed through the connecting vestibule into the next car. Then she stood and began to walk behind her, keeping half a car's distance between them. At the front end of the car, Jasmeen went into the restroom, slid the door closed, and locked it. Sarah came up and stood right beside the locked door. She pretended that she was waiting to use the restroom next.

Inside the restroom, Jasmeen opened the paper towel container and pulled out the agent's phone. She set it on the floor. Then she removed one of the high heels and knelt down. She held the shoe like a hammer, and whacked the phone with the heel. It made a loud noise, but it didn't break the glass. She realized that she wasn't going to get enough leverage using her arm.

She stood and turned on the water in the sink. She also pressed the button next to the toilet to flush it, hoping the flushing noise would mask what she was about to do. She stared down at the phone on the floor. Her left foot was bare; one of the high heels was still on her right foot. She raised her right leg above the phone. She took a deep breath, and then stomped on the phone with all her might. Then she stomped again. And again. And again. At last the glass broke. She stomped a fourth time and the phone split open like a shattered piece of ice. Jasmeen was breathing heavily. She had dunked the phone in water. Then she had smashed it open. She was certain that had to be enough to stop it from working. She reached down and scooped up the pieces of the phone and flung them into the toilet. Then she flushed the toilet, and when it was finished, she flushed it again.

Outside the restroom, Sarah heard the toilet flush. The she heard a series of loud bangs, as if Jasmeen was in there hammering a nail into the floor. Sarah couldn't imagine what the woman was doing. She heard a total of four loud blows. Then she heard the toilet flush twice more. Then the restroom door slid open. Jasmeen stood there and looked right at her. She was carrying a purse and wearing high heels. Sarah said, "Is everything OK?" She figured it was better to acknowledge that she'd heard all the banging than to pretend that she hadn't.

Jasmeen said, "Yes, everything is fine, thank you." Then she headed down the aisle, hobbling slightly.

Sarah stepped into the restroom and closed the door. She looked around. She couldn't piece together what had just gone on. There was water all around the edges of the sink—and a few drops on the floor. The top of the cabinet that held the paper towels was tilted out—as if it had been opened. She looked inside and saw only paper towels.

Jasmeen walked slowly and carefully back through the cars to the seat where she found the sleeping woman was still asleep. She repeated her earlier gesture. She sat her purse on the empty seat across from the woman. She stood in the middle of the aisle and leaned down to remove her shoes. Then she swapped the red heels for her own shoes. Then she stood up, lifted up her purse, and sat down in the empty seat across the aisle from the sleeping woman.

She thought about what to do next. She had to get off the train soon. She thought it might be a good idea to change her look. The agent had seen her from behind. He might have described her hair and her blouse to someone else. She opened her purse and took out her hijab. She put it around her head and tied it. Then she changed her mind and took it off. She also removed the pearls from around her neck and dropped them in her purse. There was nothing she could do about her blouse. She didn't have another one.

Jasmeen thought about the woman who'd asked her if everything was OK. She'd seen that woman before. The woman had smiled at Kareem in a strange way when she first boarded the train. Jasmeen had noticed it because she knew Kareem had been embarrassed by such an inappropriate gesture. Jasmeen thought about the coincidence. Now she'd found the woman had been eavesdropping on her in the restroom. She was sure of it. Maybe it was just a coincidence. But maybe not. She opened her purse again. She still had one of the two sugar packets left.

TWENTY-FIVE

Special Agent Chin called Agent Cassidy to see what progress he'd made in finding King. But his phone didn't ring. It went directly to voice mail. She thought he must be talking to Walters. So she waited five minutes, then called him again. Once again, her call went straight to voice mail. Then she called Special Agent Walters and asked him about Cassidy.

"Were you just talking to Cassidy?"

"Negative."

"Would you go find him and ask him to report in? He isn't answering his phone."

"Roger that."

Walters got up and went to find Cassidy.

Three minutes later, Walters called Chin to tell her the news.

"Cathy," he began. He rarely called Special Agent Chin by her first name. He hoped it would prepare her for the news. "Cathy, I don't know how to tell you this. Something terrible has happened. I think Cassidy … Jay … is dead. He's in a seat in the back row of the car where the phone was. He's just slumped against the window. He's not breathing. He has no pulse."

"Jesus! How is that possible?"

"I don't know."

"Is he shot?"

"I don't think so. I'm sitting next to him right now," said Walters. He stood and leaned over Cassidy, looking for signs of injury. "I don't see any sign of a wound on him. No bullet. No knife. No blood. No bruises. Nothing. It's like he just went to sleep and died."

"I just talked to him about twenty minutes ago," said Chin. "He'd found Tyrone King's phone. He said a woman had it. He was going to get a picture of her. He said the woman was nicely dressed. Green silk blouse, pearls. He said she looked Middle Eastern, and that she'd been sitting with a Middle Eastern man who went to the café car. He was going to go find him too."

Walters looked around the car. "I don't see anybody that fits the description."

"Check Jay's phone. See if he got a picture of her—or of anyone else."

Walters searched the dead agent's pockets. Then he searched the seats and seat pockets around his body. "Cassidy's phone is gone," he told Chin.

"Gone? OK. Just a minute. I'll see if Marsh can find it." Chin put Walters on hold and dialed Special Agent Marsh. "Robert, something terrible has happened. Walters has just reported that Special Agent Cassidy … is dead. Walters can't determine the cause of death. There's a chance that Cassidy may have taken a picture before he died of the woman who had King's phone. But Walters can't find Jay's phone. Can you locate it on tracking?"

"Jesus. Just a minute." Marsh checked his computer. He had all the agents' phone numbers programmed into his tracking program. But now there was no reading coming from Cassidy's phone. He told Chin, "I can't find a location for his phone. Something has happened to it. There's either no signal coming out of his phone at all, or something is jamming it."

"What about King's phone?"

Marsh checked his tracking program again. "King's phone is still working, and it's still where it's always been. It hasn't moved."

Chin switched back to Walters. "Marsh isn't getting a signal from Jay's phone. But he says King's phone is still in the same location. Can you go look for it?"

"Where is it?"

"It should be about half way up the aisle. That's what Jay reported twenty minutes ago."

Walters walked up the aisle to an empty pair of seats near the middle of the car. He saw a phone in the seat back pocket. He took out a handkerchief from his pocket and used it to pick up the phone. He carried it back to the seat next to Cassidy's body.

"I got the phone," he told Chin. "There was nobody in the seats where I found it."

"Are you sure you got the right phone?"

"I think so. Why don't you ring it and see?"

Chin called Marsh and asked him to ring King's phone. A moment later, she could hear the phone ring in the background through her connection with Walters.

Walters said, "You heard that, right?"

"I heard it. Put it in an evidence bag. We'll need to find out who's been handling it. Then you'd better search the train for that woman. She's in a green silk blouse with pearls. She has black curly hair."

"You said she was Middle Eastern. Was her head covered?"

"Cassidy didn't mention it. He would have mentioned a head covering if he saw one. So no, no head covering." Chin paused, then said. "Listen Tom, watch yourself. This woman may be very dangerous. Same for the man she was with. If you see anyone that meets the woman's description—or if you see King, for that matter, don't do anything. Just make the ID and call me."

Jasmeen looked at the sleeping woman across from her. Her lips were scarlet red, the same shade of red as the high heel shoes. Her hair was blond, but with streaks and roots and an unnatural stiffness. Jasmeen looked up at the small suitcase sitting on the overhead rack above the woman's seat. Maybe she could do something about her blouse after all. She stood and took down the woman's suitcase. She carried it to the restroom at the end of the car. Inside the restroom, she opened it and looked for a blouse. She found a white one and tried it on for size. As with the shoes, the blouse was one size too big, but that was of little concern. She just draped it and tucked it until it looked OK. She wasn't sure what to do with her green blouse. If she carried it around, someone could still spot her with it. Probably the safest thing to do was to put it in the woman's suitcase. It was unlikely the woman would look in her suitcase until she got wherever she was going.

She found the woman's lipstick and considered putting some of it on. She'd never worn lipstick. She knew it would disguise her even further. But then she remembered her disgust at how the bleached blond woman had looked. She dropped the lipstick back in the suitcase and put her own blouse in as well. She closed it, and left the restroom. She carried the suitcase back to the woman's seat, and put it back on the overhead rack. The woman continued to sleep, undisturbed.

Now Jasmeen needed to change seats again. She pulled the paper tab with her stop off the seat and walked toward the next car. In the next car, she saw the woman who'd asked her if everything was OK. She averted her head and walked quickly past that woman, and went on to the next car.

The train was coming to a stop at Poughkeepsie. Jasmeen had been thinking about getting off at Poughkeepsie. But now as she looked out the window and saw the small number of people getting off, she thought better of it. If she stayed on the train all the way to Penn Station in New York, she'd be among a much bigger group exiting all at once. If they were looking for someone of her description, she'd stand out too much at Poughkeepsie. But at Penn Station, she'd be just one person among hundreds.

She decided that she should stay on the train. Now that she no longer wore the green blouse, the pearls, or any other marker that the agent might have used to describe her, how could anyone recognize her?

She waited until the train stopped. Then after a pause, she walked into yet another car. Jasmeen knew she'd be more noticeable if she sat alone. So now, she acted as if she'd just boarded the train. Pretending to place some luggage in the overhead rack, she discreetly stuck the paper tab with her stop in the strip above a vacant seat that was next to a young woman. She sat down, smiled and said "Hello" to the young woman. At least this one wasn't wearing any garish makeup. The woman nodded, and Jasmeen pulled the on board magazine from the seat pocket and began to thumb through it.

Sarah saw Jasmeen walk past her once again. This time Jasmeen was walking normally, but she'd changed her blouse. She was no longer studying women asleep. Now instead, she seemed in a rush to get to wherever she was going. Sarah's curiosity was aroused. As soon as Jasmeen passed into the vestibule between cars, Sarah got up and followed her. She watched through the glass window in the door at the end of the car while Jasmeen stuck the paper tab above a seat next to a young woman and sat down.

Sarah went back to her seat and thought about what she'd seen. Why had Jasmeen changed seats? Why had she changed her blouse? Why was she sitting with that woman? Why had she been studying women asleep earlier? Why had she been hobbling? And most of all, what had she been banging on in the restroom? Sarah couldn't think of a reason for any of these things.

Since they'd overheard Kareem talking about a planned attack in New York City, Sarah assumed Jasmeen wasn't about to blow up the train. But her erratic behavior made Sarah certain that something out of the ordinary was already going on. "All you have to do is follow her," King had said, "and she'll lead you to the others." What if she'd already met up with the others? Sarah didn't see how that could have happened. Now Jasmeen was sitting next to a woman who looked more like a college student than another terrorist. *I'm not cut out for this detective stuff,* she thought.

Special Agent Chin had Cassidy's body removed at Poughkeepsie. They did it as discreetly as possible, with an ambulance and a stretcher, and the pretense that he was a man taken ill. Cassidy had been fifty-three years old. There was an outside chance he might have died from natural causes. But Chin doubted it. It was too coincidental. They would perform an autopsy right away and find out.

Chin tried to imagine what Cassidy had discovered. He might have discovered something about the woman who'd had King's phone, or about the man she'd been seated with—or, and this seemed least likely to Chin—he might have discovered something about King himself. Whoever killed Cassidy had done so without a trace. She found it difficult to envision how he could have been caught off guard so completely. He had a weapon. He had extensive training in self-defense. But somehow, he'd been killed without anyone on the train noticing. There didn't seem to have been an altercation of any kind.

King's phone, which had first appeared in the third car of the train back in Niagara Falls, had ended up abandoned. Whoever last had it must have figured out it was hot. Melanie Kahn's call must have been the tip off. The woman who put her hand on the phone when Kahn called must have realized that Cassidy had spotted her. Had he taken her picture? Had she killed him just to get his phone and destroy the photo? If so, it was crucial to identify her … and follow her. There had to be a reason she was so desperate to remain unknown.

When the Empire Service train arrived at Penn Station, Jasmeen again contemplated putting on her hijab. On the one hand, wearing it would hide her hair, which was one of the few things that the FBI man could have described about her. On the other hand, it would make her stand out in the crowd at Penn Station. And she knew they'd be scrutinizing everyone who got off the train. In the end, she decided to tie her hijab around her neck like a scarf. As she was leaving, she stuck close to the young woman who'd been her seat companion. She'd engaged the girl in some innocuous conversation about sightseeing in New York. The girl was a New York native and knew about all the sights.

Now, as they walked, Jasmeen chatted with her about visiting the Statue of Liberty. The girl told her the most she could do on such short notice was to get a ticket to take a boat to Liberty Island and see the monument at its base. There were only a limited number of tickets to go inside the monument and up to the crown. Those were always sold out for months. Jasmeen nodded and gestured, willing herself to appear casual and cheery, doing all she could to blend into the sea of humanity flowing through the maze of the station.

Sarah, for her part, followed Jasmeen as discreetly as she could. She stayed three deep in the crowd behind her. Jasmeen, she noticed, had tied a scarf around her neck. Now she was talking in an animated way to the girl she'd been sitting next to. Sarah heard the girl say something about the Statue of Liberty. She also said something about getting tickets for the crown. Sarah didn't like the sound of that.

She wondered where King was at this point. She didn't think he could already be in New York. She wished she could talk to him, to see if he could make sense of the strange behavior Jasmeen had exhibited. She wondered if he'd managed to follow Kareem, if he'd heard Kareem ask anyone about the Statue of Liberty.

Once Jasmeen made her way out of the maze of Penn Station and got up to the street, she broke away from the girl she'd been using as cover. She'd planned to take a taxi to Abdul's apartment on the Upper West Side. But she didn't want to get in a cab until she was confident no one was following her. To be certain of that she decided to walk a haphazard route. She snaked her way up and down the streets of the Garment District between Eighth Avenue and Ninth Avenue, then back east to Seventh Avenue. She changed direction in unexpected ways. The closer she got to Times Square, the more crowded the streets became. That only made it harder for her to see if anyone was following her. So she headed west on 39th Street to Tenth Avenue, and walked uptown into Hell's Kitchen. There the crowds thinned out.

Jasmeen didn't like being on the streets alone. Everywhere she looked, there were coarse men. And in this neighborhood, there were poorer people. Occasionally she'd see a cluster of men standing idly about, talking loudly, using what sounded to her like vulgar language. Each time this happened she crossed the street to avoid walking anywhere near those men.

She stopped in the doorway of a shop that had big windows. She could see in their reflection anyone coming behind her. She couldn't abide stares from the men any longer. She took the hijab from around her neck and tied it onto the top of her head, covering as much of her head and face as she could.

Just as she was tying the headscarf tight, she caught a glimpse of a woman walking toward her. The woman stopped walking abruptly at another shop four doors down, and ducked into its doorway. But Jasmeen saw the woman's face before she stepped out of sight. It was that same woman she'd found eavesdropping outside the restroom on the train. And a new thought suddenly occurred to her. *I wonder if that is Judith Goldman.*

Jasmeen adjusted her scarf, then opened her purse and dug around inside. Without looking, she found the packet of C&H sugar with her fingers. She slipped it out of her purse and wrapped her fingers around it. She held it tightly in her fist and continued walking.

<h1 style="text-align:center">TWENTY-SIX</h1>

King stared at the looming skyline as the bus approached Manhattan. He'd spent some time in New York a decade earlier. He'd visited the city long enough to adopt the classic "great place to visit but wouldn't want to live there" attitude. For him it wasn't just that the energy of the city was intense; it was also that he was so affected by it.

King had cultivated what his friend and teacher Walter called his 'empathic ability,' his capacity to read the feelings and thoughts of other people. In his Aikido training this helped him gauge another person's *ki*. But it also improved his work skills. As a private investigator, he had to get inside people's heads. He'd gotten pretty good at it. Walter observed that King was reading other people so well that his empathic skills verged on the telepathic. But King was not yet so good at what Walter called transparency—the ability to read other people's energy without being affected by it. He knew he'd have to get better at that before he'd be able to live in New York and handle the rush of vitality swirling around Manhattan.

As he looked out the bus window, he was trying to get inside the head of Kareem who sat beside him. It was a challenge to his skills. He couldn't get a clear reading of his thoughts or *ki*. What he got from him was a jumble of contradictions. Sometimes Kareem gave off an overbearing self-righteousness. At other times, he seemed embarrassed and awkward. The simple explanation was that Kareem was the product of a culture that was so repressed that his behavior was skewed to extremes. He was full of judgments that probably were intensified by his own shames. Walter would have said that Kareem most likely needed to get laid.

But Kareem seemed dead set against taking any bites out of what he called "bad apples." He was staring out the window. His eyes were wide. He was coming to New York with the intention of eating baklava and carrying out some new terrorist act. King couldn't imagine how anyone could commit such cold-blooded, calculated violence. That he couldn't imagine it worried him. He worried that his idealism about humanity would lead him to misread Kareem. He wanted to project a vision of innate goodness onto everyone, even onto the man sitting next to him.

When he looked at Kareem, he saw and felt the temperament of someone who seemed so much like an ordinary man, someone who liked whipped cream and pistachios. After all, Kareem had once been a baby, then a child, then a boy, then a teenager, then a young adult. There were universal aspects of these experiences that everybody shared, even in Iraq. He would have been subject to some variation on the kindnesses and cruelties that life hands to everyone.

But despite these human experiences, something had expressed itself in Kareem that was crucially different. He had developed a fatal flaw. It couldn't be written off as cultural or environmental, nor could it be excused by anything in his circumstances. It had to be a matter of his character. Something in his character was capable of terror. There had to be something evil in the man to be able to do what he had done and planned to do again. Of all the things that King had encountered in his life, evil was the most difficult for him to comprehend.

Walter believed that evil was just a synonym for inability. Walter was an idealist too. He said that people were evil because they hadn't yet learned the ability to be good—that in experiencing cruelty, some people learned cruelty. But Walter, who believed so strongly that the seeds of goodness lay dormant even in bad people, would certainly agree that Kareem had to be stopped, that he had to be prevented from ever again attempting such harm.

King thought that he sensed this evil as a kind of dark or empty place in Kareem. He considered that this reading of darkness might just be because he knew what Kareem had done. Yet he'd gotten an even darker feeling from his sister Jasmeen, even though he hadn't seen her do anything except leave her suitcase behind on the train.

Then there was Sarah. When he thought of her, his emotions lifted like something inside him lit up. He knew some part of this lighting up, maybe the largest part, was because he was so strongly attracted to her. But he trusted his sexual desire enough to believe there was something about her beyond her beauty that attracted him. Maybe they were on the same frequency because they'd both come from mixed parents. They each were a synthesis of parents whose differences had become a source of attraction. King felt that both his parents' differences and their attraction to each other lived side-by-side inside him. He'd always felt a balance between the poles that had formed him.

Sarah's mother, on the other hand, had raised her. She'd told him she was only now beginning to embrace the part of herself that came from her father. King was eager to meet her father. At the moment, he very much wanted—he needed—to connect with a good Muslim. Because that was how he was. He always had an impulse to balance.

He wished he still had his phone. He'd promised to take Kareem for a slice of baklava. That Kareem even had an equivalent to a cold shower was a point on which he hoped to build some common feeling. King was used to being able to open an app on his phone to find whatever he wanted. Now they were about to arrive in midtown Manhattan where there were a thousand places in a thousand directions. It would be impossible to know in which direction to set off to find a Turkish or Middle Eastern bakery.

Then there was the question of where to go after the pastry. Kareem would expect King to go on to his destination at the home of Sarah and her father. And even though he'd practically invited Kareem to come with him, he knew he couldn't actually bring him and his sister there without Sarah's father's permission. Dropping by with a couple of terrorists would not be a good first impression.

Besides, he had no idea where Sarah's father lived, and he wouldn't find that out until he found a pay phone and called her. What he really wanted to do was to find some way to stay with Kareem. But he knew he couldn't just tag along, go with him to a hotel, then go from there to the terror cell the next day. The best he could do was to find a reason to make a date with Kareem to see him again. He'd have to come up with some place to meet that would suit Kareem's standards of purity.

When he'd been working counter-intelligence in Afghanistan, he'd been able to meet Reema only because she'd been an exception. She'd been willing to meet him because she didn't adhere to the strict Islamic rules that separated men and women. But with Kareem, he'd have to follow the rules to the letter. And since it was Thursday, the most obvious way to do that would be to suggest joining him for prayer at a mosque the next day. King knew that the congregational prayer, Jumu'ah, always took place at noon on Friday.

King looked at his watch. They were still an hour away from arriving in New York. He said to Kareem, "When we get to the bus terminal, I want to stop and call my sister, to let her know I'll be late."

Kareem nodded. "I need to call my sister, too." He fished out the piece of paper on which Jasmeen had written the contact number. "Will they have public phones at the bus terminal?"

King shrugged. "I hope so. There aren't many public phones around anymore. But if they're gonna be anywhere, they'll be at the Port Authority."

"Tell me something, Omar," Kareem said. "Have you ever been to the Statue of Liberty?"

King kept his face expressionless, but inside he winced. Why was Kareem interested in that? He hoped it was the normal interest in the famous landmark typical of visitors to New York. But given what he knew about Kareem, he feared it wasn't as simple as that. King himself had long wanted to visit the monument. Months ago, he'd arranged to visit the Statue as part of his vacation. He'd never seen it up close.

He kept all the tickets he'd bought for New York events in his wallet—so he still had them with him. He said, "I've never been there, but I plan to visit it this weekend. I have tickets for the crown."

"What does that mean? What is a ticket for the crown?"

"To visit the Statue you take a boat to Liberty Island. But only a few of the people who go to the Island are able to go inside the monument itself. Even fewer people are allowed to go up to the crown. The crown has an observation platform built into the Statue's head with windows that look out on New York harbor. Anyone with a ticket for the crown can climb up there to look out from those windows. The Park Service only gives out two hundred tickets for the crown for any given day. But every day more than twelve thousand people go to the Island."

"How do you get a ticket for the crown?"

"They're reserved many months in advance. I made my reservations eight months ago. I've been planning this visit for a long time."

"You are going with someone?"

King hesitated before replying. He'd reserved two tickets for the crown. He thought he might get lucky and meet someone in

New York. He knew that if he did, a ticket to the crown would make for a great date. Since meeting Sarah, he'd been planning to invite her to go with him.

"I was planning to go with my sister," he said.

Kareem nodded. "I would like to see it too," he said. "I didn't know it was so hard to get tickets."

"Don't worry, you can still see it. You can get a ticket to go to the island on short notice," King said. "It's just that you won't be able to go inside the Statue. You'll only be able to walk around the base of it on the island and see it from there."

Kareem nodded. "Maybe I will go to the island when you go. When is your reservation?"

"I'm going Saturday morning. I have to check in at 11:15."

"I will speak to Jasmeen about our plans for Saturday. Is there some way that I can contact you if I decide to go?"

"I don't have a mobile phone," King said. "Well, I have one, but it broke. So I don't have it with me. But my sister has a phone. If it is all right with her, I can give you her number. Then you can call her and ask for me. I don't think she'll mind. But let me check with her first."

King knew that if he gave Kareem Sarah's phone number that might provide the authorities with evidence of a link between Kareem and Sarah. He'd have to ask her if she was willing to take that risk.

"Yes, of course." Kareem nodded.

That he understood the need to ask a woman for permission to give out her phone number didn't surprise King. Now that he knew Kareem was interested, he decided to sweeten the bait. He said, "I'm not sure if my sister will want to go to the Statue. She lives in New York, but she's never gone to see it. I don't think she'd mind at all if you came in her place."

"Does she not wish to see it?"

"She told me she's willing to go to keep me company, but she doesn't like heights or small spaces. They make her nervous. I don't think she really wants to go up in the crown."

Kareem nodded. "I would like to go up to the crown," he said. "It must be a wonderful view."

King decided to press his luck further. "Maybe you'd also like to join me for prayers tomorrow. We can go to a masjid for Jumu'ah in the city."

"Perhaps. If it is not too far from where I will be staying."

"You should join me, Kareem. Call me to let me know if you want to go—once you know where you're staying."

"Yes, Omar, I will let you know—about Jumu'ah and about visiting the Statue."

Sarah followed Jasmeen up Tenth Avenue to 41st street, then east to Ninth Avenue. On Ninth Avenue Jasmeen went into a coffee shop called Empire Coffee. After a suitable interval, Sarah followed her inside. Huge sacks of roasted coffee sat in rows on the floor along the wall. The smell alone was a stimulant. There was a short line at the counter. Some people were buying coffee beans; others were ordering coffee to drink in the shop.

Sarah got in line two places behind Jasmeen and heard her order a cappuccino. When she got to the front of the line, Sarah asked the barista for a macchiato, a shot of espresso with just a 'stain' of milk. She avoided making any eye contact with Jasmeen. Despite this, she had the feeling that Jasmeen was watching her as closely as she was watching Jasmeen. Could Jasmeen have recognized her from the train?

While Sarah was waiting for her macchiato to be made, someone tapped her on the shoulder.

"Excuse me..."

Sarah turned and found Jasmeen looking right at her.

"Are you Judith?" Jasmeen asked.

Sarah was startled by the question. The name rang a bell, but she couldn't remember what the connection was. She hadn't expected Jasmeen to speak to her directly, but now that she had, she could try to find out something about her. However, she wasn't going to give this woman her real name. She said, "No, I'm Ruth. Have we met?"

Jasmeen studied her for a moment, then said. "I saw you on the train earlier. You look like a woman I once knew named Judith. I haven't seen her in a long time. I thought perhaps you were she."

"No," Sarah said. "Sorry."

"Well," said Jasmeen, "it was just a possibility. And then the chance of seeing you on the train and again here, I thought it was too much of a coincidence."

"Small world," said Sarah.

Sarah's coffee arrived and she paid for it. She stepped over to the condiments counter

Jasmeen followed her. "What's that you ordered?" Jasmeen asked.

"It's a macchiato," Sarah said. She looked at what Jasmeen was drinking and saw that it was a cappuccino. She pointed at Jasmeen's cup. "It's like a cappuccino, but with less milk."

"Ah," said Jasmeen. "Do you put anything in it?"

"Just sugar," said Sarah. "Since it has less milk, it's stronger. I can't drink it without sweetener."

"I'm the same way," said Jasmeen. "I took two sugars to put in my cappuccino." She held out her hand to display the two sugar packets. "But so many calories!" She rolled her eyes. "I really should just use one. Here, you want the other one?"

"Thanks," said Sarah.

Jasmeen handed her the extra packet of sugar.

Sarah poured the sugar into her coffee and picked up a stirrer. She saw that there was more sugar at the counter and she thought about taking a second one. But then she didn't particularly want Jasmeen to see her using two when Jasmeen herself had just resisted that temptation. Jasmeen was already stirring her sugar into her coffee.

Sarah stirred hers and held it out toward Jasmeen. "You want to try it? You might find you like macchiato."

Jasmeen's face flashed with some kind of agitation, but then quickly recomposed itself. "No, thank you," she said. "It's kind of you to offer, but I don't like coffee so strong."

Sarah nodded and withdrew her extended hand. She looked at the cup and shrugged. "But that's what makes it good," she said.

Jasmeen looked around the coffee store. A few people stood in line. She held up her coffee cup and said, "Do you mind? I'm going to take this outside to drink it."

"Good idea," said Sarah. "There's a bench out there."

"Yes," said Jasmeen. "Let's sit there."

The women went outside and sat on the bench. Sarah blew on her coffee, but didn't drink it. "They always make it so hot," she said.

"Yes, some people like it scalding hot." Jasmeen blew on her cup too. "But I think mine is not as hot as yours because I have more milk."

Sarah nodded and looked at the people walking down the street. "So many people," she said for no particular reason. Finally, she took a sip of the coffee. "Wow," she said. "You're right. The coffee's strong. I'm glad I added some sugar."

Jasmeen's eyes went wide and she nodded. "Yes, but I like more than a splash when it comes to milk." She laughed. She held her own cup to her lips but didn't drink. She was watching Sarah intensely, as if she was waiting for Sarah to say something.

But Sarah didn't know what else to say. She took another drink of her coffee and then—since there wasn't that much in a shot—she drank it all down.

Jasmeen stared at her. She'd raised herself an inch off the bench, as if she was about to stand up. She had a strange look on her face. She held the look so long that she began gradually to tilt her head to the side.

Sarah instinctively put her hand to her mouth. She wondered if there was something wrong with her face. The way Jasmeen was looking at her, she thought she must have drool on her lips.

She wiped her mouth with her hand, then raised her hand to her head to make sure her hair hadn't blown into a mess. Her hair seemed OK. She couldn't figure out what Jasmeen was staring at.

But Jasmeen was still staring. Finally, she said, "Are you OK? You look a bit queasy."

Sarah shook her head. "I'm fine. Just a bit buzzed is all."

Jasmeen nodded, sat back down, and took a sip of her coffee. Then just as she was sipping, she abruptly pulled the cup away from her mouth and looked down at it. All of a sudden, a wild look came into her eyes and, without warning, she spat the coffee out of her mouth. She sprayed coffee all over the sidewalk. Then she stood and walked to a trash receptacle and poured all the coffee directly into the trash.

"Hey," said Sarah. "Are you all right?"

Jasmeen turned round and looked at her, but said nothing. Then she ran back into the store, went to the barista at the cash register, and spoke to him. After a moment, he handed her a cup of water. Instead of drinking it, she swished it around in her mouth like mouthwash, and spat it back into the cup. Then she came back outside and said, "I have to go now." She walked back to the curb, stuck out her hand and waved it at a cab. The cab pulled up, Jasmeen hopped inside it, and in a flash, she was gone.

TWENTY-SEVEN

When King and Kareem arrived at the Port Authority Bus Terminal, they found public phones on the second floor. Without discussing it, they each chose a phone far enough away from the other to allow a private conversation. King found a phone next to a Hallmark store. Kareem went to one forty feet away near a Hudson News stand.

Sarah answered King's call on the fourth ring. "Hello."

"Sarah, it's Ty."

"Is everything OK?"

"Yes, I'm fine."

"Where are you?"

"I'm at the Port Authority. Where are you?"

"I'm at my father's apartment."

"Were you able to follow Jasmeen?"

"Up to a point. When I got into the city, I had a strange encounter with her. I followed her into a coffee shop on Ninth Avenue. Out of the blue, she spoke to me—asked me if I was named Judith. It was weird."

King thought about it a moment. "By Judith, she must have meant Judith Goldman. That's the name I put on the phone. She must've figured out the phone was a plant and thought you were behind it."

"I told her my name was Ruth. Anyway, she was suddenly very chatty with me. We bought coffee. Then, at one point, we sat down on a bench outside the shop to drink it. She took a sip of hers, then suddenly spat it out and began to act crazy. It was bizarre. She dumped all her coffee, ran around for a minute, then jumped in a cab and went peeling off down Ninth Avenue. I got in a cab and tried to follow her. But my cab driver lost her. I guess it doesn't work like in the movies."

"Did you actually say, 'follow that cab'?"

"Yeah, I did. I think he thought I was joking. Pretty lame, huh? So that was it. After I lost her, I came here." She paused. "What about you? Did you catch up with Kareem?"

"Yes. We rode to town together on the same bus. He and I are now best buddies."

"Nice. How'd that happen?"

"It's a long story. I sat next to him on the bus and talked to him. So far, he hasn't recognized me. He's over at another pay phone talking to Jasmeen. I'm about to take him out to go get some baklava."

"Baklava?"

"Yeah, do you believe it? He likes it. But I have a tactical problem. I told him I know a good place to take him. But I don't. Could you use your phone to find a place that sells baklava somewhere near the Port Authority? Look for a Turkish place—don't make it Greek. He's picky."

"Seriously?"

"Yeah, I'm trying to get close to him and he wants Turkish baklava."

"OK, but I'll have to hang up and call you back."

"While you're at it, can you also look for a mosque where I can take him for prayer tomorrow? Somewhere open for Jumu'ah."

"Hang on, I'll ask my father."

"No, wait. Don't ask him. I don't think we should get him involved. Couldn't you just Google it? Look for a masjid. It would be better if it's one that's not anywhere near your father's mosque. Also, see if you can find one that's Shia. I'm pretty sure Kareem is from Iraq. So he's probably Shiite."

"OK, give me the number of your pay phone. You are at a pay phone, right?"

"Yes." King read her the number. "I'm just going to stand right here and guard the phone till you call."

"OK."

King hung up and looked at the Hallmark store where Kareem was still on his call. He paced around the phone. He hoped she had time to find the information and call him back before Kareem finished his call and wandered over.

Down by the Hudson News Stand, Kareem hung up his call and began to walk toward him. But halfway, he nodded and gestured, and made a detour toward the men's room across from the Hallmark. King wasn't sure what to do. He didn't want to lose sight of him. If he lost track of him now, it would be impossible to find him again.

He looked at his watch. He paced. He was just about to head toward the men's room, when the phone rang. He picked it up after the first ring.

"OK. I found a place called Troy Turkish Grill at Ninth Avenue and 40th Street. It's on the corner. They have baklava and you can eat there or take out. Can you remember all that, or do you want me to repeat it?"

"No. I've got it. Troy Turkish Grill, on the corner of Ninth and 40th."

"Right. Now about the mosque, there's a problem. As far as I can tell, all the mosques in Manhattan are Sunni or Sufi. The nearest Shia mosque I could find is in Brooklyn. You want the address for that?"

"Yes. I guess so. If that's the only choice, it will have to do."

"It's at 543 Atlantic in Brooklyn. You can take the 2 or the 3 subway, get off at Atlantic Avenue. It's a two-minute walk from there."

"OK, 543 Atlantic. I got it."

"Are you writing it down?"

"No, I told you, I have a good memory."

"If you say so."

"Listen, I don't have much time." King said. "What about you? Where do I find you?"

"My father's place is on West End Avenue near 99th street." She gave him the address. "Are you sure you can remember all this?"

"Yes. I'm sure."

"OK. When you get here, tell the doorman you're visiting Mr. Gaber in Apartment 16A. It's the penthouse."

"Fancy."

Sarah sighed. "Yeah. Like I told you, he's a rich guy."

"OK. So listen. Assuming I can make a date with Kareem for Jumu'ah, or to visit the Statue of Liberty, I'll come to you as soon as I'm done with the baklava. If not, if I can't get him to agree to see me again, I'm going to try to keep on his tail."

"The Statue of Liberty? What's that about?" There was alarm in Sarah's voice.

"He wants to visit it."

"Jesus."

"I know," said King. "I don't know what I'm going to do about it yet."

"Listen Ty, I overheard Jasmeen ask a woman on the train about the Statue of Liberty. She asked her how to get tickets for the crown."

"Kareem asked me the same thing." King paused. He wasn't sure if he should tell her the next part. But then he couldn't see any way around it. "Sarah, the strange thing is I already have two tickets for the crown—for this Saturday. I reserved them a long time ago. I told Kareem about it and he said he might like to go with me."

"You have tickets already?"

"I do. I was going to visit it. I was planning to be here on vacation, remember?"

"Right. And you have two tickets." She thought about this. "Why'd you get two tickets?"

King hesitated. He was embarrassed to confess his reason to Sarah. "Well…it's because I figured visiting the Statue would make a good date. I didn't have anyone in mind. I just wanted to have two in case…you know…just in case I happened to meet someone. I'm single, right, and single people date. Like the boy scouts say, 'be prepared.'"

Sarah didn't say anything. She was astonished. Was he so sure of his sexual prowess that he could count on meeting someone?

King filled in the awkward silence. "Sarah?"

"I don't know, Mr. King. It sounds to me more like a smooth operator move than a boy scout move."

"It's just how I am, Sarah." He felt defensive. "I like to plan for contingencies…more than most people. And look, I met you didn't I? If this had turned out to be a normal vacation, I would've asked you to go on a date with me in a heartbeat. In fact, I told Kareem that I was planning to take you."

"I see."

"Actually, I told him you were my sister. Then I made up a story about you being afraid of heights. I thought if I offered to get him into the crown, he wouldn't be able to resist. So I suggested that—given your fear of heights—he and I could go visit the Statue together."

"Nice." Not knowing what else to say, she stated the obvious. "I guess the Statue of Liberty must be where they plan to do their next attack. Sounds like a fun date for you. Take a ride out to see the Statue of Liberty with a terrorist and wait for him to try to blow it up."

King smiled, but then he realized Sarah couldn't see him. "I don't think it will be as simple as that." Across the corridor, he saw Kareem coming out of the men's room. "Listen, Sarah, I have to go. Kareem is moving and I don't want to lose him. I'll need a way for Kareem to contact me about getting together tomorrow. Is it OK if I give him your mobile number?"

"It's OK."

"If he has your phone number it will be evidence linking you to him if it ever comes out."

Sarah thought about it. "I understand. What does it matter? I'm already involved in this situation up to my neck. Don't worry about it."

"You're sure?"

"I'm sure. In the meantime, if you can't get here in the next few hours, call me. Let me know what's happening."

"I will."

They hung up and King ran over to Kareem. Together they walked out onto 42nd Street, where the air carried the smell of exhaust from a bus idling on the street. The exhaust stench mixed with the smell of meat cooking beneath the yellow and blue umbrella of a Sabrett hot dog cart and the nutty aroma wafting from beneath the red and white umbrella of a Nuts 4 Nuts cart a few yards away. The sun was low in the sky and the September air had grown crisper.

A handsome young man in plaid shorts and sandals stood idly behind the hot dog cart. He poked at the grilling links with a pair of tongs. He grinned and nodded at Kareem to urge him to buy some food. But Kareem made a face, turned to King, and asked, "Is it far to the bakery?"

King shook his head. "It's two blocks south of here, a five minute walk."

As they walked toward Ninth Avenue, they waded through a broad wash of people walking the opposite way. King glanced at Kareem from time to time and tried to analyze his thoughts. As they navigated down the street, Kareem had a wide-eyed look as he watched people approaching. He avoided making eye contact with any of the women, but he looked openly at the approaching men, as if each of them was fascinating and exotic. But if anyone looked back at him, he turned his head away as if he didn't want to be observed himself.

When Kareem turned in King's direction, King asked him, "Have you been to New York before?"

"I have never been here," he said. "Is it always this busy?"

King nodded. "This part of the city is always busy."

On Ninth Avenue, they passed a row of newspaper vending machines. There was a tall yellow case labeled Gotham Writer's Workshop, a boxy red container for the Village Voice, a shorter yellow box labeled Gay City News and a squat blue case labeled A1 News. Kareem eyed these with curiosity. "Are all these newspapers free?"

King stopped and looked at the machines. "Yes. Do you want one?" He reached down, opened the door of the Village Voice box, and pulled a copy out. "You might want to take this one if you're looking for things to do."

Kareem glanced at the boxes. He stared at them with an expression that was both fascinated and aghast. "No, no," he said, shaking his head emphatically. "I do not read such papers. They're full of vulgarity and obscene pictures."

"I suppose," said King. "That's why we're going to eat baklava, remember?"

Kareem nodded and King put the Village Voice back in its box. As they approached 40th Street, they saw the sign for Troy Turkish Grill on the corner. Inside the restaurant were a deli-style counter and a grill. Towering vertical spits of lamb stood next to the grill. Behind the counter glass sat trays of prepared food. On the other side of the room was a long row of tables and chairs.

The young man behind the counter looked Turkish and wore a mouche, a small patch of facial hair just below his lower lip. He asked them, "What can I get you?"

King said, "We'd like desert."

"We have our famous Turkish desserts…," the server said, "… such as Kazan Dibi and rice pudding and the baklava. They are made here by our chefs." He held up a bowl of pudding. "The

Turkish Kazan Dibi is really famous. You see it is a pudding with a caramelized top. Very delicious."

"The baklava," said Kareem.

King said, "I think I'll try the Kazan Dibi."

"Anything to drink? Coffee? Tea?" asked the server.

King looked at Kareem, who nodded and said, "Coffee."

"Yes, two coffees," said King.

They took their deserts to a table and sat down. Then Kareem stood, went to the counter, and brought back a sugar packet. He tore it open and stirred it into his coffee.

King spooned into his pudding, which looked like a crème brûlée, and took a bite. He nodded. "This is pretty good. Have you ever had it?"

Kareem forked off a piece of pastry, swallowed it, then took a sip of coffee. He nodded. "Yes. I had it in Istanbul. It is good, but I prefer pastry to pudding."

King set down his spoon and wiped his face with a napkin. "If you don't have other plans tomorrow," he said. "Since it is Friday, would you like to join me at noon for Jumu'ah? There is a Shia masjid in Brooklyn. It's easy to reach on the subway."

Kareem chewed for a moment and looked into King's eyes. "That is kind of you to offer. I would like that."

King nodded, then stood and went to the counter. He asked the server for a pen, and took a napkin from the holder on the counter. He wrote down the subway line and the address of the mosque in Brooklyn. He thought for a moment and added a phone number. Then he returned to the table and handed the napkin to Kareem.

"This is the address. I've written down the subway line. You can take a 2 or 3, which you can catch anywhere along Broadway. Take it to Brooklyn, and get off at Atlantic Avenue."

Kareem studied the napkin. "The 2 or 3 to Atlantic Avenue Brooklyn. Yes, I see."

"I should be there by noon. I've written down a phone number where you can reach me if you change your mind."

Kareem nodded again.

"That's my sister's mobile phone," King said. "I'll be with her, so just ask to speak to me when she answers."

"I won't call unless there's a problem," Kareem said.

"I'll try to get there by quarter to 12," King said. "I'll wait for you outside, so we can go in together."

"I understand," said Kareem. "And if I arrive first, I'll wait for you."

They finished their deserts and left the grill. Outside, King turned to head east toward Times Square and the Broadway subway. Without saying anything specific about where he was headed, Kareem said he was going to walk north on Ninth. They shook hands and parted.

As King crossed the street, he watched Kareem walk slowly up Ninth. He watched long enough to see Kareem pause and glance again at the row of newspaper vending machines halfway down the block. He stepped toward them, craning his head as if he was re-reading the names of the papers. Then he stopped and looked up, startled, as a young couple walked toward him and the boxes. Abruptly Kareem turned and kept walking up Ninth Avenue. As King walked into the canyon of buildings on 40th Street, he wondered if he'd ever see Kareem again.

TWENTY-EIGHT

King rode the subway up to 96th Street, then walked from Broadway to 99th and West End Avenue. He announced himself as Mr. King to the doorman, who phoned the penthouse to announce him. When the elevator arrived at the 16th floor, the door opened on a small, mirrored lobby that served the entrances to two apartments. Sarah stepped out from the doorway of 16A into the lobby, and offered King a hug.

"I'm glad you're safe," she said.

King kissed her forehead. "You, too," he said. "No one has recognized me." He looked in the mirror and cocked his head. "I hardly recognize myself."

"It's lucky Kareem didn't recognize you," said Sarah. She inspected his face. "Your beard is beginning to fill in." She rubbed her fingers on the facial hair below his left sideburn. "It's time to dump the fake one and shape your real beard into a goatee."

King peeled the false beard off his face. "Thank God. This thing itches."

They both turned to the doorway, where a man with piercing brown eyes, who was dressed in immaculately pressed slacks and shirt, stood quietly watching them.

"Father," said Sarah. "This is Tyrone King."

"Ty, this is my father, Abrahim Gaber."

King and Mr. Gaber shook hands. "Salaam," said King.

Mr. Gaber registered mild surprise at this greeting. "Salaam," he said and bowed slightly without taking his eyes off King. "You can call me Abe. That's what most of my friends call me." The older man's grip was strong; his searching stare was wary. "My daughter has told me of your heroic acts on the train," he said. "And of your decision to pursue these radicals on your own." He let go of King's hand, turned and pushed open the door to his apartment. "Come in and make yourself welcome."

"Thank you," King said. He stepped into the apartment. "I'm sorry to have involved you and your daughter in this," he added.

"From what my daughter says, it appears she chose to become involved in this matter."

King looked at Sarah, who rolled her eyes. He was beginning to understand more about the relationship between Sarah and her father. "Well, I'm glad to have met your daughter," he said. "Despite the circumstances." He smiled at her with a look of pride. "If she hadn't kept the detonator away from him, the bomber would have set off the bomb much sooner. We might all have been killed."

Abe Gaber shuddered. "Yes, well, God is most great. There are men, however, who are not."

King turned to survey the room. The furnishings were heavy and sumptuous. A large embroidered antique panel hung on the wall behind a dark leather sofa. On the adjacent wall was a dark red calligraphic panel with yellow script. King studied the Arabic calligraphy.

Following King's gaze, Abe Gaber said, "That piece is from the early 19th century. It's by a Turkish calligrapher. It says, 'There is no God but He, the Lord of His prophet Muhammad, peace be upon him, and…'"

King broke in to finish the translation, "'…the Lord of all that has been created.'" He leaned in close to inspect the panel. "It's a beautiful piece."

"Sarah tells me you're fluent in several languages."

King nodded and continued looking around the room. "These are pieces from the Ottoman period, aren't they?"

"Yes," said Mr. Gaber. "My ancestors."

"You're from Turkey?"

"My father grew up in Istanbul. I was born here in New York."

"As it happens, I just had some very good Kazan Dibi, at a Turkish deli by the Port Authority."

"Sarah, why don't you show Tyrone the terrace? Would either of you like tea or coffee?"

"Tea, please," said Sarah.

King nodded. "I'll have the same."

Sarah led King through a door and onto a rooftop terrace garden. Across a brick parapet, was a sweeping view toward the Hudson River.

King walked to the parapet and leaned on it with his elbows to take in the view. "Sweet," he said.

"Yes," said Sarah. "It's nice."

King turned. "And look at this garden; it's beautiful."

Sarah sat on a wooden bench and motioned for King to sit next to her. "What about the Statue of Liberty?" she asked. "Thinking about it is driving me crazy."

"What do you mean?"

"Are you taking him there?"

"I don't know. He hasn't decided. I guess he has to check in with his co-terrorists."

Sarah frowned. "OK. Please tell me you're ready to bring the FBI into this. Don't you think you know enough at this point to tell them what's going on?"

"I expect to find out more about it tomorrow. I'm meeting him in Brooklyn at noon for services. I hope by then he'll have worked out the plans with his accomplices."

"And you think he'll tell you what their plans are?"

"He might. He seems to trust me, as much as he trusts anybody. Whether he trusts me or not, if their plan involves the Statue, he'll need my ticket."

Sarah took King's hand and squeezed it. "What if they decide they need to get rid of you to cover their tracks? These people are crazy dangerous, Ty."

King squeezed her hand back. Don't worry," he said. "If they want my ticket, they'll need me to take him to the Statue. If their plan is to commit some act of mass terrorism, getting rid of me personally is going to be the least of their worries." He could see from Sarah's expression that this analysis was not reassuring. "OK, look," he added. "Once I find out for sure what they plan to do, we'll tell the FBI about it. They can pack the place with agents and make sure nothing happens."

"OK, promise me we'll call them tomorrow—whether you find out about their plans or not. I can't take anymore vigilante heroism."

As she spoke, her father stepped onto to the terrace with a tray of tea. "What's this about vigilantes?" he asked.

"I was telling Tyrone," Sarah said, "I don't think we should go on handling this situation by ourselves. It's time to turn it over to the FBI."

Abe Gaber set down the tray and began to pour tea into the cups. "I see," he said.

"It would be better if I talk to the FBI on my own," said King. "I see no reason to mention Sarah or you."

"It's a delicate matter for me," said Abe. "I have many friends. Some of them do not trust the government. They would be uncomfortable and embarrassed if the media connected them to something like this." He finished pouring the tea and handed the cups to King and Sarah. "I understand my friends' misgivings," he continued. "But I'd rather make a few of my friends uncomfortable than stand by while something terrible happens. You don't have to protect me if doing so jeopardizes anyone's safety."

"I appreciate that," said King. "But I can't see how telling the FBI about Sarah or you would help them—or how not saying anything would hinder them."

"Use your judgment," said Abe.

King took a sip of the hot tea, which tasted of mint. He pondered his next move. "I'll call them," he said. "But not until after I see Kareem tomorrow." He was playing a game of chess, not only planning his next moves, but also thinking about the moves that would be made against him. "I have to see what happens with him in Brooklyn. He can't count on seeing me after tomorrow. So if wants me to take him to the Statue, he'll have to ask me for the ticket when he sees me in Brooklyn. I want to find out more about their plan before I call the FBI." He looked at Sarah. "And I want the FBI to understand that I have to be the one who takes Kareem to the monument. He won't trust anyone else. That way they can't detain me while this thing goes down."

"I think Ty should stay here tonight," Sarah said to her father. Then she turned to King. "The less time you spend in public, the better."

"Yes," said Abe. "I agree. You're welcome to stay here."

"Thank you. That's very generous."

"Do you need money? Sarah told me you left all your belongings behind on the train."

"Sarah loaned me three hundred dollars yesterday," said King.

Abe nodded his approval.

"You see, father," said Sarah. "I'm not so different from you after all."

Abe took a seat and leaned back in his chair. For a moment, his eyes glazed over. Then he focused them on his daughter. "Just wait," he said. "The older you get, the more you'll see how true that is. I just hope you won't regret it."

"That sounds ominous," Sarah said.

"I'm only speaking from my experience," said Abe. "I never wanted to be like my father. But now I find I am."

"I wish I could remember him better," said Sarah. She turned to King. "My grandfather died when I was eight. I was just thinking that what I remember most about him is how he laughed. His whole stomach shook when he laughed. He played Parcheesi with me while we ate popcorn. I can't think what there was to laugh about playing Parcheesi."

"He laughed because you were so earnest," said Abe. "Whenever you captured someone else's piece, you'd dance a little jig. That made him laugh. Then after your dance, you'd come back to the table and be all serious again. You'd forget to eat your popcorn because you were so focused on strategy."

"I was focused on strategy?" Sarah laughed. "How can that be? What strategy is there in Parcheesi?"

Abe smiled. "Well there is strategy of a sort. Each player must decide which pieces to move, which ones to keep on a safe space. You never cared about staying safe. Even then, you were a risk taker. All you cared about was capturing everyone else's pieces—and damn the safe spaces."

"Really?"

"Oh, yes. Your mother and I played too."

"When was the last time you played?" Sarah asked.

"When you were eleven or twelve. After that, you were too grown up."

"Maybe we should play again."

"It's better to play it with a child." He looked at her and smiled. "If you have a child one day, I will play with her."

There was an awkward moment of silence. King, who'd been listening to this discussion of Parcheesi without speaking, suddenly felt like he should say something.

"I never played it," he said. "But I think it originated in India."

Sarah and her father looked at King as if they'd just remembered he was there.

"I suppose you speak Hindi," said Sarah. Then she gave him a peculiar look. "Or maybe, in your case, Sanskrit."

"No. Neither one." He was trying to figure out what she meant by 'in your case.' What kind of person had 'Sanskrit' written all over him? It didn't sound very sexy. Then he noticed the half-smile on her face. He said, "But I hope to learn a few more languages before I die. I might give one of them a try."

"As I mentioned, Ty speaks eight languages," Sarah reminded her father. "And I've noticed that he doesn't think there's anything he can't do."

"Then he is like you, no?" her father replied.

Sarah seemed surprised by this. But after she thought a moment, she said, "Yes." She looked at King. "I suppose together we're completely unbearable."

TWENTY-NINE

Abdul stared at his brother and sister. He was a tall man with a harsh and swarthy, V-shaped face, made less pointed by a carefully trimmed beard. His slate-black hair was slicked back perfectly. The expression on his face was one of skepticism. He'd been listening to Kareem and Jasmeen's explanation of what happened at Niagara Falls. Kareem's account of a man with dreadlocks, who took his gun and then kicked away his detonator, was improbable enough. But the idea that this meddler did not use the gun to stop Kareem from retrieving the detonator and blowing up the bomb seemed far-fetched.

"He took the bullets out of the gun, and then he just put the gun back in the luggage?"

"Yes." Kareem nodded.

"Why would he do that?"

Kareem shrugged his shoulders. "I do not know."

They sat in the living room of Abdul's apartment on Riverside Boulevard. He lived on the twenty-third floor of a Trump building that housed a high-end day-care center and an organic grocery. Abdul spoke English with little trace of an accent. As far as anyone in the building knew, he worked on Wall Street and was, accordingly, as wealthy as everyone else who lived in the building.

"I've seen this man's picture on the news. He is an American," Abdul said. "But he understands Arabic. He was trained as a soldier, but he does not care to use a gun. Something about this does not add up."

"Yes, it is a mystery," said Kareem.

The living room was large and lit with dappled light. One wall was all windows, but covered with vertical blinds open just enough to allow thin slits of light. Kareem and Jasmeen sat facing the blinds on a large sofa, bathed in bright vertical stripes of light.

Jasmeen held her hand up to shield it from a band of light. "I think he was FBI," she said, "or CIA. We were coming from Canada."

"That is even less likely." Abdul shook his head. "If he were with the government, he would not have let Kareem escape." He stood and walked over to the couch, his body casting a shadow on his brother and sister against the bands of light. He glared down at Kareem. "And tell me again, why was it that you didn't shoot him when you had the gun?"

"I did shoot the gun," said Kareem. "But I missed him."

Abdul slapped Kareem across the cheek. "You are pathetic."

Kareem felt a surge of acid in his stomach. He hung his head and looked straight down at the antique Persian carpet in front of the couch. He nodded, then ran his palms over the knees of his pants.

"He is not to blame, Abdul," said Jasmeen. She touched her hand on Kareem's shoulder, but looked at Abdul. "You did not train him enough with the gun."

Abdul shot her a threatening look.

"I see. And you, on the other hand," he said. "You managed to kill an FBI man."

"He'd taken my picture. What was I supposed to do? I could not allow him to keep it."

Abdul raised his hand, but he did not strike his sister. "You should have taken his camera when he wasn't looking."

Jasmeen glared at Abdul, but she did not speak. She simply lowered her hand from Kareem's shoulder back to her lap.

"Between failing with the bomb and killing this FBI agent," Abdul continued, "you've both managed to put our next operation at risk."

Kareem looked up at his brother and tried to recover his composure. He clasped his hands together and swallowed. "Listen, Abdul, about the man I met on the bus yesterday, I believe Allah has led me to this man." He spoke firmly but calmly. "This man, Omar, can get me inside the Statue." He turned to his sister. "This opportunity cannot have come by chance. Allah is watching over us."

Abdul shook his head. "And why should we trust this strange man?"

"He and his mother gave me a ride when I was hitchhiking. How many people would do that?" He waited for Abdul to say something, but his brother did not speak. "Besides," Kareem continued, "he is Muslim. I am to meet him at the masjid in Brooklyn tomorrow. It is a Shia masjid."

"Too many coincidences," said Abdul.

"Coincidence is the hand of Allah," said Kareem.

"Where is this Omar staying?"

"He is visiting his sister here in New York. I do not know where she lives. He offered to introduce me to her. She is unmarried. He wanted to take her to the Statue. But she is afraid of heights. That's why he said I could go with him instead."

"How convenient," said Abdul. "So you and Omar would go up to the crown alone? You will have no way to protect yourself up there, Kareem. They do not allow weapons."

"No one can do anything to me in the Statue. We will be surrounded by tourists."

"He has only to grab the camera from your hand," Abdul

said. "And with you holding the camera, even a woman could do that."

"How would Omar know about the camera? You said that no one would ever guess."

"No one would guess," said Abdul. "But you apparently cannot stop yourself from talking about things."

"I won't say anything about it, Abdul." Kareem tried to smile. "I don't even understand how it works."

"I've explained it to you. The camera uses an infrared beam to focus. The beam in this camera works like a homing signal. It will look just like an ordinary camera at the security check. But when you press the button to focus it, the infrared beam will guide the rocket right to you."

"So then," said Kareem. "This stranger's ticket is a perfect opportunity. How else am I to get inside the crown so quickly?"

Abdul scratched the beard on his chin. "Perhaps." He turned and went to the window. He slowly opened the blinds until the room flooded in bright light. He gazed out at the panorama of buildings, trees, and water. His apartment had a sweeping view of Riverside Park and the Hudson River. "We would have to get boat tickets for Saturday."

Jasmeen spoke. "This should not be a problem. I've done some research on the internet. The Circle Line boats hold 200 people." She turned to Kareem. "The tour boats leave the dock at 11:30. We should arrive near the Statue at 12:15. What time is your admission to the Statue?"

"Omar said check in is at 11:30 on Saturday," said Kareem. "I don't know how long it will take us to climb the stairs."

"The timing really couldn't be better." Jasmeen turned to Abdul. "If Kareem climbs up to the crown by noon, our boat will pass by the Statue just at the time Kareem is inside it."

"Another coincidence," said Abdul. "Let's hope it doesn't take you more than 30 minutes to climb to the top."

"This opportunity is our best chance," said Kareem. "And there are some coincidences that not even the FBI can arrange."

Abdul thought about this. He paced in front of the window for a moment, then stopped to gaze out again. "Perhaps," he said. Then he turned back to his brother. "But this will be your last opportunity, Kareem. If you fail this time, you won't get another chance to redeem yourself." He leaned down and spoke directly into Kareem's face. "You understand me, don't you?"

Kareem nodded. "I will die a martyr. The Statue will fall. You will honor me, Abdul. And you will honor your promise."

Jasmeen looked at them. "What promise?"

Abdul glared at Jasmeen. "It does not concern you." Then he turned back to Kareem. "You will have your wish, little brother. But when the time comes, you must stand right in the middle of the viewing platform in the head of the Statue. Stand there and wait for us. Be sure that you see our boat. The boat will sound its horn when it turns. Jasmeen will call your phone just after the boat turns."

"Will we use the walkie-talkie?"

"No. A two-way radio would look suspicious to the security guards. You will use a regular mobile phone. At that point, it won't matter if they're monitoring us. It will be too late. They won't have time to do anything. You will keep the phone in your pocket. You must be sure it's turned up loud so you can hear it. When she calls you, she'll let it ring twice. Don't answer it. Just hold the camera and press the button to focus and focus it on the boat. Do you think you can manage that?"

"Yes." Kareem swallowed again. "How long will it take?"

"How long will what take?"

"For the rocket to reach the camera from the boat?"

"I suppose it might take as long as ten seconds," said Abdul. He narrowed his eyes. "Maybe five or six. You will have just enough time to say a very quick prayer."

Everyone was silent. But soon Jasmeen began to rub her hand on the sofa's armrest. Finally, she said, "There is no reason to dwell on that." She stood. "You must put your thoughts on paradise, Kareem. Or perhaps you can empty your mind—just like a meditation. That is what I would do." She looked at Abdul. "I could do it." She turned to Kareem. "I will do it if you have changed your mind. I will carry the camera."

"I have not changed my mind." He smiled at his sister. "It is a brave thing to offer." He looked at Abdul. "But the camera is my mission. I am prepared."

Abdul walked from the window to Jasmeen's side and took her hand. "Sit down, sister." He guided her back down to the sofa. "We will not change our plans now." He waved his hand toward the dining table on the other side of the room, on which sat a stack of metal components. "Two people must carry the sections of the weapon. You and I will go on the boat as a couple. We will have backpacks, but we will hold hands. It will draw less suspicion."

Jasmeen nodded. She took Kareem's hand and held it. "Jannah, Jannah," she said. "We are on a train to Jannah. We will meet in that Paradise."

THIRTY

King and Kareem sat side-by-side on the floor of the masjid. King was intent on following tradition. He silently recited a prayer known as *tahyatul masjid slah,* which means "the prayer to greet the mosque." But his nose twitched as he became aware that Kareem smelled of cologne.

They were in the fifth row of the congregation. There were four more rows of worshipers seated behind them. A man in the first row gave the *adhan,* the call to prayer. After that, the imam began his sermon with a few words in Arabic, as is traditional. Then he began to speak in English about the responsibilities of marriage.

"In the Qur'an," he said, "the pictures we receive of marriage are those of peace, love, tranquility and harmony. In chapter 30, verse 21, we're told: 'And among His signs is this: that He created for you mates from among yourselves that you may dwell in tranquility with them.'"

The imam paused to look out over the congregation. He continued, "So you see, God has described it as a sign that He gave us mates from among ourselves. The Arabic word of the verse is *taskunu*: which means a place in which someone feels at 'home.' The word for home, *sakan*, comes from the same root word."

Now the imam stepped out from behind his podium and stood beside it. "In another verse, the Qur'an describes spouses in this way: 'They are your garments, and you are their garments.' What does a garment do for you? It protects you from cold and heat. It hides the faults that are cloaked below the garment. It covers what others should not see. And..." The imam smiled. "...it adorns your body to make you more beautiful. Is that not a good description of what spouses do for each other?"

King glanced sideways at Kareem. The garment metaphor was intriguing. He knew his own faults. But he wondered what malicious plans hid beneath Kareem's white shirt.

Before the service, Kareem had spoken to King about the tickets. He'd asked if he could accompany King to the Statue. King had agreed, but not without obtaining a promise from Kareem to join him for dinner that evening after the prayer service. King wanted to find out as much as he could about Kareem's plans. Before he talked to the FBI, he wanted to know enough about the operation Kareem and his conspirators were planning so that everyone involved could be brought to justice.

Whatever scheme Kareem hid beneath his garments, he now sat peacefully, with his legs folded, listening to a sermon about the joys and responsibilities of marriage as if matrimony were the only thing on his mind. King wished that were true. He wondered if he could find a way to talk Kareem out of his plans. He closed his eyes to contemplate how he might do that.

His intuition told him that Kareem was not at all like the violent men he'd encountered in Afghanistan. They had been men who were filled with an absolute sense of right and wrong, men whose chests were puffed up with self-righteous certainty and blood lust. They were crude, rough, violent men. Kareem, by contrast, seemed, at least on the surface, to be gentle and serene. King could not reconcile the tranquil energy emanating from the man who sat quietly beside him with a vision of terrorism in New York harbor.

The one thing Kareem had in common with the warriors in Afghanistan was self-righteousness. Kareem's admonitions about sexual temptation were sanctimonious—the product of religious idealism. Idealism was something King shared with Kareem. It was idealistic to hope that he could simply avoid the tragedy by appealing to Kareem's gentle nature.

Many things baffled King about his fellow humans, but the will to violence was one of the most mysterious of all. How could he change something he didn't understand? Something was missing. He wondered if there was some crucial insight that would explain the behavior that was hidden from him. If so, he would search out that insight in the same way a detective unravels a mystery. He thought about how he might work his way around the problem in conversation, brushing past it, using empathy to uncover the missing pieces of the puzzle.

The imam finished the first half of his sermon and sat down for a moment to offer silent prayers. It was an intermission. King had been sitting with his eyes closed while he thought about his mission. Now he shifted his posture and opened his eyes. As he did so, he saw that Kareem was staring at him. Kareem quickly glanced away when King caught him looking. King could see that his face was red, as if something had embarrassed him.

The imam stood again to deliver his final admonishments for matrimonial duty. King was pleased to hear the imam's concluding remarks were about the evils of domestic violence. That, at least, was something that King could use later. It gave him a way to bring up the topic of violence with Kareem.

When the sermon was finished, a man in the front row stood again to give the call to prayer. In response, the congregants rose and everyone moved until they were standing shoulder-to-shoulder as they formed a straight line facing Mecca. When Kareem lined up, he pressed his shoulder tightly against King's shoulder. Then they performed two cycles of the ritual prayer—

standing, bowing, prostrating, and sitting—following along with the imam.

For King, this was the most affecting part of the service. King was not a true believer in any formal religion. But whenever he performed the formal movements that accompanied Islamic ritual prayers, he felt inspired. The collective enactment of humility by all the men in the room, combined with the heightened awareness of the East—of their orientation on the earth's globe in relation to a distant land—and the physical stimulation of stretching and bowing, which, like yoga, heightened King's body awareness, made him feel a burst of gratitude and aliveness. These rituals took him briefly out of his mental obsessions, away from the endless chatter of his mind. And he just breathed.

When the prayer was over, Kareem shook the hand of the man on the other side of him. Then he turned and shook King's hand and said, "May Allah accept your prayers." King nodded. In that moment, he was ready to use every means possible to achieve his goal, even the power of prayer. He thought it very likely that the man shaking his hand was plotting to blow up the Statue of Liberty. King would do everything he could to stop it, but he had to find his own way of doing it. He would seek some avenue into the terrorist's heart—and then try to transform it—to turn that heart away from violence. It was a high stakes mission. But King was bound to try.

THIRTY-ONE

Special Agent Chin was worried. It had been more than 24 hours since Special Agent Cassidy's death, more than 24 hours since the train he was on had arrived at Penn Station, and they still hadn't found Tyrone King. The team in the field had recovered King's phone, but Cassidy's phone was still missing.

She felt certain they'd come close to finding what they were looking for. Cassidy, apparently, had come too close. She didn't have the autopsy result yet, but she couldn't imagine that his death was from natural causes. Whoever had killed him must have taken his phone. How this happened, and why it happened, was now a matter of national security.

She'd come home from work early. She knew from experience that sometimes she had to step away from a case in order to make progress. In this instance, however, she hadn't been given a choice. Franklin, her boss, had gone ballistic when he heard what happened. She'd made a terrible mistake with the Red Caps. She should have known they were nearly obsolete. He informed her that Amtrak didn't have Red Caps at all the train stops—only at the big city stations. Franklin told her that she must have watched too many old movies. He was right. She must have been replaying some movie from the fifties in her head.

Franklin hadn't formally taken her off the case, but he'd told her to go home and wait while he decided what to do. It was Friday evening. She sat in her living room petting Edgar, her dog. They were in her apartment in downtown Buffalo. Edgar, as usual, was happily oblivious to the problems that troubled her. He nuzzled her lap. He was trying to get her attention. He wanted something—probably to go out.

She stood and walked to the back door of the apartment. She took the dog out to the porch, then down the stairs to the back-yard. Edgar darted around the yard for a while, sniffing, and then did his business. All this was as expected. She thought about Edgar's instinctive ritual. Instead of getting right down to his business, he always ran around the yard and sniffed around for a while first.

She wondered what instincts were guiding Tyrone King's behavior. She didn't have evidence beyond a reasonable doubt, but she was sure he was not a terrorist. She guessed that he must have become caught up in what happened on the Maple Leaf. Now he was in hiding. She knew from the files that King had been a counter-intelligence agent in the Army, and that after his discharge he'd become a private investigator in civilian life. With that kind of background, his instincts would be to investigate whatever situation he'd stumbled into. Like Edgar, he'd want to sniff around before acting. But why not come forward and work with the agency? Maybe he was carrying a grudge about his discharge. Maybe, like Cassidy, he'd gotten too close to the truth. He might already be dead. Or the terrorists might be holding him hostage. But what she hoped, and the theory she would have to act upon, was that he was still out there trying to catch the bad guys.

The evidence suggested that King had started out as a tourist on a vacation in Toronto and New York. They'd pulled his credit card records and found that he'd planned a busy weekend for himself in New York. He had a ticket on the Maple Leaf from Toronto to arrive in New York City on Wednesday. He'd booked a room at a boutique hotel called 'The Jane' in the West Village. He had a pair of tickets for two Broadway shows, one on Thursday night and one on Saturday night. He had a pair of tickets for the Statue of Liberty on Saturday at noon. And he had a pair of tickets for a Yankee's game on Sunday at 1 PM.

All this had sent Franklin into a panic. Franklin said he didn't know which was worse, the prospect of a bomb going off in a Broadway theater in Times Square, at the Statue of Liberty, or at Yankee stadium. But Chin doubted there was any connection between King's vacation plans and a terrorist plot. In any event, King hadn't shown up at his hotel. And his pair of seats at the Broadway play on Thursday night had gone empty. The fact that he'd bought two tickets for each event suggested that he knew someone in New York. But that had turned up yet another puzzle.

The events that lead to Cassidy's death appeared to have begun with the phone call to King's phone from Melanie Kahn. The first thing Chin had done after Cassidy's death was to have Melanie Kahn brought in for questioning in the Chicago office. The FBI investigators found out that Kahn worked for King. During questioning, she admitted to knowing him quite well. She claimed that if King knew someone in New York, she had no idea who it was. As far as she knew, he'd gone there by himself on vacation. But on Wednesday, King had left her a voice mail telling her that if she got a call from him, she should answer by saying "Hi Judith, how's Niagara Falls?"

When they recovered King's phone, they found the name Judith Goldman listed as the phone's owner. The contact list included names and addresses in New York. But these names and addresses appeared to have been made up. In King's voice mail, he told Kahn that if she received a call from his phone, it would be from a man named Kareem. But Kahn said she didn't know anyone named Kareem; nor did she know Judith Goldman. None of the other names listed in King's contact list were familiar either.

It seemed that someone, probably King, had invented these names and put them in King's phone. He'd certainly been the one to put in the name of Judith Goldman, since it matched the name he left Kahn in his voice mail.

In the meantime, Chin's team reported that there were hundreds of Kareems living in the New York City area. And there were nearly as many Judith Goldmans. No one on her investigative team could find any connection between anyone named Kareem or Judith with Tyrone King.

Chin sat down at her desk, flipped through her files, and found Melanie Kahn's phone number. Kahn answered on the second ring and Chin explained who she was.

"What's happened? Do you have any news?" asked Kahn.

"No, nothing's happened. I just thought of another question I'd like to ask you."

"OK. Sure, anything to help."

"You said Tyrone doesn't have any friends in New York."

"No, not that I know of."

"Is it possible he could have been planning to meet up with a friend who lives somewhere in the region? Maybe a friend in Philadelphia, or Boston, or Washington?"

"As far as I know, he has friends here in Chicago and the rest of his friends all live on the west coast. If he knows someone on the east coast, I never heard about it."

"Do you think he might plan to rendezvous with any of his Chicago or west coast friends in New York?"

"I suppose," said Melanie. "But I think he would have told me. When he talked about the trip, he didn't say anything about meeting any friends. That angle doesn't add up."

"So you don't have any idea why he bought two tickets to the shows and the ball game?"

"Well ..." Kahn hesitated. "I've been thinking about that. It wouldn't totally surprise me if Ty bought two tickets to everything just so he'd be in a position to take a date in case he met someone."

"In case he met someone?"

"Yeah. He's single, and he probably had the idea that he'd go out and meet somebody in New York. He likes to plan everything in advance, and I mean everything. He probably figured he'd have all these exciting things lined up so he could take whomever he met out on dates. He's done that kind of thing before."

"He'd be that confident—that certain that he would meet someone who'd want to go out with him?"

Melanie laughed. "Oh yeah. You don't know him. He's totally conceited that way." She paused. "But to be honest, I guess it's not all that crazy for him to plan something like that. He never has any trouble meeting people."

"But how could he be so sure he'd meet someone that *he* wanted to date?"

"Well… I don't know that he would be completely one hundred percent certain about it. But with him, the odds are pretty good. He has broad taste if you know what I mean."

"No, I don't."

"He's bisexual. He likes girls and boys. Take your pick. On top of that, he's handsome. The odds of his meeting someone and hitting it off are pretty high."

Chin laughed, despite herself. "I never thought about it. I guess the odds would be double."

"Yeah, well, he says his pool of potential partners isn't as wide as most people think. He points out that just because he's bi doesn't mean he's hot for everyone he meets. Like everyone, he's only attracted to certain people. Personally, I think the combo of his being bi and good-looking gives him great odds of meeting someone. But he says being bi is more of a curse than a blessing."

"Why is that?"

"Because it makes people uncomfortable. No matter what kind of person he meets, he's gotta come out to them at some point. He says there's no good way to do it. And no good time. Though I suppose it's somewhat easier with gay men."

"I see."

"So anyway…if I were you, given how he thinks, I'd go on the theory that he was planning to pick up a man in New York. Gay guys are generally easier than women to pick up on short notice. At least, that would be my guess."

"OK." Chin decided to take another tack. "I understand you work with him as an investigator. Is that right?"

"Right. I'm his assistant. Sometimes. Depends on the case."

"In a situation like this, if he got mixed up somehow with a group of terrorists, what do you think he'd do?"

"He'd do whatever he could to stop them. He's non-violent, a pacifist. He's like the opposite of a terrorist."

"Do you have any idea why he's disappeared?"

"No idea. That's why I'm worried about him."

"OK, well, thank you for your help."

"Listen, Agent Chin, can you keep me in the loop? If you find out where he is or what's going on, will you let me know?"

Chin thought about it. "I promise. If circumstances warrant it, I'll let you know as soon as we find Mr. King. And if you should hear from him…."

"I have a feeling you'll know about that before I do," said Melanie. "You seem to be wired for sound over there at the FBI." She let that hang in silence for a few beats, then said, "Fortunately, I don't have any secrets. But I hate to think my gossip sessions with my girlfriends are being recorded for posterity."

Chin hesitated. She couldn't deny what was obvious. "Any incursions on your privacy will end when this episode is over. I promise you that."

"That's good."

THIRTY-TWO

King and Kareem met for dinner at 8 PM on the Upper West Side at a restaurant Sarah recommended. Although the restaurant was pleasant, King wasn't sure how to get a conversation going. And so they finished their food without saying much more than a few pleasantries.

They ordered coffee after dinner. As King sipped his drink, he decided to try discussing the sermon they'd heard at the prayer service. "How do you feel about what the imam said?" he asked. "What do you think about domestic violence?"

Kareem shrugged. "I do not approve of such violence." He shook his head. "No, of course, it is wrong. If I were married, I would try to be, as we are taught, like the garment. I would provide protection and comfort."

"So you don't think violence is ever justified?"

"A husband should not hurt his wife. There are better ways to handle problems. But some men are harsh by nature."

"Yes, but aren't there times when everyone feels harsh? Even the most holy man sometimes is angry."

"I suppose," said Kareem. "But my mother taught me to count to ten."

"Not everyone can."

"That is true. My brother is angry all the time. My mother did not teach him the same as me. He is more like my father."

"You have a brother?" King was surprised. This was useful information.

"Yes."

"Would he be violent?" King tried to ask it casually, but he immediately felt that he should have come around to the question more gradually.

Kareem held his cup in the air and didn't answer at first. Then he put his cup down with a bang and said, "I would rather not speak about my brother." He sighed.

King nodded. "OK, but you seem to be upset about something."

"I am," Kareem said. He put his hands on the table and looked, suddenly, quite animated. "I am disappointed. I wish my life had turned out differently. There are things I must do that I don't want to do." He turned and looked around the room. "But it is not something I can talk to you about. It is personal."

"I understand," said King. "I too sometimes have to do things that I don't want to do."

"Yes, of course. That is how life is. But I do not think I have been a good dinner companion tonight. I have too much on my mind." He stood and signaled the waiter for the check. "But you must let me pay for dinner," he said.

King stood too, suddenly afraid that Kareem was going to run out and disappear. "You haven't changed your mind, have you? You're still planning to go with me to the Statue tomorrow?"

"Yes, Omar, I plan to go. Where shall I meet you?"

"My sister lives at 99th and West End. Where are you staying?"

The waiter brought the check. Kareem scooped it up and handed it back to the waiter with a hundred-dollar bill. "Please keep the change," he said. The waiter's eyes went wide. It was more than a thirty-dollar tip.

'Thank you," he said and turned and walked away, leaving the two men standing beside their table.

Kareem turned to King. "I am staying near 67th and Riverside."

King nodded. "We have to go all the way down to Battery Park to get the boat to Liberty Island. I could walk down Broadway and meet you at 72nd, then we can take the subway together down to Battery Park."

"Yes, all right. What time shall we meet?"

"We have to check in at the boat dock by 10:15. I think we should meet at 72nd at 9:15. No point in having to rush."

"All right, Omar, I'll meet you tomorrow at the subway stop at Broadway and 72nd Street at 9:15." Kareem was all business now, and it was clear that he was eager to leave. He extended his hand and King shook it.

"OK," said King. "I'll see you then."

Outside the restaurant, which was at 83rd and Columbus, Kareem turned right to head south toward 67th. King went left to head north toward 99th. But after walking half a block, King paused, gazed with great interest at a shop window, and then turned to look back south.

Kareem was walking at a leisurely pace, as if he had no place special to go. At the corner of 82[nd,] he paused in front of a row of newspaper vending machines. He opened the lid of one of them and took out a paper. Holding the paper under his arm, Kareem stepped backward and then looked around in all directions.

King quickly stepped into the alcove that formed the entryway to the shop. He peered back through the glass and saw that Kareem was again walking south on Columbus. Now King stepped out of the alcove, crossed the street, and began to walk south following Kareem. After half a block, Kareem abruptly turned and walked into a shop. As King approached from across the street, he saw that Kareem had gone into a Starbucks and was waiting in line at the counter.

There was a liquor store across the street from the Starbucks.

King went into it. From the front window, he saw Kareem place an order for something. The cashier handed Kareem a cup of something. Was he drinking more coffee? It was already 9:30 PM. Kareem took his drink and sat down at a table.

King pretended to study the wines in the cases near the front window as he watched the shop across the street. Kareem had set his newspaper on the table. He turned through the pages as if he was looking for something. After a while, he began to turn the pages more slowly. Then he stopped turning. He was reading something. He took a sip of his coffee.

Kareem took out his cell phone and called someone. He spoke on the phone for a minute. Then he closed the phone, stood, left both his newspaper and the barely touched coffee sitting on the table, and left the shop.

King wondered if he might be able to get across the street and see what it was that Kareem had been reading before someone cleared the table. But he was worried that if he did that, Kareem might hail a cab and disappear. So he left the liquor store and stayed on the opposite side of the street following Kareem who continued to walk south.

Kareem continued walking straight south on Columbus, from the 80's to the 70's to the 60's. They passed by Lincoln Center where crowds of people were coming out of some event. King had to hustle to stay close enough to keep Kareem in sight. They continued on Columbus past the New York Public Library and still Kareem kept walking south. At 59th Street, Columbus became Ninth Avenue. They were entering the Hell's Kitchen neighborhood.

There was a time when this had been a dangerous area. It had once been the rough and tumble setting that inspired the musical West Side Story. But now the vacant lots and shuttered stores were gone. Gentrification had recast the neighborhood with trendy shops and restaurants. Kareem continued walking on Ninth all the way down to 51st Street, where he turned left.

On West 51st Street, Kareem turned and walked down a few

stairs into a doorway between Eighth and Ninth Avenues. King stopped across the street and stared at the building. The unmarked doorway looked like it housed a bar. King crossed the street and peered into the building from a 45-degree angle. The glass doors were propped open. Inside he saw a booth labeled "Classic Photo Booth." Behind that was a long narrow space that looked like a flattened-out subway tunnel, with the walls rounding up slightly as they turned into the ceiling.

King stepped closer to the door. The room was jammed with people. Kareem seemed to have disappeared into the crowd. On one side of the room, a cushioned, red-leather-upholstered bench ran the length of the wall. Half a dozen small tables were lined up in front of it. On the other side of the room was a long sleek bar. Patrons sat in or stood next to barstools in front of a long chrome-countered bar that was inlaid with a foot wide strip of solid ice that glowed from lighting hidden beneath the bar.

The bouncer at the front door eyed King. "Are you here for party?" he asked.

King nodded and quickly stepped inside as if he was an invited guest. The bouncer let him through, and then repeated his question to another man who had come in behind King. The man behind King said, "The habibi party, yes!"

The room was pulsing with a mixture of loud music and voices. As King's eyes adjusted to the light, he noticed that the room seemed full of Middle Eastern men. He knew the word *'habibi.'* It was an Arabic word that meant 'my beloved.' *'Habibi'* was the male form of the word, the feminine form was *'habibati.'* But King didn't see any women in the room.

At the back of the long room was a wide flight of stairs leading up to a second floor. King couldn't see Kareem anywhere. *He must have gone up the stairs*, he thought.

King stepped up to the bar. If he was going to blend into the party, he figured he'd better have a drink.

"What's good?" he asked the bartender.

"Infused vodkas are our specialty," he said, and handed King a card with a long list of flavors.

King surveyed the list, then picked one at random. He said, "Let me try the one called…" He read the name of the drink he wanted from the card. "….vodka mint with pepper and a splash of raspberry."

While the bartender prepared his drink, King turned to the man standing next to him who wore a t-shirt that said, "Hummus is Yummus." King smiled at the man and said, "My first time at a habibi party."

"My third monthly party," the man said.

King nodded. He was trying to understand the situation. It seemed like a party for a group of Arabic men. But drinking vodka in a bar didn't match with any Islamic practice he knew of.

The bartender set King's drink down on the ice part of the bar. King said to the man next to him. "This glowing ice thing on the bar is amazing."

"Yeah," the man said. "Keeps your drink ice cold.

King nodded.

"You live in the city?" the man asked.

"No," King said. "I'm just here on vacation with a friend." Then he added, "I think my friend went upstairs. What's going on up there?"

"They usually have a show up on the second floor. There's a small stage. Tonight it's probably belly dancers."

King nodded again—as if this made perfect sense. "I see," he said. "Well, that fits. My friend likes belly dancers."

He'd begun to wonder if *Habibi* was an underground organization for Arab men to pick up prostitutes. It was clear that Kareem had not come for baklava.

As King sipped his vodka, he noticed that the man with the hummus t-shirt was staring at him. King felt himself blush. He suddenly realized it was *that* kind of stare. All at once, everything became clear to him. The room was full of gay men.

THIRTY-THREE

King stepped back from the bar and tried to grasp what was going on. King saw a copy of a newspaper sitting on one of the tables on the other side of the room. He stepped over and picked it up. It was the Gay City News. He thumbed through it quickly. Eventually he found a display ad on a page near the back.

Habibi, the New York chapter of the Gay and Lesbian Arab Society, was having its monthly party at Vlada, a gay bar in Hell's Kitchen. This must be the ad that Kareem had been looking for, which led him to West 51st Street.

"Jesus," King thought. He wondered if this party was the object of Kareem's planned attack. If it was, there may only be seconds to do something about it. But then he thought about his plans with Kareem for the next day. Why would he have made those plans if he was going to carry out an attack here?

King knew that conservative Muslims despised gay men as much as conservative Christians did. But he couldn't think of a precedent for making gay men the object of a terrorist attack. He looked around the room at all the Arabic men. He assumed there had to be Muslim men in the room.

He decided he'd better find Kareem quickly. He had to find

out what he was up to. He made his way up the back staircase. As he neared the top, he heard the rhythmic beat of Middle Eastern dance music. On the second floor he found another bar, a lounge area, a dj booth, and a room with a small stage at the far end. On the stage, three female dancers dressed in pink sequined burqas wiggled their bellies with spectacular agility.

The crowd of men was facing the stage, egging the dancers on with catcalls and finger snaps. King scanned them from behind until he saw Kareem standing with his back against a side wall. He stood beneath a black and white photo of a nude male torso. Two men in front of him were holding hands, but his attention was fixed on the stage. He had a faraway look in his eyes.

On stage, the three dancers in unison flipped off their burqas, revealing—in case anyone wasn't sure—that they were all men. The muscular bare-chested men wore armbands and billowy pantaloons. The crowd cheered. Kareem now looked riveted. The men's dancing grew more frantic and the crowd began to clap. Once again, the three dancers choreographed a move in unison. This time they each pulled a string and the pantaloons fell as a group to the floor, which elicited a roar of approval from the audience. Now the men wore only skimpy thongs, which left little to the imagination. Instantly the stage lights dimmed and a spotlight shone on the men's thong-clad torsos. In one beat, the three men whirled around and the spotlight shown on their bare butts, which they wiggled with the same fevered agility they'd demonstrated with their bellies. Another roar of approval rose from the audience. An enigmatic smile appeared on Kareem's face.

King didn't know what to do. If Kareem spotted him, it would be obvious that King had followed him. How else could he explain being there? But if it was true that Kareem was gay—and at this point King could not think of any other explanation for what he saw before his eyes—then maybe there was an opening for King to further his goal of dissuading Kareem from another attack. There must be an area of empathy he could make use of.

But how could he win Kareem's trust if Kareem knew he'd been followed? King backed out of the room. He sipped the last of his drink and went back down the stairs to the main bar. He had to think about what to do.

As soon as he got back to the main floor, he set his empty vodka glass on the bar counter. As he did so, the man with the hummus t-shirt came up to him. "Did you find your friend?"

"Yes," King said. "He's watching the show. You were right. Belly dancers. All men."

"So is your friend also your boyfriend?"

"No." King shook his head. "He's just someone I met recently."

"Is he as good-looking as you are?"

King blushed, and stammered, "No. I don't know. I mean, yes —he's good-looking. But we're just friends."

"Sounds like maybe you want it to be something more?"

"Well…yes, I want something from him. But he doesn't know I'm here." King wasn't sure why he was telling this to a stranger, but he needed time to think of what to do. "You see, I followed him here without his knowing it."

"Wow," the man said. "You're stalking him? As sexy as you are, he must be really hot."

"No, it's not like that."

"What's it like then?"

"Well, my friend doesn't know…doesn't know I'm gay."

The man nodded. "Well this seems like as good a place as any to let him know."

"Yes, but I'm embarrassed for having followed him. I'm afraid it'll make him angry. I wonder," King began. He was straining to come up with a plan. "Would you be willing to help me?"

"Help you what? Tell him you're gay?"

"Yes, in a roundabout way. You see, I was thinking that if he came down here and found me with you, and if you and I were —I don't know—doing something intimate, then my friend would know I'm gay, but he wouldn't think I'd followed him here." King looked at the man plaintively. "Does that make sense?"

"So what? You want your friend to think he just happened to bump into you, and caught you at a gay party?"

"Something like that."

"What do you have in mind by us doing something intimate?"

King blushed again. "I don't know, I guess maybe you could put your arm around me in an intimate way."

The man looked at King skeptically. "Are you sure you have a friend upstairs? Or is this some kind of wild pickup technique you have?"

"No, I really do have a friend upstairs."

"What's his name?"

"His name? His name is Kareem. My name is Omar. I'm visiting the city."

The man nodded. "Omar, I'm Ali. I live in Astoria."

"I'm visiting from … " King was struggling to remember his cover story. "… Rhinebeck," King said.

"Omar, I really think you should just go tell your friend Kareem the truth. Tell him you're gay. He's gay. You're gay. Everyone here is gay. It's all good. You don't need me to do anything."

"No, I do. I can't explain why." King looked anxiously back at the stairs from the second floor. The show must have finished, because a surge of men were coming back down the stairs. "He would hate it if he thought I'd followed him here."

Ali shook his head. But just then King saw Kareem coming down the stairs and King quickly turned around.

"He's coming," King said.

Ali looked at the men coming down the stairs. "Which one?"

"He's wearing a white shirt. It's pressed. Black pants. Also pressed. He's fastidious."

"Oh, all right," said Ali and he put his arms around King's head and drew him into a kiss.

King's eyes went wide. Ali was kissing him hard on the lips. And he wasn't even sure that Kareem would notice him in this situation. He had his back to the stairs so he couldn't see Kareem. But Ali was watching the men behind King while they kissed. And when the man in the pressed white shirt and pressed black pants got just behind them, Ali released King from the kiss and said, "Wow, Omar. That was hot."

King almost bumped into Kareem. And as he did so, Kareem's eyes went wide. "Omar?" There was no avoiding the confrontation.

King did not have to pretend to be embarrassed. He turned red with the awkwardness of the moment. "Kareem?" He spoke as if he was taken aback completely. He looked around wildly. "I was just...." Ali stepped forward, his arm still around King's shoulder. "I wasn't expecting to see you until tomorrow," King said. He tried to recover his composure. "This is Ali," he said to Kareem. "From Astoria." He turned to Ali. "This is Kareem."

Ali and Kareem shook hands clumsily. Ali said. "Hi, Kareem. Omar was telling me about you."

Kareem said, "He was?"

"Yes, I think he has a crush on you."

Now it was Kareem's turn to flush red. "He does?"

King stammered. "I...well...I didn't think it was possible," he said, "that such feelings would be acceptable. I mean, I didn't think that you would be here also. I didn't know that you...." He couldn't finish the sentence.

"Well," said Ali, "now that you two have that straightened out, or should I say, now that you've both got it un-straightened out, I think I'll leave you two alone." And he left.

Kareem looked down. "It is very strange to find you here, Omar, at this party."

"Yes," said King. "I ... I don't know what to think." He gave Kareem a sidelong look. "You didn't follow me here, did you?"

"No." Kareem shook his head. "No, I did not. I swear it."

King nodded. "Well, I guess it is quite a strange coincidence."

He paused. "I am embarrassed that you should see me doing something so ... so haraam."

"Do not worry about it." Kareem waved his hand. "Who was that man you were with?"

"Ali? I don't know him very well. I just met him."

"But you talked to him about me?"

"Well I was making small talk. I told him I'd just met you—and I must have mentioned your name."

"Why did he say that he thought you had some kind of feelings for me?"

"I don't know. I guess he thought ... you know ... given where we are ... that I was like that. And so, for some reason, he must have thought that." King was flustered. He tried to think of an explanation. "But then Ali kissed me. I think he was just trying to hit me up."

"You don't need to be embarrassed, Omar. I understand. You and I are alike in this way."

"We are?"

"Yes. But I am sorry that I cannot return your feelings, Omar —if you have such feelings. I have a very special friend back in Iraq. Although you are a handsome man, I am faithful to Muhammad."

"You mean you have a lover?"

Kareem nodded.

"So you are ..." King waved his wrist.

Kareem nodded again. "Yes, but I did not come here to betray Muhammad. I was not expecting to meet anyone here tonight. I just came here to be with men who are like me. I don't know anyone here in New York who is gay."

"Yes, I am ... well ... I am actually bisexual," King said. "And sometimes I come to these parties." King looked around the room again. "It isn't anything I would do if I was married."

Kareem nodded.

"So do your sister and brother know about your situation? I mean about you and Muhammad?"

"My brother knows," Kareem said. "But my sister does not."

"How does he feel about it?"

"I would rather not talk about my brother," said Kareem. "Abdul and I do not see eye to eye on most things. He is not a good man."

King had heard Kareem and Jasmeen talk about Abdul. Now he understood that Abdul was his brother. "I'm sorry," said King. "Your friend Muhammad is in Iraq?"

"Yes. He is in Sadr City."

"I am glad you have a friend. It is not easy to meet gay Muslim men."

Kareem brightened. "But this must be the hand of Allah; that you and I should meet here in this way. I am sure of it. I do not think there is any such thing as coincidence."

"You don't think so?"

"No, I don't. I felt there may be some bond between you and I —even when we met." He paused, choosing his words. "It was as if I'd met you before."

"Yes. I felt something too," said King. "As if we'd known each other from somewhere in the past."

Kareem reached out and took King's hand. This time he held it rather tenderly. "It is good for me to have a friend on this night —a friend who will not judge me."

"I won't judge you, Kareem. I don't judge you," said King. "You're right. It is good that we met here. It makes me realize how small the world is." He squeezed Kareem's hand and let it go.

"Yes. It is a small world."

Now they both stood awkwardly. King considered if he should offer to buy Kareem a drink. But he wasn't sure that Kareem drank, since to do so was haraam. He was trying to process the information about Muhammad. And Kareem's brother. But he said, "I hope you will still plan to join me tomorrow."

"Yes," said Kareem. "In fact, I think I should go home now,

and go to bed. I want to be alert tomorrow." He looked around the room one more time. "And I should leave you to your party. Perhaps your friend Ali is still here."

King shrugged. "I do not care about Ali."

"But you should find a friend too," said Kareem. "Perhaps Ali is Muslim."

King nodded. He could see that Kareem was determined to leave. He didn't think he would be able to find out anything more from him at this point. He said, "Well, I will ask him."

"I'll meet you at 72nd Street tomorrow morning," said Kareem. As he left, he reached up and kissed King gently on the cheek. "Good luck."

King remained standing at the bar and watched Kareem leave. Then he ordered another drink. He needed it.

THIRTY-FOUR

King stayed up late. He wanted to talk to his friend Lieutenant Colin Zeller in Iraq. At midnight in New York, it was 7:00 A.M. in Baghdad, just about the time Colin would be on his second cup of coffee.

King had served with Zeller in Afghanistan. He was a seasoned intelligence officer. About a year before the Iraq war wound down, the brass reassigned him to Baghdad. Zeller had spent many years in the thick of the action in Afghanistan, long enough to be exhausted by the violence. He claimed he was getting preferential treatment going back to Iraq, since casualties in Iraq were down. But in truth, he was one of the best at what he did. His new job was to build a network that would keep intelligence flowing about all the activities beneath the surface in postwar Iraq. He had spent more than a year building his network. King was confident that by now Zeller would have a substantial set of connections.

Colin had been a good friend during King's "Don't ask, Don't Tell" investigation. He was straight, but he'd been the kind of friend that King could trust. When Colin stumbled onto facts that revealed King's standing in the center of the Kinsey scale, he stayed firmly in the "Don't Tell" camp. But being a good intelligence officer, he'd also used the knowledge to build up a new branch on his information chain. King hoped that Colin had built up a similar chain in Iraq, one that would allow him to find out information about Baghdad's gay scene.

When the call came, Zeller didn't recognize the name on the caller ID, but he answered the call from New York anyway. "Zeller."

"Hey buddy, it's Cappuccino." He used his nickname because he knew Colin's personal phone might be monitored. Only a few close friends knew him by that name.

"ID says, Sarah Gaber, Cap."

"Let's just say I'm focusing on the lower-numbered side of the Kinsey scale at the moment, and her name is Sarah."

"Well, hello to you, too, buddy. What the hell kind of a mess have you got yourself into? You know we get the news here too."

"Oh, you mean about my honeymoon trip at the waterfall? I'd rather not go into that." He hoped that this reference would be enough to prod Zeller to avoid revealing anything more about who he was.

"Yeah, well I gather you had a real bang-up honeymoon. So her name is Sarah, huh?"

"Yeah, Sarah. She's amazing. But the real reason I'm calling is to see if you can dig up some intel for me on someone who is gay."

"You do know they repealed that law, right?"

"Yeah, yeah. Don't worry. It's nothing like that. I'm looking for info about a civilian."

"A civilian he or a civilian she?"

"An Iraqi named Muhammad. He's got a boyfriend named Kareem who is currently here in New York. But I need you to see if you can find out something about Muhammad asap. Any info you can find out might help me keep from blowing the second part of my honeymoon—if you know what I mean."

"How close are you to blowing it?"

"I've got an outing with Kareem tomorrow morning. Any news you can dig up on his buddy before then may help me keep Kareem from doing something ugly."

"OK. I get it. It's that important?"

"Yeah, it's like 'give me liberty or give me death' important."

"OK, Patrick Henry. I'll see what I can do. Have you got anything else to go on—just Muhammad and Kareem?"

"Are you typing this down?" King knew that Colin's memory was not as good as his own.

"I will. Hold on." There was a pause. "OK, junior, shoot."

"I don't have any last names. But Kareem has a sister named Jasmeen and a brother named Abdul. I'd guess they're all in their twenties. They have a father named Omar. The family is Persian, came over from Iran. The boyfriend Muhammad is in Sadr City."

"Out in the burbs, eh?"

"Yeah, so you'll want to tap the local underground hummus queen circuit…you do have connections there, don't you?"

King could hear the smile in Zeller's voice. "I may have."

"Good, then see if anyone has been scooped up by the Mujahedeen for being nancy. I have a feeling they're using Muhammad to pull the strings on my boy Kareem to get him to do something hazardous over here."

"What makes you think Kareem needs his strings pulled? There's no shortage of eager beaver jihadists, you know."

"It's just a hunch. But you know how it is with me, Colin. I put a lot of faith in intuition. I've spent time with Kareem. He doesn't fit the profile."

"What? You mean because he's gay?"

"Actually, that does have something to do with it. But it's not just that. It's everything about his manner, his energy."

"His energy, huh? So you've gone clairvoyant?"

"Yeah. I took a reading on him with my psychic wand."

"I miss you, Cap. Since you left I don't talk to people with your colorful view of reality."

"OK, you want logic?"

"It wouldn't hurt, especially since I'm going to have to go out on a limb based on this hunch of yours."

"OK here goes. My boy Kareem is gay. But he's stuck in a fundamentalist Muslim family. He grows up and falls in love with his friend, Muhammad. As you know, where they live, there isn't much privacy. Kareem's big brother Abdul's a mujahedeen, a true believer. Given the lack of privacy over there, what are the odds big brother catches Kareem and Muhammad doing the nasty? And that's like a real horror for the true believer. It would be a stoning offence if Abdul turned him in. But Abdul sees an angle. He sees a way to gain control of his kid brother. The kid can redeem himself by carrying out Abdul's plan for international glory. Except when the time comes, the kid blows it. So Abdul ups the ante. As far as Abdul is concerned, the boyfriend is *shath*—abnormal. It's disgusting. Abdul doesn't hesitate to have him kidnapped."

"And in the next outing, your boy is really motivated."

"Something like that. Tonight at dinner Kareem said, quote, there are things I must do that I don't want to do, end quote."

"I suppose it's plausible."

"I'm just asking you to look into it, Colin. Put your ear to the ground and see if you can find out what's happening with the boyfriend."

"OK. So, do you just want me to find out about this guy Muhammad, or do I need to do something about him?"

"If you find out he's been kidnapped by the long beards, you better get him out of there. Get him to safety. We need to cut the string that's pulling Kareem. The sooner the better."

"By when?"

"By noon tomorrow. New York time."

"Geez. You couldn't call me sooner?"

"I've been busy."

"I noticed. Listen, if it turns out I need to pull this guy out of the weeds, you know I can't make that happen on my own. I'm going to need approval from higher up."

"Can't you improvise?"

"Those days are gone, cowboy. In case you haven't noticed, the war is over, over here. Besides, I couldn't improvise with the Mujahedin even if it was the old days. They don't play nice."

"OK. I understand."

"So is anyone working with you on this or are you on your lonesome saddle again?"

"I haven't called in reinforcements yet."

"What're you waiting for?"

"I don't want my wings clipped. I'm so close."

"You sound like my old girlfriend."

"OK, look Colin, if they've got Muhammad tied up, you better call the cavalry. Tell them what's going on. Get the approval. It's a very high-risk situation. Given what's happened already, they'll understand."

"High risk, huh? Where are you and this Kareem going on your outing?"

"How secure is this line?"

"Well, it's still early here. The switchboard guys haven't arrived at the office yet. I don't think my phone is on their list. But if it is, this call will be at the end of their overnight tape. They won't be getting to that until later tonight, if they bother at all. Things have been pretty quiet around here lately. And given where I am, I doubt I'm on anyone's short list in connection with you."

"OK, Colin, Here's the deal. I got a couple of tickets for the Statue of Liberty—the crown. Kareem is my date."

"Sounds like a fun date."

"That's what Sarah said."

"You couldn't just take him to Jersey? I got an uncle there that could take care of him."

"Kareem is not the problem, Colin. I mean he's only part of it. If it was that easy, I'd take care of him myself. But I want to find out about everyone involved. I don't know all the other players yet. Unless you hear from me, you have to give me until 11:30

tomorrow my time before you call anyone. If I get the whole picture sooner than that, I'll call you right away and you can sound the alarm."

"I don't know, Cap. Sounds like you're taking a big risk on your own."

"I am. But what can I do? You know how it is. The government red tape will just get in the way. This guy trusts me at this point. I can get him to talk to me. Besides, the security at Liberty Island has got to be totally tight. I'm sure he's not gonna be able to do anything there on his own. He'd have to have other people working with him. Just getting him out of the way won't stop them from acting." King paused.

"OK. I'm listening."

"Colin, if the fed pulls me in to chat about everything, I won't be able to snag the critical intel. And you know the moment you call them, they'll have to pull me in."

Colin was silent for a moment. "OK. I'll try it your way. But you know this will come down on me like a ton of bricks if it goes bad."

"I know."

"Which cavalry do you suggest I get in touch with when the time comes?"

"I don't know. Check the paper. Find out who's been babysitting my honeymoon adventure. I'm sure any branch of our government will be happy to connect you to the proper authority. Just be sure you call me before you call them."

"OK."

"And Colin, I'd rather you don't say anything to them about Sarah. She just stumbled into this thing."

"Same old story for you, Cap. You're always getting innocent women in trouble."

"Yeah, well it's just my luck. Speaking of that, have you heard anything from Reema lately?"

"No. Sorry. But I guess no news is good news, right?"

"I hope so."

"How am I supposed to reach you, Captain America? On this phone?"

"Yes. It's Sarah's phone. Call her. Either I'll answer or she will. You can tell her to get a message to me if I'm not around."

"So it's Sarah, huh? Sounds kind of serious. Does that mean you've finally seen the light of heterosexual sex?"

"Come on, Colin. I've always seen the light. You know that. It's just that I see the light in everyone … even you."

"Me?"

"Yeah—too bad you're so narrow-minded in your focus. You're kind of sexy, Colin."

"You and I? That would be a mistake. You and I wouldn't last two days. Too much testosterone."

"You see, you just don't get it, Zeller. Sometimes a big helping of testosterone is what's wanted."

"Yeah, well I'll stick with the yin yang."

"Your yin getting any yang lately?"

"None of your business."

"OK, just checking. Call me when you have something."

"Roger that. And good luck, Cap. Don't wait too long to phone. I know I don't need to tell you, but I'll say it anyway. It would be better for you to miss getting some of the bad guys than to let something bad happen in New York."

"Believe me, I know it."

THIRTY-FIVE

King awoke early the next morning on the sofa in the Gaber's living room. After his conversation with Colin Zeller, he'd stayed up talking to Sarah about what he'd learned about Kareem, his brother Abdul, and his lover Muhammad. He'd told her about his encounter with Kareem at the gay bar. But he'd decided not to tell her everything. He didn't tell her about his own bisexuality.

There was no question in his mind that he'd tell her about himself eventually. He'd definitely tell her before anything sexual happened between them. The trouble was he couldn't be certain how she'd react. It was such a wild card. He knew enough about her to expect her to accept it in an enlightened way. But what if she didn't? Normally that possibility wouldn't cause him to hesitate. He'd tell her and let the chips fall where they may. But under the circumstances, given what was at stake with Kareem and Jasmeen, he thought it was better to defer the big conversation for a less complicated moment. Once they could put the threat of international terrorism behind them, they'd have a more normal situation in which to assess their relationship and their feelings about each other.

They'd planned to get up early so that Sarah could go down

and stand watch at 67th and Riverside Boulevard, where Kareem said he was staying. King would meet Kareem at the Broadway subway stop at 72nd Street. But he wanted Sarah to keep an eye out for Jasmeen, Abdul, or anyone else Kareem might be staying with. King assumed they all had to be involved in any plan for the Statue. There was no way Kareem could act alone given the security at the monument.

He hoped that if Sarah could track the movement of Jasmeen and Abdul, while King stayed with Kareem, they might be able to identify all the members of the operation and inform the FBI before anyone got too far along with their plan—and before anyone got away.

The first rays of morning light cut through a crack in the heavy drapes and shone on King's toes. Since the plush sofa was too short for the length of his body, he had to unfold himself before getting off it. He stood and stretched the kinks out of his joints. He could hear the shower running in the bathroom down the hall. He knew it was Sarah in the shower, since her father had a private bathroom off the master bedroom. He was wearing only the boxer shorts Sarah had bought for him. He wondered if she'd come out of the bathroom wearing just a towel, or if she'd brought her clothes in with her so she could get dressed.

He wasn't sure why he was feeling frisky. He knew it was going to be a difficult day. He needed to focus on getting ready. But he reminded himself that if things went well, he'd be in a much better position to spend a leisurely day with Sarah tomorrow.

When Sarah came out she was wearing just a towel—a big mint green bath towel. King smiled, stretched out his arms and yawned. He knew he was being flirtatious, but he didn't care. Sarah eyed him and said, "You're up."

"Nice towel," King said.

Sarah came into the room, picked up the blanket from the couch, and began to fold it. "Wait here a minute. I'll go get you some more clean underwear," she said. "My dad has a whole room dedicated to clothes." Then she left.

King sat with his arms spread across the back of the sofa and his legs stretched out on the floor. He conjured up a picture of himself repeating this same pose the next day when there wouldn't be any terrorist plots to distract him. Then he pulled in his legs and leaned his elbows onto his knees in a more modest pose.

Sarah came back in with a pile of clothes. She picked up the underwear from the top of the pile and dangled it. "No boxers, just these turquoise briefs. And they're kind of skimpy at that. Can you believe my father?" She tossed the clothes to King who caught them.

"Thanks. Any messages yet?"

"You mean from your friend Zeller? No. Just a message from my mother telling me to be careful because there are quote crazy people in New York City close quote."

"I think she's right."

"I'm going to go get dressed, then I'll make us some breakfast."

"What about your father? Is he here?"

"He's already gone to work."

"On Saturday?"

"Yeah. He works six days a week. I don't think he has much of a life, apart from his underwear."

After they got dressed, they went in the kitchen where Sarah fried eggs while King prepared toast.

Sarah plugged in the coffeemaker. "You said you prefer tea instead of coffee, right?"

"Normally, yes." King dropped two slices of bread into the toaster. "But I could use the caffeine. So coffee's fine."

Sarah stuck a carafe under the machine's spout and watched while it worked its way through the brewing cycle. After a moment, she asked, "What makes you so sure Jasmeen and her brother are going to have anything to do with this thing today?"

"I'm not sure." King pulled the hot toast out of the toaster and set it on a plate. "It could be that Kareem is only doing reconnaissance today. Maybe they're going to do the real operation on a later date."

"Let's hope so."

"But there is a chance they'll try something today. And if they do, I think it's going to have to involve his brother and sister as supporting players." He paused while he worked butter onto his toast. "I got an email from the national park service when I bought my tickets. You can't bring anything with you up into the monument except a camera and prescription drugs. Everything else, you have to check at the base—bags, purses, everything. They have lockers. There's no way Kareem can take a bomb up there."

"What about a camera? Is there such a thing as a camera bomb?"

"I seriously doubt it. If there was, it couldn't be very powerful, and anyway, I'm sure they have equipment to detect that kind of thing. We still have to go through all the security checks."

"So then how would Jasmeen and Abdul be able to do something? Unless they have tickets for today, too."

"I don't know. But that's why you need to watch them and see what they're up to."

"What if Abdul comes out of the building by himself? I won't have any way of recognizing him."

"I know; it's a long shot."

"And if Jasmeen comes out, how am I supposed to keep her from recognizing me?"

"Wear sunglasses and a big floppy hat."

"Oh, right."

"I'm serious."

"I don't have a big floppy hat."

"Do you have a friend you can call? It might be better if you were with somebody anyway. You'd be less noticeable if you were with a friend."

"I don't have any friends here."

"No girlfriends, no boyfriends?"

"No any friends."

"What about your father?"

"I told you, he's at work."

"No, I mean maybe he has a hat you can wear. Like a baseball cap or something."

"I don't know. Maybe." She set plates of eggs and coffee cups on the kitchen table. "I'll look around after we eat."

After breakfast, Sarah went back into her father's dressing room. A few minutes later, she emerged wearing a black t-shirt and a Yankee's baseball cap.

"Yankees!" King said. "I forgot to tell you. I have two tickets for the Yankee's game tomorrow. We can go."

"Again with the two tickets."

"Yes, I have two. So do you want to go or no?"

"You should ask my father. He's the Yankee fan."

"I don't want to go with your father, Sarah. Come on."

"We'll see. We have to get through today first. For all I know we might be in Guantanamo Bay by tomorrow."

"Don't you like baseball at all?"

"I don't know. Canadians are mostly into hockey."

"You like hockey?" King was surprised.

"I didn't say that." Sarah shrugged. "Actually, the one sport I like is lacrosse."

"Lacrosse? That's like hockey without the ice, isn't it?"

"Sort of."

"How come you like that?"

"I played it in high school, OK?"

"Well look, even if you're not all that into baseball, going to a game is fun."

"Can we just focus on today for a minute? I'm too nervous to chit chat about sports."

"All right." King stood up. "Let's focus on today. If you see

Abdul and Jasmeen, all you have to do is keep your distance, and you should be fine."

"So you say. But you want me to follow them if they go somewhere."

"Right. Did you ask your father to borrow his phone?"

"Yes. I have it here in my bag." She took her handbag off the counter and set it on the table. She pulled two phones out of it and handed one of them to King. "Here. You can use my phone."

"Good, then you call me as soon as you see where they're going."

"What about the FBI?"

"I'm gonna have Colin take care of contacting them. There's no reason for you to get involved with them." King handed her his sunglasses. "Here, put these on."

Sarah put on the glasses, took a hand mirror out of her bag, looked at herself and made a face. She took the glasses off. "I don't like these. Besides, you need to wear them. You're still a wanted man." She handed the glasses back to King. "I'll go borrow a pair of glasses from my Dad."

When they were ready, they stood by the door.

"There is something I want to ask you before we leave," said Sarah.

"OK. Go ahead. Ask."

"If you saw that someone had to take Kareem down today, would you do it?"

"Of course."

"So you haven't gone all soft on him just because they might be putting the screws on him with his lover?"

"I'm not sure what you mean by soft. I've studied Aikido so I can defend others and myself without hurting anyone. But it isn't soft—and it has nothing to do with someone's guilt or innocence. Even if he were a purely evil person and not being blackmailed, I'd still try not to hurt him."

"So it's like a Hippocratic oath with you?"

"If you mean 'do no harm,' yes." King stared at Sarah.

"Frankly, it bothers me when people think non-violence is soft. There's nothing inherently brave about violence. But it always takes courage to stand up to violence with non-violence."

"OK. OK. I only want to be sure you're not going to get hurt. That's all. I'm not trying to step on your principles."

"So the same goes for you."

"The same what?"

"I mean, I want to be sure you don't get hurt either. Don't take any chances. Call me as soon as you see who's with them and what they're up to. But don't get too close."

"Yeah. OK. What do I do if they get in a cab?"

"Hail another cab and follow them. If you can't, just get the number of the cab they're in and write it down. Do you have something to write with?"

She nodded. "In my purse."

"If that's what happens, and you get their cab number, call me and I'll call Colin and he can tell the FBI."

"Seems kind of complicated."

"I'd call the FBI myself, but I'll be using your phone and I don't want them to get your phone number. You made it clear you don't want to end up in Cuba, remember?"

"All right. All right. I guess I'm just a little nervous about today."

"Being nervous is totally appropriate." He looked at her wistfully. "I'm truly sorry to have dragged you into all this, Sarah— even though I'm glad we met. I wish it was you and me going to see the Statue today. I wish it had just been the two of us going to see the Broadway show."

"Yeah, me too."

"And I wish you liked baseball instead of lacrosse." He smiled.

"OK." She rolled her eyes. "If it will make you happy, I'll go see the damn Yankees with you. But I want something from you in return."

"Sure. What?"

"When we get back tonight. I want to lie on the couch, and I want you to give me a foot rub."

"A foot rub? Really?"

"Yes, I plan on doing a lot of walking today."

"I see."

"And..." She looked at his arms. "You look like you have a strong grip."

He smiled. "I do. Very strong."

"And I want you to play some music. And, I want a glass of white wine, and—uh, let's see. Oh yes, you should be shirtless, and light a fire in the fireplace before you begin."

"Wow. This favor is getting more and more interesting. What are you wearing during all this?"

"Just something comfortable. Something made out of silk, I think"

"Hmmm. Maybe we should forget about the terrorists. Let's just skip right to the foot rub."

"Easy, soldier. We have a job to do. The nation is counting on you. I just wanted to be sure you have a good reason not to do anything foolish. So do we have a deal?"

"It's a deal."

"Good, then I'm ready to go out and fight for the home team." She turned the brim of her Yankees cap to the back and raised her arms in a cheer.

King picked up a pair of sunglasses from the table, opened them, and gently placed them on her head. Her arms remained in the air as he did this. Then she lowered them behind his back, encircling his body. But before her arms were completely around him, his hands darted behind her and pulled her toward him. He kissed her, gently at first, then with a desire that he couldn't hold back. And, for a few happy moments, they forgot about the task that lay before them.

THIRTY-SIX

Kareem watched as Abdul and Jasmeen methodically divided the rocket launcher components into their respective backpacks. When then had everything packed, the backpacks were bulging at the seams. Jasmeen strapped her pack onto her back, then walked up and down the room to model it.

Kareem looked at her warily. "Is it very heavy? Can you carry it?"

"Of course I can carry it," she said with a bit of annoyance. "But how does it look?"

Kareem assessed her profile. He lightly touched the top of the backpack. "I think you should put a small umbrella in here at the top," he said. "Use one of the small collapsible umbrellas. They're very light. Then you can let the handle of it stick out of the top flap. People will see the umbrella handle, but they won't know how long the umbrella is. If they think there are more things like umbrellas inside the pack, they will be less suspicious."

Abdul frowned at this suggestion, but then, after a moment, he seemed to change his mind. He went to the closet to get their collapsible umbrellas. When he returned he said to Kareem, "You must leave now. If you miss the rendezvous with your friend who has the tickets, our covenant will be broken. You must honor Muhammad."

"What is this covenant that honors the prophet?" Jasmeen asked.

Abdul glared at her. "I've told you," he said. "It is nothing to do you with you. It is a matter that concerns only men."

Jasmeen turned to look at Kareem, as if he might answer her. But he merely smiled at her, and asked, "When will you leave?" He felt his emotions begin to rise. This would be their final goodbye.

"We should leave at 10 o'clock. We can walk along the riverfront. We need to arrive at the boat dock on 42nd Street at 11 o'clock," said Jasmeen. "That is when the tour boat starts boarding. Before they board the boat, the operators march all the passengers through a parking lot where they have a camera and a back drop set up. They take a photograph of each party. Then later they attempt to sell you a copy of this photograph, for a very high price, of course."

"But that is not good," said Kareem. "You don't want the boat company to have your picture, do you? They may be able to use it to identify you later."

"Don't worry. We'll tell them we do not wish to have our picture taken. Then we will walk by the camera without stopping," said Jasmeen. "Not everyone wants to have their picture taken. It will not make them suspicious."

"You must leave now, Kareem," Abdul repeated.

Kareem glared at his brother. He did not regret saying goodbye to him. But when he turned toward Jasmeen, he had to lower his eyes. He could not look at her directly. He did not want to allow tears to form. He went to her and hugged her. He could hear that she was crying. He squeezed his fists as he hugged her, then he turned and went out the door.

Abdul looked at Jasmeen and said, "It is for the best." Then he walked over to the washroom, entered, and closed the door.

Jasmeen sat on the couch and tried to guess what the terms of the covenant between Abdul, Kareem and the Prophet Muhammad might be. "Something that concerns only men," she murmured aloud. Then she bowed her head and prayed that Kareem would enter Paradise. "I will join you soon," she whispered.

Sarah leaned against a fence that surrounded a dog park just across the street from the luxury high-rise buildings near Riverside and 67th Street. She stood on the park side of Riverside so that she could watch the entrances to the buildings across the street. She wasn't sure which of the several buildings near the intersection to watch, so she systematically turned her gaze from one to the next. Then she started over again with the first one in the series. Her neck began to hurt.

Their plan had been for her to arrive early enough to spot Kareem leaving for his rendezvous with King at 9:15. It was already 8:45. She was worried that he might have left early. But five minutes later, she saw him. Kareem walked out of the Trump building directly across the street. He wore clothes similar to those he'd worn on the train: dark pants, with a pressed, pale green dress shirt. He carried a camera in a strap around his neck. Looking straight ahead, lost in thought, he kept up a steady gait. He walked to 67th Street and turned east. He hadn't notice her. She hadn't thought he would. But she knew it wouldn't be so easy with Jasmeen.

King stood at the 72nd Street subway entrance watching for Kareem but thinking about Sarah. Her plans for a foot rub in front of a fire with a glass of wine clearly meant she was ready for a new level of intimacy with him. He'd have to tell her everything about himself tonight. He was suddenly overwhelmed by the twists and turns his vacation had taken. As frustrating as it was to find himself caught up in Kareem's brother's holy war, he didn't regret the circumstances that allowed him to get to know Sarah. He felt fully alive. His senses were in a heightened state. The mixture of adventure and romance had so focused him in each moment, that, now that he had a moment for introspection, he realized he had spent a rather long time out of his usual introspective state. But as he stood quietly watching the bustling New Yorkers flow into and out of the subway, he knew that he was again in a reflective moment. He was once more an observer, witnessing and assessing the life around him from an outside vantage point with a detachment that allowed him to feel a part of but protected from reality. He watched the scene unfold before him the way a reader might read a novel. He knew he was a player in the plot. Yet he could also see himself from a higher vantage point, as if he was watching himself in this story without being at any personal risk.

When he saw Kareem walking toward him with a camera around his neck, dressed like a tourist, but wearing a solemn expression, he marveled at the mystery of the world. How could a gentle gay Muslim be blackmailed into becoming a terrorist? Kareem's love for Muhammad must be strong. But to be unable to generalize that love, to not see the rest of the world transformed by the overflow of his personal affection, was a mystery to King. He felt his own capacity for love enlarged by Sarah. And as happened whenever he felt himself falling in love, he was in love with all the world.

So when Kareem joined him and they sat together in the subway bound for the Battery, he was aware of the contradictions of the man beside him, who seemed sincerely religious, and yet, must be oblivious to the souls of those whom he was willing to murder. Last night he'd allowed himself to feel sympathy for Kareem, knowing what it was like to be a persecuted sexual minority. But now as he weighed the moral choices that Kareem appeared to face, he could feel no patience for a man whose love for another, no matter how deep, drove him to evil. If there were seeds of goodness in Kareem, King would have to find them quickly. He sensed from the emotional pall that hung over Kareem, that today's outing would not be a scouting mission.

"You seem lost in thought today," he said to Kareem, as the train rumbled down toward Lincoln Center.

Kareem nodded. "Yes, but so are you, Omar."

"Yes, it's true," said King. "I've been thinking about our meeting last night. You said that you and your brother do not see eye to eye."

"We don't."

"And you said you do not think your brother is a good man."

"He is not."

"So how does a good man deal with a man who is not good?" King asked.

Kareem was perplexed. "What do you mean?" Kareem slid slightly on his bench to make room for a woman with several shopping bags.

"I was just wondering," King whispered, "if you have given your brother too much power."

"I would rather not talk about Abdul," Kareem said. "He and I are bound as brothers, but I do not share his feelings."

"Then why do you let yourself be bound to him?"

"It is not my choice," said Kareem. "He has bound himself to me." Kareem frowned. "Let us talk about something else." Kareem looked around. The woman with the shopping bags had stood up and made her way to the door. They were again alone on the bench. "Were you able to make friends with Ali last night?"

"No, I wasn't really drawn to him in that way."

Kareem nodded. His eyes were narrow and focused on King's eyes. "Have you never been in love, Omar?"

"Yes, once."

"What happened?"

"I was in love with a woman, but she fell in love with someone else."

Kareem's eyes went wide. "With a woman?"

"Yes."

"Then you are not gay?" Kareem suddenly looked mortified.

"No, I'm both. I'm both straight and gay. Many people have a hard time understanding it. But it feels natural to me. For me they aren't mutually exclusive."

Kareem was skeptical. "Is this really true?"

"Sometimes I'm tempted to hide it," said King. "But I'm being honest with you about it, Kareem. I think it should be easier for a gay man to understand what it's like to be different from others."

"You are right. I'm sorry." Kareem closed his eyes for a moment. "But if you have a choice, why would you choose to be gay?"

"I can't choose who I'm attracted to. Certainly you must understand that."

"But you could ignore those feelings that make you different."

"No. I can't. I can't control it one way or another any more than you can, or any more than anyone can for that matter. Love and desire are powerful forces."

"So you were in love?"

"Yes."

"With a woman." Kareem's tone was still skeptical.

"Yes, we were married."

"Married!"

"Yes. It happens."

"But then your wife fell in love with another man?"

"No. With another woman."

Kareem threw up his hands. "I have not heard of this happening before."

"It kind of surprised me too. But it happens."

"You must be very angry with her for this betrayal."

"I was sad and hurt, at first. But it was a long time ago. I've put it behind me." King was flustered. He had intended to draw Kareem out in order to find out something about his relationship with Muhammad. But instead, he'd been the one to reveal intimate facts about himself. But perhaps he could use this to advantage. He knew that to gain trust, one had first to offer it. "What about you, Kareem? You said you are faithful to your friend in Sadr City."

"Yes, I am. I would never betray him."

"But why do you travel so far away from him?"

"It is not something I have chosen. I have a mission to fulfill."

"A mission?"

"I have to do something that will help keep him safe."

"Is he in danger?"

Kareem looked around the car to assure himself that no one was eavesdropping. "Yes, it is very dangerous to be gay in Iraq."

"Perhaps he could seek asylum here, in the United States?"

"You Americans do not offer asylum to gay Iraqis."

"Have you spoken to anyone about it?"

"No. I know from the newspapers. There is much hatred here for gays, and for Muslims."

"But Kareem, not everyone feels this way."

"Perhaps. But those in power regard us, you and I, Omar, as the enemy.

"You mean because we're Muslims?"

"Yes. And then… as for gays, even for Christians it is haraam."

King shook his head. "It seems to me, Kareem, you paint all Americans with the same brush. How are you different from those in power?"

"You do not understand. I do not think of Americans as the enemy. I have met many people that I like. You and I are friends, are we not?"

King nodded. "Then you don't think of America as the Great Satan? You don't feel, for example, as Al Qaida feels?"

"Al Qaida?" Kareem looked around again. "They are hardly sympathetic to me. But I understand the importance of jihad." Kareem was focused now on a man who'd sat down on the bench opposite them. "This is not the place to speak of such things, Omar."

"OK." King looked out the window and saw that they were now down to 14th Street. He decided to change the subject. "I see you brought your camera."

"Yes, I want to take some pictures. It is a rare opportunity, as you have told me, to go to the crown."

"What kind of camera is that? It looks expensive."

"It is a good camera. Would you like to see it?" Kareem lifted the strap off his neck and handed the camera to King.

King took it and looked it over. He could not see anything suspicious about it. If it held an explosive of some kind, it was a small one indeed. He was tempted to try to take a picture, to see if Kareem objected, though he didn't relish setting anything off. He thought perhaps he might pretend to take a picture. "Can I take your picture?" he said.

"No!" Kareem's voice was suddenly loud. "Do not waste a picture on me. Why don't you take a picture of the boat or of the Statue when we get there?"

"All right. But it would be nice if we had a picture of us together. Perhaps someone will take it for us."

"No, Omar. I do not like to see myself in pictures. I do not look good in pictures."

"But why? You are a handsome man, my friend."

Kareem blushed, but shook his head. "I do not think so. But it does not matter. My brother would be angry with me. He has strong feelings about it. He believes it is haraam to let oneself be photographed. There are strictures, you know, against depiction of the human form. It is idolatry."

"That is what your brother believes. But what about you?"

"I told you. I don't like how I look in photographs."

King decided to let it drop. He handed the camera back to Kareem. "Where are your brother and sister today?" he asked.

"I do not know." Kareem shrugged. "They are probably at my brother's apartment. Why do you ask?"

"I was just wondering. Do they know you're going to the Statue?"

"Yes. I told them. My sister was envious to see the view."

"Perhaps I will meet her someday."

"Yes," said Kareem. "Perhaps."

Then they were silent, as the train lumbered along making all stops on its way down to Battery Park.

Back on Riverside Boulevard, Sarah felt the brim of her Yankee's cap, checking it again to be sure all her hair was tucked up inside it. She tried staring sideways at the entrance to the building across the street, but it was hard to do that with her sunglasses on. She was afraid that if Jasmeen walked out of the building, she'd immediately look across the street and spot Sarah standing there. She needed to do something to make herself less conspicuous. She noticed a woman walking on the park side of the street with two small dogs in tow. As they approached, she knelt down and stretched out her arm to engage the dogs. The dogs came up to her eagerly.

"They're beautiful," she said to the woman. "What kind are they?"

"They're Corgis."

"Like the Queen's?"

"Yes." The woman nodded knowingly. She'd heard this comparison many times before.

Sarah was trying to think of some way to prolong the conversation. "What are their names?"

"This is Annie." The woman pointed to the lead dog. "And this is her friend Leo Stein."

"Leo Stein. Oh, just like the art dealer." Sarah stole a glance at the building across the street. "How cute! Is he named after Gertrude Stein's brother?"

"Yes." This time the woman looked more impressed. "That's right." She opened the gate to the dog park, and the two Corgis bounded inside. "Do you have a dog?" she asked.

Sarah shook her head. "No, I... Well, my father has a dog. I'm visiting him."

"Oh, I see." The woman looked around. "Are they here?"

Now Sarah felt foolish. "No, I'm waiting for my father." She gestured toward the building across the street again. "My father is slow, I'm afraid." Just as she spoke, the front door of the building was opened by the doorman. Sarah caught a glimpse of Jasmeen emerging behind a man who wore a backpack. Jasmeen had a backpack as well. "Oh dear," she said and whirled around, turning her back to the building. "You see those people with backpacks coming out of the building across the street?"

The woman stared at the couple emerging from the entrance across the street and nodded. "Yes."

"Those are my father's neighbors," Sarah said, suddenly improvising. "I don't want them to see me. They asked me to go hiking with them today, but I said I couldn't because I was going out of town." Sarah's mind raced to invent a story. "If they see me they'll want to come over and talk to me."

The woman with the Corgis nodded, though her expression was perplexed. "Hiking?" she said.

"Yes, they're avid hikers. They take the train to the Poconos just about every weekend. But if they see me they'll come over here and want to talk my head off. And she, and she, that woman ... " Sarah wasn't sure what to say. "... She hates dogs!"

"I see," said the woman, who clearly didn't see at all what this was about.

"Are they still there?" Sarah didn't dare turn her head around.

The woman nodded. "They're walking downtown. I suppose they must be going to Penn Station."

"Yes. Probably so," said Sarah. "I'm sure they'll walk. They hate to take cabs."

"You said they're hikers?" said the woman.

"Yes. If they got in a cab, I'd be shocked. They just love to hike. They aren't hailing a cab, are they?"

"No." The woman shook her head.

"That's good. I mean, I hardly see the point of taking a cab if you're going on a hike."

The woman, at this point, appeared to decide that Sarah's babbling had become sufficiently crazy that it would be best to leave her alone. She turned to go into the dog park.

"Wait," Sarah pleaded. "Can you just tell me if it's safe for me to turn around without them seeing me?"

The woman narrowed her eyes and glanced at the couple across the street who had now walked half a block south. "Yes," she said. "You can turn around now." Then she herself turned around and walked into the dog park.

Sarah wanted to call after the Corgi woman to thank her. But the woman had moved rapidly into the park in search of her dogs. Sarah turned around in time to see Jasmeen and the man with the backpack as they arrived at 66th Street. They were walking straight south. Since they hadn't hailed a cab, she hoped that meant they were going to walk to wherever they were going. But she also knew they might just be waiting to get a cab on West End or another of the busier north/south streets east of Riverside. She couldn't afford to let them get too far ahead of her. Cautiously, she walked up to 66th on the park side, then turned to follow them on their side of the street, walking about half a block behind them.

She quickened her pace, wanting to get as close as she could so she could see better what is was that they were carrying. As she came up behind them, she saw that each of them was carrying a backpack that looked heavy. She'd invented the idea of a trip to the Poconos, but now she wondered if they were, in fact, heading out of town. If so, she could hardly follow them just anywhere. She'd have to call Tyrone if they got on a bus or train out of town.

Even though Jasmeen and the man, whom she assumed was Abdul, were walking at the same pace, it seemed to Sarah that Jasmeen struggled under the weight of her backpack. Abdul was striding, almost marching, while Jasmeen's pace was uneven.

From time to time she shifted the weight of the pack on her back, as if she hoped to find a more comfortable position.

Riverside ended at 62nd Street where Jasmeen and Abdul turned left toward West End Avenue. Sarah followed them. At West End Avenue, they turned right. They continued walking straight south, down through the 60's and 50's even as West End turned into Eleventh Avenue. By then it was obvious to Sarah they weren't going to hail a cab. But now she wondered if they were heading toward the Port Authority. She didn't want to call Tyrone prematurely. She knew he was with Kareem. But if Jasmeen and the man were in fact going out of town, she didn't see how Kareem's trip to the Statue could be anything more than an outing. She'd already made note of the fact that Kareem had carried nothing except a camera. The thought that this might all be a false alarm began to turn over in her mind. She could sense how relieved she'd be if it were.

THIRTY-SEVEN

Special Agent Chin knew that Tyrone King had made plans to visit the Statue of Liberty. He hadn't checked in at his hotel or appeared at the Broadway show for which he'd bought tickets. But that didn't mean she could ignore the rest of King's plans. Her team would have to watch both the noontime Statue of Liberty tour on Saturday and King's seats at Yankee stadium during the game on Sunday, just to be safe.

For the Statue surveillance, she'd dispatched two agents to board the ferry to Liberty Island at the time that corresponded to King's ticket. She'd briefed the National Park Service, which managed the monument, and Homeland Security, advising them to raise their internal security alert level, but also clarifying for them that there was no concrete intelligence upon which to act. As far as Chin was concerned, there was as yet nothing about the situation that would warrant a public announcement or a closure of the monument.

Everyone Chin spoke to was confident that the security measures routinely employed at the Statue of Liberty were impossible to circumvent. She was told that every visitor to Liberty Island must pass through a standard airport-style screening to check for weapons or liquids before boarding the boat. Then, once at the Island, any visitor going into the monument itself, would have to pass through an even more thorough screening. No one was ever allowed to bring anything potentially dangerous inside the Statue structure. A visitor was allowed to carry a camera and bring any necessary medications. Everything else—backpacks, luggage, purses, water bottles, shopping bags, anything big enough to conceal an explosive—had to be checked in a locker.

Chin's speculations about King's plans had been pushed in a new direction by her conversation with Melanie Kahn. If King was really the non-violent pacifist that Kahn had described, it meant someone else was responsible for Cassidy's death. The evidence showed that King's phone had been on the train. She reasoned that Cassidy must have discovered who had the phone. She also thought it likely that Cassidy had been killed to hide the killer's identity. But it made no sense for King to kill Cassidy just to protect his identity. King had already been identified in the media as a suspect. Cassidy must have discovered someone else, someone unknown to them. But why would someone other than King be carrying his phone? That was a riddle she couldn't answer.

The fact that King had not come forward troubled her. Was it because he was dead or being held captive? Or was he up to something? She didn't like the fact that his plans included outings to two high profile potential targets. The FBI and Homeland Security constantly monitored potential threats. The protocols were well established. But Cassidy's death had raised a new level of concern throughout the government. For the time being, she was still leading the operation. But she was prepared for someone higher up to take over her role at any moment. She figured she still had a small window of opportunity to break the case before she was replaced. Although both the Statue and Yankee stadium might be at risk, the only surveillance she could be sure of leading was today's surveillance of the Statue. She decided to go all in. If the Statue was where King's next move would be, she would be prepared for him.

Before they could board the boat for Liberty Island, King and Kareem had to wait in the security check line. King purposely let Kareem go through the security check ahead of him. He watched as Kareem placed the camera, his mobile phone, his belt, and his shoes onto the conveyor belt that went through the scanner. Kareem wore a bracelet on his right wrist and a watch on his left. He first removed the watch, then the bracelet. Then he dropped them, along with a ring of keys, into the basket meant for small metal items. He walked through the metal detector without raising an alarm. King was so preoccupied monitoring Kareem that, after removing his belt and shoes, he almost forgot to take the phone Sarah had loaned him out of his pocket. He couldn't afford to call attention to himself in any way. Just before stepping into the scanner, he held up his hand to let the agent know he wanted to wait a moment. Then he dumped his phone in the basket, and walked through the scanner without incident. On the other side of the scanner, King watched as Kareem, apparently at random, had to undergo a secondary screening. An unsmiling agent patted Kareem down, then scanned him with a wand. After a moment, he let him pass through.

When they got on the boat, they followed the crowd and took seats on the upper deck. It was a beautiful day. Most of the passengers were in a cheerful mood, chatting and already taking pictures, even though the boat hadn't yet left the dock. But Kareem was subdued. He stared out at the waters of New York harbor with a glazed expression. His mind seemed to be somewhere else. In response, King remained quiet. He contemplated the various objects—camera, watch, bracelet, phone, keys—that Kareem had brought through the security line. He'd made sure to look closely at the phone. It was a regular cell phone and not a walkie-talkie. He knew a cell phone could still be rigged as a detonator for a bomb. But he couldn't see how Kareem could hide a secret bomb among the small objects he'd brought along.

He thought about Sarah and decided he'd better talk to her to find out what was happening with Jasmeen. He told Kareem he wanted to go down to the snack bar on the lower deck to get a drink. He asked Kareem if he could get him anything. Kareem asked for a bottle of water. When King got to the lower deck, he immediately dialed Sarah.

Sarah, when she answered, was slightly out of breath. "Where are you?" she asked.

"Kareem and I are on the boat. We're about to leave the dock. Where are you?"

I'm following Jasmeen and a man that I assume is Abdul. We're at a dock on the Hudson at 42nd Street. They just bought tickets for the Circle Line tour. So I bought a ticket too."

"The Circle Line?"

"Yeah. Circle Line. Blue boats. They go around the island. It's a boat tour. The tour leaves at 11:30."

"That's in fifteen minutes. Do you recognize the man with her?"

"I've never seen him before. But I'm sure it must be Abdul. I can see a family resemblance."

"What about security? Does it look like you're going to go through a security check before you board the boat?"

Sarah craned her neck to try to see past the people standing in line. "I can't tell. The line goes down the dock, then it makes a right turn. It looks like it goes into a parking lot or something."

"Well, if you find yourself getting on the boat without going through security, you'd better call me right away."

"OK. Hold on." Sarah moved into the queue. "I'm getting in line. I'm at the back of the line. There's no one coming after me." She paused a moment. "Let's see, one, two, three, four...." She continued counting. "There are about thirty people in line between me and the you-know-whos. By the way, the you-know-whos are both carrying some giant backpacks."

"Backpacks?"

"Yeah. Like with umbrellas and stuff."

"There's no rain in the forecast."

"Well…they have umbrella handles sticking out of their packs. And the packs are stuffed. They look heavy. Jasmeen looks like she's ready to fall over from carrying hers."

"Heavy backpacks are not good. Where does this Circle Line tour go?"

"Hold on a minute, I'm looking at the brochure I got at the ticket window." Sarah paused again while she read the description of the tour. "Oh, nice," she said. "It looks like we go straight down the Hudson past Wall Street, and then head out into the harbor for a ride by the Statue. Then we circle back and go up the East River. We go under the Brooklyn Bridge, and then we go up to the United Nations."

"Damn it. That's a lot of targets along the way. But you'll be in a boat the whole time, right? You don't go ashore, do you?"

"I don't think so. The brochure doesn't say anything about docking at any of these spots. I think we just ride past all the sights. It's a two-hour boat tour."

"Sarah, this can't be a good sign. Do you think you could find out what's inside their backpacks?"

"I'm having a hard enough time keeping Jasmeen from spotting me. I'm wearing sunglasses and the baseball cap and I keep turning around every 10 seconds so she won't notice my face. I don't see how I'm going to be able to get close enough to her to check out her backpack."

"Maybe you can get close to Abdul. Keep watching in case there's a moment when they separate. If she leaves him alone, you might have a chance to get close to him and see what he has in there."

"I doubt it. And anyway, what am I supposed to do, stick my hand in his backpack and feel around for a bomb while I distract him with my charming smile?"

"You're right. I don't know what you can do. In fact, I don't think you should get on that boat, Sarah. If they have bombs in those backpacks, you aren't going to be able to stay safe. It's time to call the cavalry."

"It's way past time, Ty. You better call them." Sarah looked at the people in line. "But I'm going to get on the boat. I have to. If the cavalry doesn't show up in time, someone has to warn all these people. I see a lot of high school kids in this line, Ty. It's like they're on a field trip or something."

"No, Sarah, please don't get on the boat."

"Listen, if it looks like something's about to go down, I'll grab a life vest and jump in the water. I'm a good swimmer."

"I really don't like this situation. It's too dangerous. But we're going to run out of time. I need to make a call."

"I'm at the parking lot now. Apparently they're taking pictures of everyone. Souvenir photos against some kind of screen. I don't see any security stuff."

"OK. Listen. I don't want you on the boat, but we're running out of options. The only thing I can think of is that you try to find someone in charge when you get to the boat, and tell them what's going on. Maybe you can keep the boat from leaving. I don't know if this will work, but maybe the Circle Line people could pretend there's a mechanical problem, and announce that they have to get everyone off. The important thing is to not let Jasmeen and Abdul get suspicious. They might just blow it all up if they think someone is on to them. It has to look like no one suspects anything. But don't get on the boat. Hold on a second." King had reached the front of the concession line and ordered two bottles of water. "I'm buying some water."

"What's happening with Kareem?"

"I left him sitting on the upper deck. I'm at the concession stand on the lower deck."

"Ty, they're getting ready to take my picture. I have to go. Do you want me to call you after I talk to someone?"

"Yes, please call me as soon as you can. Don't worry about Kareem. I'll step away from him so we can talk privately."

"OK. Bye."

"Bye. And Sarah, don't get on the boat!"

"Got it." Sarah hung up. She didn't have much time to think about how she was going to pull off what she needed to do. She had to find someone to talk to in order to stop the boat from leaving the dock. But she couldn't let Jasmeen see her. She would talk to whoever was taking the tickets and tell him what was going on. That way she could avoid being seen, warn the authorities, and stay off the boat.

There was a kid standing in front of a rope that blocked the path into the parking lot. He appeared to be in charge of organizing people to take the photographs. He'd been letting people past him in small groups. He spoke to Sarah. "Are you by yourself today, ma'am?"

Sarah nodded.

"OK. Just step in front of the screen up ahead of you. Gary over there will take your picture."

Sarah looked around. "I'm the last one in line, right?"

"Yep. You're the last one."

"They won't leave without me, right? I mean the boat."

"No, don't worry, ma'am."

"Can you tell me who I'd speak to about a security matter?"

"Did you say security?"

"Yes, I saw something suspicious earlier, and I want to talk to whoever is in charge about it."

The kid shrugged his shoulders. "I guess you better talk to Peter. He's the guy taking tickets. I'm not really sure."

Sarah sized the kid up. She didn't think he was the right person to count on at this moment. "OK. Well, do I really need to have my picture taken?"

"Not if you don't want to."

"Then, I'm just going to go talk to Peter, OK."

"OK." The kid waved her ahead. "Go on." He also waved to the cameraman with a signal that indicated she wasn't getting a photo.

Sarah trotted past the photo screen, then turned left to go toward the boat. By the time she got there, she saw that everyone else had already stepped onto the boat. She ran down the gangway that lead on board toward the man waiting to take her ticket, whom she assumed was Peter.

Peter watched her with an impatient look. He was holding out his hand to take her ticket. "Hurry up," he said. "All aboard."

Sarah ran up to him with her ticket held out in front of her. Peter grabbed it.

Sarah said, "Can you hold the boat a minute?" But just as she spoke, the boat blew it's whistle, which drowned out what she said.

The cameraman, who apparently had been following behind her, stepped onto the boat and slid the gate on the gangway behind them. Sarah turned around and saw two men on the dock who began untying the ropes that held the boat. A third man began to pull the metal gangway back onto the dock.

"Wait, wait," she yelled at him.

But Peter had already hopped down onto a side section of the boat where he was pulling one of the ropes away from the dock and winding it onto the boat. Another crew member was doing the same thing with the other tie line. The cameraman walked straight into the doors of the main cabin and Sarah was left standing by herself.

Suddenly the engine began to churn loudly and the boat began to move. Sarah tried to yell again, but she couldn't make herself heard over the noise of the engine. She decided she'd better get up to the captain and talk to him right away. There might still be time for him to pretend there was a mechanical problem and return to the dock before they got too far along.

She stepped into the main cabin of the lower deck, removed her sunglasses, and looked around. She needed to determine how she could get up to the bridge on the top of the boat. A few people were milling about, but most people were seated and facing the windows. She walked past a set of stairs that went down to a lower level that held a sign that indicated the restrooms were below. She turned around and saw that there were stairs going up on either side of the main door she'd entered by. She went to the stair on the right and climbed to a landing, where it joined with the stair from the left. She turned onto the landing and walked straight into Jasmeen, who stood in front of the next flight of stairs going up, blocking her path. There was no one else on the landing. Jasmeen wasn't carrying her backpack. She pulled a gun out of the pocket of her windbreaker and pointed it at Sarah. "Don't say anything," she said. Though her hand trembled, she spoke calmly. "I won't hesitate to use this if you do."

THIRTY-EIGHT

King went to a chair by a window on the lower deck and put down the two bottles of water he'd purchased. He pulled out the phone Sarah loaned him and dialed Colin Zeller.

"What's the word, Cap," said Zeller by way of a greeting. "I thought I might hear from you by now. I've been sitting by the phone, tapping my foot."

"You'd better sound the alarm," said King. "I hate to say it."

"What's your boy Kareem up to?"

King reflexively glanced up toward the upper deck in response to hearing Kareem's name. "It's not Kareem I'm worried about. Remember I mentioned that he has a brother and sister?"

"I remember."

"My friend Sarah just tracked them to a tour boat that's headed to Liberty Island."

"Oh right, Sarah, your girlfriend. You've got her involved now, huh? It's no wonder women don't want to date you, Cap. So what about it?"

"I doubt that the boat tour has much security. What worries me is that the brother and sister are carrying heavy backpacks. No reason to carry big backpacks on a boat tour." King let that sink in a moment before he continued. "I told Sarah not to get on the boat. I think you need to let the cavalry know about it. Let them know they have to act discreetly. Keep the boat from leaving, if they can, then evacuate everyone, but write it off to mechanical trouble. If the brother and sister suspect we're on to them, they might blow themselves up before anyone can get to them."

"What tour boat is it?"

"The Circle Line."

"OK. I've heard of that. When does it leave?"

"Sarah said the boat leaves at 11:30." King looked at his watch. "What time have you got?"

"It's 11:30 eastern now, if my math is right."

"Same here," said King. "You better act fast, Colin."

Colin hesitated a beat before replying. "Listen Cap," he said. "I'm going to have to do some digging around on my end to find out who to talk to about the Circle Line. Then I'm going to have to do a whole lot of explaining. I don't know how fast I can get the cavalry in play."

"What about Kareem's boyfriend Muhammad? Have you found out anything about him yet?"

"I have. I got intel on Kareem and his buddy Muhammad. Muhammad disappeared three weeks ago. My contact in the gay underground thinks he was kidnapped by the Mujahedin in Sadr City and taken to Fallujah. I have an agent trying to track him down. If my agent finds him, we'll send in a rescue team, but it could be dicey."

"I have to get to Kareem. If we could take the squeeze off him, I think I could get him to tell me what their game plan is."

"Is he carrying a backpack?"

"No. He has nothing with him but a camera."

"Did you check it out?"

"Yeah, it's an ordinary normal size camera, nothing special."

"Could they have something already planted on the island?"

"I suppose."

"Well, listen Cap, there isn't much time. I better get busy with the Circle Line. Call me if something breaks."

"Ditto. Especially if your team pulls Muhammad out of Fallujah. I might be able to convince Kareem to tell me what's happening if I have that leverage."

King closed his phone and picked up the water bottles. He wanted to call Sarah again, but he decided it was more important to get back to Kareem, who by now would be wondering what happened to him. On his way up to the top deck, he turned the corner on the stairs, and almost crashed into a sailor. The sailor had come up the other stairs carrying a pair of water bottles identical to those King was holding. As they stepped to each side of the stairwell to avoid each other, they both processed the fact that they were on matching trajectories with matching bottles of water —almost a mirror image of each other—and they each smiled. It was the first time King had smiled all morning. King nodded at the sailor, who nodded back. It reminded him, for a fleeting moment, that the rest of the world was oblivious to the danger that King was unable to ignore.

After the death of Special Agent Cassidy, Agent Chin had recommended that Special Agent Walters take some time off. But he'd refused. Walters wasn't going to stay at home mourning while whoever killed Cassidy was still at large. He'd asked Chin if she'd keep him on the case, and she agreed. She'd paired him with a new partner, Agent Torres, and assigned them to do surveillance at the Statue of Liberty.

At 11:35 Chin called Walters on the boat going to Liberty Island.

"Did anything come up in the security check?" she asked him.

"Nothing unusual. A woman set off the alarm with her earrings. A man set off the alarm with the key chain in his pocket. Another man set off the alarm with his wristwatch. But they were all clean."

"OK. When you get to the island, check in with security at the monument and stand by for further instructions."

"Roger that."

Chin checked the schedule. The boat was due to arrive at the island at 11:45. Those going into the monument would go through the secondary screening in a facility at the base of the Statue. At noon, she planned to have Torres go up to the crown first, so that Walters could stand at the base of the stairs and eyeball everyone going up after him.

Jasmeen put the gun back in her pocket. In a low, firm voice, she told Sarah that if she made any move to escape, she'd take the gun out of her pocket and, without pause, shoot her. She ordered Sarah to follow her to the top level of the boat. The top level had both an exterior and interior section. In the center of the exterior section were a series of chest-high metal cases that bore stenciled lettering indicating that they each contained 30 life preservers. On both sides of the cases, rows of seats faced the bow. All the chairs were filled except for two seats next to Abdul, who sat on the center aisle on the starboard side of the life preserver cases. The two backpacks sat on the deck floor, wedged behind the seats in front of him. Jasmeen told Sarah to sit on the chair next to Abdul. Jasmeen took the next seat so that Sarah was sitting between them. When she sat, Sarah's left foot was just to the right of one of the backpacks. She imagined they contained bombs like the one Kareem had on the Maple Leaf. Turning her head as little as possible, she moved her eyes, scanning the area around her to assess how she might escape. She considered that if she could manage to grab a life preserver and get to the railing, she might jump in the water and swim clear of the boat. But the life preservers were shut inside the metal cases, and she couldn't see how to open one of them quickly enough to avoid arousing either Jasmeen's gun or the detonation of the bombs.

As the boat started down the Hudson, the tour guide stood

between the interior and exterior parts of the upper deck. He faced the passengers seated in the exterior section and spoke into a microphone. He began with a speech about the safety features of the boat. Then he announced that two special groups were on board for the tour: the Jackson Jaguar marching band from Jackson Memorial High School in New Jersey, and a delegation from the American Association of Women Surgeons, whose convention was underway in midtown Manhattan. Sarah could tell that the high school students were on her side of the deck, the starboard side. Most of the passengers in front of her were kids.

Across the aisle, on the other side of the deck, the rows were filled mostly with people whose heads were turned toward the port side view of lower Manhattan. Since their heads were turned, Sarah couldn't make out anyone's face, but she felt certain they were mostly women. She thought about what she might have to do and who she might have to rely on. She didn't want to get any of the high school kids involved. If she needed help, she'd look to the surgeons. She hoped she would be able to count on one or more of them to stay steady in a difficult moment.

The tour guide was asking everyone to remain in their seats. "I know many of you want to take pictures," he said. "But remember that all the folks around you paid to come on this tour to see the sights, just like you. None of them paid so they could sit here for a couple of hours and stare at your backside. But if you stand up to take pictures, folks, that's all the people around you are going to see—your backside. So please, folks, stay seated while you take your pictures. And remember we're going to go down the river and go past the Statue in one direction, then we'll come back around and go past the Statue in the other direction. So both sides of the boat will get a chance to face all the attractions. That means you don't need to get up and run over to the other side of the boat for a picture if you see something on the other side. Everyone will get a good view and a good shot when we turn around. So please stay seated at all times."

Since they were on the right side of the boat, Sarah assumed the Statue of Liberty would come into view on their side before the boat turned around. She tried to imagine what Jasmeen and Abdul's plans were for the bombs. She didn't think they were planning to lob them off the boat in the general direction of the Statue or the Brooklyn Bridge or the United Nations. But she also didn't see why they'd want to blow up the boat just offshore from one of those sites. Since Kareem was going with King to the Statue, she assumed the Statue must be their main target. But how would they use the bombs? She didn't have much time to figure it out. The boat was rapidly heading down the river toward the harbor. She calculated it would take them twenty or thirty minutes to reach the Statue. For the moment, Jasmeen and Abdul sat quietly on either side of her. Without looking directly at either of them, she could tell they were more intent on watching her than in looking at the sights.

Sarah kept looking straight ahead and slightly down. She glanced to the right. She could see that Jasmeen held her right hand inside her pocket. If Sarah was going to make a move, she'd have to start by knocking Jasmeen off balance before she had time to pull out the gun. Sarah thought about King. For the first time, she wished she too had studied a martial art. The best she could do was imagine how a martial artist might go about disabling Jasmeen. She vaguely imagined a series of punchy movements with her arms and legs. But where should she aim? She shook her head. She could feel the weight of her mobile phone in her pocket. What would she do if King called? She wished she could talk to him just for a moment. She wanted his advice. She almost smiled, as she realized how much that would please him.

Kareem drank his entire bottle of water in a series of long gulps. Next to him, King sipped his water slowly as he watched the skyline of lower Manhattan recede into the distance. They were halfway out into the harbor. King wanted to ask Kareem about

Muhammad, but he was mindful of the fact that they were in a public place where private conversation would be impossible. He assumed Kareem would be embarrassed by any conversation that touched on his sexual orientation. So King would have to broach the topic using the coded language he'd learned himself at a young age.

"I was surprised to see you at the party last night," he began.

"You must believe me, Omar. I did not follow you there. That was just a coincidence."

"I know," said King. "But I was glad you were there. I wouldn't have guessed that you'd be there."

"I would not have guessed it about you either," said Kareem. "So I too was surprised. But it was a pleasant surprise."

"Really?"

"Yes, of course. It is always nice to meet a friend who can understand you."

"Yes, I know," said King. "That's how I felt too."

Kareem turned to face him. His eyes moved back and forth as if he was scanning King for something. He clearly had something on his mind. "I was also pleased for other reasons," he said.

King said nothing. He could tell that something was coming.

"Omar, you see, I believe it is not only my sister..." Kareem paused, looking around, choosing his words carefully. "... who would find you attractive."

King knew what Kareem meant, but he said, "I'm not sure what you mean."

Kareem grimaced. "Omar, this is not a good place for me to tell you what I mean." He looked around again. "Perhaps we can go somewhere else to talk."

"Somewhere on the boat?"

"Yes, somewhere more private."

King looked out at the horizon. The Statue of Liberty was not too far away. "OK," he said. "But we're almost at the Statue. There isn't much time. Where do you want to go?"

"Follow me," said Kareem. He stood and walked to the stairs

descending to the lower deck, looking back to be sure that King was following him.

King followed at a slight distance. He wasn't sure what was happening. If he had to describe the look in Kareem's eyes when he glanced back at him, he would describe it as seductive.

Kareem walked through the interior of the lower deck toward another descending stairwell. The sign over this stairwell indicated that it went down to the restrooms.

King shook his head. He was trying to read Kareem's mind. All he could imagine was that Kareem was about to hit on him. If that was about to happen, he wasn't sure how to play it. He wanted to gain Kareem's confidence. He needed Kareem to feel confident enough to tell him what he and his friends had planned. It was a standard Mata Hari espionage situation, very much like what he'd trained for in Afghanistan with Reema. But with the boat rapidly approaching the Statue, he wouldn't have much time to segue from a seduction scene to intelligence gathering. And he couldn't help but think about Sarah. How would she feel if he let himself cross an erotic line with Kareem—even for the sake of gaining crucial intelligence? He wasn't sure how he felt about it himself. Reema had been an innocent participant, caught up in the politics of the war, herself a victim of a repressive culture. Kareem, on the other hand, had detonated the bomb in the Niagara River that might otherwise have killed hundreds of people. Even if he was, in fact, being blackmailed, Kareem had crossed a moral line. King had a moral line too, but he couldn't decide on impulse exactly how that line played out in the current situation. He was aware that on a purely physical level, a level he had mostly held at bay, he found Kareem sexually attractive. The disjunction between his sexual desires and his emotional desires was a source of great anxiety. He felt his heart begin to beat rapidly.

Kareem walked into the men's room and looked around. No one else was in the room, which was not surprising, given how close they were to arriving at the island. Kareem waited until

King entered the room. Then he walked over to one of three toilet stalls and walked into the one on the far left, which had a wide door for wheelchair use. He held the door open and gestured for King to follow him into the stall.

King, despite himself, flushed red. He had sensed this might be coming, but he hadn't expected Kareem's desire to be so urgent. Were they going to have sex in a bathroom stall? Surely if they just needed to talk privately they could do that standing at the sink. Besides, if they both went into the same stall, how could they have a conversation without drawing attention to themselves if anyone else should come into the room?

Not wanting to make a scene, he followed Kareem into the stall. Kareem, without speaking, closed the stall door, then put his arms around King's waist.

"You said you wanted to talk," King whispered. "Can't we talk by the sink?"

Kareem lifted his hand up to King's head and ran his fingers through King's hair. "You are so beautiful, Omar," he said.

"But you have a lover," said King.

"He is so far away, and I don't have much time."

King felt Kareem's hand slide down his back. He put his other arm around him and seemed, for a moment, to have clasped his hands behind King's back. King could hear the jangle of the bracelet on Kareem's wrist.

Kareem leaned into King's chest. "Please, Omar, I know you have been following me. I know that you want this too."

"Following you?"

"Yes, of course. You have followed me ever since the Maple Leaf."

King took a step backward. "Since what?"

"Since you took my gun on the train in Canada. I knew when you did not shoot me, when you let me escape, that you were my guardian angel. You kept the bomb from harming anyone. You saved me from committing a horrible act. Without you, I would have had no choice."

"You mean you've known all along?"

"Yes, of course," Kareem smiled. "I don't know how you managed to arrange to pick me up with the woman you called mother. That was very clever, Omar. But of course I recognized you. How could I not? You are beautiful with or without your hair and beard." Kareem lifted his head and moved his lips towards King.

King tried to digest what he'd just discovered. If Kareem knew who he was all this time, what was going on? King had thought that he was fooling Kareem. But it had been just the opposite! He could feel Kareem's lips touching his. He couldn't think clearly enough to decide what to do. He tentatively pressed his lips back. He felt Kareem pulling on his arm. Felt the caress of his fingers moving over his forearm. Kareem pressed so hard against him that King stepped back and bumped into the wall of the stall, which made a thumping sound. Then he heard a click, as if the lock on the stall door had been turned.

King felt something metallic on his wrist. In an instant, he heard another click.

"I am sorry, Omar," said Kareem. "I cannot let you get off the boat."

King tried to pull his arm away from Kareem's grasp, but he realized that his arm was handcuffed to the grab bar in the toilet stall.

"Kareem," he said. "What are you doing?"

"You may have noticed the bracelet I was wearing. It is a double bracelet that opens into handcuffs. The small key that I am taking off my key ring will open the handcuffs." He held the key up in front of him. "I'm going to leave this key on the shelf above the sink outside the stall. In a little while, the boat will begins its journey back to Manhattan. Sooner or later, someone on the boat will come in to use the toilet. You can ask whoever comes in to unlock the handcuffs for you."

"Why? Why are you doing this?"

"It is not safe for you, Omar. I don't want you to go on the island. You are a beautiful and kind man. If I had not already given my heart to Muhammad, I would wish to spend time with you. But I cannot. I have no time left. I must do something horrible again. And this time you cannot stop me."

"Don't do it," King said. "I know you love Muhammad. But this price is too high. Whatever you are planning. Please, Kareem. You can't do it. You must have doubts. Don't be like the people who have hurt you."

"You cannot know what is in my heart, Omar. I have had doubts all my life. All my life, I have hidden myself from my family and everyone I know. Only Muhammad has ever loved me as I am. I'm sorry, my friend. But, don't worry. You will be safe. I must go now."

Kareem opened the stall door and stepped out. King heard the tiny clink of the key as Kareem placed it on the metal shelf outside. "Wait," King shouted. "Wait. Kareem, don't do it!" But he was gone.

King heard the abrupt sound of the engines reversing, which he knew meant the boat was maneuvering into the dock. At this point, everyone would be queued up by the exit door ready to disembark. It seemed unlikely that anyone would come to the men's room before leaving the boat. It would probably do no good to shout or call for help. Kareem had timed everything care-fully. King banged his cuffed hand against the stall door, and loudly yelled, "Fuck."

THIRTY-NINE

Lieutenant Colin Zeller had to talk his way through nearly a dozen groups of people before he finally got connected to Special Agent Connie Chin. He told her what he knew about Tyrone King's situation, about Kareem and Jasmeen and Abdul, and about what King had reported about Jasmeen and Abdul and their heavy backpacks on the Circle Line tour.

Since all of what he told her fit into her own earlier speculations, she saw no reason to doubt him. "Where is Mr. King now?" she asked.

"As far as I know," said Zeller, "he's with Kareem on the boat to the Statue."

"Can you hold for a minute?" she asked. "I want to check on the status of that boat."

Chin called Walters, who told her that the boat had just docked. He had been watching everyone disembark. The last few passengers were filing past him on the gangplank. He hadn't seen anyone who looked like King.

"He must be there," said Chin. "I've just had confirmation that he was on the boat. You'd better go to the monument and tell them to stop letting people into the Statue. Have them evacuate it immediately."

Chin switched back to Zeller. "Who did you say is following the people on the Circle Line boat?"

"Her name is Sarah. She's a woman King met on the Maple Leaf. She's been helping him follow the terrorists."

"How long have you known this information, Lieutenant Zeller?"

"About 24 hours."

"And you're only now reporting this to us?"

"King knew that if he came to you, you'd detain him for questioning—just like you are questioning me right now. He was afraid that coming forward would compromise his ability to track the suspects. I agreed with him. I know him and I trust him. If I were you, I'd save your questions about who knew what when for a less urgent moment."

"All right, Lieutenant. I'll talk to you later. I'm going to contact the Circle Line now."

"Good idea."

Chin disconnected Zeller and keyed a search string into her computer. She had access to thousands of unlisted phone numbers. She doubted she'd be able to place a call directly to the Circle Line tour boat, but she might find someone who could.

King leaned back against the grab bar to which he was cuffed. The bar pressed against his pocket and he felt it push the contours of Sarah's phone against his leg. His right hand was cuffed. The phone was in his right pocket. He reached around to put his left hand into his right pocket. He had to lean away from the grab bar in order to do it. He carefully lifted the phone out of his pocket. He thought for a moment about who to call. If he called Sarah, she'd be warned that something was happening, but he didn't see how she could help him escape. If he called Colin

Zeller, he might be able to contact someone who could come uncuff him before the boat left.

He decided to call Zeller. It was a challenge to dial the phone with only one free hand. He had to balance it on the grab bar with his free left hand while he pushed the buttons on the virtual keypad with his cuffed right hand. After he dialed, he pulled the phone up to his left ear with his left hand.

"The cavalry is on its way," said Zeller when he answered. "Where are you?"

"I'm handcuffed in a stall in the men's room on the boat."

"Oh Jesus. That doesn't sound too good, Cap. Sounds kind of kinky though."

"Colin, I need you to find someone to uncuff me as soon as you can."

"I just talked to the FBI agent who's been looking for you. I'm pretty sure she has an agent on the boat. I can have her get the agent to come find you."

"No, Colin. Not yet. I don't have much time. I can't deal with an FBI agent just now. Now more than ever I have to get to Kareem, and no one but me knows what he looks like."

"OK then. Who exactly would you like me to call?"

"Earlier I ran into a sailor on board." King scanned his memory. The visual memory of which he was so proud worked like a video recorder. He replayed the tape of the moment when he and the sailor bumped into each other. He visualized the sailor's nameplate. He could see the letters spelling the name 'Giller.' "The sailor's name is Giller," he said.

"Did you notice his rank?"

King scanned his memory again. "He had a yellow bar. So what's that? Ensign?

"Yeah, ensign.

"OK. See if you can get a mobile number for an ensign named Giller from your database, probably on leave in New York, and call him. He was on the boat, but everyone's probably off the boat now except me. You'll have to ask him to come back on board and get me. Tell him it's the guy who bumped into him with the pair of water bottles."

"Sounds like a long shot, Cap."

"If you can't find Giller, then call the FBI agent."

"OK. I'm on it."

"Wait. Before you go, Colin. What did you find out about Muhammad?"

"We got him."

"You got him?"

"We pulled him out about five minutes ago, Cap. Even as we speak, the rescue party is taking him to Camp Baharia. That's the closest U.S. base to Fallujah."

"So he was a hostage?"

"It was just like you said. The long beards were holding him captive. They've got some real homophobic Mujahedin over here, Cap."

"What else is new? OK, Colin, please find someone to get me out of here."

"Roger that. Keep an eye out for Ensign Giller or the FBI. One or the other." Zeller hung up.

King looked at his watch. He finally had the information he needed, but it may have come too late.

The Circle Line boat had traveled ten minutes past the southern tip of Manhattan. The tour guide was beginning his spiel about the Statue of Liberty. He was giving a stirring speech. The story of the gift of the French people was a moving one. As Sarah watched the giant figure with her torch held high come into view, she felt the symbolic weight of it. This was the worldwide symbol of liberty, a global symbol of freedom. To attack it was to attack one of the great monuments of civilization.

On her left, Sarah felt Abdul stirring. He reached down and opened the cover of one of the backpacks. He removed the umbrella and tossed it aside. Then he carefully began to pull a large tubular metal piece out of the pack. He opened the second pack, discarded its umbrella, and took another large metal tube out of it. Then he took the first tube and attached it to the second, making a single tube about five feet long. One end of the tube was open, like the barrel of a gun. The other end was capped with a thick round cap of metal. It looked like a small cannon. A long handle protruded from the bottom of the tube.

Sarah gulped. It wasn't a bomb. It looked like some kind of rocket launcher. She looked around. Everyone's eyes were on the Statue of Liberty. Some of the kids from the marching band had stood up, despite the instructions from the tour guide. No one was paying attention to Abdul.

Jasmeen rose from her seat and said to Sarah. "You must come with me now. Do not forget what will happen if you do not comply." She wiggled her hand within the pocket of the windbreaker to underscore her point. Sarah stood up. As she stepped in front of him she saw Abdul holding something that looked like a tiny telescope. He reached down, as she passed, to attach it to the top of his weapon. She looked up again at the Statue. It was still about five or ten minutes away. Jasmeen had moved into the aisle where she waited for Sarah to follow. Sarah got up and stepped in front of Jasmeen.

"We're going to the bow," said Jasmeen. "You walk first, and don't turn."

Sarah began to walk in what felt like an unnaturally slow way. Everything had begun to move in slow motion. They were headed toward the doors that opened into the enclosed main cabin of the upper deck. Beyond the main cabin was another small exterior deck at the very front of the boat. In front of her, off the starboard side of the bow, the Statue loomed, as if Lady Liberty had just risen to lift her lamp.

King heard the sound of footsteps coming down the stairs from the deck above. After a moment, the door swung open. King smiled. It was the sailor, Ensign Giller. King had opened the stall door. Now he stood at the threshold feeling like a dog on a chain. "Thanks for coming," he said. "The key to these handcuffs is over there on the shelf above the sink."

"This is a weird scene, bro. What's going on?"

"What did they tell you?"

"They just gave me orders. Told me what I had to come and do. They said go to the head and uncuff the guy you saw earlier with the two water bottles. They told me it was a matter of national security."

"Right," said King. "There isn't time to explain. I'll come find you later and fill you in. But for now, just unlock me." He rattled his cuffed hand against the grab bar.

Giller picked up the key from the shelf. King presented his hand with the cuffs. After a moment of careful tinkering with the key in the tiny lock, the cuffs came open. King grabbed the cuffs and squeezed Giller's arm. "I need the key," he said. "I want to take it with me."

Giller handed him the key.

King shouted "Thanks!" and ran out the door. He bounded up the stairs to the main deck. There were already new passengers walking in through the front door. More were coming up the gangplank to board the ship. King had to push his way past all of them. Once he was back on land, he stopped for a moment to dial Sarah's phone number. Then, while it was ringing, he ran as fast as he could toward the monument. He listened to the phone switch over to voice mail. He left her a brief message.

"Be careful, Sarah. Something is going on. Kareem handcuffed me to the boat. I'm free now, but I've lost track of him. It looks like the Statue is their target. Call me as soon as you get this message."

When King arrived at the base of the monument, he saw people coming out of the building. But nobody was going in. When he got to the door, a man blocked his path.

"The Statue is closed," he said.

"But I have a ticket."

"Doesn't matter," the man said. "There's a security alert."

King looked around. He hadn't seen Kareem. He couldn't take any chances. It was entirely possible that Kareem was already inside the monument. "Yes, I know," he said. "I'm the one who called it in. You need to let me inside. I know the man we're looking for. I've been tracking him for several days. He had me handcuffed on the boat. I just got out."

"What's your name?"

"I'm Tyrone King."

"You're King?" The man's expression changed. "Hold on a minute." He picked up his phone.

Now it began. King knew the man was probably an FBI agent. He was about to call the agent in charge. They would want to bring him in for questioning.

"There isn't time," King said. "I'm sorry." In a swift series of moves, King executed nikyō, the same wristlock he'd used on Kareem on the train. The agent at the door had no time to react. King forced him down to the floor in four and a half seconds. He had learned something from his experience with Kareem. This time he dialed back the amount of force he applied. He didn't want to cause the man any lasting pain. "It may hurt for a moment," King said. "But you'll be OK." He reached under the man's coat and pulled the gun from his shoulder holster. He'd wanted to save the handcuffs for Kareem. But he couldn't take the chance of having this agent chase after him. He cuffed the man to the emergency exit bar that ran across the inside of the door. He kept the key in his pocket.

There was a security-screening checkpoint ahead of him. Already two of the security guards were coming toward him. King didn't have enough time for more Aikido. He pointed the gun at them. He told them to stand back. They held up their hands and stood to one side. King held the gun steadily on them as he took the weapons from their holsters. He tucked the security guards' guns into his waistband. He kept the FBI agent's gun in his hand. He ran straight through the metal detector without stopping. An alarm bell went off. King kept going. At the base of the staircase, a sign informed him that there were 354 stairs to the crown, equivalent to climbing up twenty floors in a building. King began to climb.

FORTY

Sarah walked through the main cabin and out onto the deck at the bow of the ship. There was a metal ladder built into the center of the deck. A pair of life preserver canisters sat on either side of it. A long thick rope hung from a rung of the ladder and spooled onto the floor behind it. Sarah assumed this was the rope used to moor the boat to the dock. The metal ladder supported the weight of, and climbed up to, a small room on the deck above them. The room was ringed with windows. Sarah assumed this was the bridge where the captain was piloting the boat. Sarah stepped toward the bow. It was crowded with people clutching the railing. Everyone was leaning out to gaze at the approaching Statue. Sarah could sense Jasmeen moving behind her. Suddenly, Sarah heard her phone ring. Then she felt Jasmeen put her hand on her shoulder and pull her back.

"Don't answer that. Stand back here by the ladder," she said. "We will wait here until my brothers have finished their work."

"What's going to happen?"

"You do not need to worry. Nothing will happen to you if you follow my instructions."

Sarah began to turn around, but she felt Jasmeen's fingers squeeze into her shoulder.

"Do not turn around. You do not wish to become a pillar of salt."

Sarah felt the breeze in her face. The boat was only a minute away from the Statue. They were going to pass very close. She'd had no idea the boat would come this close. She thought about the weapon that Abdul was assembling behind her. Once again she pictured in her mind a vague series of martial art moves with her arms and legs. She'd have to swing around quickly. Jasmeen had removed her hand from her shoulder, but Sarah could tell approximately where Jasmeen was standing. She'd try to knock her over. Then maybe she could do something with the rope.

Sarah took a deep breath and whirled around with as much speed as she could muster. Her arm was thrust straight out and her fist was balled. She hit the top of Jasmeen's head, causing her head to whip to the side, but it didn't knock her over.

Jasmeen pulled the gun out of her pocket. Sarah lifted her foot and kicked Jasmeen hard in the stomach. Now Jasmeen fell. She fell on her back and rolled slightly to her right side. She held the gun firmly in her hand, but she had to support the weight of her body with her right arm. She couldn't aim the gun.

Sarah stepped to Jasmeen's left side. Once again she aimed her foot like a slingshot. She slammed it out and down towards Jasmeen's right hand. She jumped and tried to land on Jasmeen's right arm with all her weight.

She did land on Jasmeen's arm and it knocked the gun from her hand. But she also lost her balance and fell. Then the two women scrambled on the floor of the deck to reach the gun. It had slid four feet away.

Sarah looked up and saw a woman was watching them. "Grab that gun. Get it and throw it overboard." The woman stared at her. Sarah remembered how it felt to be in this exact situation. She remembered what King had said to her. "Do it now."

The woman stepped back, as if she was going to walk away.

Her face was filled with fear. But then she stopped. She continued to watch them as they wrestled. The look of fear on her face was mixed with curiosity, like someone who couldn't turn her eyes from an accident.

"Do it," Sarah said again.

The woman crouched down, but didn't move toward the gun. She seemed afraid to move at all.

"It will be OK if you get it." Sarah tried to keep her voice calm. "Pick it up and throw it into the water. Then everyone will be safe."

The woman did nothing. Why was she hesitating? What was she waiting for?

"Do not listen to this woman," Jasmeen shouted.

"This woman is a terrorist," Sarah shouted in return.

Now the woman began to move toward the gun. The word 'terrorist' had animated her. She picked the gun up—just as Sarah had done on the Maple Leaf—as if it was a bomb about to detonate. She held it out in front of her at arm's length.

Jasmeen yelled something loud in Arabic. The woman stepped to the railing, and, without making a sound, tossed the gun over the side of the boat.

"Get help," Sarah shouted to the woman. "Get the surgeons to help me."

The woman nodded. She walked into the main cabin, while Sarah and Jasmeen continued to wrestle. Jasmeen was jabbing her elbow into Sarah's ribs. Sarah, in turn, was thrashing her arms to pound Jasmeen's head.

King climbed the stairs of the circular staircase inside the Statue of Liberty. He was taking two stairs at a time and panting hard. But adrenaline was pumping in his veins. He could hear the sound of footsteps coming up the stairs twenty feet below him. He wouldn't have much time once he got to the top.

He passed a fenced-off section that led to the arm holding the torch. As he climbed, he could see the entire inner structure of the Statue. He was coming up through the trunk. He saw the metal armature narrowing above him as it formed into the neck and head. The crown was only ten or so feet above him.

Like a sprinter, he focused all his thoughts on the last hurdle. He pumped his legs and began to count the stairs to keep his mind clear. It was hot inside and he was sweating profusely. As he burst up past the top stair, he saw that Kareem was alone in the crown. King thought there was supposed to be some kind of guard at the top, but he couldn't see anyone except Kareem.

Kareem stood in front of a window that was propped open, tilted out from the bottom. It was one of a row of windows that formed a decorative part of the crown. King glanced around. All the windows were propped open. King felt a breeze drift past him. The cool air magnified the damp sensation from the sweat on his arms. Kareem held the camera up to his eyes. He looked like he was planning to take a picture down through the opening in the window.

"Kareem," King shouted. "You don't have to do anything. Muhammad is safe."

Kareem turned and looked at him. But then he looked back out the window. His attention was riveted on something far below. He put his hand on the camera shutter.

Sarah saw them coming through the interior cabin. They were marching toward her, a mob of women with a mixture of fear and anger on their faces, led back to her by the woman who'd disposed of the gun. Then in an instant, they burst onto the bow deck. Half a dozen arms reached down and grabbed Jasmeen. Another half dozen hands grabbed Sarah and pulled her upright. Both women were pulled up and stood on their feet.

"There's no time," Sarah said. "This woman's brother is back on the main deck. He has a weapon."

One of the women nodded. "She's right," she said. "There's a guy out there with some kind of bazooka thing."

"We have to stop him right away," Sarah said. "He's going to blow up the Statue of Liberty."

"You cannot stop him," said Jasmeen. "It is too late."

The women holding Sarah let her go. She wasn't sure how they knew to trust her. But she didn't stop to think about it. She ran straight through the interior cabin and out to the main exterior deck. Abdul had climbed up on top of one of the metal life preserver canisters. The cannon device rested on his shoulder. The open end of it was pointed toward the Statue. He held the handle of the weapon with his right hand. He had a gun in his left hand, which he rotated around in a steady circular motion.

"I will shoot anyone who comes near," he was saying.

The kids from the high school marching band had all moved from their seats. Some of them had made it into the interior cabin. But others were still pressed against the door. The panic had caused them to get stuck. The students closest to the door couldn't open it because the doors opened outward and the people behind them were pressing too hard against them.

On the other side of the deck, the remaining passengers were all crouched down behind chairs, trying to stay out of the line of sight of Abdul's gun.

"He's a terrorist," Sarah shouted. "He wants to blow up the Statue. We have to stop him."

Abdul fired the gun in Sarah's direction and a collective scream went up from the people on the deck.

Sarah heard the bullet whiz by her, but she couldn't tell if anyone behind her was hit. "We have to all go at once," she yelled. "There isn't time."

"Stay back," Abdul yelled. "I'll shoot all of you."

King pointed his gun at Kareem. "Stop what you're doing," he said.

Kareem didn't take his eyes from the back of the camera. "It is too late," he said.

"I have a gun," said King.

"It does not matter to me, Omar" said Kareem. He was leaning down, pointing the camera down through the open window. "You can shoot me if you want to."

"Muhammad is safe. He was rescued by American soldiers. I spoke to a military agent in Sadr City."

"How could that be true, Omar? Why would a military agent listen to you? You are a wanted terrorist. Do not speak untruths to me, brother. I know that you do not agree with jihad. But I have no choice."

Kareem leaned down and stuck his arms out the window. King saw his finger pressing hard on a button on the top of the camera.

"I don't want to shoot you. But I will stop you," King said. He lowered the gun and stepped toward Kareem.

Kareem leaned even further out the window. He held the camera with his arms extended as far out as he could.

King looked out the window and saw the Circle Line boat in the harbor below. He could just make out the commotion on the top deck of the boat. A figure stood alone in the center of the boat on top of some platform. He held a rocket launcher on his shoulder. Suddenly, it all became clear.

The National Park Service security men from the base of the Statue had arrived at the crown. They were creeping toward King. King whirled around and pointed his gun at them, waiving it in a gesture that meant "stay back."

"They have a laser-guided missile in a boat down below," King said. "This man has the laser to guide the missile to the crown. I'm going to stop him but I don't want to hurt him. Stay back."

Kareem at this point was leaning as far out the window as he could without falling. King came behind him and grabbed hold of his legs. He spoke to Kareem in Arabic. "Drop the camera,

Kareem. Muhammad is safe. I swear by Allah, he is safe. You don't need to do this."

"Do not swear untruths, Omar."

"I speak the truth."

Kareem was having trouble holding his precarious position. He'd leaned so far, his feet had left the floor. Instead of restraining him, King found that he was holding him by the legs to keep him from falling.

"I won't let you fall, brother," King said in Arabic.

"You swear by Allah? You swear he is safe?"

"I swear it."

"I cannot turn back. It is too late for me. They will execute me."

"No, Kareem. No one has yet been hurt. There is still time. I will tell them. You have been blackmailed. You will not be executed."

"It will not matter to them, Omar. The Americans will hate me."

"I will stand by you."

"Omar, I think I'm going to fall."

"I'm holding you, Kareem. You're safe. Drop the camera and I'll pull you in."

While King was focused on Kareem, one of the security men had sneaked up behind him. Now he felt someone grab one of the guns from his waistband.

"Don't move," the man said. "I have your gun and it's pointed at your head."

Sarah looked toward the women on the other side of the deck. She cupped her hands around her mouth and called out. "I'm going to count to three. On the count of three, everyone rush him at once. We'll stop him." She couldn't tell whether or not any of the women were with her. But she decided to count anyway. "One." She paused for a moment. She could feel her legs trembling. "Two." Another beat. She steadied her legs. "Three!"

Sarah rushed toward Abdul. Nearly all the women on the other side of the deck rushed with her. A group of marching band kids rushed too. It was exhilarating. But then shots rang out. There were screams. Sarah heard chairs crashing. She didn't know if the chairs had been knocked over in the rush or if someone had been hit and fallen into them.

Eight women reached the life-preserver cases at the same time. Abdul pointed his gun down into the crowd and fired. This time, Sarah saw a woman collapse to the ground, as blood spurted out of her shoulder.

Sarah grabbed at Abdul's legs. He dropped his gun, which freed his other hand to reach up and pull hard on the trigger of the launcher. A loud "Whop!" sounded and the weapon seemed to explode as a missile shot out from the end of it and streamed up toward the Statue. He'd wobbled at the last minute when she pulled on his legs. She couldn't tell if it had affected his aim.

Now there were five women climbing onto the case. They tackled Abdul and pulled him down from his perch. In a moment, he was on the ground. A dozen legs stomped on his legs and torso.

King felt the muzzle of the gun pressing against his head. "Hurry," he said to Kareem in Arabic. "There is no time."

Kareem was hanging almost entirely out the window at this point. He swung his body to gain momentum and flung the camera as hard as he could toward the left side of the Statue, out and away from the arm.

King saw the rocket streaming toward them. He watched as the camera hurled in a wide arc, flying past the base of the torch. The missile was honed onto it. As the camera began to fall, the missile curved down toward it. The path of the camera's fall led the missile down. It shot beneath the arm, missing it by a mere ten feet. But the missile couldn't recalibrate its trajectory fast enough to follow the camera completely. The camera was plunging to the ground. The missile, instead, bent and curved downward but not quickly enough to keep it from arching out across, then past the Island. It hit the water 200 feet from the shore and exploded.

When it exploded, King pulled Kareem legs back across the fulcrum of the window ledge far enough for his toes to touch the floor. He tentatively let go of Kareem's legs and was about to ask him if he was able to stand on his own when someone grabbed him from behind. He knew it was one of the security guards. The guard grabbed King under his arms and yanked him back from the window. To counter it, King jerked forward. He'd just let go of Kareem's legs, and now he tried to grab hold of them again. But Kareem had become unsteady. His legs flew up like the weightless end of a see saw. Kareem did not cry out as he fell. But after a deafening silence, a woman's scream rose up from down below. As King looked out, he saw the Circle Line boat moving through the water a hundred yards off shore. And he knew that the scream had come from Jasmeen, just as Kareem's body crashed onto the wide stone base of the monument.

King stared down at Kareem's body. He wished he were the sort of person whose mind did not process chunks of thought so quickly. Maybe if he could have slowed his thinking down, he might have found a way to avoid the conclusion he knew he must come to. But he couldn't roll back his mind. He knew he would never be able to roll it back.

Of course, there would be consequences for what he'd done. He knew his independent actions would be judged. He had known the FBI wanted him for questioning, and yet he'd intentionally hidden from them. In the final frantic moments of pursuit, he'd handcuffed an FBI agent. He'd pulled a gun on the National Park Service guards. He fully expected the mechanics of the justice system would be engaged to decide if what he'd done warranted punishment.

But he also knew that the judgment of the justice system would be of little help in resolving his personal guilt. He didn't think he'd ever be able to exonerate himself for the carelessness of his final actions. In a moment that had called for the utmost care, he'd acted recklessly. He'd been holding the legs of a man whose life depended on the strength of his grip. It should have been a moment for caution.

He'd spent four days probing the soul of that man. He'd tried to understand what made him tick. He'd sensed a good and gentle quality in him. All the while, he'd hoped he could find a way for that goodness to prevail. And in the final moments, it had.

Kareem had flung the camera hard enough and far enough to stop the horror. But it had come at a price. Kareem had teetered on the edge. And in that moment, King found himself holding everything that mattered. He'd held the prospect of redemption for a gentle man driven to unconscionable acts by the evil of fundamentalism. He'd held the balance of a man who'd been willing to die for love. He'd also held the weight of a man who was willing to kill for love. But everything he held, he lost. And in the end, Kareem had killed no one except himself.

It would not matter to King whether the courts decided to punish him or pardon him for his vigilante actions. They would never be able to take up the real questions. They would never be able to consider the real forces that had led to the final moments.

All his training should have taught him what to do. He should have been steady. He should have been deliberate. He should never have let go. Even the surprise of someone yanking on his shoulders should not have distracted him when a man's life hung in the balance. His reflexes could have moved his arms more forcefully. He could have grabbed Kareem's ankles, his shoes, anything. He knew he'd see those moments again and again, for the rest of his life—always reaching out but never able to grab hold.

He wanted to cry out, like Jasmeen. But he slumped to the

floor. His mind reached to find an anchor, to turn his attention away. He thought of the poet Rumi.

The universe turns on an axis.
Let my soul circle around the table
Like a beggar, like a planet
Rolling in the vast, totally helpless and free.